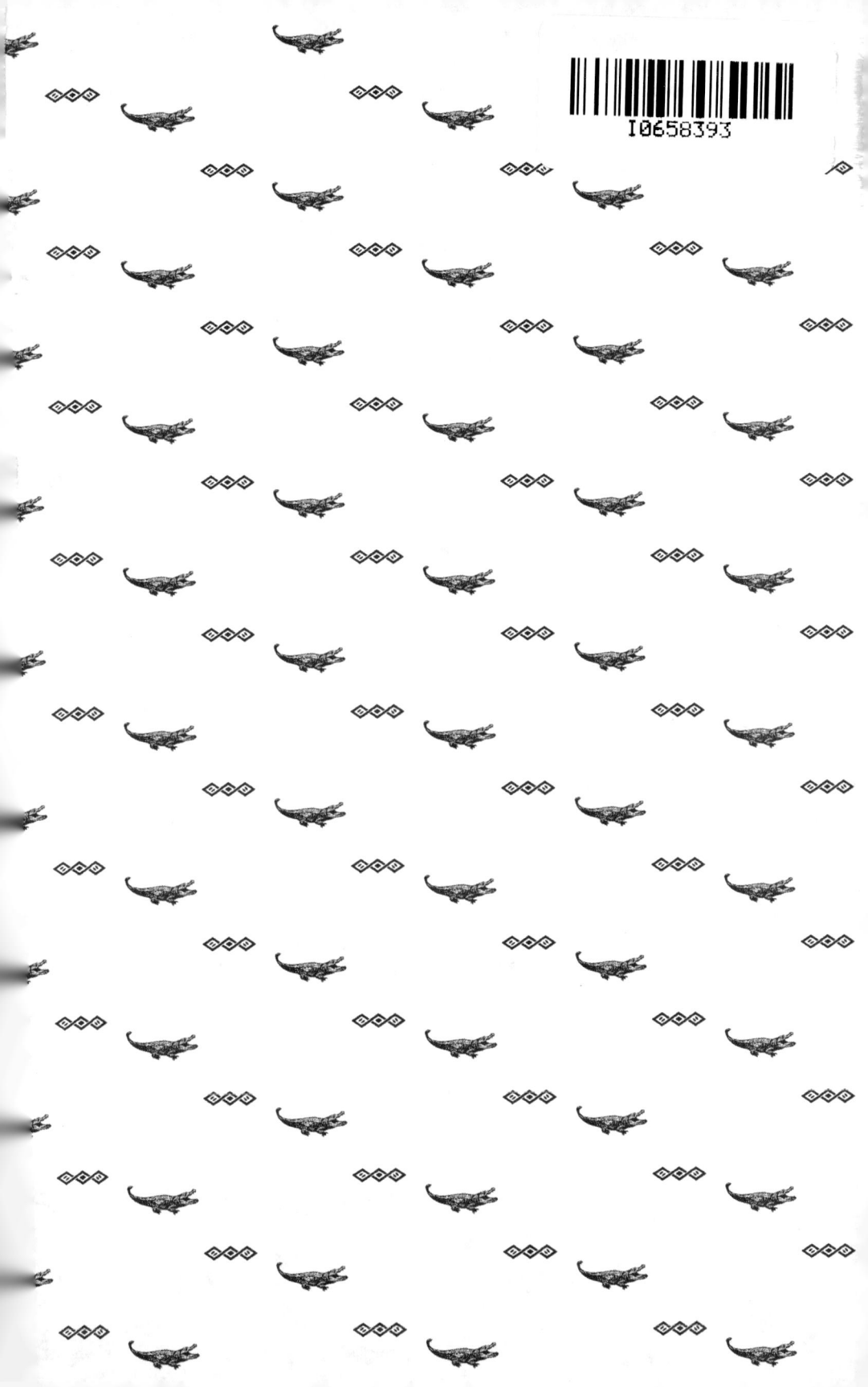

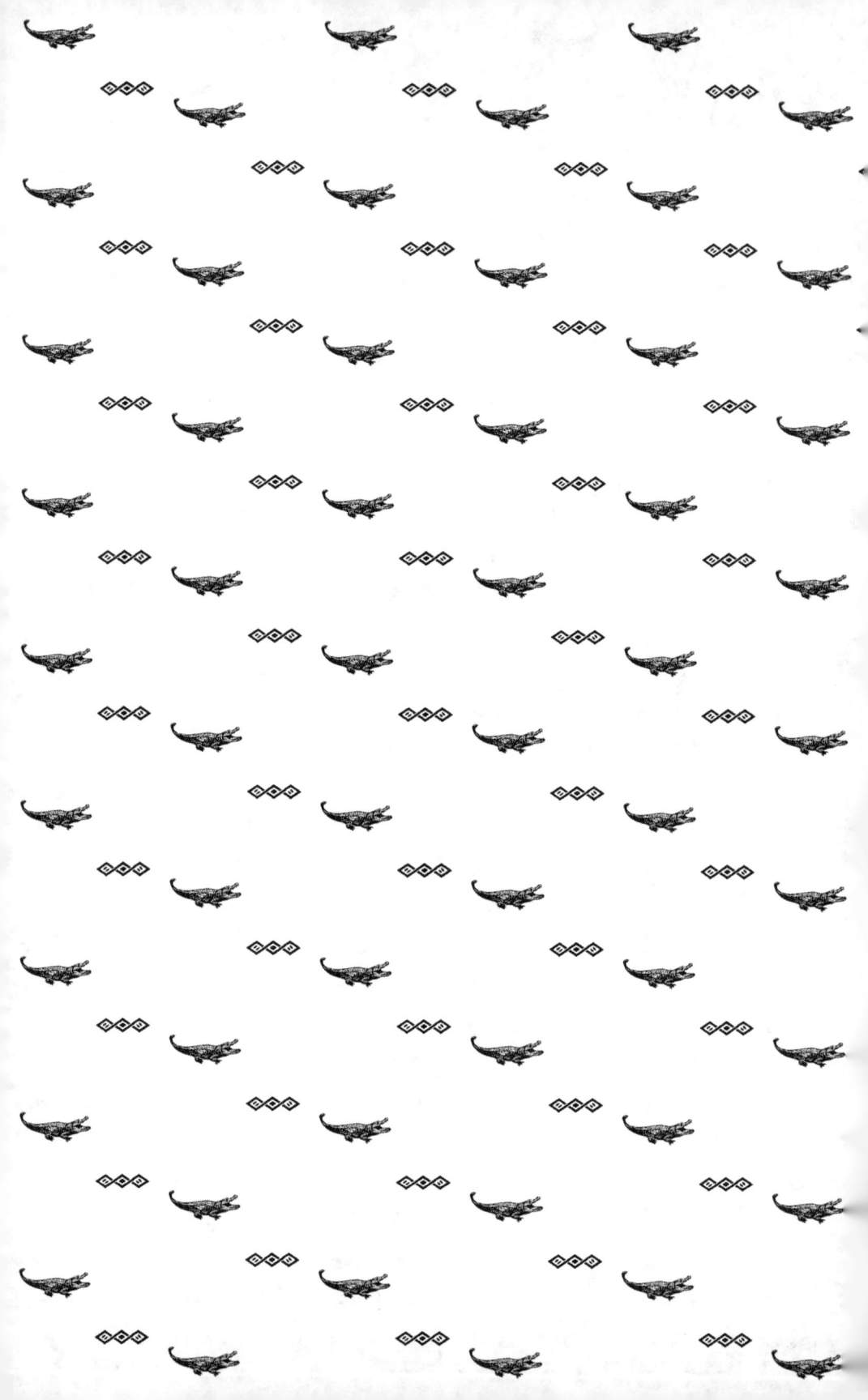

THE INVISIBLE VAZIMBA

SUSAN DWORSKI

THE BLUE ONE • VENICE • 2010

THE BLUE ONE
www.theblueone.com

Library of Congress Control Number 2001117037
Dworski, Susan
The Invisible Vazimba

Design and typography • The Blue One

Cover photograph of an *aloalo,* a funerary sculpture carved from *katafa* wood. These erotic figures, measuring one-half life size, decorate the tombs of the Sakalava tribe, who inhabit the arid lands of western Madagascar. The Sakalava—*People-of-the-Long-Valleys*—count their riches in cattle, and believe that no greater tribute can be paid to their ancestors than to celebrate their lust for life.

For CWH, ATB, and JND

Avy tsy nangeha ny raza.

The ancestors come into our lives
like guests who need no invitation.

I am going to tell you a story.
It is a lie, but not everything in it is false.

MALAGASY
LEGEND

In ancient times there was only Sun and Moon and Stars. The earth was a red, mountainous place. It was covered in a salty mist and surrounded by the sea. One day when GreatCreator was not paying attention, the earth cracked and the sea began to rise and lap at the edges of the land. The Great Red Island was being born.

Deep in the secret hollows of the Great Red Island the SpiritAncestors lay sleeping. GreatCreator looked down and realized that because of his neglect they were in danger of drowning. He ordered Sun to shine a ray of bright light into a crack in the earth.

It woke SpiritWoman. Feeling Sun's warmth on her eyelids, she stretched and began to give birth to children. Sunbirds flew out of the cleft in her chin. Hedgehogs nestled in her eyebrows. Frogs sprang from her toes and tortoises trundled out of her bush. Chameleons counted their steps as they emerged from her navel. Boars wallowed in her nostrils and serpents slithered out of the hair of her armpit. Lemurs swung from her fingers and played games between her knees. Bees circled about her lips, and fleas, small as mustard seeds, sprang to life in the valley between her breasts.

It was night by the time SpiritWoman heaved her tired body up out of the mud. GreatCreator ordered Moon to rise. Its silver light cracked open SpiritWoman's eyelids, and out crawled two more children, a boy and a girl. These children were not like any of SpiritWoman's other children, for they only had hair-at-the-top. They were very small and very dark and very wild. SpiritWoman was pleased and named them Vazimba, the Little People, decreeing that henceforth they would be ruled over by queens.

Many years passed and other peoples sailed to the Great Red Island. The Vazimba were set upon and much perplexed by these newcomers. Wearied by the constant fighting and praying to GreatCreator for help to defend their villages, they decided to ask him for a god who could live on earth with them. "For," they said, "O GreatCreator, you live too far away, much too high. It takes too much time for our prayers to rise up to you and your help arrives too late."

"Very well," GreatCreator answered, "I shall give you a god who will live with you, though under my command. He is in this closed box. Above all be careful not to open it. If you do, great misfortunes will befall you."

The Vazimba promised not to open the box, and they thanked GreatCreator for his bounty.

But as soon as he had left, curiosity became too strong and the bolder ones opened the box. There they found a white man—the first *vazaha*. They wanted to close the box, but they could not manage it.

GreatCreator had foreseen this and had not gone far away. He came back down to earth and called a great *kabary*, saying, "You broke your promises and opened the box in spite of my taboo. Since you do not wish to have a god with you who would be under my command, I shall put this *vazaha* among you. He will be wise and clever and you will listen to him." And GreatCreator took his box and went back up to the sky, leaving the *vazaha* on earth.

But the Queen of the Vazimba was dismayed and cried out to SpiritWoman, her AncestorMother, saying that the *vazaha* was too crafty by far, that she feared he would soon enslave them and her brothers and sisters, the animals. She refused to obey the *vazaha* for he was full of tricks and had no respect for *mahery*, the power of wild things.

SpiritWoman wept for she knew the truth of her daughter's words. She told the Queen to burn her village and flee secretly with her people to the safety of the Blue Rain Forest, commanding her to build a new village at the edge of Lake Marovoay and call it Andrebabe.

The Queen did as she was told and, having done so, she died. She was placed in a pirogue, another was placed on top of her, and the canoe was pushed out into the water by the grieving Vazimba. Her body slowly sank into the sacred lake. As it slid into darkness, so many giant crocodiles arrived to escort her home that it was as if the lake were planked by drifting logs with iron nails set in them. After the Queen disappeared, balls of light could be seen bobbing above the water, and sometimes children, dressed in white, guarding the shore.

Upon learning of the death of her beloved daughter, SpiritWoman withdrew in mourning to the secret hollows of Mount Ambondrombe and the Vazimba faded into the subterranean rivers of memory. Men listened to the *vazaha* and his descendants and soon forgot the way to Andrebabe, or that the village had ever existed.

Legend recounted to Archdeacon Wilbert N. Harvey, in November, 1863, Antananarivo, Madagascar, by Rasombaona, chief of the Antambahoaka tribe. Ref.MS Personal Box No. 3, London Missionary Society Archives, School of Oriental and African Studies, London.

PREFACE

People said I was crazy when I told them I was going to Madagascar to find James, at least the ones who knew where Madagascar was. But it was simple, really. James was my favorite brother and he had disappeared into the wilderness. If he was lost or in trouble, then it was my job to find him. And let's be honest—I was at a dead end. Cycled out. Lonely. In a drought. Farmers, lovers and artists, we've got one thing in common: a dread of dry spells. Well, I was in one. A major internal drought. I needed action. A purposeful mission to a far-away place, preferably with some hot blue sky and sea to match. A place where the rain is the same temperature as your skin and orchids grow wild for the picking.

I got my wish, in spades.

How to begin. How to make sense of it all? I'm a practical cat. I'll begin with my desk, with the journals and sketchbooks that clutter its surface. As an illustrator, I'm an obsessive keeper of notes, collector of photos, accumulator of all sorts of visual flotsam. Scrap, it's called in the trade. Very useful when creativity wanes and a deadline looms. You'd probably call it junk. Sometimes I wonder if it's the reason I've never married. All that scrap lying around.

Fact is, I'm very warmhearted, but not a naturally tidy person. *Tu tienes corazón, pero tengo que ir*, is how my old boyfriend, Raul put it as he packed his bags. *Lo siento mucho*, but gotta go. He waded through the piles of scrap without looking back once.

Corazón.

I ask you, what good is heart if they walk?

Four years ago I slammed the door on my heart and nailed it shut. Four years is a long time to live alone if you're blonde and thirty and smothered in scrap. You get weird. Stiff. Stale and bent.

I've waited almost a month since my return before beginning to sift through the evidence. Malagasy scrap. Grimy business cards. Torn pages from telephone books. Letters of introduction officially rubber-stamped in red and purple REPOBLIKA DEMOKRATIKA MALAGASY. Letters of love tied in a bundle. Pages of research carefully printed out in blue in Father Soren's neat hand titled *Le sens de la mort et les ancestres de Madagascar*. A fuzzy photocopy of a Vedantic mandala from Dr. Rabansoro's treatise on metaphysics. A thick, handmade Antemoro postcard embedded with daisies and dried cosmos that says, *In Morondava men make love eternal. Why not us? J.* I found that card tucked into a box jammed with Rexworthy's field notes and a bunch of Malagasy proverbs. But the biggest pile by far is a stack of yellowed telegrams addressed to my brother: James Artema, Ph.D., International Wildlife Consortium, BP 3309, Antananarivo, Madagascar. Telegrams cancelling his funding, demanding his immediate return. My journey really begins there, with that stack of unanswered telegrams. The University had sent those. James had never bothered to answer them. Or, couldn't.

So I headed for Madagascar to find out why.

1

"Come, let me show you our little town."

The Honorable Robert Theron, United States Ambassador to Madagascar, took my arm firmly and steered me along the edge of the terraced lawn of the embassy garden. It was a cool October evening, the end of the dry season on the high plateau. The clay path was sticky from the afternoon downpour and the neatly trimmed borders of grass were splashed with thick, red mud. Antananarivo's twelve pointed hills poked up into the night sky in weird shadowshapes. A bright handful of electric lights prinked the darkness here and there, but they offered as many clues to the real shape of the city as planets standing in the heavens. The Ambassador and I stood on top of one hill and tried to make sense of where the other eleven began and ended.

"Some people find it very beautiful."

It was a question hidden in a statement.

"Yes," I said. "Very."

Ambassador Theron gripped my arm as we circumnavigated

the lawn. A lobe-shaped moon was rising between two witchy roofs whose rounded tiles bumped against the blue-black sky. As we strolled I saw kerosene lanterns dimly glowing in the windows of shuttered houses on the hillsides of the valley. The soft flames fluttered like rosy handkerchiefs, beckoning and seductive.

"How do they live?"

The Ambassador's melancholy took me by surprise. Was it a response to beauty? A gust of homesickness? Or did it refer to the many strands of barbed wire strung along the top of the embassy wall? Clearly Antananarivo was a hardship post, lowest grimace on the foreign service totem pole. I noted the Ambassador's gold signet ring and crisp monogrammed cuffs, wondering what sort of promises might have induced a man like Theron to accept a position in an obscure Third World capitol. A future posting to London? Or perhaps Madrid? It never occurred to me that Theron might be on the way down.

We passed the entrance where a brace of armed Marines stood rigidly at attention. The Ambassador's blue wool blazer was hot and scratchy against my bare arm, as ominous and stifling as the barbed wire. I removed my elbow from his hand, suddenly overwhelmed by a sense of diffuse, inchoate anxiety which I hadn't been able to shake since arriving on the island.

"Ambassador Theron, I need your help."

Three fat ducks scrabbled noisily among the Madagascar periwinkles bordering the path, snuffling for snails.

"Tristan, Isolde and Gretel." Theron leaned down and patted a fat rump. "Hansel was eaten by an owl last week." He peered at me mournfully, bringing his face very close to mine. "Thing *eat* things in Madagascar, you know."

"I've been here a week and I'm getting nowhere."

Ambassador Theron reached into the pocket of his blazer, extracted a few kernels of corn, and tossed them at the ducks. "Things take time *au bout du monde*," he said.

A huge moth zoomed past and braked. Hovering like a dark, satanic hummingbird, it fed in the throat of a trembling blossom near my right ankle.

"You know people. Your name..."

Theron reached down and plucked a sprig of periwinkle.

"*Catharanthus roseus.*" He brandished the branch of flat, magenta flowers like a baton. "Sixty alkaloids in one, small plant. Revolutionized the treatment of Hodgkins disease, childhood leukemia. Fifteen tons of leaves to make just one ounce of vincristine. A hundred thousand dollars a pound!" His eyes gleamed and his voice rose. "There are things to be discovered in Madagascar! Out there..." He shook the periwinkle at the moon.

"My brother James, for one."

Why was he making this so difficult?

"Ambassador, you have cars, contacts..."

Above the wonking clubber of the ducks we could hear the *zzzipps* of night flyers sucked into the florescent mouths of insect lamps hung in intervals around the perimeter of the garden. As we approached one, Theron stooped down and picked up something winged and grey. I thought it must be a small bird.

"*Acherontia,*" he said, turning the creature over so I could see the death's head marked on its thorax. It was the carcass of the sphinx moth that had been feeding at my feet a few moments ago. Electrocuted. Fried on the wires.

Things eat things in Madagascar.

"They call them *lolo* in Malagasy," Theron pronounced it *lool*, lowering his voice to a confidential whisper. "The Malagasy believe they are the lost souls of the dead who have been deprived of the right to be buried in the family tomb."

I put out my hand.

"You're not afraid," he asked, placing the insect in my palm.

"I used to collect them. With James."

He looked startled. "Moths... or souls?"

"Both," I said, studying the pink surprise of the sphinx's underwings.

"Is that why you're here,?" Theron teased. "To add to your collection?" He wrapped an avuncular arm around my shoulders and began steering me towards the lighted embassy. "If it's butterflies you're after, Miss Artema..."

"Eva."

"...you'll probably find plenty in Madagascar. More than 3,000 species. Most of them unique." He looked down at me, his beefy cheeks hanging like chops in a stall. "But souls...? How'd you plan to go about catching those, Eve?"

"Eva." I placed myself squarely in front of him, blocking the way, bringing the cremated sphinx up right under his nose. "Well, if I had a car I could begin."

The moth lay in my hand like a sparrow, or a linnet. Its great, bulging eyes were misted over, and one of its feathery antennae had been sheared completely off by the jolt from the contraption that hung overhead. Its hollow, black tongue extruded like a long whisker, dying in a curly spasm.

"Just what kind of souls you planning to catch?"

The Ambassador's voice had an edge. He wasn't used to being toyed with.

Ease off.

I let the moth float soundlessly to the damp path.

Walk softly.

Stay low to the ground and look for another opening.

"Souls?" I said. "Why, old souls, of course." I turned on a bright smile and took his arm. "*Monsieur l'ambassadeur*, shall we dance?"

I pulled him towards the flagstone stairs which led to the living room where someone was playing a Cole Porter tune on the piano and men in white jackets circulated with trays of drinks.

"Old, huh?" Flattered, Theron was back on top. "Playful, even. How old?"

"Very old," I said gaily. "Vazimba souls."

"Vazimba?" He dropped my hand. "You're insane. The Vazimba have been dead for four hundred years... *if* they ever existed."

But I was already in motion, taking the stairs two at a time, abandoning the Ambassador to the moonlight.

2

The American Embassy was a cavernous pile, more suited for official receptions than living quarters. With its broad stone entry stairs, walls three feet thick, and barred windows, it dominated the crown of the hill with a sweeping view of more hills over which crawled a dark and muttersome cluster of steeply gabled houses, their edged chiseled white by the moon. Towering over this jumble, the embassy loomed—a bastion, an *edifice publique*, built by the French prior to Malagasy Independence in 1960 and intended, no doubt, for important glove-touching and deal-swapping between colonials and the motherland.

I paused for a moment in the entry to catch my breath, assessing the guests. Nasal American accents ricocheted around the vast living room like pinballs. Groups of Malagasay stood in tight, nervous knots, as if trying to avoid being struck. Their polysyllabic conversations hummed and burbled, evaporating into the air like soap bubbles. I noticed a certain formality, a *politesse*, about them. The way they stood. Nothing at all like the loose body movements and ragged bursts of laughter that erupted from the Americans.

In the center of the floor, three mauve velvet sofas squared off theatrically around a glass-topped coffee table in which was displayed a collection of mounted butterflies, each identified in meticulous Latin script written on tiny cardboard flags attached to the pins.

"Endemic. Theron collects them. Recognize any?"

A man slouching against one of the sofas pushed off with an effort and headed towards me. Not tall, hardly taller than I. Curly dark hair, prematurely grey at the temples. A thick moustache. A handsome, rough-edged man, he wore mirrored sunglasses. He saluted me with an empty glass, cocked his head, swaying slightly.

"Nice hair," he said. "Refreshing." He circled closer. "We don't get much white pussy here in Tana."

"You're drunk." I stepped quickly away towards the piano. "And crude. Whoever you are."

"No doubt," he said, following me. "Jack Mooresby."

I slipped in between several men in coats and ties at the piano, joining them to sing the last bars of *Night and Day*.

"*Hola*. A *nuevo* soprano." A tall man with a paunch, capped teeth and a Panhandle drawl shoved his hand at me. "Howdy. Paul. Paul Cummins. CANTEX Oil. Welcome to Tana. This here's Stephan Giardini, World Bank. And Eli Mazan."

"IRRI. International Rice Research Institute," said Eli. His hand was cool and dry, like paper.

"Eva. Eva Artema. Tourist."

There was a pause. Infinitesimal, but telling. Enough to indicate a subtle shift in the weather.

"Good timing." Paul Cummins took another drink from a passing tray. "You just missed the rains. Country's impossible then. Nasty typhoon couple of months ago in Tamatave. Blew out the harbor, sea walls. Roads washed out, bridges caved in. Potholes big enough to swim in. Ask Jack. He's flown over most of them. I'm telling it straight, Jack?"

The man in the mirrored glasses stepped into the circle. "Straight up," he said, extending a hand. "We haven't met. Jack Mooresby."

"We tried. It failed." I crossed my arms over my chest, wishing I hadn't worn the red silk blouse. It had a way of making me angry.

"Jack here's our man from New Mexico. Makes it all possible."

"All?"

"Oil, honey. CANTEX's sewed up the southeast quadrant tighter'n a drum. Looking for crude."

I must have looked puzzled.

"Exploration. Petroleum companies divided up Madagascar. Drew a few blue lines, bought off some government big-wigs, and chopped it up. It's nothing new. Same as your missionaries did. Catholics in the north, Lutherans in the southwest, Anglicans in the east. Madagascar gets its infrastructure built for free, a percentage of every barrel pumped and a shit-carload of used Land Rovers. Everyone's got a piece of the action and nobody steps on anyone's toes. It's a lottery, but it works."

Stephan Giardini snorted. "Sure, Paul. Until someone actually strikes oil. Then we'll see some blood on the tracks."

I turned to Jack. "Are you a missionary?"

I caught my reflection in his mirrored glasses. My forehead bulged, my eyes bugged out like a sphinx moth, without the antennae.

"Of sorts." He drained his glass, picked a full one from a tray. "I fly birds."

"Best damn helicopter pilot in the business," said Stephan.

"When he's not boozing or *cherchez*-ing *les femmes*. Right?" Paul Cummins laughed and punched Jack's shoulder. "Hey, there's Rakotomana."

A tall, heavy-set Malagasy man in a three-piece suit stood at the doorway with Ambassador Theron.

"Excuse us, Eva. Boys? Showtime." They began walking away.

Stephan Giardini stopped and turned. "Artema...?" he said.

I felt my heart squeeze. "I have a brother, James Artema. He's a biologist. He's been working here for almost a year on a grant, studying lemurs. Perhaps you know him."

"Not offhand. Name seems familiar, though. Here's my card. Be careful. There's been an outbreak of typhoid in Tana. People dying every day. Nobody's talking. They had to airlift Theron's wife to Reunion on Wednesday." He bowed sightly and left.

I turned to Jack. "Is that true?"

"Could be." Jack shrugged. "Don't ask me. Last month I heard it was bubonic plague. I spend most of my time in the bush." He reached over and touched my hair where it curved around my earlobe. "Nice hair." His voice was husky. "What're you really doing in Madagascar, Eva?"

"Don't touch me."

"CIA?"

I retreated into the curve of the piano.

Jack grinned and moved closer, trapping me. "On a secret mission for World Health? Counting periwinkles for Eli Lilly?"

I could feel his warm breath on my collarbone.

"What kind of underwear do you wear, Eva? White, I'll bet. White cotton..."

"You're disgusting!"

The sound of my voice disappeared into his laughter. I tried to twist away, but he held me tight.

"Play," he ordered.

The pianist obeyed.

Jack put his arm around my struggling waist and steered me out onto the parquet floor in an awkward fox-trot. Bright chevrons of light reflected from the crystal chandeliers and bounced off his mirrored glasses as we moved across the floor.

Damn his eyes!

"I don't dance with blind men."

"So. Be my cane."

Jack Mooresby tightened his grip and executed a swooping turn so that now I had a clear view of Rakotomana. He was pressed into a corner, almost buried by Paul Cummins, Stephan

Giardini and Eli Mazan. Ambassador Theron had one arm draped around Stephan and Eli's shoulders, listening. His florid face looked bloated, used-up.

"Rakotomana? Isn't he the Minister of Waters and Forests? James often mentioned him in his letters."

"Not quite." We swirled around the couches. "Michel Rakotomana's the Director of the International Wildlife Consortium, a quasi-United Nations of scientists looking for fame and funding south of the equator. New Age imperialism wearing academic robes."

"Harsh words from an 'oily' being paid to rape and pillage." I tried to pull away, but his hand tightened around my waist.

"Rakotomana's a powerful man. Comes from an old Merina family. Very well connected. They say he's amassed a personal fortune by gouging western scientists for permits to study in the Reserves, then appropriating their equipment when their visas run out. Handsome, though. Don't you think?"

The pianist segued into *My Melancholy Baby*. I whirled past dark cheekbones, thick Polynesian eyelids, a pronounced overbite disguised by a tightly curled beard. Rakotomana reminded me of a monitor lizard James had once brought home from Surinam. Watchful. Toothy. And dangerous.

"Introduce me," I said, and stopped dancing. "Please." It was an order, not a question.

"Whoa." Jack's fingers dug into my waist. "Listen up and slow down. This is a rough country. Outside these walls, beyond these pathetic strands of barbed wire, these little tin soldiers... you're *nada*. Understand? Nobody. Just another *vazaha*. Helpless as a blind, albino croc. Nothing on this island is what it seems. These people will stonewall you with kindness and eat you alive. You're in a fancy duet with one of them, calling it a friendship, smiling and scraping and *pas de probleme*-ing—then suddenly you look down and find your money's run out and your leg's half chewed off."

"Things eat things in Madagascar, right?" I wrenched backwards. The red silk stuck to my flesh, pasted under his damp, sweating palm. "Well, I don't buy it. None of it. I've been here for a week. I want some answers. Somebody in this room must know my brother, starting with Rakotomana. You'll excuse me. This dance is over."

But he held on. "Don't push the river, Artema." The teasing had disappeared, replaced by something hard and unyielding. "And never, ever, confront a Malagasy dead-on with a question. They'll do anything to avoid saying no. You circle around..." He swung me out away from him and twirled me back again without missing a beat, "...and you make heap big small talk. Lots of it."

"I haven't got time for small talk. I've got an agenda."

Tough talk. Meaning: I'm scared.

He grabbed me so close to him that I stumbled. "Take a look around, Eva. Everybody in this room wants something. Everyone's got an agenda. It's Code Blue, babe." His mouth was almost in my ear. "*Azul*. Can't you feel it, my little blind albino *vazaha*?"

I jerked away, stung, wanting to hurt. "Code Blue my ass, pilot." Tracers, shot over my shoulder as I headed for the door where Ambassador Theron was helping Rakotomana into his overcoat.

"Excuse me..."

I approached the Director, arranging my mouth into what I hoped resembled a smile. Then, turning to Theron, "Ambassador, I haven't yet had the pleasure..."

"How thoughtless of me..."

Rakotomana surveyed me with an unhurried calm from under half-closed eyelids. The well-tailored Saville Row suit and starched white collar did nothing to offset the tremendous darkness that exuded from him. It was like standing in front of an open elevator shaft.

"*Enchanté*," said the Director, somewhere between a purr and a growl. "Mademoiselle, if you will excuse me, I am late for dinner." He clicked his heels, bowed and walked briskly through the foyer and down the wide stairs towards his waiting car.

Square One. Again!

"Sir..." I ran alongside him. My red blouse had come untucked, my hair hung in ropy hanks. "I've been trying to... Would it be possible for me to meet with you in person in your office one day? Tomorrow, perhaps? It is a matter of some urgency."

Pathetic. Begging.

Rakotomana assessed me coolly, one muscular, pinstriped thigh already inside his car. "Madagascar would be honored," he finally said, and slid inside. The door slammed shut, and he was gone.

I watched the car pass through the embassy gate, saw the Marines salute, then retreat to the safety of their bullet-proof sentry boxes.

"*Soyez en garde, ma cherie.* Michel has a penchant for blondes and Scotch, preferably enjoyed together."

Ambassador Theron came alongside me and held out both arms like a supplicant. "As I recall, mademoiselle, not so long ago you invited me to dance. May I accept?"

Under the white light of the moon, he looked like a cadaver. His face had caved in somehow, folded onto itself. Like a deflated punching bag, I thought, suddenly feeling a surge of pity for him, lost in the Third World in a prep school blazer.

"*Pourquoi pas?*" I allowed.

3

The moon had set by the time Ambassador Theron put me into a cab. During the waning hours of the party I had received lectures from various guests on astrology, *ayahs*, schistosomiasis and the therapeutic value of celibacy. From Madame Clouseau, a French textile exporter, I learned where to buy the best brioches, on which days the cheese shipments arrived from Antsirabe, and why Antandroy tribesmen made the best watchmen.

"Spears and genes." Madame Clouseau blinked rapidly and made queer, nibbling movements with her mouth. "You see, the 'Tandroy are genetically *sauvage*."

I'd successfully avoided Jack Mooresby for the balance of the evening by dancing with the Cultural Attache and his weedy young assistant more often than I would have liked. Nonetheless, I'd managed to collect a promising pocketful of Malagasy business cards.

I felt good.

It was only a matter of time before I would locate James. A

matter of days, probably. Tananarive was a small town, Madagascar a small island. Jack was wrong. Being a *vazaha* was all right. It gave you visibility. Opened doors.

My fingers closed over the packet of cards and a sense of ease and relaxation stole over me.

Things were moving now. It was only a question of time.

The pre-war Citroen deux-cheveaux barreled down the curving street, squealed around a deserted square and dove into a tunnel. The blatting of the taxi's ancient motor racketed along the stone walls like an exploding sewing machine. The driver's head and shoulders were hidden in the folds of a thick, cotton blanket which protected him against the night chill. Another passenger, similarly wrapped, swayed from side to side in the front seat next to him. The driver carried on a rapid-fire conversation in Malagasy, gesticulating and joking. Apparently, the passenger was an old friend, for the driver did not seem to be put off by his lack of response.

Leaving the tunnel, we passed a series of arched doorways where beggars slept, huddled around open charcoal fires. Their bodies lay on the sidewalk, as lumpy and misshapen as bags of potatoes abandoned in the fields. I saw a flash of obsidian gleam from among the folds of cloth where a mother lay, and recognized it as the wakeful eye of a nursing infant—a glimmering shard of humanity, thirsting for life among the rags.

The battered taxi shuddered and clanked over the uneven cobblestones as it spiraled downhill, twisting around corner after vertiginous corner. Occasionally, the headlight beams would smear a quick wash of light across red and blue graffiti letters painted crudely on the side of peeling colonial mansions: PKOMNA/AKR. PPKM UNITE. ARASN. Political acronyms. Cryptic logos of splinter parties whose philosophies and dreams were as unfathomable as the reveries of the ragged beggars who slept curled in the doorways where coal fires burned. Codes to

Malagasy passions I could only imagine.

God, I prayed, let James be alive. Let it not be typhoid. Or plague.

The cab hurtled along a wide avenue past a bronze statue of a general on horseback, then skirted a murky, leaf-choked lake guarded by a circle of chestnut trees. Ours was the only car, and the driver drove wildly, willfully, erratically careening through the night without regard to lanes or laws, as if the three of us, entombed in this antiquated Citroen, were the only people alive.

"Slow down! Please! I beg you!"

Why didn't the other passenger speak up? Was I the only one who feared for my life?

Undeterred, the driver pressed on through the night.

I closed my eyes, assailed by the onset of an immense exhaustion. I must have dozed for a second or two, for I awoke with a jerk when the cobblestones ended, abruptly giving way to dirt.

I felt oddly alert, like a warrior in enemy territory. My pupils dilated. The back of my neck prickled. There was a tinny humming in my ears. Nothing had changed, yet somehow everything was different. A curious ground fog hung along the edges of the roadway, cloaking the reedy bushes in grizzled witches' hair. I peered out, trying to guess where were were, but we had entered a section of town that was utterly unknown to me. Perhaps it was a shortcut.

The car picked up speed. Now we were racing down a narrow, clay road lined on either side with two-story, red brick houses leaning in upon each other like an armada of terra-cotta galleons. Shoulder to shoulder, the buildings brooded over the unpaved street, so densely packed together that not even a hungry dog could slip between them. Kerosene lanterns shone here and there through cracks in tightly shuttered windows. Smoke seeped through the chimneyless, thatched roofs, the only sign of human habitation.

I saw it first. A tiny white smock.

"*Arretez!* Stop!!"

But it was too late. The child's body slammed against the bumper, then hit the windshield with a sickening thump. It arced over the road, its legs thrown unnaturally wide, splayed in the glow of the headlights like a poorly-mounted butterfly. Its eyes flashed past, huge and dazzling as mirrored coins.

I clutched the front seat and screamed. "We've hit a child! We've hit a child!" I pounded on his shoulders with both fists, nearly hysterical. "Now! Stop the car now!"

The taxi skidded to a stop. I threw open the door and leapt out into a choking cloud of red dust which temporarily blinded me. Fighting clear of it, I saw something small and white lying on the road a short distance away, like a discarded rag. It was crawling down into a drainage ditch which ran alongside the raised, dirt embankment.

"Wait!" I ran towards it. "Don't be afraid!"

But the rag kept moving, scuttling awkwardly along the ground through the misty bushes like a disjointed crab.

Omigod. My heart pounded and my throat was dry. We've broken its arms and legs. What if it dies. I *can't* let it die.

By the time I'd reached the edge of the ditch I could no longer see the child, but I could hear it thrashing around in the bushes. It appeared to be making for an opening between some rocks where a trickle of fresh water flowed.

"Don't be afraid," I scrambled along the bank, trying to keep from slipping into the fetid mud as I called to it, coaxing. "I won't hurt you. I promise."

Stupid, inept words.

I grabbed onto a stand of wild grasses for support, but they slid uselessly out of my hand and I skidded down into the ditch, one knee painfully bent under me.

Brick houses loomed overhead, somber and impregnable, plumes of smoke like malevolent spirits, leaking from their rooftops. I remembered that I'd read somewhere that rural Malagasy will not venture forth after dark, shutting themselves up inside their homes, fearing witches and ghosts of their unburied

Ancestors who roam about the countryside on the lookout for unwary victims. They fear most of all the blue-eyed foreigners—"heart-stealers"—who suck the blood of Malagasy children, piercing them with pointed, vampire teeth. *Vazaha* teeth.

I lay quietly on the chilly mud nursing my twisted knee, listening for the child. Alone. Afraid. No moon illuminated the blank, shuttered buildings. Not a single star shone.

I thought, because of me, someone's child is dying. Followed immediately by an acute panic: And if they find me, they will kill me.

I shivered, trying to pull myself together, recalling the convivial, lighted embassy on a hilltop somewhere not far from here. This was Tananarive. A civilized capitol, not the bush. Malagasy in Tana sent their children to France to be educated. Ate brioches. Wore three-piece suits and took skiing holidays in Switzerland. Passed out engraved business cards and invited *vazahas* like me to dinner parties after dark. Accidents happened, didn't they?

There was a rustle nearby. A feeble movement among the grasses. I caught a glimpse of white cloth. Evanescent, silvery as a phosphorescent firefly.

"Please, I'm here to help you," I implored in a hoarse whisper. "I'm your friend." I dragged myself closer, reaching blindly through the reeds toward the faint light. "Come. You need help. A doctor..."

There was a splash. Something wriggled away through the shallow water. I lunged at it, throwing myself full length at the sound.

A leg!

I grabbed onto the slippery limb. It was small and slick as a mossy twig. Impossibly small... for a human.

"Be still!" I commanded, suddenly angry.

I wallowed forward on my knees, flushed with certain victory. But as I pushed aside the remaining vegetation which separated me from the child, it lashed out in a frenzy to escape, kicking and hissing, churning up the foul water. A demonic whirligig.

What kind of wounded child was this?

I held fast, trying to get a good look at its face.

Was it male or female? Was this slippery bone and flesh I grasped an arm? Or a leg? It felt more like a wing, or a flipper.

A wild, keening cry rose from the creature, an unearthly wail of anguish taut as a wire from hell.

Terrified, I relaxed my grip and the child sprang forward. I plunged after it, managing a last grab before it disappeared into a cleft in the muddy bank. On my hands and knees, I peered into a fissure no more than a foot wide from which poured a clear stream. It formed a miniature waterfall that dropped into the base of the drainage ditch, creating a pool, a small, crystal umbilicus in the middle of a filthy mire.

The opening was so narrow and forbidding it seemed inconceivable that a child, no matter how frightened, would attempt to take refuge in it. As I leaned closer, I realized it must be the opening to an underground cave. I sniffed a peculiar odor, a mixture of sea spray and night-blooming jasmine overlaid by the acrid scent of tarnished silver blowing from somewhere far away, deep in the earth.

A cock crowed. Voices muttered behind wooden windows. A shutter banged open. There was a shout. A lantern swung out over the road. The taxi pulled up alongside.

"Help me!" I begged the driver, yelling above the sound of the running motor.

His eyes rolled wildly from side to side. "Mademoiselle, it is dangerous. Leave it! You must leave it and come away!"

A warning whistle echoed in the street. And another, answering.

They were searching for the child!

Just then I noticed a curious object lying beside the pool on a rock just outside the entrance to the cave. It looked like a handmade toy of some sort, dropped, no doubt, by the fleeing child. It was incredibly ugly, but I picked it up. Perhaps it meant something. A clue. Or a sign.

A door opened and a shaft of light fell like a guillotine across the drainage. Ghostly wisps of ground fog smoldered upwards through the slatty reeds, as if the ditch itself were on fire. Unknown men called to one another loudly behind the closed doors, gathering strength, like a pack of hounds. At any moment, they would burst forth and be upon me.

"*Vite! Vite!*" The taxi driver gunned the engine.

I hauled myself up the bank, threw myself into the cab and we were off, wheels spinning, gouging ruts in the soft roadbed.

I leaned over the front seat. "This child. A crime..."

"No, mademoiselle. It is nothing. You must let it pass."

"Nothing? To run down a child, *and let it pass*?"

"It did not die." He spoke slowly, deliberately.

"What?"

"There is no crime. There was no... child."

"Wait. *You* saw it too, didn't you?" I tugged at the fine-textured red silk cloth which shrouded the passenger seated silently next to the driver. "It was a little child," I continued. "Four or five years old at most. Wasn't it?"

I shook his shoulder—not roughly. But the passenger slumped sideways at my touch, sagging across the dashboard as if I had punched him in the gut. His head tipped over at a peculiar angle, like a puppet whose strings had suddenly snapped. The cloth wrapping which hid his face slid backwards, exposing a wizened skull, and, to my horror, I found myself staring into the empty eye sockets of a grinning, partly-decomposed corpse.

"*Jesus!*"

I shrank back into a corner of the taxi, shriveling into a ball, trying to put as much distance between myself and the mummy as possible.

"My uncle, Rasolo," said the driver. "Five years have passed, many things have changed in Tana. I'm showing him around town, bringing him up to date."

James, James... where are you?

"But, he's... *dead.*"

"*Au contraire,* mademoiselle," the driver chuckled. "Rasolo lives."

"I... I don't understand," I groaned, clutching my rapidly-swelling kneecap.

"Yes, of course."

The driver shifted into second and we began climbing a hill. The sky was beginning to pale in the east, and we were once again rumbling over cobblestone pavers.

"But... the child? What about the child?"

"*Kokolampo,*" he declared.

4

The street vendors on the sidewalk outside the Hotel Le Terrace were rolling up their blankets and beginning to set up shop by the time Uncle Rasolo and I screeched to a halt in front.

I handed several hundred Malagasy francs to the driver, but he refused to take them, shaking his head vehemently. *Pas necessaire, pas necessaire* he kept repeating, his eyes darting back and forth as if terrified one of the street people would recognize him. The instant I set foot on the pavement the turquoise Citroen roared off, enveloped in a cloud of diesel fumes. I staggered to my room and flung myself onto the bed.

Sleep was out of the question. I peeled off my silk shirt and headed for the communal bathroom down the hall. Le Terrace was rated 'pension' in the Guide Bleu, which meant it had running water somewhere on the premises and no cockroaches in the rooms—although there was a grand-daddy in the watercloset. He had seriously interfered with my bodily rhythms for a few days until I realized that it was the sudden burst of light from the naked bulb that set him off, causing him to streak out of his hiding place under a flap of loose linoleum and charge up the wall in a blind rage, taking up a quivering, defensive posture on the pull-chain, effectively turning my colon to concrete. I had considered several solutions, including a large brick, but was not convinced that Le Terrace's commode could withstand the repeated blows which might be necessary to terminate such a macho *Blattaria*. Instead, I usually compromised and took a flashlight in with me, then switched it off and stood on top of the toilet seat, just in case grand-dad got any wild ideas.

In addition to its convenient location next to the railway station, the Hotel Le Terrace had one other advantage not mentioned in the guidebook: the downstairs bar was *estacion central* for Tana's hard-working *femmes de la nuit*. It was where I first met Rangita, a smoldering Malagasy beauty clad in a skin-tight leopard print unitard and a blonde wig.

Rangita turned tricks for wristwatches, though I never could figure out why, as she was never on time. In fact, like most Malagasy, she didn't believe in it. At least not the way we Westerners do. *Time is a circle, and we're always at its center*, was one of her favorite sayings. Confusing? Not to her. To her, it's we who go round in circles. Her favorite expression, accompanied by a permissive motion of her left hand, was: *Moramora, moramora.* Which translates roughly as: Relax. Simmer down. Don't rush things. Go with the flow. Or: Yes, the plane may arrive today but if it doesn't, stick around, it will certainly arrive tomorrow or the next day and is tomorrow really so much different from today anyhow if you reach your destination sometime? All this I learned much later, but you might as well practice sliding around now, loosening up about time. That way you'll be ahead of the game when things make a bee-line for the rabbit hole. It'll feel perfectly normal then—or at least familiar.

Rangita had quite a collection of watches, including a slick little Goofy model with a tri-color neon strap. Her favorite was a battery-operated rhinestone bracelet that spelled out T E N N I S.

A cunning little trap door hidden in a brilliant, *faux* tennis ball opened so you could read the hour. The battery had long since given up the ghost but *moramora*, it had been redundant anyway. *Le grand montre*, a Rolex, The Big One, still eluded her, but she was logging a lot of sack time with an Indian named Aziz who owned a match factory, and she was optimistic that his Rolex would soon be *en bras*.

The shower was lukewarm and coffee colored. I sloshed around, making the most of the trickle. It wasn't the River Jordan, but it went a long way towards restoring my soul. I was returning to my room in remarkably good spirits considering that I'd just run over a *kokolampo* in the company of a corpse, when Mme. Moreau, the concierge, accosted me. She was carrying a pail and a mop, and a cigarette hung from the corner of her mouth. Her cheeks were crinkled like potato skins and she smelled faintly of garlic and talcum powder. Her stockings were rolled onto rubber bands well below her varicosed knees, yet her white cotton blouse was buttoned primly at the neck, like a proper French schoolgirl, which she must have been—a half-century ago.

"Koreans keep you awake?" she inquired. "You know. The engineers."

"Why no, not at all." I edged past her.

"Cooking in their rooms, Kung-fu, Ken-po, ping-pong..." Mme. Moreau ripped the fag off her lower lip and took a deep, disgusted drag. "Do we *need* that dam in Manajarka? Do we *need* twenty-four used Soviet MIGs? We do not, thank you *monsieurs les Russkies*."

She flipped the butt into the soapy, grey water and watched it expire with a tiny *hissst*. "*Mon Dieu*, Madagascar does not have an airstrip sufficient to land those jets upon! National defense? A joke. What's to defend? Nothing here but rice, and even that is running out. I heard yesterday that the United Nations sent a battleship filled with rice to Tamatave after the cyclone last February and still it sits in the harbor, rotting. No way to unload it. Some *voyou* stole the rice bags and sold them to the charcoal men, *et comme toujours*, Madagascar starves."

I inserted my key into Number 27. After a week of Mme. Moreau's hospitality, I'd learned to hit the ground running when she hove into view. Sixty-two years in Madagascar, first as a member of the French colonial ruling elite and now as a beached and forgotten exile, she had more than a few opinions, which she shared freely with any guests who would stand still long enough.

I affected a tremendous shiver, pulled the towel around me, sneezed, smiled and shut the door.

That's when I got a really good look at the toy.

It crouched in the middle of the bed like a squashed tarantula: a handful of blackened twigs, mud, red beans and a tooth, held together by a wisp of plaited straw. An ominous bundle. A mute, miserable little mess with all the charm of a shrunken head or the remains of a small rodent vomited from a cat's stomach.

I circled it slowly, drawn to it, and yet unwilling to sit down next to it.

What sort of child would create a plaything like this? Or was it part of something larger? A primitive game, perhaps?

James would have known.

I pulled one of his letters from the stack on the bedside table. It had been written to me soon after his arrival. He had just established his solitary camp in the rain forest near Ranomafana, which probably accounts for the frenzied, over-the-top ecstasy— call it madness—in his initial descriptions of the wilderness:

"Nature in Madagascar is so exuberant that it invests the seething excesses of its vitality in royal whims, or fancies. The day to day struggle for existence plods on, and yet everywhere you look, nature's at work, creating a surrealistic world, a sumptuous place where everything is like a fairy tale, a fairy tale which, in Madagascar, becomes a reality.

"Jungles run riot in their fertility, animals hold power over the fortunes of men, men live the lives of plants and animals, rivers and mountains

transform themselves into rapacious beasts or friendly spirits, and the senses become even more rapacious and intoxicated. Everything which surrounds you is both reality and chimera, a network of dreams and evidence, both sun and shadow.

"On the lower levels of existence, fear and death are a cruel reality. And yet, in the higher planes, there's this amazing, what should I call it?——this amazing splendor of life, that indulges itself in dreams and incarnates them in unaccountable forms, imposing upon nature exquisite follies with which to conquer the spectre of death."

A network of dreams and evidence... exquisite follies... with which to conquer the spectre of death... This was definitely not the kind of field report you'd expect from a post-doctoral scientist

I rifled through the stack of letters. There were other letters like this. Lots of them. They made me very nervous. This was not the James I knew.

My brother was a biologist schooled in the linear, left-brain laboratories of Yale and Cornell. A pale, short, skinny kid, even in junior high school he was known as a dogged worker and a teacher's pet. A grueler. Nothing changed as he grew taller. He didn't become a tough man, or a poetic one. He was a worker bee. A foot soldier. At university he gained a reputation as someone to be counted on to deliver a solid piece of research. A man of superior intellect and modest ambition. In our family of four brothers and a baby sister, he was the only one we could send out for pizza who was guaranteed to return without having eaten a single slice.

In short: James was our nerd.

Maybe that was why I loved him so much. We were a lot alike—shy, self-effacing loners in a family of swaggering half-breed Italians who threw spaghetti against the wall yelling *al dente!* even when we had people over. The fact that mama was a WASP from Ohio didn't seem to matter. In fact, I think she was the one who originated the spaghetti test. "Eat Italian, or die!" was one of her favorite sayings.

James hid out behind his intellect, fiddling around in a little laboratory he'd set up in his clothes closet. He grew things in there that belonged in far-away, exotic places. For instance, he mid-wifed millions of Brazilian walking-sticks, coaxing them out of dried egg cases sent to him from Bahia by a collector named Tito Guzmeyer in exchange for a pair of Giant Rain Beetles James had captured in a mating mosh on Interstate 80 outside Kingman, Arizona.

I hid out myopically behind thick glasses, my four eyes trained on the outer world with a mixture of suspicion and wonder. Pens, pencils and brushes were my antennae and defensive artillery. After dinner, in the hour before dark, our older brothers would run outside to shout and throw the ball around, one-upping each other with baseball averages and farting jokes. James and I would retire to his lab.

In the lab, I was important. I was James' right-hand, his artistic batman, a court painter whose job it was to faithfully catalog each specimen in his growing collection of fantastic insects. Perched on a high stool, James would crack open an aromatic Monte Cruz cigar box and reverentially extract a perfectly stretched specimen of, say, a *Phasmatidae philoptera*, a rare Indonesian grasshopper with iridescent purple underwings and brilliant orange abdomen. I'd begin by first drawing its outline delicately in india ink, then I'd lay on veils of sheer watercolor wash, ending—often long after bedtime—with a blip or two of Chinese white gouache for brilliance. As I painted, James would read to me in his old-fashioned, scholarly voice about *philoptera's* life cycle.

Outside, we would dimly hear the *aacckkk-aacckkk* of Papa's rainbirds and Mike, Ernie and Paulo hollering back and forth as they tackled each other on the lawn. In the lab we were warm and safe, embalmed in the sickly sweet odor of cigars, carbon tetrachloride and old tennis shoes. The cocoon of a gigantic Cecropia moth from Ohio hung on a broken branch. Somewhere inside that gossamer, brown silk pouch, astonishing, metamorphic life was going on, life which could burst forth any moment as a glorious, feathery creature with twelve-inch wings marked by owlish, cobalt blue eye-spots.

Those evenings spent drawing bugs in the closet with James were the happiest hours of my childhood. When mama died, I tried life with my grandparents for a while, squeaked through high school, and ran away to San Francisco to become a struggling artist. Papa had his hands full with the rest of the boys and more or less forgot about me. But not James. When he left home to study at Cornell, he sent me a set of Dutch charcoal sticks in a red tin box with a corny little card that read: ART SAVES. DO IT. I still have the card and the box, even though I used up the charcoal years ago.

I stared at the bed where the toy lay bristling on the white bedsheet. It looked like a spavined tenrec—one of those miniscule Malagasy hedgehogs about the size of your thumb. Or maybe a Hairy Shrew.

I reached out to touch it, then withdrew my finger.

It was a beastly little thing, yet there was something undeniably compelling about its wretchedness. A portentous, powerful little rat's nest, I found myself thinking, capable of wreaking horrible, unforeseen damage. Capable of... altering reality.

I pulled on my clothes, eyeing it superstitiously.

What are you, crazy? an inner voice warned. Dump it now.

But, I didn't. I gingerly picked it up by one, twiggy leg and dropped it in my knapsack instead.

To this day, I'm not sure why.

Maybe it was simply too ugly to throw out.

5

There was a guard sleeping in the doorway, dozing against a sun-baked wall, his mouth slack as his empty holster. He cradled a pistol in his lap while he snored.

I slipped past him and into a gloomy building which housed ministers and other government functionaries. Several windows on the ground floor had been boarded up. A grim tracery of bullet holes in their shutters indicated an abortive coup attempt. More ominous were the walls themselves, glazed dark green, black and maroon.

The colors of revolution and torture, I thought, as I climbed to the second, then the third floor.

It was slow going. I was exhausted, and my knee was painfully swollen from last night's fall into the ditch. I limped past nameless doors swaddled in puffy, black leatherette. Soundproof. Probably bulletproof as well. I felt certain of it.

At the end of a long corridor I arrived at another padded door which boasted a small, brass plaque INTERNATIONAL

WILDLIFE CONSORTIUM. I rang, and after a long pause a lithe young man appeared and ushered me through another upholstered door into a reception area where three men were wrestling with a brace of antiquated telephones, poking feverishly into the dials, repeating themselves into the receivers. They were banked by file cabinets which overflowed out onto the floor. Stacks of papers and stamped documents bundled together with ribbon and twine were piled in corners and behind chairs. In one corner a very old man in a brown tweed overcoat pounded laboriously on a large, black typewriter, pausing every now and then to stop and blow his nose. Poor Sisyphus. I felt for him, buried under all that Malagasy scrap.

"I am here to see the Director."

"Do you have an appointment?" asked the lithe, young man.

"No, but..."

He went around behind a bare desk and put on an official face. "The Director is occupied this morning." He began to fiddle surreptitiously with a ball point pen, snapping and un-snapping it somewhere beneath the desk.

"Please tell Monsieur Rakotomana that Eva Artema would like to speak with him."

The pen stopped but the man's Adam's apple was working overtime. "I'm sorry. The Director's schedule does not permit."

"The Director gave me his personal assurance that he would see me this morning." I hunched up my shoulders closer to my ears, trying to make myself more imposing. "I am sure Monsieur Rakotomana is a man of honor and would not lie." I turned up the volume at the end to make sure I got my point across.

It worked. The young man blinked and opened his mouth once or twice.

Taking advantage of his confusion, I added haughtily, "Remind the Director that as I have come to honor Madagascar, I expect Madagascar to honor me." I sat down in a straight chair near the door. "I will wait here."

He disappeared, looking extremely chagrined.

I looked around. Posted on one wall was a large map of the island with notations of the areas set aside for wildlife Reserves marked off in colored pen. I was surprised at how limited a patchwork it was; the protected Reserves constituted barely 6% of the total island, and yet James had written that fully 95% of the bird species were endemic, over 86% of its flowering plants, some 99% of its reptiles were unique, including 148 of its 150 species of frogs.

I studied the outlines of the Reserves at close range, trying to recall James' descriptions. Soalala: famous for its caves and cave fauna. Andohahela: a combination of southern rainforest and desert flora on a granite base. Perinet: home of the wailing black-and-white indri indri lemurs. Nosy Mangabe: a mere speck of an island off the northeast coast where a special Reserve had been created for the nearly extinct aye-aye, a bizarre nocturnal mammal with bat ears, beaver teeth and skeletal prehensile forefingers that it uses to strip bark from fallen logs and impale the fat grubs hidden inside.

"Some superstitious villagers believe that the aye-aye brings bad luck or death into a village, and if one is found nearby the inhabitants hunt it down and kill it, even going so far as to burn down the entire village and relocate it elsewhere in order to escape the aye-aye's baleful spell. In 1966 nine animals were captured with great difficulty in the coastal rainforests along the eastern escarpment by Andre Peyrieras and Jean-Jacques Petter. They released them onto the beach on the island of Nosy Mangabe where the aye-ayes promptly disappeared into the bush, not to be seen or heard from again until 1987 when one was briefly sighted, its eyes gleaming like orange marbles in the beam of a flashlight."

"The Director will see you in his office," said the young man, holding open the door.

I swept past him.

Rakotomana's office was palatial, but spartan. Twenty-foot-high ceilings accommodated several roomy, turn of the century glass-front armoires filled with dusty fossils, amonites, amethyst geodes and a few woodcarvings. Open bookshelves housed a modest scientific library in French, Malagasy and German. Very few volumes were in English. On the walls were a collection of sepia photographs of 19th century Malagasy notables dressed in frock coats and hoop skirts. They looked hot and serious; not one of them smiled.

The Director had his back turned when I entered. He was talking earnestly into a cell phone. From behind, he was even bigger than I remembered, almost as large as the President, whose garish, oversized photograph dominated the wall over Rakotomana's desk. It occurred to me that the President sported an unconscionably large assortment of military medals on his uniformed chest, given the fact that Madagascar had not been involved in any recent wars. Maybe they were tributes to the Malagasy infantrymen who fought with France during the Second World War.

Rakotomana turned and holstered the phone on his hip.

"Ah, Mademoiselle Artema. Please be seated." He indicated a large cut-velvet settee to one side of the room, settling himself at the far end. "I regret my hasty exit last evening. A family affair. Here in Madagascar we put our family responsibilities first, before everything." He reached for a carafe on the table and poured two tumblers.

"Scotch?"

Blondes and whiskey, taken together...

"Why not?" I said, gamely lifting my glass to match his.

James, at 10 a.m., this one's for you.

"You are enjoying your stay *au bout du monde*?" Rakotomana inquired, and drained his glass. A drop of Scotch clung to his lower lip, where it glistened like honey. In the morning light the disparity between his impeccable tailoring and raw energy was blatant.

I clenched my hands tighly around my wounded knee and eyed him evenly, trying not to blink. The whiskey helped.

"I would like to say yes, but unfortunately I cannot. My brother, James Artema, is missing—has been missing—for over seven months. I'm afraid that something may have happened to him."

The Director poured another glass for himself before answering. He settled back into the velvet cushions with the studied ease of a card player holding a straight flush.

"Mademoiselle, Madagascar is not a violent country like America. We have no gangs, no drugs, no random shootings in our schools. A little petty thievery, a few pickpockets at most."

"Seven months is a long time."

Reaching into my bag, I withdrew the stack of letters. "For over a year James has written to me once a week, without fail. And then, suddenly, silence. Nothing." I fished out another packet and brandished them, saying, "And these telegrams from his University... returned, addressee unknown."

"There is something you should understand, mademoiselle..." he tipped his glass. "The status of foreign scientists is, how should I say... *problematique* in our country. Missions, delegations from your universities, they stop here for a few months or a year training their microscopes and binoculars on Madagascar's plants and animals..." Rakotomana leaned forward to pour. "Do they ever take the time to visit the University of Tananarive and lecture on their findings? Do they arrange reciprocal research fellowships for Malagasy scientists in their own countries?"

He emptied his glass before continuing.

"Imagine, if you will, a party of German biologists arriving in Florida to study your native alligators with not so much as a nod to their American colleagues. Madagascar is a world heritage, yes, but it is also *our* heritage. Why should foreign scientists come to Madagascar and then act as if we Malagasy do not exist?"

The morning light slid across his face and caught a bead of perspiration. It ran down his left temple, disappeared under his beard and re-emerged to slide into the cleft of darkness underneath a fleshy ear lobe.

I tried another tack. "Monsieur Rakotomana, I have heard that you have a list, a record of every foreign scientist working in the Reserves."

33

He hitched up one pant leg and gazed past me at the glaring, primary colors of the Presidential photo. His eyes faded oddly, became dull and flat, like the eyes of a hooked fish. It was as if a scrim had suddenly dropped between the two of us, rendering him present, but not accounted for. I immediately regretted my words.

Never confront a Malagasy dead-on with a question. Circle around. Make heap big small talk.

"May I..?" I proffered my glass. "Johnny Walker Black. Excellent whiskey."

He poured generously. "A taste acquired abroad, at the University of Strasbourg."

"Then you're a biologist yourself?"

"I'm a taxonomist by training. I was called home while in the midst of completing my thesis on the comparative anatomy and taxonomy of Madagascar's *Tenrecidae*. Pseudohedgehogs, you call them in the West." He cracked his knuckles as if to punctuate his point. "Called home. Family duties. A long time ago..." he trailed off, lapsing into silence.

"The list..." I soldiered on uphill, ignoring the personal opening, "...of scientists."

"It is our duty to protect our Reserves from incursions."

I pressed the opening. "Then, such a list does exist?"

"So many species still unaccounted for. A taxonomist's paradise..."

The Director dropped his voice to a hoarse, urgent whisper, hunching closer to me until our thighs were touching. The antique sofa creaked under the shifting weight of his body. I recoiled, as if an extraordinarily dense and radioactive meteorite had suddenly cratered next to me.

"Miss Artema," he said, "you understand, there are things to be discovered in Madagascar."

Ambassador Theron's very words.

The Johnny Walker roared in my ears, tasted brassy behind my tongue. This was a far cry from my usual 10 a.m. routine of lukewarm black coffee, gulped down while pacing alone in an unheated studio, waiting for my paints to warm up and my brain cells to ignite.

"Yes, I know. James came to Madagascar with the hope of discovering some of them." I searched for flattering words, soothing phrases. "He often described the island as a floating laboratory. I think his exact words were 'a Noah's ark that drifted away from the mainland of Africa over 65 million years ago.' He considered it a paradise for scientists like himself. A once in a lifetime opportunity to study rare, endangered species in the wild."

Unfortunately my words, calculated to calm, had just the opposite effect.

"As I have told you, mademoiselle, the status of foreign scientists in Madagascar is a small and short-term problem." Rakotomana's voice rose imperiously. "Conservation education, however, is a complex and long-term problem. Guarding the forests and the very existence of the named and as-yet-unnamed species is the largest problem of all, for it is intertwined with the day-to-day economic needs of the Malagasy people. In our country, science must lie down before empty bellies."

The scrim between us had thickened, along with his speech. He spoke fiercely, yet somehow I couldn't help feeling that his words were forced, his passion rehearsed. Was it the Scotch talking? Or, was there something he was trying to hide?

I struggled to reel him in, none too sober myself.

"You will forgive me. I certainly appreciate the difficulties inherent in your work..."

Should I go down on my knees now, or later?

"Would you... could you please check your computer for the date when you issued James a research permit, and for which Reserve?" I took a deep breath. "It would be a beginning."

In a single, bellicose gesture, the Director shot his cuffs and his chin towards me. "Mademoiselle, are you aware that there are only fifty computers in Madagascar? And that half of them are broken, hopelessly in need of repair and spare parts? As for a list..." He waved angrily in the direction of the outer office. "You have seen our *systeme*. Phillipe, Jerome, the boys..."

Azul. Can't you feel it, my little blind albino *vazaha*? It's Code Blue, babe. Jack's words swarmed in my head.

At that moment the door opened and Rakotomana's assistant entered, handed him a sheaf of documents and withdrew. The Director frowned and leafed through the pages, carefully inspecting the stamps.

"Ah, just so," he said slowly. "Dr. Artema is a primatologist, yes? Lemurs are his specialty?"

I nodded eagerly, hunching closer to him.

"According to these, he was permitted for Zaohitra Reserve on March first."

Zaohitra. I recalled James' description clearly: *"Leaving tomorrow for Zaohitra. Escarpment rain forest. Leeches and lemurs. Isolation. Ecstasy."* That letter, posted in Ranomafana, was the last letter I'd ever received from him. Its pages were filled with that exalted prose I'd found so unlike him.

Rakotomana's face darkened. "It seems that your brother has overstayed his *sejour* in Madagascar by many months." He tapped the papers against his open palm. "He is in violation of his permit, and his visa expired as of July 13th. It is October, and there is no indication here that he has renewed it."

My heart turned over painfully in my chest. "Then I am right, he *is* in danger."

"Legally, yes."

"He could be anywhere! Ill, lost, captured... murdered!"

"Please, do not jump to such grave conclusions, Mademoiselle Artema. All that is known for sure is that your brother is in violation of the permit granted to him by the I.W.F. to conduct research in Zaohitra Reserve."

Rakotomana swirled his manicured forefinger around and around the rim of his empty whiskey tumbler, causing a low and mournful toning to rise and fall in the empty space between us, where it vibrated like a sine curve in the still air. He stared at me with unsmiling, leaden eyes.

"The matter of his visa is a separate, more serious problem. Our Consortium is not the Malagasy government..." He spoke slowly and deliberately for emphasis. "However..."

...suddenly you look down and find your leg's half-chewed off...

"Are you saying that it's a hopeless quest?"

He recrossed his heavy thighs. "*Au contraire*. Not hopeless, just ill-advised."

Upon seeing the look on my face, he shrugged and softened slightly. "Zaohitra is a beginning. Something, after all. Perhaps you have a better idea. Who knows? It is possible you'll get lucky and find him camped somewhere in the rain forest with his lemurs. Zaohitra is a small Reserve, only 731 kilometers in all, uninhabited and largely unexplored. In our country, it is known as the Blue Rainforest."

Only 731 kilometers? Camped somewhere in the forest? I snorted softly, acutely aware of the pathetic impossibility of my task.

"Well then, shall I plan to catch a plane or a train down to the small, blue rain forest?" It was hard to keep the disappointed sarcasm out of my voice.

"Neither." He blew right past the irony. "You will need a pirogue—a dugout canoe."

I slapped my forehead, surrendering to the absurdity and the whiskey.

Hang on, James. We've hit a snag. A small *probleme* with a dugout.

Rakotomana continued. "This time of year you cannot fly to the southeast coast. Air Madagascar flights have been booked for months. You'll need to take a bush-taxi or hire a four-wheel drive to take you to Mananjary. From there, if you're very lucky, you might find someone with a pirogue who is willing to take you up the Pangalanes Canal as far as the village of Ambohitsara. There is a chance you will meet Pere Soren, a missionary, making his annual *tournee*." He chuckled, "This month is *sambatra*, and *sambatra* makes the Christians a little nervous."

"Nervous? Why?"

He leaned towards me. "*Sambatra* is a mass circumcision ceremony."

I blanched and gulped.

Azul. Azul.

"It is a special celebration that takes place only once every seven years in Mananjary." He lowered his tone confidentially. "However, in the village of Ambohitsara, they hold another, even more archaic ceremony. *Tres symbolique.* Myself, I have never met a Westerner who has ever witnessed it. I believe it is taboo, but I do not know for sure..."

He drained his glass and placed it on the table, studying my reaction carefully.

"Unfortunately, one must pass through Ambohitsara in order to reach the Blue Rainforest."

"Surely there is another route."

"There is no other way to enter the forest today," Rakotomana stated firmly. "The trails from the northeast were demolished during the cyclones last winter, and as far as I know, no one has ever scaled the Tanala escarpment that runs along the western border. There is a mountain..." he began, then checked himself. "The southernmost border is naturally protected by miles of salt water marshes and tidal sloughs. I'm sure you can see why Zaohitra is our least-popular Reserve."

"And... s*ambatra?*" I blurted out. "Who attends that celebration?"

"Hundreds—perhaps thousands—of young men from all over Madagascar. Most of them travel on foot. One must take great care while driving. The roads will be jammed with people, including many small children."

"Children? You mean... *kokolampo?*"

The word flew out of my mouth unbidden. It ambushed me, like a quail that flurries up, flushed from under a hedge the moment you raise your booted foot above the trail.

Michel Rakotomana stared at me without speaking. Only his flaring nostrils indicated he had heard me, but I felt certain he was startled and making an effort to disguise it.

"*Kokolampo*? Where did you hear that word?" His face broadened into a smile but his eyes stayed behind the scrim—dark, prowling, wary.

I raised my eyebrows naively. Two can play this game. "Oh, I must have overheard it last night, at the Ambassador's party. I'm curious. Tell me, what exactly is a *kokolampo*?"

He hunched forward, frowning. "*Kokolampo* are demons. Water sprites. Malevolent spirits. The rural people believe they inhabit our forests, lakes and streams. Some foolishly insist that they live underneath Tananarive in underground rivers and subterranean grottos. Of course, no one has ever actually captured one and dissected it. Therefore, we scientists cannot assign them a *réalité*, can we?"

There is no crime. There was no... child.

"You're speaking as a taxonomist, Monsieur Rakotomana? Or as a metaphysician?"

It was his turn to raise his eyebrows.

"Both," he said smoothly. "Anything less would place one's soul in peril."

Mademoiselle, it is dangerous! Leave it! You must leave it and come away!

A fleeting image flashed across the back of my retina, the image of a white rag, crawling into a ditch. I drew a deep breath. "These... *kokolampo*. They're merely figments of the Malagasy imagination then?"

"But, of course. Mere prehistoric memories of our Indo-Polynesian ancestors. A part of our racial dreaming, you could say. As for their supposed 'habitat'... Speaking as a scientist I can assure you that Tananarive is built on gneiss and granite overlaid with lateritic schist. Underground rivers? Subterranean grottos? Pure fantasy!"

"And, speaking as a metaphysician?"

As soon as I spoke I regretted the flirtatious lilt in my voice, but it was too late to call back the words.

Rakotomana looked down at my flushed face. Smiling slowly, intimately, his gaze tracking the hollow where the clavicle curved away under the open collar of my denim workshirt.

"It is a pity you are not a scientist, Mademoiselle Artema." His tone contained an unsettling mixture of threat and longing. "A great pity. You have so much... else."

I stood up and shook his hand fast and hard. Quickly. Like a man.

"I am eternally in your debt."

Looking straight ahead I stepped past him, in a hurry to reach the safety of the outer office occupied by Phillipe, Jerome and the typewriter's comforting clack.

Rakotomana crossed the room quickly and caught me at the door, pressing one hand flat against the thick leatherette, barring my way. His body felt huge and hot next to mine. His voice rumbled around in his chest like apples in a barrel.

"I strongly advise you against undertaking this journey, mademoiselle. The Blue Rainforest is a place very few Malagasy have ever visited. There are legends. Rumors. I do not recommend... for a woman alone."

Fighting words.

"Monsieur, take care. You're talking about my brother. *Family.*" My cheeks flared, brushed with warning fires.

He backed off and bowed slightly, retreating into an official *politesse.* "Of course. My sincere apologies, Mademoiselle Artema."

"Please. Call me Eva."

It was the least I could do.

After all, it *was* a beginning.

I should have been pleased, but the meeting left me strangely depressed and more at sea than before. Relieved to be sprung from the catacombs of the Ministry, I decided to walk back to my hotel, hoping that the fresh air would help me sort things out.

It was an error. I'd forgotten that several steep hills separated me from Independence Square and the Hotel Le Terrace. I hadn't walked more than a hundred yards when my knee went on strike, swelling until it resembled the trunk of a baobob tree. The midday heat didn't help, or the gaping cavities in the sidewalk where large chunks of paving stones had crumbled away to reveal deep muddy pits big enough to swallow a crippled *vazaha* without a trace.

Kokolampo... kokolampo...

The words beat a cadence in time to my throbbing knee. Malagasy rushed by, swaying nimbly and effortlessly, crowds of them separating to glide past me in that uncaring, muscular way a pod of dolphins will part to plunge past a lone and clumsy human swimmer. Many were barefoot, carrying their shoes and stockings in a neat bundle atop their heads to keep them fresh for arrival at their destinations. It certainly made sense. Looking down, I saw my ankles tattooed with red clay mud, my calves encrusted in rusty knee-highs, dress code for an obscure tribal ritual. My knapsack bumped against my hip, and I shrugged it around to the front, clutching to my chest all that linked me to my missing brother—a bunch of dog-eared letters and telegrams. I had no eyes to lose them to the prying fingers of a thief.

...a few pickpockets, at most.

Rakotomana had sniffed at my fears, but only yesterday I'd seen a pair of golden hoops snatched from the ears of an elderly *vazaha* in broad daylight near the train station. She'd screamed and dropped her shopping basket, cupping her hands over her bleeding earlobes as tomatoes and onions tumbled out in the dust at her feet. There had been an encouraging tumult and some fist waving as solicitous Malagasy rushed forward to pick up the vegetables, dusting them off and returning them politely to her basket, but nobody seemed motivated to give chase and the thief disappeared into the crowd without a trace.

This morning, I'd taken the precaution of removing my zircon studs. Not out of fear, but for love.

My ears used to be a favorite erogenous zone. No sense sacrificing a known pleasure dome for $39.95 worth of phony diamonds. *Bésame, pajarita,* Raul used to whisper, nibbling, biting, feasting. Oh, he was a *nosher* of ears all right. He could take me out standing up, right there in the kitchen backed up against the stove with the chicken frying and the garlic smoking, his tongue in my ear *bésame, bésame* with my skirt hiked up over my waist and who cared? It's a known fact. You can count on my ears as a solid base hit, if not an RBI.

Something else I should mention. My pain threshold is low. I was even hospitalized once for poison oak. It was a Catholic hospital, and when I saw the nurses swooping up and down the halls in their starched white wimples, I thought they were angels and I'd died somewhere between 622 Jasper St. and the door of my room at Mother of Mercy. I was six at the time and being Catholic scared me even then, though I didn't know what being Catholic meant except that there wasn't much of a margin for error or you'd end up in a spooky, damp place like Our Lady of Perpetual Sorrows forever and ever, amen.

Hobbling around a corner, I arrived at Lake Anosy, a stagnant, jade pool lying placidly in the center of a busy roundabout. Towering above the lake to the east brooded the Palace of Queen Ranavalona the Cruel who, in 1835, pulled the plug on the Christian missionary effort in Madagscar by spearing the first Malagasy saint, a woman named Rasalama. After that, there was no stopping Ranavalona. Countless thousands of believers were flogged, stoned, poisoned, plunged head-first into boiling water or burnt alive before they were thrown off the front porch of her palace, kicked tumbling down the sheer granite cliffs to meet their Maker in the brush surrounding Lake Anosy.

Traffic swarmed around the lake's perimeter in a circular blur. Cranky deux-cheveaux Citroens jostled with bush-taxis crowded with wide-eyed peasants newly arrived from the countryside to buy and sell in the Zoma market. Occasionally, a late-model Land Rover with familiar, First World acronyms stencilled on the door panels would rumble into the roundabout. I scrutinized the pale *vazaha* faces inside and felt a blast of envy as they tooled loudly around the lakeshore in their shiny imported trucks on their way to governmental conferences, riding smugly to the rescue of the Developing World, their humanitarian devotion back-stopped by the knowledge that their paychecks were being deposited in an overseas bank, secured by a gold standard and immune from the disastrously sagging currency of their host country; that whatever inconveniences they had to endure here were only temporary and would be more than offset by the bounty of technological advances and cosy comforts that would engulf them upon their return home. But, why be envious? Let's face it: My brother James was one of them, hunkered down into his narrow professional niche, skilled at keeping his personal opinions under wraps, trying to publish a paper or two as leverage for next year's funding. Dedicated, well-meaning. Harmless.

What had happened to him? Why had he abandoned his government sinecure? It wasn't like him to let his visa run out. He was a bear for details like that. Nausea arose in my throat. The taste of bile. Of fear.

Gentle James. The way you removed your gold-rimmed glasses, carefully wiping them, then replacing them on your nose as if you were saying a silent Eucharist. James, James, you should have been a priest.

At the edge of the road was an open-air barbershop consisting of six straight-backed chairs placed in a row under a stand of tall chestnut trees. I crossed the street, dodging taxis in a disorderly scramble, and sank onto one of the empty chairs to rest my leg and bask in the cool air lifting from the surface of the water, watching the barbers work. They leaned forward from the hips, as waiters do, patiently shaping their clients' sideburns, their chromed shears flickering like a school of jack smelt in the leafy shadows. The dirt underneath the chairs was furred with soft, black tumbleweeds clipped from the heads of the patrons. They skittered aimlessly across the packed earth, propelled to and fro by an errant breeze.

It was then I noticed that a small crowd was gathering at the edge of the lake. The knot of people was increasing rapidly. Bands of raggedy children dashed back and forth shouting excitedly, "*Le sacré croc! Le sacré croc!*" Shawled women wrapped in white *lamba*s huddled together in groups, pointing at something in the shallow water.

Curiosity has always been one of my character defects. I say that because it has gotten me into trouble more often than out of it. I'm a sucker for novelty, too. So, naturally I abandoned my shady chair and joined the ranks of the curious at the lakeside, peering over the heads of the Malagasy.

There, beached in the sludge, a mossy veil of lime green bouillon draped raffishly over its snout, was an enormous crocodile. Its yellow eyes bubbled up on the top of its gargantuan head like fiendish, primeval periscopes scanning the present from the vantage of a far distant, antediluvian past. Its great jowly neck surged and bulged as it squirmed up the bank, the leathery scales forming a writhing boa of armored, grey platelets.

The crowd pressed closer, chattering nervously. Men dressed in Western suits competed for a view with peasants wearing raffia caps and the traditional *malabar*—knee-length plaid shirts.

"*Pauvre croco*," muttered a tiny, wizened crone at my elbow. "Just look at her, the sacred crocodile of Anosy, our beloved ancestor, smothered in slime. Yet, she lives! And still beautiful. *N'est ce pas?*"

The old woman clung to me, grinning toothlessly. "They say she is a Vazimba Queen." Her fingers stabbed into my elbow as newly arrived onlookers jostled past us for a better view. "*Vazaha*," she hissed, "give this to her. Appease her." She placed a bottle of rum in my hand, pumping it up and down, making a sprinkling gesture.

"Who, me? I'm... I'm a tourist!"

I backed away from her, trying to blend into the crowd. but was instantly catapulted forward, flung toward the beast by the momentum of the throng, a reluctant acolyte waving a sacrificial bottle of home-brew.

As if on cue, the crusty old saurian heaved herself up out of the water on spraddled legs, opened her repulsive pink jaws rimmed with a double row of crooked fangs, and headed straight for me at an alarming speed.

Holy shit! This was no *kokolampo*! This *sacré croc* meant business!

I sprang back, struggling against the wall of humanity.

The croc lunged.

People cheered.

A man began plucking merrily on a *valiha*, a sort of bamboo ukelele-in-a-tube. Two women in brightly patterned *lambas* started a fast, rhythmic clapping, and *bingo*, I was thrust forward once again, against my will, pushed right to the very edge of the ooze, helpless as a surfer about to eat it on a coral reef.

One whip of her mighty twelve-foot tail brought the croc nose-to-toes with my muddy kneecaps and then...

She stopped, unhinged her jaws and emitted a horrible *chhaaachht!!*

"Pour, *vazaha*! Appease her. Appease our Queen!" the old crone hissed at my elbow, her creased face shining like a betel nut.

I didn't need any encouragement. I poured, I dumped, I flung the entire bottle of rum down, down, about six feet down into the pinkish-white throat where it ricocheted against the sacred glottis and disappeared, joining the bones of who knows how many unfortunates as her jaws closed with a resounding *snappp!* And all the while the *valiha* twanged and the *lamba*-ed ladies of Tananarive clapped and sang, driving the hag at my side to execute a frenzied jitterbug, completely carried away by the joy of it all.

Then the crocodile lowered her gruesome snout, swinging it from side to side several times before aiming it directly at me!

The crowd fell silent.

I braced myself. Yea, though I walk through the Valley of the Shadow, Raul, Papa, James... wherever you are, trust me, I had *corazón*. Right up to the end.

The monster took two short steps forward—I could feel the breath from her nostrils hot on my calves—and, amazement! she gently, ever so gently, laid her ugly head at my feet! Obeisance, that's what it was. Obeisance pure and simple. There was no mistaking it.

A communal shiver swept through the assembled Malagasy. Strangers put their arms around each other. People crossed themselves. Mothers hugged their children. Hands reached out to touch me. The gigantic reptile lay docilely in the slime as if drugged, the pupils of her eyes reduced to hairline slits.

"*Voici la reine de Vazimba*," whispered the clinging crone in a hushed tone.

The Queen of the Vazimba? Was she referring to the crocodile? Or to me?

I tiptoed backwards. Always quit winners, Papa used to say as he swept the matchsticks off the edge of the card table. I threaded my way back up the shore towards the roundabout, retreating to safety with the old woman glued to my side. Now the crowd parted magically around me, falling aside in waves like the Red Sea. I knew in that instant how the Pope must feel. And, I confess, I didn't dislike the feeling, either.

We must have created quite a sight gathered there on the side of the roadway, for a jeep swerved out of the streaming traffic and bore down on us, honking as it came. A man in mirrored sunglasses leaned over and opened the passenger door.

"Hey, Artema. Need a lift?"

Jack Mooresby, no less.

He grinned and motioned to me from the jeep, "Hop in."

As if last night was nothing, had never happened.

"C'mon. Jump in." His smile broadened. "I won't bite."

I felt the old woman tugging at me and looked down. She reached between her withered breasts and pulled out a grubby card with an astral chart drawn on one side. I turned it over and read:

Dr. R. A. Rabansoro, Ashram Vedique, 24 Rue Malombaoro, Antananarivo.

"Go to him," she said, pinching my fingers around the card. "Go now. Before it is too late."

"Artema, let's roll." Traffic was beginning to pile up behind the jeep.

I don't know exactly what made me do it. Maybe it was seeing the word "ashram" that set me off, and memories of a month spent trekking in Nepal. But it just didn't seem as if *ciao* or *au revoir* would cut it at a moment like this. So I pressed my hands together with the card held tightly between, and I bowed, touching my forehead with the tips of my fingers—first towards the old woman, then to the congenial rabble, then towards Lake Anosy and the sacred crocodile.

"*Namaste,*" I said. I see the god in you.

They solemnly returned my bow. All except the Old Queen herself, who had slunk down to the lake and vanished into the ooze while no one was paying attention.

"Where to?" Jack said, as he pulled out into the traffic.

When I told him the Hotel Le Terrace, he laughed. It was a wicked, knowing laugh, but I chose not to respond, wondering if he indulged in the activities that went on in the bar downstairs and in rooms No. 40 and 42, which Madame Moreau rented by the hour. Rangita preferred No. 42. It had a small balcony overlooking the Zoma market. She'd waved me into No. 42 the afternoon I'd arrived, thirty-one hours out of San Francisco with my metabolic clock going backwards, registering somewhere around 2 a.m. Pacific Standard Time.

"*Americaine?*" She was fluffing her wig. "Come in. Come in. You have my blessing."

Rangita had been "between sets," as she delicately put it, and while she washed and dried I hung over the wide railing, looking out on the vast open market below, dazzled by the sea of white canvas umbrellas that stretched up and down Independence Square, disappearing into the steep side streets like the snowy tails of a receding glacier.

"Today's Friday. Market day. Streets around the Zoma will be jammed. How about lunch instead?" Jack's smile was so boyish I almost forgave him his trespasses.

"No thanks. I'm not hungry."

"No? Why not? You still got a hard-on about last night?"

Nothing modest about Mooresby.

"Let's just say some things take time, *au bout du monde.*"

He laughed again. "You sound like Theron. Say, what were you doing out there by the lake, anyhow?"

"Nursing my knee and anointing a crocodile." I pulled up my skirt and showed him the swelling.

He whistled. "In any particular order?"

"I... I don't know. It's a long story, and weird. You haven't got time."

"Try me," he said, wheeling a U-turn.

We rumbled down a side street, narrowly missing a brightly painted rickshaw loaded with cassava. The muscular, bare-chested driver of the *pousse-pousse* was shouting and singing at top volume as he dragged the heavy, wooden cart over the cobblestones, as oblivious to danger as a pit bull in combat.

"*Omelette aux herbes,* or *bifsteak au poivre?*"

"I said I'm not hungry."

"Right," said Jack. "Chinese it is."

We ended up not far from the Zoma market after all. Entering a narrow alley behind a burned-out arcade that housed Air Madagascar, we ducked into L'Indochine Restaurant under a sprawling jacaranda tree that dripped purple blossoms into a tank filled with lazy koi.

It was cool and dusky in the restaurant, except for a few beams of sunlight that pierced a carved screen covering a window. The tables were neatly appointed with white nappery and tiny porcelain cups. I held one up to the light. It was the finest porcelain I had ever held in my hand. The light fell through the translucent rice pattern, spattering the white cotton tablecloth with pale, cobalt blue ovals. It reminded me of the light at Chartres, falling in long rays from the great rose window, falling soundlessly, full of motes and incense, to shatter into colored confetti on the worn, stone floors where worshippers shuffled and genuflected.

"Here, give me your leg," said Jack, kneeling in front of me, pushing up my skirt and placing my leg over his. He pulled a half dozen dripping tea bags out of the pot that was steeping on the table and began squeezing out the excess liquid. "Great for bruises. Something about the tannin..." He applied the poultice in a rough tourniquet, grabbing extra napkins from other tables until I was completely swaddled in white.

"I suppose you're going to take charge of ordering my lunch, too?"

"Already have," Jack said, flashing that smile. "Any more questions?"

I took a deep breath. "Is hit-and-run a capital crime in Madagascar? Why do Vazimba queens masquerade as a crocodiles? Are all the taxis filled with sightseeing corpses? What in the hell happens at a mass circumcision, and do you ever take off those bloody mirrored glasses?"

Jack threw his head back and roared. "In any particular order?"

"The shades, for starters. I'm an old-fashioned girl with old-fashioned needs—like eye contact."

"Fair enough," he said, and removed his glasses.

Big mistake.

His eyes were brown, with swimming gold flecks and a few odd bits of turquoise. His lashes were long and tangled, like a girl's. They were the kind of eyes that ate your clothes and spat them out and then spent a lot of time going over the rest.

"What's the matter? Leg hurting?"

"Yes. No." I fumbled around, staring intently into the bowl of soup the waiter had just set down in front of us. "I... I'm allergic to shrimp."

"*Garçon!*"

A distinguished old man with pomaded hair and an exceedingly gracious manner glided out of the shadows bearing two more dishes, one of which was a large, brilliant, boiled fish that looked suspiciously first cousin to the koi in the patio tank outside.

"Specialty *du chef*," said Jack, plunging his chopsticks into its steaming midsection and offering it up to me. He nodded at the retreating waiter. "Kwon Duc must be eighty-five at least. He emigrated to Tana during the 1950s when Madagascar and Indochina were both French colonies and *le Metropole* still called the shots in a big chunk of the Third World."

"I take it you're not a Francophile?"

"Imperialists, like cowboys, were born to be overthrown."

"You say that with too much conviction not to be one—or the other."

"Try the other." He took a sip of tea and tipped back in his chaair. "I was born in Bozeman, Montana, in the back of a two-ton pick-up. My mom flagged a Greyhound as soon as the cord was snipped, cutting Pop and me loose to float. We followed the rodeo circuit until he was stomped by a bull in Albuquerque. I was nine then. He died before the rodeo clowns could pull him out of the ring. My uncle Crick was one of those clowns. Crick never got over it. Guess that's why he took me home to raise."

"It's quite a stretch from Montana to Madagascar."

"Lotta years in between, Artema. Lotta *agua*."

The scent of jasmine tea filled the air between us, softening the bitterness in his voice. It started me thinking that maybe those shades were hiding something more than a fly-boy's vain ego. He pulled some more tea bags out of the pot and got very busy fooling around playing doctor with my knee. When he finished, he slouched back into the laquered chair, crossing his arms over his chest.

"Now, what's this about a hit-and-run?"

So I told him the whole story, up to and including the business with the sacred crocodile. I neglected to mention my ears and

Raul. After all, why muddy the *agua?* We went through a couple of pots of tea, and I could tell that he was as skeptical about my story as I was about his doctoring, but I felt a lot better for having laid it out the way I did. I mean, it sounded almost sane, if not plausible.

"I'm no expert on Malagasy customs," Jack said. "But I do know that they're into some serious ancestor worship. In fact, chances are you'll run into a *famadihana* almost anywhere in the *haute plateau* from now on during the dry season. They refer to it as the '*retournnement des morts*', the 'turning of the dead'."

I must have wrinkled my nose, for he continued, "It's not like that. I've never seen one, but I hear it's more like a gigantic block party, with music and dancing and plenty of rum. The astrologer sets the day. Then they open the family tomb and take out the mummified corpses and bones of their ancestors that are laid on some kind of shelves inside, wash them and re-wrap them in new silk shrouds, and then carry them around town so they can see what's gone on since they died."

"Hence, Uncle Rasolo. Who didn't die."

"Hence, Uncle Rasolo."

"But that doesn't explain the *kokolampo*, or this." I reached into my bag, pulled out the toy and handed it across he table to him.

He took one look at it and said, "*Ody.* Get rid of it."

"What're you talking about?"

"*Ombiasa* make these things. For Malagasy. Not for *vazahas*."

"Hold on a minute." I didn't like his tone. It was a reprise of last night. "Translate, please."

Jack took his chopsticks and pushed the *ody* into a neutral zone between our tea cups, speaking as if I were a child—a not very bright one.

"An *ombiasa* is a sorceror, a magician. There are supposedly thousands of *ombiasas* here in Madagascar. Some of them specialize in white magic, others black. These *odys* are part of their magician's bag of tricks. They use them to prey on the superstitions of the villagers. As a subtle means of control. I hear tell some of these *ombiasas* are very rich and powerful."

"Something's not kosher here. On the one hand you're trashing these magicians, and on the other hand you're making it sound like I'm in some kind of danger."

Jack stood up and reinstated his shades.

"If I were you, Artema, I'd put that thing back where I found it. Pronto. And I wouldn't show it to anyone in the meantime. As far as the crocodile scenario goes, I'd put it down to just another crazy, Third World one-off. And I'd make damn sure to keep my mouth shut about it, too. The Malagasy go on about their ancestors, the Vazimba, the way we go on about Jesus. Larger-than-life heroes, easy to worship—now that they're dead."

"But," I tried to lighten things up, "nobody ever dies here. Remember Uncle Rasolo?"

"Don't be a fool." Jack seemed shaken and angry, even behind the mirrors. "People die here every day. Ambassador Theron's wife died this morning. Typhoid fever. I flew her to the hospital on Reunion Wednesday. Friday she's dead."

It was my turn to be shaken. And curious. If a bunch of little sticks and a few beads were sufficient to get Jack Mooresby worked up like this, then maybe the *ody* was worth hanging onto. What if the *kokolampo* had left it behind on purpose, to help me find James? It sounds crazy, but I really thought that. That's how far gone I was, hearing about Theron' wife and black magic in the same breath, and me fresh off the plane from San Francisco, treading water *au bout du monde*.

I fingered the card in my pocket and decided to pay a visit to Dr. Rabansoro in his ashram after lunch. A little Om-ing with a respected yogi wouldn't hurt. I could use some old-fashioned centering. Especially after Jack's parting thrust.

"The Blue Rainforest, you say? Watch out for the leeches, Artema. The little suckers are regular vampires. I hear tell they've got teeth *and* wings."

His wicked laugh followed me all the way out to the street.

8

"Ny fanahy no olona. The spirit is the person. The person is the spirit." Dr. Rabansoro's words floated on wreaths of cigarette smoke. Raspy. Quavering. Barely audible. The men crowded against the walls of his study hunched closer, leaning forward to hear their teacher.

"He is ninety-one years old. A living monument," the man seated next to me whispered when I slipped into the chair beside him. The lesson had already begun.

Whiffs of incense and burnt sugar drifted into the room, mingling with the acrid scent of clove cigarettes and the smell of burning charcoal from cooking fires in the courtyard below. There were no curtains on the windows, only dusty panes of wavering, French colonial glass through which I could see the shadows of people passing by in the street outside. Great throngs of them, many barefooted, moved across the sun like shades from the underworld, their voices muted and indecipherable. They crossed the cobblestones on softly padding feet, an indiscriminate swirl of human energy, disconnected and strangely mournful, like Dante's trimmers.

"You understand, the Vazimba are still alive," the yogi wheezed out the syllables. "But," he rapped the table with one bony fingertip for emphasis, "they are invisible. They exist in another reality, on the astral plane."

Wooden chairs screaked as the men moved forward, their dark faces an immobile frieze of ebony, mahogany and teak, like carved masks in a pagan temple. From somewhere in the bowels of the ashram a rooster crowed. The edge of the plastic tablecloth flapped twice, lifted by a sudden breeze from an open window. The air was heavy, charged with a taut, metallic expectancy. In the stillness, I could hear my heart thumping: *invisible, invisible.*

Dr. Rabansoro continued, "If they wish, the Vazimba will manifest themselves, but only to true believers, the pure of heart."

Dr. Rabansoro sipped from a glass. Nobody moved. A fly settled on a cracked oil portrait of a high-collared, 19th century Malagasy cleric in sideburns suspended from the gunwales of the ceiling by a rusty wire. The fly crawled around the priestly face as if searching for a fissure where the soul flew out. The men leaned close together, their smooth faces packed and shining. Impassive icons. Believers.

"The Vazimba are... invisible?" My voice sounded thin and dry. I felt pale and irrelevant in my white skin.

Dr. Rabansoro turned to face me, gazing at me quietly for a long moment before he spoke. "*Bien sur*, mademoiselle. Invisible. *Pourquoi pas?*"

Indeed. Why not?

A terrible loneliness filled my chest. A kind of shame. An acute sense of being a spiritual poseur; a voyeur with no role in life but to peer into the lighted windows of other people's faith, into other people's secret worlds. I wasn't the only Artema who suffered like this. My brother James shared this affliction. "Loneliness is the curse of the nerd," he had once said, jokingly. I had lost myself in art; he had disappeared into science.

"Sometimes it hurts to be alone," he once wrote. *"Not only with myself, but even in the midst of others. Often then I am most separate, most horribly alone. I will do anything to avoid that pain. I believe it is why I do my best work solo, in the field, surrounded by untamed nature. With no human companions, something wild inside me resonates with the wilderness without, goading me to rise and try to understand its magnificent otherness. I bite off the fieldwork in great chunks, tearing into it like a man obsessed. I hunch all night under a plastic tarp in the driving monsoon, fighting off demons and spirits and leeches, scratching observations in a soggy spiral notebook until dawn finds me, more often than not slumped on the ground asleep, my flashlight still burning and my boots filled with rain water."*

James had his lonely passion; it was a blessing. But what about me? Was endless peering through lighted windows with a paintbrush in my hand to be my fate?

No. I had Rangita's promise.

"Come in. Come in. You have my blessing." Fluffing her blonde wig, she had welcomed a weary *vazaha*.

"Sister," she then said, and placed my hand upon her warm breast.

Sister...

The word had contained no hint of irony, but could one go so far as to call it affection? Or even friendship? Were we—Jack's words—merely executing a fancy duet, a tired *pas de deux* between the new world and the old with a few shiny trinkets as bait?

Leaning over her balcony in the tropical sun, I'd been charmed by the flotilla of pristine, white parasols shading the Zoma market, but what did I really know of the Malagasy who swarmed and bustled beneath them, buying and selling and exchanging gossip, interdictions and—most certainly—blessings? A combination of ignorance, luck and a sacred crocodile had brought me to Dr. Rabansoro's ashram. But why? What questions could I possibly expect to ask, or to have answered, within these peeling walls? And could these questions ever be more than presumptuous,

First World scratchings on the door of an unknowable, unfathomable darkness?

The seamless, almond skin of Dr. Rabansoro's face caught the dying rays of the afternoon sun, outlining him in a golden aura.

I stared, transfixed by this halation, half-expecting to see his body X-rayed next. Embarrassed, I looked down, studying my freckled hands—*vazaha* hands. I stuffed them deep into the wide pockets of my demin jacket and was shocked to feel the outline of the *ody*, bristling and unmistakeable. I'd forgotten that I had grabbed it off the lunch table in haste, ignoring Jack's warning words.

Mine, I thought, squeezing it bravely, defiantly. *Mine.*

The room suddenly became quite dark. The sun disappeared, the sky grew surly. There was a low rumble of thunder in the distance. Through the dim, watery glass, human shadows swirled faster, picking up the pace before rainfall.

I lifted my head and looked directly at Dr. Rabansoro. If anything, his halo was even more radiant than before.

The room darkened.

The yogi incandesced.

My chest tightened and I blinked.

The old yogi... glowed. Around his shoulders pulsed a saffron light, lapped in streaming rays of silver. I tried not to think of the Buddha, but images kept coming up.

Things were getting a little out of hand.

"You mean, these Vazimba are... they live... this village is completely, um... astral?" I stammered stupidly.

The assembled men swivelled and glared at me with opaque eyes, like a school of brown ciclids.

James, I thought. You owe me one.

Across the table, Dr. Rabansoro shone peacefully, his bald head luminous as a gibbous moon. His eyes were mere slits, his breathing slow and regular.

Was he sleeping? Or about to levitate?

"Mademoiselle," he said in a low voice, "you are wondering

why it is you are here in Madagascar."

I held my breath.

Rimpled plaints of thunder ripped across the sky, hovering outside the mullioned windows, knocking against the weary glass.

"Andrebabe, mademoiselle. The invisible village. You must search for it." The old yogi's voice faded to a dreamlike whisper, "It is why you are here." Then he began reciting in a queer, nasal sing-song:

"*Believe me, believe me not. If you believe me, it will be fine...*"

A man to his left picked it up. "*If you do not believe me, it will rain...*"

"*Ah, aha, it is not I who tells lies...*" another follower sang, nodding his head rhythmically.

"*It is the Old Ones, the Wild Ones, the Sly Ones, the Ones who inhabit the lakes and streams...*" added a young boy in a checked shirt. "*...It is the kokolampo who have told me this story.*"

The men chanted the last line in unison, pumping out the words in a sonorous, resonating baritone, lobbing them one after the other into the murky air, repeating them softer and softer until they disappeared like stones dropped into a bottomless cenote.

There was a tremendous clap of thunder and one of the windows slammed open. The priestly portrait slewed across the ochre wall and rammed into a plastered corner, blown by a gust of rain-laden wind. In the lurid, blue lightning immediately following, I noticed a jagged tear had appeared in the painting, severing the minister's right ear and its mutton-chop from the angular cheek-bone, exposing a raw canvas edge and some garish pink underpainting, like a duelling wound.

The yogi's acolytes jumped up and began rushing around, securing the remaining windows against the driving rain. Only Dr. Rabansoro and I remained seated.

Things were going south fast.

Rain drummed against the tiled roof of the ashram, beating down upon the plattery leaves of a banana tree in the open courtyard, drenching the yogi's *dhotis*, which hung disconsolately from a sagging rope, emptied of flesh or spirit.

Clearing my throat, I conjured for a definitive exit.

"Doctor, please understand, I am in Madagascar for one reason alone: that is to find my brother."

"Yes, of course." he sighed. "There is that, too."

The living monument smiled, closed his eyes and leaned back, pressing his hands together in front of his chest, oblivious to the tumult going on in the room. Chairs scraped, windows banged and a dozen men swiped at the wet, wooden floor with torn bits of colored cloth. Nothing they did seemed to disturb the shimmering aura that illuminated the yogi's head and shoulders.

"If you do not believe me, it will rain..."

Dr. Rabansoro hummed the words softly, like a lullabye. Rocking back and forth, he waved a thin, saffron hand vaguely in my direction.

Was it a curse, a blessing, or a dismissal?

Before I could decide, he uttered one word, *Namaste,* and clapped his hands together. The interview was over.

Namaste.

To see so many gods in one day was pushing it, believe me.

Out on the sidewalk, I huddled under a black, silk umbrella that Rangita had loaned me, clutching my shoes in one hand and a book on Malagasy metaphysics—a gift from Dr. Rabansoro—in the other. The word DIOR was stamped in large gold letters on the umbrella handle. It had been a special present from a banker-client with tentacles in many cyclone-ridden capitals. All around me, the gutters ran red with swift-moving, muddy foam, and the cobblestone street was pocked with deep, terra-cotta puddles. The taxi I'd paid to wait was nowhere to be seen. Across the street a hump-backed zebu cow sulked under a tin shed, harnessed to a wooden cart piled high with bags of charcoal. Its owner squatted under the wagon smoking a cigarette, in no hurry to move until the rain stopped.

I yanked the umbrella down, covering my face. "God damn you, James!" I shouted against the silk, thrumming with rain. "To hell with your lemurs!"

I was about to consign Raul, Jack, and Rakotomana to a worse fate when, just under the edge of the umbrella, I caught sight of a small child dressed in a hooded white smock emerging cautiously from a crack between two buildings opposite me. It paused for a brief moment, perched on a flap of soggy matting above a roaring gutter that poured loud gallons of brick-red foam into an open drain tunnelled under the cobblestones. Hovering like a silvery dragonfly above a tumbling brook, it looked nervously up and down the deserted street. Then, in one swift motion, using the broken bit of matting as a sort of water-toboggan, it dropped into the churning maelstrom, twirled around twice, and disappeared! – –sucked down into the drain below the street.

The *kokolampo*! I could have sworn it.

I opened my mouth to yell but nothing came out. There was only the sound of rain and more rain, coming down.

I spent the next half hour negotiating with the charcoal vendor to deliver me within walking distance of Le Terrace. After the deal was struck, I settled back against the lumpy bags next to the driver, prepared to to let the town unfurl under his cracking whip. A slow slide through Tananarive in a *charrette* pulled by a lyre-horned zebu seemed like a civilized diversion after spending a morning in the company of a distempered crocodile, lunch with a horny cowboy and an afternoon hallucinating about demonic midgets whose existence was up for grabs.

I took out my notebook. It was time to make a list.

I'm a big believer in lists. Crisply numbered lists. Arranged alphabetically, prioritized chronologically, or weighted emotionally —the organizing principle isn't what matters. The point is the numbers. Big black numbers with periods after them. *Uno. Dos. Tres.* They set the boundaries. I figure, if you're taking a header off the edge of the earth, you might as well define the edge. You may not know where you're going, but it helps to know where you've been. Lord knows I was spun out, sailing around the big blue bend faster than you could yell Christopher Columbus. Things were getting mighty slippery around the edges.

"Here in Madagascar, it is everywhere *le temps elastique.* Rubber time."

Rangita had announced this with great good cheer yesterday afternoon, slapping her empty wrist as she headed downstairs to work the early bar crowd, a visiting contingent of Latvian agronomists whom she hoped might offer something novel in the way of Eastern Block time-pieces. She had dropped in uninvited, bearing gifts: a ripe mango and a black and white raffia lemur. I'd thanked her and begun carving the mango with my Swiss Army knife. Meanwhile, Rangita happily rummaged through my cosmetic bag. She opened each tube or pot with a tiny gasp of pleasure, placing the colors around her in a circle. She finally chose a glistening coat of cyclamen lip gloss which she daintily applied with the tip of one pinky, blinking her freshly mascaraed midnight blue eyelashes in a rapid spin-dry. She followed this cosmetic transformation with a deft and experienced lifting, squeezing and centering of her ample cleavage so as to show off her breasts to best advantage in the bosom of her spandex leopard jumpsuit.

"*Elastique!*" She had laughed and placed my hand on her chest where the leopard's spots were stretched and distorted into round owlish eyes. Then she took her own small, dark hand and put it squarely on my breast, looking gravely into my eyes.

"Sister," was what she said.

Her breast was as soft and brown and abundant as mine was girlish, pale and—okay, I'll admit it—skimpy. There was no mistaking the intensity and warmth of her gesture. Although it seemed a slightly histrionic response to a few layers of Maybelline, I accepted it gratefully.

"Sister," I answered, "have a mango." And offered her the sweet golden flesh to bite.

The charcoal wagon rumbled along wide asphalted avenues built by the French. Spilling into them from all sides were the old alleys of ancient Tananarive—broken, winding, steep, hidden. The hillsides swarmed with two- and three-story Malagasy houses built of red earth. The setting sun, shot from beneath the rain clouds, fired them in a blazing Umbrian palette: sepia, sienna and Venetian rose. It seemed as if the whole town had burst into flames. Windows of the stepped houses caught fire in the dying sun like glowing topazes. The valleys between the hills were punctuated with pools of viridian and Hooker's green where trees and hedges overhung the walls and private gardens of the proud Merina aristocracy.

Rubber time...

No. What was happening was worse than that. Rubber time I could deal with; a mere *moramora* problem, easily solved by taking a few deep breaths. But rubber *reality*. That was something else. I propped my notebook on my knee and pulled out a pen.

KNOWN:

1. James permitted for Zaohitra January 1st
2. James' visa expired July 13th
3. Today's date: October 10th

UNKNOWN:

1. How to find/rent/borrow/steal a four-wheel drive?
2. How to find dugout canoe?
3. How to find missionary Father Soren?
4. How to find Blue Rainforest?
5. How to find James' camp in Blue Rainforest?
6. What to do if James: sick, wounded, insane, dead?
7. What to do if money runs out?

I crossed out the word "if" and wrote the word "when," then continued.

8   What to do if my visa runs out and none of
above tasks completed?

Then I wrote:

BEYOND THE UNKNOWN
1.   What about the *kokolampo*?
2   What about the Vazimba?
3.   What about Andrebabe, the invisible village?

I hesitated, then scribbled:

4.   What about Jack?

I studied the list for a long time. I was tempted to cross off the
last entry, but left it on and tore up the entire list instead.
    Square One.

The zebu clopped steadily forward. The sun slid down behind a
bank of shifting rain clouds. Houses that a short time ago radiated
a feverish warmth darkened and turned purple. Night was falling
swiftly. Kerosene lamps were being lit in makeshift stalls along the
avenue. Each one displayed identical small piles of tomatoes or
bananas, perhaps a thermos of coffee, some matches, cigarettes,
newspapers and boxes of soap powder. Throngs of people wrapped
in *lambas* filled the streets, hustling past as if apprehensive of the
coming darkness. In spite of the traffic and the crowds, there was
none of the clamor that you'd expect in an Asian or African city.
The sound that arose was more like the stifled murmuring of
contented bees, punctuated now and then by the vaguely
querulous, rising intonations of French. Perched on the planked
seat of the charcoal wagon high above the padding crowds, I felt
equally a queen and a fool.
    Voici la reine de Vazimba. The words sprang into my head.

65

What had the old woman meant, as she clung to my arm at the edge of Lake Anosy? Had she been referring to the old myth about queens who turned into crocodiles? Or was it crocodiles who turned into queens? It was all incredibly confusing. I scoured the passing crowds, straining in vain to find some answers in their faces, but what I saw there did nothing but heighten the sense of separation and aloneness that, almost hourly, threatened to swamp me.

You... said the guarded eyes of the high-cheeked Malagasy, flashing in the lamplight spilling out of the stalls, *You are different. You will never be one of us, for you are a foreigner. A vazaha.* There was a wary ambivalence in those eyes, a lively curiosity reined in by a carefully controlled reticence.

I remember James saying, "The Merina tribe, living on the high plateau, refer to themselves as the Elevated People but, like all Malagasy, they're extremely reluctant to display aggressive emotions, especially anger."

Maybe so. But right then, I certainly felt it. Hidden anger, girdled by fear, expressed as an intense, patronizing haughtiness. A constrained, hostile, and possibly dangerous, indifference.

"Have no fear. We Merina are Christian, not *barbare*," Rangita had joked, trying to set me at ease.

I wanted to believe her. But how to explain the barbaric little *ody* nestled in my pocket. Or the business with the sacred croc?

Night fell. The streets grew quiet. Only the steady beat of the zebu's hooves metronomed our passage. A stray dog appeared, kept pace with us as the wheels turned a dozen times, then disappeared. The driver whistled, lightly touched the zebu's left haunch with the tip of his whip, and we pulled onto a broad colonial avenue.

A blue light of great intensity filled the valley, like a winter sky before a heavy snowfall. Against this numinous, sapphire backdrop the kerosene lamps shone like cut steel, hardened into a brilliance so unlike their earlier, insubstantial waverings that I had to look and look again to make sure that some secret switch had not been snapped on, sending a halogenic charge throughout the town. Grumbling thunder from the retreating storm rolled across the horizon, bounced against the western mountains, reverberating over mirrored rice paddies now dulled by the velvety paws of night. In its wake returned the unbearable exhaustion and attenuated loneliness that had haunted me since arriving on the island.

Au bout du monde...

I lay my head back against the lumpy bags of charcoal and let the meaning of the words wash over me.

...the end of the world.

There was no getting around it. That's where I was. At the end of the earth. On a crazy mission. Without a friend or lover to believe in me, let alone hold me. I was hitting the pity-pot pretty hard. In fact, I would have fallen in feet first if I hadn't looked up and seen the sign. In the night sky high above our charcoal wagon hovered two words, faintly etched in red neon on the top of a tall, modern building: MADAGASCAR HILTON.

I felt a sudden surge of self-confidence. It was pathetic, really, the rush of renewed self-esteem. A minute ago I had been wallowing in terminal self-pity, yet at the sight of a familiar word or two— words that at any other time would have symbolized crass, commercial, cookie-cutter tourism—I was bouyant as a thistledown, ready to take on the world.

Leeches be damned! I know where I am *now*, Jack Mooresby!

The Hilton meant civilized pleasures. A tennis court. Hairdressers. To know that only a few blocks away, people were soaking in tubs of steaming hot water, reading the Paris Tribune, sending chirruping faxes to factories and offices in Europe and America. Things *worked* at the Hilton. Phones, for instance. James had called me last July 22nd on my thirtieth birthday from one in the downstairs lobby.

My birthday...

A day I'd rather forget. And why not? Raul did. I didn't wait up.

I drank the entire bottle of champagne, scraped the pink roses off the top of the cake and devoured them, one by one, then fell asleep on the couch with my clothes on. Oh, thirty was a real stinker. The only thing that rescued the day was hearing the excitement in James' crackling, overseas voice, going on and on about tenrecs and aye-ayes and giant lemurs that were supposedly extinct, but maybe they weren't after all. It was a bad connection and I couldn't quite catch every word, but it helped me forget the whole nasty B-day. How I had envied him then, a carefree biologist, happily beating the bushes for exotic, undiscovered species.

"You can stop here." I thanked the charcoal seller and scrambled down from the wagon.

As I waited for traffic to clear, something drew my attention to a sign on one side of a darkened alley that twisted its way down the steep hillside, emptying into the avenue where I stood. It was nothing special, just another sign; but, a very odd kind of sign. A single light bulb illumined a weathered board that had been nailed to the wall of an abandoned building. *Hotel Kokolampo* was printed on it. The words were painted in faded, cobalt blue lettering. Next to them a flotilla of children's hand prints had been pressed onto the wood. These hands were also blue. They drifted across the splintery wood like skeletal leaves. A painted arrow pointed down to a small, arched door—a small, blue door.

I was in the throes of an exhausted, giddy euphoria so encompassing that my intuitive feelers were as useless as the waving legs of an overturned beetle. Poised at the entrance of the alley, I failed to recognize that I had arrived at a turning point, a place where the known horizon ends and begins its descent, curving with infinite, inexorable subtlety down, down to meet the unknown. In all fairness, I could not have understood it differently then. For, like Columbus, I still believed in one, singular reality, that it went on and on, forever the same; that if you kept sailing you'd simply find more ocean and the same sun shining, somewhere.

The door to the hotel was no more than four feet tall and very narrow—a troll's door. Hanging from the rounded lintel was a silver bell suspended from a dirty leather thong. Knobby, old-fashioned, flat-head iron nails jutted out around the door's arch. They had been pounded in at severe angles. It was very peculiar.

I made a rough viewer with my fingers and sighted through it, framing the sign, the arrow and the door, the way I would before beginning a sketch. Thus isolated, the shiny little bell, the rusted iron nails, the odd, raccoon-like hand prints presented a strange tableau, like the entrance to a pagan temple.

Suddenly, quite distinctly, I heard a tiny, silvery *tinggg.*

I squinted. Blinked.

The bell was trembling; the air was dead calm.

I looked up and down the alley.

Nobody there.

Hotel Kokolampo, the sign said.

BEYOND THE UNKNOWN, my list had read.

The building was silent as the grave. Whatever it had been in the past, the hotel was clearly not expecting guests today.

Or was it?

Tinggg. The bell rang again. A silvery tinkle. Playful and inviting. *Ting ting tinggg.*

I cocked my head, twisted it from side to side. Without letting the bell out of my sight, I walked slowly backwards. Perhaps it was merely a question of me changing my perspective. A simple shift, like surrendering to the notion of rubber-time. I crept deeper into the shadows, never taking my eyes off the entrance to the Hotel Kokolampo, silently challenging the bell.

Ring. Go ahead, try me. I'm watching.

I pulled the corners of my eyes out slant-wise, the way I used to as a near-sighted kid when I wanted to see with more clarity.

Clarity!

I'll be honest. I desperately wanted someone to come out of that door with some clear answers. To reassure me that everything was perfectly normal. To tell me that the little door led into a hostel for wayward children, or a shelter for orphans.

It might be a snack-bar for school kids, I thought. Run by somebody small. A little person. Maybe a dwarf.

"Ring, dammit!" I tried to sound fierce.

But the bell hung lifelessly from its thong, under the watchful, neon moon of the Hilton logo.

Annoyed, I circled back down the alley, skulking along the gutter, sneaking up on the hotel until I stood directly in front of the door, my fists jammed into my pockets. As my fingers clenched the *ody*, I distinctly heard a voice urging: *Go on, Eva. Knock. What are you afraid of?*

Afraid? Who, me?

Feeling pretty ridiculous, I dropped onto my good knee and rapped gently on the little door.

Just then something behind me in the street began snarfling through a pile of refuse. It was joined by another something, much larger, and they began to fight, screeching and kicking garbage into the center of the alley. Banana skins, chicken bones, shredded paper, onion peelings and human excrement exploded all over the place.

Rats!

They panted past me in the Stygian gloom, their hairy bodies brushing my legs, their scaly tails lashing my ankles. Thank God I couldn't see their eyes. I already knew what color they'd be. Ruby red. Or yellow. Take your pick. I refused to to think about their teeth. Nothing terrorizes me more than rats. One crawled inside my sleeping bag in Katmandu. You won't catch me eating granola bars in bed again.

The rodent war heated up. Rats closed in from every direction. Gnashing teeth shrieked like chalk on a slate, interrupted by bleating, high-pitched squeals.

Trapped, heart pumping, I pounded on the blue door, jangling the bell. "Somebody! Hear me! Let me in!"

A flying melon rind blind-sided me across the left temple. I staggered sideways, landing directly on top of a muscular, bristled rat.

"Get *away!!*"

I lashed out, kicking wildly at the squirming creature, hooking my toe under its fat belly. It *whoompfed* up against the wall, ricocheted onto the cobbles and raged off into the night, bawling in protest,

I pounded on the door as hard as I could.

"*Kokolampo! Kokolampo!!* Open up!!"

A small *click*... and the door swung slowly inwards, opening onto an even blacker blackness than my night. I had a sense of something hovering expectantly nearby as I squeezed inside. Then the door blew shut behind me, and I was alone, in total darkness, blind as a Texas snake.

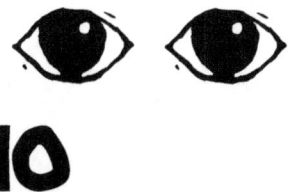

10

No matter how wide I opened my eyes, there was nothing but night. Thick. Furry. Palpable.

I blinked rapidly, expecting my pupils to adjust, but nothing changed. It was as if I'd been swallowed up in an immense, underground tar pit. I stretched my arms out in front of me, but they were lost in velvety darkness. In rising panic, I felt for the edges of my body with my mind, but it was guesswork where my skin left off and the velvet began. The boundaries had disappeared. I had ceased to exist.

Code Blue, Artema. You're in one now. I heard Jack Mooresby's cowboy twang, his cackling laugh.

"Let me out!" I bellowed, punching futile fists into the dark. *Owowoo, owwouuut...* The syllables echoed down, down, fading away like the howls of a wounded coyote.

Get a grip, girl, I thought. You got in. You can get out.

Carefully, on all fours like a rooting bear, I felt behind me for the wooden door, but my fumbling hands discovered only dank, seamless rock.

Where was it? There must be a handle around here somewhere...

I worked my fingers higher, feeling my way blindly across the walls for the entrance.

Nothing but handfuls of damp stone.

Impossible! I just came through that door.

Without thinking, I stood up quickly, cracking my head against the low roof. The blow stunned me onto my knees. I rolled into a fetal ball clutching my head and promptly passed out.

I awoke with a splitting headache and no sense of how much time had passed. I could dimly hear running water somewhere in the depths far below, a slow, gurgling, sucking noise, occasionally interrupted by an ominous thump and a heavy splash, as if a body were being dumped overboard. It was not an encouraging constellation of sounds.

Listening, I became aware of two glowing discs, floating about waist high a short distance ahead of me. At first I thought they were the buckeyes of a phosphorescent moth, an obscure Madagascar species of *lolo* especially evolved to survive undergound.

But, no. On closer inspection I realized that they were real eyes! Hugely dilated, strangely silver, they were about the size of fifty-cent pieces, completely round, and they were watching me intently. They swung gently back and forth in the void like ethereal Japanese lanterns, giving off a weird fluorescence, throwing pallid beams of light across the stony ground like the rays cast by a pair of weak flashlights.

Fear jammed my mind. My chest constricted. I scrambled for rational explanations. This must be a bad dream. Or else a bizarre reaction to the various tropical jabs I'd had to endure before leaving the States. It was too soon for malaria; I'd only been in Tananarive a few days. Perhaps it was a stress-related illness, a disorientation induced by isolation in exotica. Or maybe a temporary, mental aberration resulting from the pervasive anxiety that had dogged me since arrival.

I glared back at the eyes.

In all probability I would wake any second to find myself in room 37 at Le Terrace, twisted in sweaty blankets, damp hair plastered against my neck, Malagasy roosters heralding the grey dawn, heir to nothing more than a hangover from a troubled night's sleep.

In all probability...

I gingerly touched my forehead.

The lump on my head told me I was kidding myself: this was no dream. This nightmare was real.

I took a deep breath and faced the spectre head on.

"What are you? *Kokolampo*...?"

There was no response.

"*Vous êtes kokolampo?*"

If it seems weird, conversing with a couple of levitating flashlights, consider: I had to cosy up to those glowing spots. They had the wattage I needed to get me out of this hellish hotel.

The thing must have heard me. Its eyes went dark, there was a muffled snort—somewhere between a chuckle and a whistle—and the incandescent orbs flickered on again, dancing ahead of me down a steep slope. The eye-beams played back and forth across the floor of what I now realized was a downward-twisting tunnel.

I balked.

Conrad Hilton, where is your neon moon now?

The beams became agitated. They moved in jerky, accelerated motions over the uneven rock, furiously whizzing back and forth, creating a solid illuminated pathway—a silvery, umbilical cord of light.

Follow me, they seemed to be saying. *Follow me!*

Half-crouching, holding my aching head, I crawled toward the lights thinking, whatever you do, for God's sake, don't take me to your leader!

Jest with life, that's all it's good for.

Voltaire was right. When you're going down the rabbit hole behind a couple of loose eyeballs, why *not* joke? Not that I was overloaded with options.

I stumbled blindly forward, tripping over a cairn of stones, trying to keep an eye on the flashing silver lights. The tunnel seemed to be one of a vast labyrinth of similar passageways that burrowed over and under each other, criss-crossing, interconnecting, merging to form a wide artery, then splitting off again into dozens of unmarked, identical worm-holes that honeycombed the earth under Tananarive.

The eyes flitted in and out in the vanguard, darting easily ahead in a series of disconnected swooping motions, apparently without recourse to such mundane appendages as legs or feet. Every now and then something—possibly the hem of its garment––would scrape across the rocks, leaving a faint trail of phosphorescent sparkles in its wake, like the mark your hand makes trailing across a July sea at midnight.

I struggled to keep up, desperate not to lose sight of what were literally my only rays of hope. The tunnel walls were rough now, studded with jutting shards of flinty stone. Squeezing around a particularly narrow curve, I tore a nasty hole in the sleeve of my jacket. When I put my hand into the opening I felt hot, wet blood.

I continued to follow the eyes downward, into the belly of the earth. My shoulder ached badly, my swollen knee was dragging. Yet I staggered blindly on, spiralling ever deeper into the darkness, propelled by a growing certainty that if I lost track of those lights I'd never find my way out.

I gasped for air in rasping, tearing gulps. The passageways became lower and narrower the deeper we went and my shoulders raked both sides of the tunnel but somehow I wiggled through, fixated on the ghostly rays that flickered just a few yards ahead, terrified that if I paused—even for a moment—to assess the horror of my predicament, I would break down entirely in a fit of hysteria.

Who was this guide to whom I had entrusted my life? Where

was it leading me? Was there a guide at all? Or had I simply gone mad from the darkness, fear and claustrophobia, imagining lights where there were none, following a chimera deeper and deeper into an endless maze from which I would never escape?

Suddenly a thought struck me: what if these caves and grottoes were inhabited?

I knew that during the eighth and ninth centuries, in Cappadocia, Christian monks had lived underground for years in tunnels like these, hiding out from the Saracens who raged through Anatolia, looting and burning. emerging only at night to replenish their water and food stores, vanishing at dawn, sealing themselves in by pulling great stones behind them. But, there had been no Saracens in Madagascar. Nobody was at war on this island. Not today, certainly. So why would humans choose to live in these dank, mole-like warrens? Unless... It hit me like a body blow. Unless... they *weren't* human!

The instant I thought that, I regretted it. It opened up a Pandora's box of horrors—a spook show. I felt like a child waking at night to find that the closet door's been left open. That sickening feeling of... *There's something alive in there!*

My shoulder grazed the wall and I shouted out loud as raw pain shot down to my wrist.

You're losing it, Eva. Stop and think. Use your head. Of course there's a way out. No doubt there were people living here once. Ancient humans. Aborigines. That's it! Aborigines! Plenty of aborigines still live in caves, in places like Borneo and the Philippines. There must have been aborigines here, too.

I paused to catch my breath, racking my brain, rifling through ill-remembered snippets of Malagasy history, and recalled a story Rangita had told me. We had been hunched shoulder to shoulder over the balcony of Le Terrace, drinking *cafe noir* and watching the teeming crowds in the Zoma market.

"Long, long ago..." she had begun. "Listen carefully, Eva, this is the story our grandmothers tell their grandchildren. Long ago our ancestors came from the east, from the land of the rising sun. They came in double canoes over great oceans. The winds carried them on and on over the waves until they reached land. We Malagasy are not African. We are not Asian. We are not black, or yellow or red. We are a beautiful soft brown, as were our ancestors who came out of the east in the long, long ago." When she finished, she had turned gracefully and beamed at me a devastating smile, as innocent and protective as the white canvas umbrellas sheltering the teeming crowds below.

We gazed down, the heat of the tropical sun welding our shoulders together as we leaned over the parapet watching the busy market below. She was right. They *were* a beautiful people—a yeasty, harmonious, racial stew. Almond-skinned businessmen in three-piece suits mingled with barefoot, ebony tribesmen from the southern deserts. Farmers in calf-length, checked *malabars* and tightly woven straw derbies jostled with turbaned Indian traders and portly Chinese. Elaborately coiffed cinnamon matrons, their hair balkanized into corn-rows, bargained for baskets with pale, slender, flat-cheeked girls straight out of Gauguin.

Rangita made an expansive gesture encompassing her fellow countrymen. "So we say, *Tsihibelambana olona*. All colors under the sun are plaited into the same mat." With a wide arm-swing like a jibing sail, she had gathered up every Malagasy in one good-humored swoop and brought them home safely, tucked tightly against her chest. "*Tout le monde*," she said.

"Everyone?" I teased. "Including *vazaha*?"

"Well, not all *vazaha*," she conceded.

"And the Vazimba? What happened to them?"

"Why, we live. As always."

We... live...?

My French was lousy, but not my hearing.

Before I could press her, she had grabbed my arm. "Come, let's go down to the Zoma. I see the man from Abovombe. He has beautiful silver bracelets made from Maria Theresa dollars." She tugged my hand, pulling me away from the balcony's edge. "Come, sister. I promise you will not be disappointed."

Rangita!

Alone, in the hideous darkness, I was overwhelmed by a burst of longing for her. *Sister* she had called me. But why? I had known her barely a week. Surely it wasn't greed or avarice. I had nothing to give her, no First World toys or trinkets other than my personal belongings, and those she had already rummaged through and dismissed.

I stood up, feeling faint stirrings of hope—real hope —for the first time since the little blue door had slammed shut behind me.

Rangita wouldn't let herself be buffaloed by a bug-eyed water sprite! No way. Demon or not, she'd zero in on the guy's wristwatch and get down to business.

I was laughing aloud in the dark when it hit me.

The Vazimba! These were *their* caves.

11

Rounding a sharp corner of the tunnel, I was impaled by a nauseating stench driven by a violent, hot wind. I'd never smelled a dead body, let alone seen one, but I had no doubt that only one thing could stink like this: rotting, human flesh.

It wasn't the smell that made me scream—it was the bodies. I tripped over them as soon as I staggered out of the tunnel, knocking the skulls loose. They rattled across the rocks— ghoulish castanets!—and rolled down an incline.

I'd entered a huge cavern. It had to be huge because of the way my screams ricocheted off the ceiling. The echoes kept going on and on, long after I'd run out of breath and the skull clattered into silence.

I'm not the screaming type, but why hold back? I had heavy company in that cavern. Corpses, heaps of them, lay all around me, not thrown helter-skelter, but neatly stacked, each wrapped in a red silken shroud. The most recently deceased lay on top, wedged between row upon row of skulls and skeletons. Feet, hands and jawbones were tangled up in shreds of rotting cloth. On the ground nearby lay a thin gold ring, glittering and poignant. The cave was not quite as dark as the tunnels had been—maybe it had something to do with the dripping limestone that formed the walls and floor.

I turned around slowly. Everywhere I looked, I saw skeletons and more skeletons. In and around them wound a slow-moving, lime green river. It was an infernal scene, a macabre vision.

I suddenly remembered Uncle Rasolo.

Was it from this underground graveyard that he had been plucked for his ghostly joy-ride through the streets of Tananarive? Or were these the ancient bones of aboriginal Malagasy, from another age, ancestors of ancestors who rode the long canoes over the waves from Polynesia? Could they be the remains of the mysterious Vazimba, who lived here before history itself? Whoever they had been, what did it matter? They were no more and I *was*. And I planned to continue. Alive. Above ground.

"Lights! Give me lights!" I yelled, twisting around, searching for the eyebeams I'd become so dependent upon.

Flinging my head backwards, I saw dozens of pairs begin to flicker on and off from a very great height. They dotted the roof of the looming cavern, swaying back and forth like silvery Christmas balls, sweeping the ground where I stood with their sallow, eerie rays.

Kokolampos! What else could they be?

My shouts must have awakened them. Gyrating and flashing and owling, their eye-beams scoured the stone floor, carving out a circle of light that lapped at my toes, nailing me to the smooth grey rock.

"Ai yai yeeeee!!!" I hollered up at them. "Ya ha eeeee!" I tried again. "*Kokolampos*, awake!!"

I clamped my hands over my aching head, listening to the echoes of my shouts as they died away, trying to reconstruct the events of last night. I conjured the rutted road, the speeding taxi, the thump and the sickening arch of the tiny, white-clad body, the grappling in the ditch. Everything was clear except a view of the creature itself.

I peered up into the shadows trying to imagine them, secreted in crevices between the rocks, sleeping like bats, hanging upside down or clinging to the ceiling, their white cloaks wrapped closely about them, like tightly furled cocoons.

Splaasshh!!

Something had launched itself into the river directly below me. The splash was followed by another, and another. The bilious surface of the water began to buckle and heave. Pale, sunken logs arose, surfaced, and sank, only to rise again, roiling and rolling. The sunken logs quickly devolved into more ominous shapes: snouts, nostrils, scales, teeth.

Crocodiles!!

Shooting up out of the maelstrom, one white monster broke loose, scrabbling on the slick riverbank with stubby, armored feet. On its back rode another, smaller reptile, jaws snapping. Its curved claws dug into the dorsal scales of the larger crocodile. They hung together for a horrid moment in the fetid air, hissing and blowing like a witch and her familiar, before falling back into the thick ooze.

But... something was horribly, horribly wrong.

These weren't your everyday, garden-variety man-eaters. Where there should have been eyeballs, there were empty, wizened sockets. Strange, opalescent film covered the holes where pupils once grew. And—more revolting—where you'd expect dark, thrusting scales rimming their backs, these crocs had sickly, anemic flanges, flapping loosely, like wedges of untanned leather.

My legs buckled. My stomach turned over. The water was swarming with blind albino crocodiles!

I recoiled, listening to them thrash like sharks in a feeding frenzy. How many years, how many eons of breeding in the dark, in this subterranean river, had it taken to create these monstrous mutations? I cowered in the lee of a rock, watching them fight, climbing desperately over each other to reach me.

I covered my wounded shoulder with my hand. Warm blood. Is that what they wanted? Wasn't there enough flesh in these body-piles to satisfy them?

The heat and the smell were unbearable. The hot, rank air whirled with eyebeams of the newly-awakened *kokolampo* suspended among the rocks high above. Their light rays played excitedly back and forth over the river, convulsing with foam and scaly bodies. One after another, in thrall to a primeval blood lust, they would surge up out of the murk, only to fall short and slip backwards, their claws gouging scarlet scimitars in each other's pale flesh.

I squeezed sideways, pressed against the rear wall of the cavern, avoiding the dead stacked like cordwood, my mind chattering like a high-speed dubbing tape.

Go back, Eva, it said. Escape to the tunnels. Now! Do you want to meet your Maker torn apart by a blind white worm the size of a Datsun with a brain like a pea?

Don't do it! The committee jabbered. You'll become lost in the maze and the darkness where you'll die of starvation, or madness. And in case you forgot... *the door disappeared.*

Score one for committees.

There is NO... WAY... OUT. Jack's cynical voice harangued.

No! I refused to believe it.

"In the name of the Father and the Son and the Holy goddamn ghost," I shouted. "Hear me! It's your daughter Eva, calling You!"

It wasn't the kind of prayer Father Michael had drilled into us Sunday mornings on the hard pews at Perpetual Mercy, but the Lord would have to make allowances—this was Code Blue.

I pinched my eyes tightly shut. Sweat poured down, pooling in the tails of my lashes. My arm was crusty with dried blood. My knee throbbed. My head was a bomb about to go off.

"Listen to me, God! I'm telling You, this island's no picnic!"

I wasn't telling Him anything He didn't already know. Hadn't James warned me? And Jack? And Ambassador Theron? Suddenly my paint brushes looked good. Very good.

Slick with perspiration, I grabbed for my bandanna, but my fingers touched the *ody* instead. The amulet radiated a strange warmth. Hot and quivering, it wriggled around in my palm like a mutating pupa. I raised my arm in revulsion, ready to fling it across the cave when I heard a soft voice—Rangita's voice—saying, *The way in is the way out.*

This was no time for riddles.

I wound up and pitched the miserable little talisman into the river.

Almost immediately I was encircled by a bright flurry of sparkling swashes. They swirled around, up and over me, like Tinkerbell's trails, coalescing finally into a brilliant sphere of light that landed on the floor of the grotto at my feet and rolled downhill, bouncing over the laddered ribcage of a desiccated corpse like an illuminated soccer ball, rolling into the whirling river, where it bobbled among gnashing snouts and lashing tails, floating downstream.

Downstream…

Of course! The river! It flowed in, it had to flow out. The way out was the river. But… how?

I didn't have to wait long for an answer. It came in a familiar form——the *sacré croc*, the old Queen of Lake Anosy.

When she surfaced the river divided. The waters swelled and washed over her mighty back like a tidal bore, surging up the bank to the very spot where I stood. Rising like a sub on reconnaissance, her dark bulk dwarfed the fighting albinos. Alongside her they resembled a handful of squabbling night-crawlers. In her long jaws rested the ball of light. She held it between her snaggled fangs as tenderly as a mother cat carries a kitten, swinging her head from side to side, just as she had earlier alongside the lake.

She hauled her gigantic carcass up out of the water and lay panting along the river's edge, her scales as rough and hoary as a thousand year-old redwood. You could carve a double canoe from a tree this big.

So, get on and ride her, a voice said. *Do not be afraid, sister. The way in is the way out.*

It was Rangita's disembodied voice I heard speaking, no question of it.

I sagged to my knees, clapping my hands over my ears. "Stop it! Stop this madness!!" No wonder Van Gogh cut off his ear. If I'd had a knife I'd have cut off mine, too—both of them.

"Take me, bite me, chew me up. Spit out my bones!" I blabbered incoherently, looking back over my shoulder towards the tunnel, that blind alley leading away unto death. The jesting was over. I was walking through the Valley of the Shadow.

"Father, forgive me," I prayed. "James... I tried. Papa... I failed. Raul, wherever you are, believe me... I had *corazón.*" My eyes filled with nostalgic, self-pitying tears before Jack took over my brain.

Corazón? Bullshit. Who you kidding, Artema? All paths are the same. They lead nowhere. They go into the bush and out of the bush. Heart, my ass. Try saving yours.

"All you know, Jack," I shouted at nobody, "is about pushing rivers and people around."

Don't push the river doesn't mean be a wimp! You planning to give up and die here, Artema?

Damned Jack!

"Mooresby," I hollered, "get the hell out of my head!!"

I'd gone round the bend. Certifiably gonzo. A blithering wreck, making no sense. I buried my head in my hands, pulling my hair till it hurt, sobbing, "White coats, come get me. It's over, I'm yours."

And they did.

Two *kokolampos.* Or was it three? I was too scrambled to tell. Each tugging on a sleeve, they led me down to the Old Queen. Their little white cloaks made silvery star-trails wherever they brushed. Their eyebeams picked out the trail.

Voici la reine de Vazimba. Appease her...

It was too late now. The die was cast. Appease her? No chance. It was simple surrender. I was her guest, or her prey; it was her choice.

The *kokolampos* helped me climb onto her back and she pushed off into the foam. With one thrust of her tail we crossed the river, leaving the blind white worms and the Ancestors to writhe in the never-ending darkness. The Queen held her head high. Guided by the ball of light in her mouth, she charged straight for a limestone wall.

I threw myself flat onto her horny scales. Foul water poured over me. Slime clogged my nostrils. I spat and blew, feeling the crocodile's powerful muscles working against my belly, her scales pressing rhythmically against the insides of my arms. Gripping her scaly back I squeezed my eyes shut, thinking Lord, if she dives, I'm a goner. James had told me stories of crocodiles who drag their victims underwater until they drown, saving them to eat later, at leisure.

Miraculously, the Old Queen slid narrowly under the rock face resurfacing in another cavern where the water ran still and black. I clung to her back like a baby lemur, hanging on just above the water line.

I don't know how long we traveled thus through the underground caverns. I lost track of time. Was it minutes or hours? There was something hypnotic about it. The lapping of the water against the rough scales, the great tail working, propelling us through the darkness, the darting shadows cast by the ball of light against the passing rocks, the occasional burst of phosphorescence in the river—all of it accompanied by the steady, pumping legs of the Old Queen, carrying me safely through the night.

Safe...

Bizarre as that may sound, it's exactly how I felt. Completely and utterly safe. I even dozed from time to time, awakening to the reassuring glow from the ball of light and the easy rocking of the

Old Queen's body.

At length the river broadened, grew shallow. A cool, fresh wind blew against my face, bearing on it the same odor of tarnished silver I'd noticed in the ditch after the accident.

Without warning the sacred croc steamed up out of the water and onto the shore. Unprepared for the sudden halt, I fell off with a bump, landing in a bank of moss, mud and swamp grass. Through a crack between two rocks I saw stars shining, and some clouds far above, drifting across the moon.

The crocodile tossed her snout the way a horse does when bothered by a fly.

Zippp!! The bright sphere flew out of her jaws and landed in a shower of dazzling sparks so brilliant that I was forced to shield my face. When I looked again I saw... the *kokolampo*! Its round eyes peeked out from under the hooded cloak. They strobed on and off with a dizzying speed that could only mean one thing: sheer delight.

I took a step towards the shimmering little creature.

At the same time it moved towards me.

We met on a grassy hummock.

It stretched out its arm—fin, flipper, hand, I couldn't tell, but what did it matter?—and dropped something into my open palm.

The *ody*.

It seemed I couldn't get rid of it, no matter how hard I tried.

"*Namaste,*" I whispered, pressing my hands together and bowing deeply.

When I straightened up they were already gone, powering back up the river into darkness, the *kokolampo* riding shotgun on the shoulders of the Old Queen.

12

Pitipitika... A shower of fine rain was falling when I slithered out from between two rocks.

Joy! Freedom! Alive!

Gratitude flowed through me like an electric current. Tears fell, salt mixing with raindrops. I raised my arms to heaven, throwing my head back, open-mouthed, letting the drops trickle over my tongue, sucking in the cool night air like a moth drinking nectar from a flower, hovering at the throat of the world, at the neck vein of life.

God, I'm still here. I made it.

I looked around. I was knee-deep in a bog, or a sump, surrounded by a thicket of water reeds, papyrus and tumbled rocks. The damp air was thrumming with frog-songs. Sharp, beetle-like chirps blended with rusty sawing and the deep, farting grunts of lovesick toads. It was the most beautiful music I had ever heard.

"Why don't you do it in the ro-o-oad..." I burst out at the top of my lungs.

I stripped off my denim jacket and let the rain wash over me. "Looked over Jordan, what did I se-e-e... Comin' for to carry me ho-o-me..." It wasn't a bad rendition. Even the frogs listened up. Not a peep out of them until I finished singing.

Yea, I had walked through the Valley...

I felt so relieved it was a sin. All tiredness dissolved into the past under the wide overarching night sky. The rain whispered down in a misty grey umbrella, beading the slender sedge grasses. It floated over me like a bridal veil, drifting right down to my toes, falling so softly you couldn't hear it landing anywhere.

"Yes," I said it again. "*Yes!*"

It's times like these people make wild promises. Take vows. Become monks. Join the Peace Corps. Get down on their knees and dedicate their lives to impossible humanitarian causes. Rush pell-mell towards sainthood.

I've done enough knee-time, I thought, twisting my hair into a donut at the nape of my neck. Enough. I've got a goal—a grail. It's called James. I need to find him *now*. Before he joins the Ancestors.

I checked my watch.

Nine o'clock.

I tapped on the lens.

No, that couldn't be right. It had to be later than nine. That would mean I'd been underground for less than fifteen minutes. Impossible! It made no sense.

I turned around slowly in a circle. It was still night, yes. But, was it the *same* night? Raindrops slid down my cheeks. *Time is a circle, and we're always at its center...* Maybe it was tomorrow night? Or yesterday night? Who cared? The rain was real, yes, and the mud I was sinking into, and the armies of invisible frogs, singing their *bufo* love songs. What did it matter? I was here. I *lived*.

"She's a ho-o-o-o-o-onnnky-tonk wo-man..." I sang, keeping time with the *krexxing*. "Gimme, gimme, gimme those honky-tonk blues..."

I rolled up my jacket and stuffed it into my knapsack next to James' letters, carefully zipping the *ody* into an inner passport pouch, patting it gently, thinking, I'm not letting you out of my sight. You're on board for the duration, pal. This island keeps a hard school. Everyone's got an agenda here, even the dead. And so do I. What's more, I have a certified Malagasy rabbit's foot to even the score. Who cares where it came from, who gave it to me, or how ugly it is.

James, I vowed, trampling the damp grass, I'm on my way. Nothing's going to stop me now.

I was in a valley at the edge of a rice paddy somewhere not far from the center of Tananarive. Perched on the crests of the surrounding hillsides were jumbles of red earth houses packed defensively together like small-scale Tibetan lamaseries. They were shuttered and silent; thin trailings of woodsmoke leaked through the roofs. High above shone the red neon beacon of my landmark, the Madagascar Hilton. It was still there! I hadn't gone mad after all. I radar-ed in on it, slogging around the edge of the swamp.

Reborn I may have been, but it's fair to say I didn't look it. My wounded arm leached sticky red rivulets that ran down into the bend of my elbow. My bruised knee bulged awkwardly.

Who cared? Hallelujah. I was free!

As I marched towards town, I hummed a little salsa tune and amused myself by composing a letter.

Querido Raulito, it began... *I'm sitting here under a palm tree in my hot pink bikini. Across a turquoise lagoon I see a sailing pirogue in the distance. Oh, here comes a man with a net full of fresh fish to choose for lunch. The thatched roof of my sunshade rustles in the warm breeze. You need shelter here from the equatorial sun, and to keep the ice in your mai-tai from melting. I've got a lei of sweet-smelling ylang-ylang flowers around my neck. Mmmmm... and on the sand at my feet there's a big pile of conch shells and cowries. Today I went windsurfing with sea turtles. Flying fish leapt out of the water to greet me. Bailando toda la noche con hombres guapos y muy amables. Tomorrow I'm off to the rain forest and James' camp. Looking forward to seeing lemurs in the wild. Hasta pues, Eva.*

Hombres guapos...

Handsome men. *That* would nail him. If the all-night dancing and the flying fish didn't.

In a sudden rush, the collected rain sluiced down off my head, filling my ears with ice cold water.

Handsome men...

I shook my waterlogged erogenous zones.

...used to be one of my obsessions.

I banged the left side my head with the flat of my palm and water poured out of my ear.

Used to be...

I smacked my right ear and more rain ran out.

...four years ago.

The paddy led to plowed fields, then to a packed earth road. Wallowing in unrequited erotic reveries, I covered the distance into town rapidly and before I knew it I'd arrived on the front steps of the Hilton. Through the expansive glass doors I saw the group of men I'd met at the Embassy clustered around the front desk. Among them were Paul Cummins, Eli Mazan and Stephan Giardini. They were talking excitedly and laughing loudly. I hurried up the steps, but two green-uniformed doormen stepped quickly in front of me, blocking my passage.

"I beg your pardon..." I tried to push past.

"*Pardon, mademoiselle,*" the taller one looked at me with disdain, if not outright disgust, "...it is not permitted to enter the hotel, *comme ci...*" He waved his hand over me the way you would over a scurvy dog that's rooting around overturning your garbage cans or defecating in your driveway.

"But, I know those men. They're my *friends*. Let me pass!"

He whistled and three more bellmen materialized. Now there were five abreast on the step above me.

This was ridiculous!

"I have business with Mr. Cummins. An important message. From his office."

I tried to make an end run around them, but they cut me off at the top step.

Then I saw why.

Reflected in the glass front of the hotel I saw my appalling self. A wild woman. A beast. A *clochard*. A bedraggled bag lady, soaked to the gills, mud stuck to her legs, a bloodied arm, no makeup, hair plastered to her lumpy forehead. A filthy, mad *vazaha* trying to crash the Hilton for free food and drink or a kip on a couch in the lobby.

"Mademoiselle, I will find you a cab. You must go home and rest." The doorman took my arm and steered me towards the standing taxis.

"No. Those are my people!" I dug in my heels. Let them drag me down the stairs.

"What's goin' on here?" Paul Cummins drawled, Oklahoma Panhandle all the way.

"No problem, sir. Just a woman..."

"Mr. Cummins," I cried. "It's me, Eva Artema."

Paul froze for a beat, then regrouped.

"Eva! My God, what in hell's happened to you?"

The other men joined him, staring down at me from the top step as if I were some sort of cockroach. A reprehensible, squashable *Blattaria*.

"I... I got caught out in the rain," I said, with the greatest dignity I could muster. "But I'm all right now, thank you." I backed down the stairs. "I'm... this gentlemen has just found me a cab, and..."

Paul Cummins descended the stairs carefully, one by one, eyes glued to my bleeding arm. "You... you ain't been out there..?" he motioned off into the darkness. "By the lake, I mean."

"Lake Anosy?"

"Yeah. I hear there's been some trouble. Some shooting."

"Shooting?" My heart raced. "You mean, civil war?" It was the only thing I could think of, recalling the tracery of bullet holes in the Ministry staircase, the political graffiti splashed on every blank wall in the city.

"Nah. More like your big game, safari stuff."

"Someone shot a wild crocodile out there tonight," Eli Mazan interrupted. "Big mother. Eighteen-footer. Shot her right through the head. Thirty-ought-six. Took a couple of rounds to put her down. They skinned her right there on the spot."

He might as well have have kicked me in the stomach.

"Good thing, too," Paul added. "Motherfucker like that right in the middle of Tana. People, kids. Anybody could've been hurt." He shook his head. "Crazy goddamn country. Hey, where you going? You better take care of that arm. C'mon. We'll give you a ride back to your hotel."

But I already had one foot in the cab.

"*Vite*," I told the cabbie. "*Vite!*"

I couldn't get away from there fast enough.

13

"Rangita will understand. Rangita will explain..." I repeated the sentence over and over like a mantra until I reached Le Terrace.

The bar downstairs was jumping when we pulled up, but I'd learned my lesson at the Hilton. A frontal assault was out of the question. Folding my bandanna in a triangle, I tied it under my chin, put on my dark glasses and my torn jacket, paid the cab with my last five hundred francs and hurried around the back alley, hoping to enter through the kitchen and slip upstairs to Rangita's room undetected.

Through the low windows, I could see Madame Moreau scrubbing at the sink, a cigarette hanging from her lips. She was changing the water in her fish tank. On the counter rested several small bowls; each contained a single, beat-up black guppy, stirring the water with bored fin flicks. An old, wooden radio blatted out the news in crackling French. Upon hearing a particularly distressing bit, a look of rage and disgust would come over her face, and she would remove her cigarette and spit with fantastic accuracy into a wastebasket in the corner.

I tapped lightly at the glass, not wanting to alarm her. "Madame Moreau, may I come in?"

She shuffled up to the window and peered out. "Who goes?" she said.

"Me. Eva Artema."

She pressed her face against the glass, fogging it with her breath.

"Number thirty-seven." I said. "*Americaine*."

She hesitated, wiping the cloudy glass with the back of one hand. "*Americaine*, are you crazy? What are you doing? You don't belong here. Go around to the front. This is the kitchen. Guests do not enter here."

"You don't understand, I have had..." I struggled for the right word to engage her sympathy, "...some trouble."

Right away I knew I should have said "an accident."

"Trouble? *Mon Dieu*, we don't need more of that! Go around to the front," she said and picked up her guppies, snapping off the light on her way out.

There was nothing for it but to do as she said.

The alley alongside the hotel was narrow and blocked by a bent iron grating. I pushed at it, trying to inch between it and the building, stepping on an inert form that I took to be a discarded mattress.

Instantly the mattress reared up and I was slammed flat against the wall, a thin forearm denting my windpipe.

"*D'argent!*" the man demanded. The whites of his eyes rolled from side to side, yellow as old trade ivory.

"I don't have any money," I choked, tearing off my Ray-bans and scarf. "Here, take these."

He took one look at my pale, ravaged visage and backed away, terror-stricken.

"*Mpakafo!*" he hissed. "*Mpakafo!*" He kept repeating the word over and over as he fled down the alley.

I fingered my neck, searching for bruises. One thing was

certain: I wasn't winning any popularity contests in Tananarive. On the plus side, you could say I was beginning to understand bravery.

Madame Moreau was lying in wait for me at the front entrance. She had Maurice, the night watchman, in tow. He was a scrawny rheumatoid with shaking hands and a perpetually smiling face. He carried a *panga*, a broad flat steel blade like a machete. Maurice was amiable enough, even wielding a weapon as formidable as a *panga*. He sat on an upright chair by the door every night after dark, the blade across his knees, keeping tabs on the clientele passing into the bar, thumbing the sharpened blade and grinning. This combination of executioner and clown was disconcerting, to say the least, but sent a powerful message to potential brawlers.

"You can't be too careful these days." Madame Moreau pushed the door open, scrutinizing me over antiquated reading glasses. "Been swimming?"

"I, er... The rain."

"Ah, of course. Of course..." She stared at my bloody arm. "It can be troublesome indeed... the rain..."

Before she could elaborate I scurried past Maurice and his *panga* and began climbing the stairs.

"Excuse me, Madame. I'm very tired. I must change."

The door of the bar blew open onto the lobby and with it a followed a gust of laughter, billowing on clouds of clove cigarette smoke. Inside I could see the usual evening crowd gathered around the tables. I searched in vain for Rangita. One of her *confrères*, Jeanine, was busy slipping her slim legs between the ankles of a stout, unsmiling man—a Romanian advisor, no doubt. There were lots of ex-Soviets hanging around Tana in cheap, ill-fitting grey suits, sticking their dour faces into Malagasy business. Nobody seemed to take them very seriously. They sat each evening at Le Terrace, backed into corner booths, nursing beers and glaring at the convivial throng, like homesick turnips. Rangita had dismissed them as humorless and stingy—a bum lay. "With them, we are like chickens, scratching among the dry gravel for a kernel of love," she had shrugged. "But sometimes, who knows, perhaps there will be a Chinese watch..."

Rangita...

The sounds of the bar followed me down the hallway leading to Number 42. I leaned close, putting my ear to the worn keyhole, expecting to hear the muffled scratchings of love, or at least a creaking bed.

Silence.

I knocked, then pushed on the door and was startled to find it unlatched. It swung open revealing a tidy, barren chamber. The sagging bed was made up with fresh linen, a pink flannel blanket folded neatly across the foot. The curtains were drawn, blocking the view from the terrace, and the place reeked of some harsh disinfectant. No trace of Rangita remained in this sterile cell.

What had happened? Where had she gone?

I looked around for any clues to her disappearance. Perhaps she'd gotten into a row with Madame and taken her trade elsewhere. It seemed unlikely, and yet... One of her clients might have whisked her away to Paris, or Jakarta. More likely she'd cashed in a couple of gold watches and lit out for the beaches of Nosy-Be. She was young and beautiful. Anything was possible.

I heard a metallic clank behind me and turned to find Maurice's grinning, lopsided face in the doorway.

"Where is she?" I demanded.

"*Phooot!*" he said. "*Comme ci.*" He made a slicing motion with his *panga*, smiling witlessly. "No problem. There are many girls coming from the country these days looking to fill their rice bowls. Soon there will be another to take her place."

"But, surely she said something to Madame."

"There was money on the bureau. That was all. *Phooot!*" he repeated, tilting his head to one side, leering benignly. "I think it is much better to have rich American tourists, like you."

It wasn't until I was alone, sitting cross-legged on my bed in my disheveled room, that the enormity of the loss sunk in—Rangita was gone. To whom could I tell my story now? Who would believe it?

Desolation and sorrow enveloped me. I had a vision of the Old Queen, lifeless, face-down in the slimy mud on the shore of Lake Anosy, her flayed and dismembered corpse stripped of its magnificent skin, her majestic snout half-buried in livid weeds, her muscular tail trampled by careless mobs of thrill-seekers straining for a last look at the mysterious, sacred crocodile who had inhabited the lake since before recorded time.

Au revoir, reine de Vazimba.

Never again would those fearsome jaws carry a *kokolampo* like a kitten, nor bring a frightened *vazaha* back to life.

In my mind's eye I approached the flensed Queen with a bottle of sacrificial rum, prepared to anoint her for the last time. I saw the rum splash over the immense, pink carcass, naked and obscene as an aborted embryo. I tried to invent a blessing but my heart hurt so much I couldn't cobble two words together.

Was this how a queen should die? Blown away by an act of gratuitous violence, reduced to a grotesque sideshow? It was unconscionable. Who would shoot her? Why? A mythic animal—a national treasure!—had been destroyed cruelly, for sport. To make matters worse, I had no one to share my grief with. I'd been abandoned by Rangita, the one person in Madagascar that I could even remotely call a friend.

Right now, I thought miserably, ten thousand miles around the curved earth, cable cars were clanging gaily, making the turn-around at Powell and Market. People were drinking double *lattes* at Starbucks and schmoozing about the Giants. People were making love. Or at least angling for a date. Down on Montgomery Street people were buying long and selling short. Macy's was having another white sale and Carol Doda was thinking about having more implants.

There was a pit at the center of my stomach. Three sharp-bladed shovels—grief, confusion and loneliness—dug into my belly. I reached for a bag of Trailmix and began stuffing nuts and raisins into my mouth. It seemed like a hundred years since lunch with Jack Mooresby. I pawed at the cellophane, scrounging for the last raisin. Not only did I feel hungry, but I felt old—older than the Old Queen. I pulled my cosmetic pouch over on the bed next to me and scumbled around in it for a mirror.

Vanity, you're thinking. At a time like this she goes for a mirror? What solace can she hope to gain there, other than a quick, narcissistic hit? The truth is: vanity is one of my main survival tools, and my mirror, sanity's handmaiden. Narcissus was no fool. He saw all human consciousness reflected in the surface of that shimmering pond. When I gaze into my mirror I invoke all the images it has ever received, conjuring apparitions from the far distant past, seeking to strip off the veil of time and see myself as a part of the human continuum. Eternally receptive, the silvered glass becomes a door through which my spirit frees itself to pass to the other side.

Looking for sanity, trying to snag a glimpse of my soul, I stumbled upon an envelope, nestled among the tubes, bottles and brushes. One word:

was written on the front in an ornate, old-fashioned hand. The envelope was heavy. It commanded respect, like an invitation to a coronation. It had been sealed with a blob of blue wax imprinted with an ornate capital letter "R." The paper was thick and smooth, a creamy vellum heavy as Arches watercolor paper. Attached to the lower left corner with another knot of sealing wax was a dainty silver chain. I tugged on it gently and out from under a bottle of moisturizer popped something long and curved, set in filagree silver. I recognized it immediately: a crocodile's tooth. The chain passed through a ring on the top shaped like a crown.

Put it on, a voice urged.

I slipped the necklace over my head. The chain was long, exquisitely fashioned into twisted links resembling tiny crocodiles, each biting the tail of the one going before. The tooth hung perfectly balanced between my breasts, curving to one side, the sharp tip almost touching my nipple. It was strangely erotic and very beautiful. I was admiring it when I realized...

...Someone was in the room with me.

There was no mistaking the feeling. It came on so fast and strong that I actually started to shake. I got up and fastened the safety chain on the inside of the door. I pulled the curtains closed and checked inside the armoire. I went to the door again and listened for somebody breathing outside.

The keyhole!

I broke off a Q-Tip and stuffed it into the eye of the lock. I knelt down on the floor and peered under the bed.

Nothing.

Still trembling, I went over by the window and sat primly on the edge of the chair, avoiding my wet clothes draped over the back. On the floor at my feet lay the *ody.* I'd almost forgotten about it. I picked it up and gave it a squeeze. "Stick with me," I whispered, glancing apprehensively over my shoulder. Then I took out my Swiss Army knife and broke the waxen seal.

The paper inside had been folded several times to form a square. I drew it out and opened it slowly. The lettering was written in a looping, spidery hand more suited to the eighteenth century than the computer age.

Sister...

...it began,
Thunder over the lake.
Oxen trample the rice fields.
Blue hands point the way.
At the mouth of a tomb, the hair stands up.
Rocks are its walls.

Eyes cannot measure how high they reach.
Evening shadows fold into eternal night.
Great White Ones guard rattling bones.
The dead release their stubbornness into dust.
O Fearful Ancestors!
The sun sets and does not return.
The day has no need to finish.
A kokolampo lights the river without end.
A solitary vazaha perseveres.
A crocodile becomes a pirogue.
She is ten thousand women with heart.
Her breath is a waterspout, rolling is her pace.
A solitary vazaha perseveres.
O hear!
The Blue Rainforest weeps bitter tears.
Bamboo breaks with the weight of a dying babakoto.
Mpakafo ride steel dragonflies.
Taboos are cracked and broken, useless.
There grass dries.
There earth shakes.
There villages burn.
There the ground smells of blood and rum.
A solitary vazaha perseveres
With a single jug she makes a thousand men drunk.
With a single kiss she takes dominion of the stars.
With a single blessing she makes the invisible visible.
O hear me!
Andrebabe, Vazimba fortress
Invisible in the Blue Rainforest
Awaits the solitary vazaha who perseveres.
She is not alone.
She is not alone.

It was signed: *Rangita, Reine de Vazimba*

In tiny handwriting across the bottom she had added a postscript: *Eva, please seek out M. Ratelifera in the Zoma. He wears a red shirt. He will have herbs to heal your arm. Have courage, my dear sister. You will need it. R.*

I stretched out on the bed, staring up at the dim, forty-watt bulb hanging from the ceiling. I'm not a fan of cryptic, metaphysical poetry, but I got the message, loud and clear: I was being set up. Co-opted. Asked to lay down my life by a Malagasy hooker wielding a quill pen and suffering delusions of royalty.

Things had gotten *way* out of hand.

Grappling to stay afloat, I reached back into the past, to the hard pews of Our Lady of Perpetual Sorrow, hearing Father Michael's booming Sunday morning voice, intoning Scripture.

Therefore, My Father loves me, because I lay down My life that I may take it again. No one takes it from Me, but I lay it down of Myself. I have the power to lay it down, and I have power to take it again.

Jesus hadn't minced any words with the Pharisees. Maybe I could tear a leaf from His book to deal with Rangita.

Then my rational brain launched an attack.

What!? Lay down your *life*? Earth to Eva. Hold everything. You're talking about a minor hike into a rainforest here, not a trip to Mars. You still have a choice. You can blow off the *babakoto*— whatever that is—and the steel dragonflies. It wouldn't take much to change your plane ticket. You can be home in twenty-four hours. Your paints are probably still damp on your palette. You could even catch the white sale at Macy's. James is a grown-up. A professional. This whole nocturnal adventure, including the blind cave crawl, has been wild fantasy, born of loneliness and frustration.

Maybe, but there was no getting around the fact that, like it or not, I now had another agenda, one that went beyond merely rescuing James. It had to do with rescuing... my life.

It's Code Blue, babe...

The glove was down. No escaping the question.

What *about* my life?

That was the real question. Did I in fact have the power to take it up and lay it down again? Courage. That's what was really at stake here. Did I have it, or did I not? Could I walk the walk? Or was I just a blind, albino *vazaha*, holiday head-tripping in the Third World?

There was only one way to find out.

A solitary vazaha perseveres...

Some serious faith was being called for.

She is not alone...

I fingered the hard, blue wax of the broken seal.

I had it in writing didn't I? Between God and Rangita, somebody was looking after me. All I had to do was believe it.

I read the verses again.

With a single jug she makes a thousand men drunk...

Now that was promising.

With a single kiss she takes dominion of the stars...

Sold.

Tomorrow I would pack my bags and head south.

I slept badly that night. My dreams were filled with fire and blood and lemurs with chattering blue teeth. One of them was swinging through the trees wearing James' gold-rimmed spectacles and a scarlet T-shirt with GO BIG RED on it.

That surprised me. I mean, James liking football.

14

Despite my best intentions, getting out of Tananarive was not going to be easy.

First, there was my wound.

The night hadn't been good to it. It had become an angry, suppurating crater. Red infection lines were streaking for my armpit. I could feel my swollen lymph nodes gearing up for a major battle.

I found M. Ratelifera, the herbalist, seated on a straw mat on the sidewalk in the Zoma market, yawning sleepily in the sunshine. He had spent the night on the pavement, anticipating early morning customers. He wasn't hard to locate. As advertised, he was wearing a bright red shirt. His wares were spread out around him in rough piles. Many appeared to have been yanked directly from the soil, for there was rusty earth still clinging to their roots. Odors of indigo, sage, resin and a piercing citrus mingled with rank gutter smells, setting my sinuses on fire.

It wasn't the kind of apothecary that took your PCS card. On the mat lay odd, radish-like, white tubers and bundles of purple twigs. Shrivelled, mushroomy things like dried bats' ears tumbled out of a basket. Stringy, celadon, asparagus stalks were stacked up next to bunches of shiny orange wormlets strung together like chilis on straw thongs. Saffron-colored beans with bright black eyes, prickly, two-tone pine cones, perfectly smooth, round nuts and indescribably hairy roots clogged with dirt vied for my attention. Off to one side was a disorderly mound of sticks that looked like kindling for a Girl Scout campfire. There was not a sign nor a label anywhere to be seen.

M. Ratelifera squinted up at me from under his straw hat and smiled. He was a leathery little man with intensely dark skin, very unlike most of the Malagasy I'd seen in Tana. "Good morning, mademoiselle. It is a fine day, is it not?" He swept his arm in a circle over the heaps of nameless vegetation. "Whatever your condition, we have a cure."

This drugstore called for a major leap of faith.

I rolled up my shirt and pointed silently to my arm.

"Aha..." M. Ratelifera took one look at me and grabbed a handful of desiccated, grey vine leaves in a basket on the ground beside him. "*Talapetraka*. One must crush these, boil them for twenty minutes, make a poultice by soaking them with a cloth. One must change the dressing every four hours. In three days..." he smoothed his own arm with a downward motion, "one has... peace." He tore off a sheet of old newspaper and began rolling them into a small packet.

"If I were you I'd try tetracycline."

There could be only one cowboy at the end of that rope.

Jack Mooresby stood behind me blocking the sun with his arms folded on his chest, eyeballing M. Ratelifera's sidewalk pharmacy with cynical amusement. He wore the same worn jeans as yesterday, but he'd changed to a tight, black T-shirt. It was most unsettling. I wasn't used to muscles like that so early in the morning.

"You don't believe him?"

Jack squatted down and picked up some wrinkled green leaves that looked like basil. "I wouldn't say that exactly." He turned to M. Ratelifera, "What's this one for?"

"We call it *mahaibe,* 'the wise one.' It is for bubonic plague. Very good medicine."

I looked at Jack. "I thought that disappeared with the Inquisition."

"Nope. Bubonic. Black. You name it. Plague's still making the rounds in Madagascar, in the boonies. It's another one of those things they don't mention in the guidebooks."

I studied the nameless weeds wrapped in yesterday's newspaper, which M. Ratelifera had handed me.

"I'm not saying those are no good," Jack nodded at the little packet. "But I'd back them up with something..."

"Something... *real?* Is that what you mean?"

Jack picked up a bunch of soft white leaves and sniffed them. "Well, something more than a panacea, anyhow. Take these, for instance. This is old-fashioned New Mexican sage." He faced the herb seller, "What disease do you cure with this?"

M. Ratelifera pursed his lips and paused for a long moment. A cloud passed across the sun, casting a shadow over the mat and the herbalist seated upon it. His face, under the broad brimmed hat, dropped away into nothingness. "Evil," he whispered. "We use it against evil."

Images of last night swarmed into my head when he said that. Endless tunnels, blind crocs, *kokolampos* hanging upside down from vaulted caverns. I felt sick and dizzy.

"Please, how much do I owe you?"

I moved closer to him, preparing to hand him a few francs from my coin purse. As I did so, the crocodile tooth on its crocodile chain slipped out of the neck of my blouse and swung directly in front of his nose.

M. Ratelifera then did something extraordinary. He reached out and took the tooth in both his hands, bringing his mouth forward to kiss it.

"So...You are the one."

He sighed and rocked back on his heels when he said it, staring at me quietly and reverentially, in no more hurry than the cloudshadow moving across the face of the sun. "Welcome. We have been expecting you, from another ocean, beyond the sea."

His eyes looked through me, not at me. And I was knowing what he saw there: blown spume and turquoise grey waters. Bent, rough-barked cypress trees and yellow coreopsis daisies knocking back and forth in a chill westerly. Twisted driftwood and steep beaches shaled with agates and moonstones. He saw fog, too, I knew it. And he heard the music of foghorns, calling to each other across a bay girdled by three great bridges. It was simple. He saw it. I knew it. And he knew that I saw it.

"Hey, I've got an idea," Jack interrupted. "Let's you and I take a run up to Tzimbazaza Park and check out those weeds before you go plastering them on that sore. I've got a friend up there at the Tananarive Zoo—Jerome Rastatondrafara—he's researching medicinal plants."

I extracted the necklace from the herbalist's hands and slipped it back into my shirt, handing him a wad of francs. M. Ratelifera pushed the money back at me, shaking his head.

"What say, Artema? Sound like a plan?"

I locked eyes with the herb-seller, ignoring Jack.

"Thank you for the medicine. I... I am glad to be here, I think..."

He took hold of my hand, pulling me very close to him, speaking into my ear.

"Prepare for danger. Trust Rangita, but guard well your immortal soul. Many souls—and lives—have been lost in the Blue Rainforest."

He released me abruptly, and I lost my balance, falling backwards against Jack, banging my hurt shoulder. I let out a yelp of pain.

"Hey, c'mon kid," he said. "Quit playing the martyr. I've got some tetracycline in my first aid kit."

I let him lead the way.

Why not? I wasn't that far out of it not to realize he had what I needed…

A car.

Jack gunned the Land Rover up the hill behind Analakely, "the little woods." Once this valley had been covered with trees, but the forest was long gone. It was crowded instead with white umbrellas sheltering the Zoma market.

We passed the sellers of endangered tortoise shell from the coast, the hawkers of litchi nuts, the vendors of fresh vanilla beans and spicy *sakai* sauce. We circled the square slowly, avoiding weavers of raffia mats and peddlers of hand-forged aluminum pots and pans. In the arcade they were selling mohair carpets, and off to one side, in tiny canvas stalls, shoppers huddled, bargaining for cut and uncut gems. Open-air dealers displayed used locks, nails and screws—all sorts of odd, old hardware ripped from crumbling French colonial houses. Under another umbrella, shoppers admired kerosene lanterns, cleverly crafted from tin to resemble many-storied Merina houses. Under the umbrellas' shade children stood guard, ready to barter over mounted butterfly collections and boxes of giant beetles captured in far-off rainforests. We passed the basket-makers and the mattress men and the stalls of the *lamba* ladies, festooned with meters of tropical-colored, printed cottons.

"So, d'you want to talk about it?" Jack said.

I sulked, looking intently out the window, counting the purple petals on the jacarandas flashing by.

I should've known he would ask that.

"I've decided to leave today for Mananjary," I announced.

He looked at me for a long beat, snorted, and burst out laughing.

"Are you kidding, Artema?"

We started climbing another steep hill. On top I could see some sand-colored, official-looking buildings.

"Say, isn't that the Directorate of Scientific Research up

there?" I said brightly.

"Cut it out, Eva. You can't leave today. First of all, it's Saturday. Tomorrow's Sunday. Nothing's open. What about your permits? Have you checked with *Eaux et Forets*? Do you have train tickets? The Antsirabe line is always booked weeks in advance on weekends. And the hotels—what few of them there are—are always full. I almost forgot, it's *sambatra* time. The southeast will be *loco* this month. Madagascar isn't like the States where you can simply fall into a Motel Six when the sun goes down."

He was becoming extremely agitated. I'll confess, I liked it. A lot.

"Well, I can always camp out." I said lightly.

"CAMP OUT!!? Alone? Are you shitting me?"

It was thrilling, watching him pound the wheel in exasperation.

"Why not? James does."

I not only liked it, I loved it.

"Your brother is a *trained biologist*!!" he shouted. "And besides, he's... he's a..." He stopped and grabbed the tails of his thick mustache.

"He's a what? He's... a man. Is that what you were going to say?"

"No. Yes. *Hell* yes!"

"You don't have to swear to make your point," I said.

"*Vazahas* don't go roaming around in the bush at night!" He was steaming. "Don't you know that last year two French geologists were killed in their camp in the forest less than a hundred miles north of Tana? *Mpakafo*, that's what the villagers called them. *Heart thieves*! They put a spear through each one and cut them loose to float south on the Mahajilo River in a dugout canoe."

"Poor guys," I said. "Maybe they would still be alive if they'd've been women."

He did have nice muscles. Anger defined every one of them as he rammed the Rover into low gear and tromped vengefully on the gas pedal. We squealed around a corner and into a parking lot.

"From what I hear, they understand strong women on this island. James says they have a long history of powerful queens, going back to the Vazimba."

"Jesus Christ!" said Jack, wrenching the parking brake. "You're *not* a Malagasy. You're *not* a queen. You're a *vazaha*. Things happen to wandering *vazahas*. Remember that."

As if I could forget!

"Mmmmm... you're probably right. I forgot, it's Code Blue here." I turned towards him, blazing my most beguiling smile.

Full court press, Artema.

"You're not traveling south next week by any chance, are you, Jack?"

He looked dazed, as if I'd hit him up the side of the head with a two-by-four.

Gotcha, I thought, watching him twirl in a machismo breeze.

"Hey, we're here." I jumped out and slammed the door. "Let's take a peek at some skeletons and check out those herbs with your friend Jerome."

It's disgusting how twinkly a person can be when she wants something and it starts to fall into her lap. Some people might even call it dazzling.

I'll be honest. It had been a long time since someone wanted to protect me. It didn't feel half bad.

15

Jerome Rastatondrafara was full of surprises.

To begin with, I suppose it surprised me that he and Jack were friends at all, given Jack's propensity for blunt language. Jerome was very small and very fat—unusual for a Malagasy. He wore a crisp, white cotton lab coat with many pens clipped to the breast pocket. Around his hips he had wound a striped cloth, Malaysian-style. His chubby, bare feet were thrust into sprung rubber thongs and he rolled from side to side as he ushered us into his small laboratory, all the while humming queer little songs under his breath. He reminded me of an inebriated hedgehog got up as Dr. Kildare. He kissed Jack and me on both cheeks twice in the French style, and appeared genuinely pleased to see us.

As for me, I felt instantly at home.

James always kept snakes in his pockets and alligators in the bathtub. Tortoises hibernated under the clothes dryer and tree frogs estivated in the begonias. Once he gave Mama a yard-long, fluorescent-green iguana for her birthday. He used to answer the telephone by braying like a donkey.

I looked around. Michel Rakotomana was right. Madagascar *was* a taxonomist's paradise. The shelves lining the walls groaned with pickling jars with an array of specimens. There were some ordinary things like salamanders, rubbery snake eggs, baby geckos and dead beetles the size of small dogs. But there were many other specimens that defied description. Every cranny was filled with something that had once been alive. Furred, feathered, scaled, skinned or finned—dusty inanimate critters hung, swung, perched and clung with claw, toe, tooth or wing to every inch of freeboard in the lab. Hanging from the ceiling was a stuffed flying fox—a giant bat about the size of my cat, Arlo. It dangled disconsolately on leathery wings, surveying the denizens of the Great Red Island with unblinking, glassine eyes. Lying atop a pile of scientific reports was a clutch of thumb-sized, brilliantly colored, mottled sunbirds ready for taxidermy.

Jerome picked one up and smoothed its feathers lovingly. "In Madagascar we're calling these little guys *mister-now-you-see-me-now-you-don't*." He chortled, delighted to surprise me with his idiomatic English. "*Et moi?* You are calling me Rasti, okay? Like my friend, Jack." He rolled the "r" like a Sicilian.

He guided us through the maze of musty Malagasy wildlife to his lair, huffing and panting and humming as he wove his way through the frozen zoo. His rubber thongs slapped against his bare heels, and he reeled off Latin and Malagasy names so rapidly I could barely keep up with him, let alone gather my wits to ask questions.

He ushered us into his laboratory.

It was small, not much larger than James' childhood closet, but it was glorious—a reeking, botanical circus. Bunches and bundles of twigs, thistles, branches, leaves, vines, stems, tubers, roots, knots, bolls, galls, petals, pods, cones, seeds, spores, and stamens filled every available niche. Unlike Ratelifera, his Zoma counterpart, everything in this pharmacopoeia bristled with tiny, handwritten labels.

Rasti heaved a contented sigh as he looked around. "There is so much magic in this room."

He picked up a lump of nondescript weeds and brought them to his nostrils, sniffing them as if they were a bottle of rare French perfume.

"*Magnifique! Mysterieuse!* So many diseases, and for every one... God makes a cure." He inhaled deeply, wrinkling his little round nose. "So many things to be discovered... So little time."

A look of deep sadness clouded his face.

"Mademoiselle, all Madagascar is burning. Dying. Going up in smoke. Each day we lose another hundred hectares of forest to ignorance and the practice of *tavy*—you are calling it slash-and-burn agriculture. Our forests and woodlands are home to hundreds, perhaps thousands of unknown species. Once they are gone—*phhhttt!*—they are gone forever. It is the same everywhere––Amazonia, Borneo, Zaire. We scientists must run, run, run, run to keep ahead of the flames and the ax."

Jack thrust the newspaper packet towards him. "Eva bought these from a fellow on the street. I thought you might recognize them."

Rasti unrolled the package and crumbled the leaves in his right hand and sniffed.

"*Bien sur,*" he said. "*Centella asiatica.* In the West you are calling it Madecassol. Very effective for healing skin abrasions." He turned to me. "May I inquire from whom you bought these?"

"Oh... a man. In a red shirt."

I knew his name. Why didn't I simply tell him? Was it that I didn't want to have to explain why, or how I knew? Was I somehow trying to protect Rangita?

Rasti was ahead of me.

"Okay, sure. Ratelifera. He is a good guy. You could say he knows as much as I do about plants, despite my university degree. More, perhaps. He has brought me many herbs and many stories of their cures, to examine under the microscopes of science." He turned towards me. "But, surely you have not been wounded,

Mademoiselle Eva?"

"A small scratch. It is nothing."

I felt Jack at my side, bursting with unasked questions. I avoided his eyes and instead I took Rasti's arm. "I haven't seen the zoo or the museum yet. It would be a privilege to have such a knowledgeable guide."

And so he was.

Together we strolled through the gardens below the research laboratory. I questioned him closely about James, and was greatly disappointed to learn that he had not met him, nor heard of his work. In fact, when I mentioned the Blue Rainforest he quickly changed the subject, pointing out various endemic plants that had been brought to the capital from remote corners of the island. He was a charming and informative teacher. He and Jack joked playfully, engaging in a verbal shorthand that poked fun at Rasti's desire to learn slang. "Street American, as we are calling it here," he explained.

Tzimbazaza Park was a gentle place, but a melancholy one. It was crowded with Malagasy families and young couples chatting and laughing quietly among themselves. Women with traditional white *lambas* wrapped around their shoulders held the hands of children dressed in blue jeans and T-shirts. They circled outdoor cages that held the living descendants of the stuffed animals we had just seen.

"Our zoo... It is a blessing which obscures a great national tragedy." Rasti spoke in a low undertone, so as to not be overheard. "For many—perhaps all—of the people you are seeing here, these are the only wild animals they will ever see in their lifetime."

He pointed to a cage nearby where a black and white lemur clung to the wire, nursing an infant. You could never mistake her for a monkey, despite the obvious similarities between the two animals. Although she resembled a monkey, with her slender body, long legs and arms, and the distinctive tail, she had a delicate and graceful presence about her, quite different from a monkey's nervous agitation. This lemur's amber eyes shone like agates above a slender black muzzle; her soft fur caught the morning sun, creating a luminous aura around her cupped, translucent ears. The infant clinging to her with spidery arms was a perfect, miniature version of its mother.

Rasti continued, "The *sifaka* there, so sad, so mournful in her eyes, is one of a small troop whose forest home is even at the present moment being hacked down and turned into charcoal to be sold by hungry peasants. These *sifaka* are doomed. Even this mother is doomed. She doesn't know it, but soon her baby will die, for we are not sure what foods these rare lemurs eat, and even if we did, we do not have the money to feed them. In the wild, she would be bounding freely through the trees, dropping half-eaten fruits and calling out noisily to the rest of her troop. Here, she is alone and silent. And yet," Rasti shrugged and displayed his palms, "without this zoo, our people would have no idea at all that they have a heritage of unique wildlife. Here, at least, they learn that it exists. Later, perhaps, they will be moved to save it." He sighed, "Let us hope it will not be too late."

We had arrived at a shallow enclosure in the middle of the lawn. Three small boys leaned over the iron fence, making faces and rolling their eyes in mock terror.

"*Voay! Voay!*" they called out.

I looked down to see what it was.

It was a crocodile.

My hand flew to my chest where the tooth lay hidden. My heart pounded, my face grew hot. I closed my eyes and felt once again the rhythmic rocking of the Old Queen, as she ferried me through the underworld.

I stared down at the lethargic reptile. This croc certainly couldn't hold a candle to *my* Queen.

Rasti joined me at the fence. "In Malagasy we have a saying, *There is nothing God does not know, but he decides when to bend down.* We say God bent down very low when He created the *voay*. That is why He gave it such great power. In some parts of our country crocodiles are regarded as sacred beings."

"Sacred queens, you say?" It just slipped out of my mouth.

For a chubby guy, the look Rasti gave me was pretty piercing.

"Queens? No, I have not heard that. I know there is a lake in the north where the villagers believe they are Ancestors and call them to shore with a bowl of fresh blood. They feed them by hand with sacrificed zebu meat. Alas, like the *sifaka*, crocodiles are becoming more and more rare. Soon, I fear they will be no more than a symbol, a legend. Like the Vazimba."

The tops of my ears went hot on that one.

"But what about the old, um... Isn't there supposed to be a crocodile right here in the middle of Tananarive, living in Lake Anosy?"

"There used to be rumors of a giant when I was a boy. Every now and then someone claims to see it, but nothing has been proven. We scientists are calling it a wishing fantasy, like your Loch Ness monster. Something to fill the newspapers when people become tired of politics."

"But, last night... I was told there was shooting... many bullets... an old female.. down by the lake."

My head was spinning.

Jack put his hand on my shoulder. "Artema, you okay? C'mon, you're looking kind of green. Let's get you out of the sun and put some medicine on that cut."

"Bullets?" Pens clinking in his breast pocket, Rasti trotted alongside us, looking concerned and puzzled. "Perhaps you are meaning the fireworks for the President's birthday. Hunting with guns for a legend? Surely that is a sport for cowards or madmen, *n'est-ce pas?*"

Rasti boiled up Ratelifera's leaves on a bunsen burner in his lab, and while they steeped he led Jack and me through the museum. We shuffled along with the crowds, peering into glass display cases.

He paused in front of a gigantic skeleton of an Aepyornis, an ostrich-like bird over nine feet tall. Perched on the platform below was a massive egg the size of a football.

Jack whistled. "Looks like a candidate for a Texas two-gallon omelette. Or else some great southern fried. Check out those mighty thighs."

The Aepyornis towered over us, its thick, three-toed feet balanced on leg bones stout as palm trees. Its long, giraffe-like neck, extending upward, was topped by a tiny skull.

"In Africa they say the kick of an ostrich can kill a leopard. I'll bet the Ancestors gave this elephant bird a helluva wide berth." Jack seemed truly impressed.

"No one knows exactly when or how *Aepyornis maximus* became extinct," Rasti said. "Hunting, egg collecting, climatic changes all contributed to its demise. You are right though, it is for sure that they were alive and well when the Vazimba roamed the island, gathering their eggs in which to store water or grain, just as the Bushmen use ostrich eggs today."

He patted the bird's great knee-joint. "*Vorounsatrasana*—the Bird No One Has Ever Seen. He is believed to be the same gigantic bird described to Marco Polo by Arab traders. You remember the story of Sinbad's legendary roc?" He leaned closer conspiratorially, pointing at the humongous egg and whispering, "Sometimes, even today, believe it or not, a wandering hunter will uncover a fresh, whole egg in the Spiny Desert of the deep south, the yolk and white perfect and unbroken... still edible!"

"Hold on, Rasti. I don't get it. You just said the Aepyornis has been extinct for over 500 years."

Practical, linear Jack.

Rasti's smile split his face in two. "In Madagascar, my friend, one must be careful not to draw the line between truth and fiction with indelible ink. It is better to use a pencil, for here even the firmest convictions can be erased in the twinkling of an eye."

No news that.

In my mind's eye I saw the little blue door of the Hotel

Kokolampo, heard the *tinggg* of the silver bell, felt the claustrophobic darkness of the endless tunnels and smelled the stench of the great cavern where the Ancestors lay.

The three of us entered a room filled with a dozen or more prowling skeletons, some with two feet, some with four. Lemurs or humans? It was impossible to tell. I tried to decipher the labels, but they were written in Malagasy and Latin.

"Which ones are the Vazimba?"

"Ah, the Vazimba. ...dolichocephalic, orthognathus, steatopygous, low in stature, and the women are longynymphal..." Rasti struggled manfully with the unfamiliar English words in a soft, sing-song voice.

Jack interrupted, "Professor Rastatondrafara, speakada English, *por favor.*"

Rasti chuckled, "That is how a missionary described the Vazimba over a century ago. He is meaning long-headed, straight-jawed and fat-rumped. Some of us believe they were very small, and dark, with crinkly hair. Others say they resembled the Bushmen of today, with pale skin and straight hair."

Either way, I thought, Rangita would not have been flattered. But, come to think of it, I'd never seen her without that blonde wig...

"I'd like to see the remains of one," I persisted. "A Vazimba."

Rasti looked blank. "I am very sorry. We do not have such a thing. Not a femur, not a tibia. Nothing."

"You don't... There's no evidence? How can that be? Then how can anyone presume to make any claims about something they've never seen?" My voice rose a couple of notches. "I mean... maybe they never existed at all? Maybe somebody simply dreamt them up?"

"There is always a dream, dreaming us."

Rasti's round face was suffused with pleasure as he said this. In fact, it glowed. Exactly like Dr. Rabansoro's.

I blinked.

Wait a minute. This guy was a supposed to be a scientist, not a yogi.

"Doesn't *anybody* know what's real on this island?"

I didn't mean to shout.

Rasti reached out and touched the back of my hand. "*Realité*? Ah, Mademoiselle Eva, when you let go of that... then you become a magician."

A woman laughed.

I whirled around and looked over my shoulder. There was nobody in the hall but the three of us and some dry bones.

She laughed again.

It sounded exactly like Rangita.

"But I am a scientist, not a magician," Rasti trundled on ahead, oblivious. "I leave witchcraft to others."

He stopped before another case filled with dusty fossils, raising one finger and tapping the side of his temple, as if he were calling forth something important and long forgotten.

"Vazimba bones we may not have, that is true. But tombs... Aha, that is another matter. We have many of those around the countryside of Imerina, often near lakes and streams, hidden from prying eyes."

The blood rushed to my cheeks. *A solitary vazaha perseveres...*

"Can I... could we... visit one?"

Rasti pinned me with a look as sharp as a dissecting needle.

"You would be very disappointed, mademoiselle. You will see nothing. A few stones, some grass, a bent twig, a little grease smeared onto a rock, perhaps a burnt coin or two. These Vazimba tombs are poor things, nothing like the grand carved and painted houses of the dead built by the Mahafaly or the Antandroy in the southwest."

Something pushed at me to press him harder, something more powerful than mere curiosity.

"Please, I'm very interested. There must be some tombs near Tananarive."

"Oh yes, perhaps some..." He sounded deliberately vague. "In the mountains a few hours' drive from here."

"Perfect. Let's make it a Sunday picnic." I moved to include

Jack. "We can pick up some bread and cheese in the Zoma on our way out of town."

"I thought you were hell-bent on leaving for Mananjary this afternoon," Jack grumbled.

"Agenda subject to change without notice." I turned on the twinkle. "It *is* a woman's prerogative?"

Prerogative? Who was I kidding? It was an order, pure and simple, hidden in a question. A sinker ball. Low and on the outside. Jack Mooresby was a proven pitcher of those. Now let's see if he could hit the ball, too.

The irritation on his face said it all.

Strike one.

He regrouped and began steering me in the direction of Rasti's lab. "Not before we finish what we came here for and fix up that arm of yours." He shook his head, speaking gruffly into my ear, "Seems like all I do is play doctor with you, Artema." He gently massaged the soft part of my underarm with his thumb. A small, subtle, nothing gesture.

Why did I hear the sound of blue jeans, being unzipped?

His hand was large and brown, with callouses on his fingers that rubbed back and forth rhythmically against my tender skin, setting off some serious alarms south of my navel.

I felt my nipples go hard.

"Don't get any wild ideas, pilot," I whispered weakly. "This body is a temple. Don't ever forget it."

He tensed, tightening his grip.

Strike two.

His thumb continued circling, kneading. Warm and insistent. "Well, Hail Mary..."

"I said temple, not church."

Undaunted, he worked his thumb slowly up into the milky white flesh near my armpit, blowing my base chakra all to hell.

"...full of grace..."

We had arrived at the end of a long corridor where Rasti's lab was located. I tried to walk faster, but Jack pulled me back into him.

"I said... blessed art thou..." He whispered the words, brushing his mustache against my neck.

I closed my eyes for a moment and heard blue denim sliding down over strong, naked thighs, landing in a heap on the floor.

"...on earth... as it is in heaven." Jack Mooresby was close enough to bite my earlobe when he said that. He kind of nuzzled around where my hair curled into my collar.

I heard the crack as the ball left the bat.

Shit. He could pitch and he could hit.

Then he stuck the tip of his tongue into my ear.

Damn!

It was a solid RBI.

I'll admit it. Right then, I lost it. I wriggled my butt up against Jack Mooresby's 501's, twitching like a honeybee dancing its honey-dance, singing a body-song about stamens and pistils, wild meadows and secret sweetness. Just thinking about it makes me ache. Thank God Rasti was leading the way. I'd have been mortified if he saw. It was pretty blatant—the wanting. Everything flew out my window. I forgot about Rangita and the Old Queen. Or even that I had a brother named James.

Ears.

You gotta watch out for them. They can get you in a lot of trouble.

16

"So ends the freeway and begins the bush."

Rasti made this pronouncement as Jack swung the Land Rover in a wide arc to avoid a deep fissure in the road bed, sending several bottles of Eau Vive mineral water and our hastily-assembled picnic rocketing across the floorboards. We were an hour outside the capitol and the asphalt had run out and the red dirt and the potholes had begun.

Rasti pointed to a worn track leading off to the right into a grove of eucalyptus and scrubby, insubstantial pines. "We are turning here, Jack."

We climbed steeply uphill, winding through a scrawny forest. A dizzying succession of naked tree trunks striped the car with sun and shadow. There was no sign of ashes to indicate slash-and-burn farming; this was deforestation, pure and simple. Stumps of eucalyptus trees logged fifty or seventy-five years ago sprouted suckers upon suckers, some of them more than thirty feet high. They created a feeble secondary forest of weak saplings and emaciated branchings. Not a bird sang, nor was there any other life in these blighted groves. I could see no movement save the slight swaying of thin, grey trunks. Certainly if there had been any lemurs in this desolate bush they had fled or been eaten long ago.

We'd left the lush, emerald rice paddies surrounding Tananarive far behind. Once beyond the city limits, we rumbled past tight enclaves of two-storied red brick houses with steeply raked, thatched roofs. On second-floor balconies lines of washing slapped lazily in the noon sun. From behind faded pastel dooways, cows stomped and blew bovine warnings from wet, rubbery nostrils. In tidy, sun-drenched courtyards, convoys of chickens stabbed at the earth for grubs and seeds. A woman with Asian cheekbones walked alongside the road proudly carrying an old-fashioned coal-fired iron nestled like a fat hen in a basket of leaves on her head. In shimmering rice ponds, laughing children leapt in and out of the muddy waters, trapping paddy fish like silver dollars in basket-sieves. Atop a dike of red mud, a line of clear white geese trotted like noisy schoolchildren, obediently following a girl who shouldered a long twig with a bright red rag tied onto the end like a flag. This could be Indochina, I thought. Many years ago. Long before it became Vietnam, before it belonged to France.

Jack slammed the truck in and out of gear, slowing for every rut and pothole. The roar of the engine made conversation impossible. I lifted up a corner of my bandage, scraping the wet leaves away from the wound, and was surprised to see that the angry red streaks were gone.

Ratelifera knew his herbs, all right.

I caught Rasti staring at me. He winked and made a thumbs-up sign, settled back and closed his eyes. Apparently we were nowhere near our destination. Not even warm.

I wedged myself into a corner between the seat and the door, trying to keep from becoming car-sick, wishing I could get out and walk. Anything but this wrenching and ramming. Fighting nausea, I pulled out a letter from the tattered packet in my knapsack.

"The Malagasy love to walk," James wrote in his fine hand. *"From the air, you can easily see their footpaths; the island is spider-webbed with bright red trails. In fact, until the French arrived in 1895, there were no roads here at all—not one. What for? The Malagasy hadn't invented the wheel—even for toys. The ruling Merina knew what they were doing. Their not-so-benign neglect of roads was a calculated attempt to quash any attempts by invaders to unseat them.*

"Their plan was doomed; they couldn't remain isolated forever. Fueled by dreams of empire the French army steamed through the Suez Canal, crawled slowly down the East African Coast. Crossing the equator under a blistering apricot sky they disembarked in the sweltering, tropical marshes of Mahajunga dressed in thick, army-issue woolens and high-topped leather combat boots designed for climbing the icy slopes of the Matterhorn. They found to their surprise that before they could fight the Merina they had to build a 250-mile long road to get at them."

I looked out at the eucalyptus scrub forest, remembering I'd read somewhere that the first thing the British built when they occupied a new country was a custom-house, the first thing the Germans built was a fort, and the first thing the French built was a road—Madagascar being a prime example of French colonialism.

"It was madness, of course," James' letter continued *"Pure insanity. But the French did it. They pushed a road through the mid-summer, malarial flats of the west coast, bridging rivers alive with crocs, crashing through the tangled thickets of the high plateau in order to strike at Tananarive—all the while fending off spear attacks by fierce Bara and Sakalava tribesmen. Building that one road took the French six months and cost them 9,337 lives—a staggering total. Very few of these deaths occurred in battle. Most were from dysentery, malaria and heat exhaustion. Dragging a heavy iron cannon, the decimated French forces finally stabbed their road into the very heart of Imerina—Tananarive itself—and they blasted four, well-aimed shells at the Queen's Palace, located high on a granite escarpment overlooking the city."*

I recalled the grim castle on the cliffs above Lake Anosy, glowering over the busy roundabout with its barbers, cars and buses.

"The last shell exploded, scattering enough shrapnel around to wipe out thirty-five Malagasy, including the Queen's own Life Guards—magnificent, tall black men in dazzling uniforms who died, mutilated, in a sunken courtyard, before her eyes.

"That was it. The great war was over. The defeated Queen Ranavalona III—a small, frightened woman dressed in a hooped, Victorian velvet gown encrusted with gold embroidery, wearing a necklace of diamonds—hoisted a white flag on November 20, 1888, and the Merina monarchy ceased to exist. In the space of four cannonballs Madagascar had become a French colony."

The forest had petered out and the road shrunk to a track hardly wider than one of James' spidery footpaths. It was strewn with exposed boulders and gullies where the rains had leached away the topsoil. In the distance up ahead I saw a strange cloud, like a small tornado, swirling upwards. It was odd. There was the barest trace of wind, and yet the air was thick and churning.

I smoothed James' letter and read on.

"Ancient Madagascar was loaded with powerful queens—some good ones, and one truly evil one: Queen Ranavalona I. Her reign reeked of persecution and bloodshed and yet, from my vazaha viewpoint, she seems almost heroic. She made a desperate, suicidal bid to defend traditional Malagasy beliefs against us foreigners and our Christianity. The Cruel One won the battle, but she lost the war. By massacring tens of thousands of her fellows, she virtually guaranteed Christianity's entrenchment island-wide.

"After her death in 1861, her successor, King Radama II, burned the infamous sampy idols and banned the ancient death ordeal by tangena poison. This Malagasy truth-torture was usually orchestrated by the local sorcerer. Those accused of witchcraft were forced to ingest three greasy pieces of uncooked chicken skin and two grated Gerbera tanguin pits, and then, accompanied by much ceremonial chanting, the victim was fed a gruel made

of flour. The accused either vomited up the whole mess and was absolved on the spot, or died a grisly death after hours of excruciating misery. The practice hasn't died out entirely, merely gone underground. Rumor has it that present-day Malagasy still commonly use tangena for suicide, or murder.

"It was no surprise that after years of this sort of thing the Malagasy rushed forward in droves to accept Christ as their Saviour. Nothing spreads faith like setting fire to a few martyrs, does it? Remember what Father Michael used to say? "Blood consecrates, my children." Certainly every Malagasy I've met counts himself a true Christian. But, from what I can see, they also hedge their bets. Sorcery, divination, astrology, magic black and white—a whole lot of mumbo-jumbo—seems to survive and thrive on an equal footing with Our Lord.

"All love, your brother, J.

P". S. I sometimes wonder about those Vazimba. What do you suppose their queens were like?"

I folded James' letter, slipping it back into the stack of tissue-thin, air mail envelopes. At the bottom of the pile lay a heavy, cream-colored envelope impressed with an old-fashioned

I fingered it for a second, then reconsidered. No way was I going to open that envelope in front of Jack and Rasti. I knew a can of worms when I saw it and shoved the letter back into the pouch, zipped it up and pondered James' post-script.

How *did* the Vazimba queens fit into this fierce female lineage? According to Rangita, they'd been well established by the 1500s when the first Kon-Tiki-style rafts arrived from Polynesia. What had happened to those mysterious Little People? Why hadn't scientists unearthed a single Vazimba bone? Had they intermarried and been absorbed into the intruders' gene pool? Could it be possible that the Vazimba still existed, living in caves or unexplored pockets of primeval forest? Or even, as Dr. Rabansoro insisted, on some...

Here I took a deep breath...

Some... astral plane?

I leaned against the car door, but it wasn't the cold, painted metal I was feeling, it was the warmth of Rangita's strong brown shoulder pressing against me as it had when we leaned together over the balcony at Le Terrace.

"Why, we live. As always," she had said.

We. Live.

Two simple words. Yet they contained meaning enough to blow my world apart as surely as those four French cannonballs had destroyed the kingdom of Imerina.

I took a slug of mineral water and passed the bottle to Jack, fixating on the dust cloud in front of us, watching it draw closer. A list. That was it. A list would harness the questions pin-balling around in my brain.

Pulling out an envelope, I scrawled on the back:

1. WHO IS RANGITA?

    a.   A jolly tart in a blonde fright wig, putting the arm on a lonesome tourist for a few bucks.

    b.   A dangerous weirdo with some secret political agenda.

    c.   A lusty bi-sexual with a thing for watches and *vazahas*.

Or... I took another breath and threw caution to the winds.

    d.   A Vazimba queen able to slip through some kind of astral time-warp who writes old-fashioned poetry, sleeps with men for money and bonds with strange *vazaha* women for no apparent reason.

    e.   Any or all of the above.

I kept writing.

2. WHERE iS RANGITA?

I knew the answer to that one. Skipped town, leaving in her wake some turgid verses and a souvenir croc tooth. But if so, why did I keep hearing her voice, her laughter? What sort of Malagasy tricks she was up to? What kind of Third World cat-and-mouse game? What did she want from me? Why had she singled me out, calling me "sister?" Or was our sisterhood merely a vengeful, xenophobic ploy to discredit a crafty *vazaha*?

What, why, when, where, how? Again and again the questions buzzed my brain... Why? Why? My cogent left-brain list quickly crashed and burned, spiralling to earth in a whine of Whys. This line of reasoning—if you can call it that—was making me seasick.

I shot a desperate glance across the front seat at Jack Mooresby. *Read my mind, why don't you?* I screamed at him silently. *Rescue me! Can't you see I'm losing it?*

But Jack Mooresby was no Ratelifera. He white-knuckled the steering wheel, oblivious to my unspoken pleas, his jaw set like Dick Tracy, maneuvering the Rover across a series of racketing, washboard gaps in the abominable road, no doubt wishing he could trade this ground-hog for a 500D helicopter.

I clamped my teeth together to keep them from chattering, but I couldn't control my jibbering brain. So I turned the envelope on its side and tried again.

3. WHAT ABOUT RATELIFERA AND HiS X-RAY EYES?

How did he know what he knew? I wasn't imagining it. He had seen right through me. How?

I paused, not daring to add the Old Queen, the caves and the kokolampo to the list. Putting them down in black and white was guaranteed to send me over the edge.

I got it! Everyone was on Rangita's payroll!

No, better still...

I scribbled furiously.

Maybe all of them were working for The Yogi Who Glowed—including The Whore Who Would Be Queen!

"Waunhhhhh!!" I crumpled the envelope into a ball and threw it violently against the front windshield. "Ahrararrggh!!" The sound that came out of my mouth wasn't a snort. It wasn't a snarl. It was a bark. The bark of a rabid dog.

Rasti's eyes flew open like uncaged birds.

Jack braked, bringing the car to a dead halt. He cut the motor and turned, training his mirrored shades on me. "Something bothering you, Artema?"

I froze, half-expecting him to reach over and wipe a clot of infected foam from my lips.

"Yes," I said, enunciating very slowly, very carefully. "Yes, there is. I... want... to know... What does it mean to be a Vazimba queen?"

Jack stared at me. "Are you *nuts*?"

There followed a terrible silence.

Rasti looked utterly stricken, as if he were going to burst into tears.

Was I? I thought. Was I nuts? It was awful. I honestly didn't know.

"*Famadihana!*" Rasti suddenly thrust his arm between us and pointed through the windshield at the boiling cloud of dust. "It is a lucky day, Mademoiselle Eva," he exulted, patently relieved to have found a way out of this sticky, emotional impasse. "*Now* you are seeing some tombs."

At that, he leapt out of the car, leaving Mooresby and me to figure out the next move.

17

"We might as well get out and walk. We're going nowhere at this rate." Jack began gathering up our picnic.

"Yes, let's," I agreed. Our car was surrounded by a milling throng. We were stuck, an awkward, metallic slub in a bright, moving carpet of Malagasy. They crowded around the Rover, pressing against its dusty flanks, staring through the hazy windows at the two *vazaha* goldfish.

Rasti was already deeply engrossed in a conversation with several village elders. He waved us over and introduced us with great ceremony. The oldest took a couple of steps forward and planted his walking stick in the dirt directly in front of me. A warm breeze lifted my hair, making me aware of a skyful of clouds moving silently from east to west. The old man spoke in Malagasy, never taking his eyes off my face. Rasti translated, clasping his hands together tightly over his stomach.

"Mademoiselle, he is their *mpanandro*, an astrologer. He predicted your arrival when he chose this date for the ceremony.

He says you are The One. They have been awaiting you since early this morning. He thanks you for coming such a great distance to honor their ancestors."

Telepathy again! *So, you are The One...* Ratelifera's words rang in my ears.

I eyeballed the astrologer. Was he a member of the Yogic League too, along with the herbalist and Rangita?

The *mpanandro* handed me a slim green bottle.

"Drink," Rasti whispered. "It is only rum."

I took a small swig. It burned all the way down, like chili peppers soaked in honey and gasoline.

"More, you must take more or they will be insulted."

I tipped up the bottle and drank again.

It was a signal for everyone to cut loose. Bottles emerged from under *malabars* and out of baskets. Suddenly everyone was celebrating, even the kids. A band of Malagasy mariachis hired for the occasion struck up a tune. Trumpets blared, drums tatted and guitars thrummed. A sextet of clarinets laid into a smoking, syncopated number with reedy vengeance while a lone saxophone riffed, fooling around on the off-beat, playing snooty games along the edge of the melody, like a cat walking a fence at midnight.

I returned the flask and bowed deferentially. "Tell him I'm delighted I could make it. It took us a while to... er, we had... some difficulty... um, finding the place..." I looked around. Rutted road, windswept hilltop, empty miles. In either direction: nothing. No sign of a farm, or a village, or a tomb. Nothing but red earth and a few isolated groves of trees that had somehow escaped the logger's ax. "But, now that I've arrived..." I took another swig of rum and threw my arms out dramatically, "...*Laissez le bon temps roulé!*"

The crowd burst into laughter and surged forward in a good-humored gust of energy, carrying Rasti, Jack and myself along on its swell.

"Let the good times roll!" Rasti clapped his hands together so enthusiastically two of his ball point pens jumped right out of his pocket. "Mr. Chuck Berry! That is a pisser, mademoiselle!" He slapped me five, then doubled over, chortling. His button nose sank into his round face like a raisin baked into a gingerbread man, and his rubber sandals pattered against his heels as he shuffled back and forth in a spontaneous sort of samba. "A definitive pisser! Right, Jack?"

I put my head down and marched straight past them both, plunging into the vibrating cloud of humanity.

I was immediately hedged in on all sides by a mass of complete strangers who were, nonetheless, expecting me at their party. It was no small crowd, either. If you counted the children, there were at least two hundred people or more, all of whom had walked up out of valleys and ravines, carrying food and babies and bottles of rum. We formed a broad, joyous river, flowing uphill. As we came over a rise, I saw the tomb: a rectangular, stone box built into the top of a hill. Unadorned by any statues or ornamentation, it had about as much charm as a concrete bunker. Yet, at the sight of it a cheer went up and many of the front-line marchers broke loose and rushed forward, arms outstretched.

Rasti pulled me to one side. "Most of them are from Ambodivorondro, a poor village a few miles from here. Some have come from as far as the capitol. *Voanjo*, we are calling these—seeds, people whose true roots lie here, in the *tanindrazana*, the land of their Ancestors. They have had no money to build great, painted tombs like the ones you are seeing in guidebooks for tourists. They say it has taken them two years to save up enough for this *famadihana.*"

The sepulcher was already opened when we arrived. Several men wearing plaid cotton *malabars* and straw hats were digging furiously in the dirt around its perimeter. The band played loudly, non-stop and a carnival atmosphere prevailed.

"The exhumation has begun. Now they are digging up the bodies of children and others who have died since the last *famadihana*. Today these will be buried properly, placed inside with the rest of their Ancestors, the *razana.*"

I glanced at the growing pile. "How many...?"

Rasti shrugged. "They tell me it is twelve years since the last ceremony. This is not just one family's tomb. This one belongs to the whole village."

My God. Twelve years. A whole village of corpses...

"That's a heap of ancestors," Jack said, completing my thought, adding in a low voice directed at me, "And this is a hell of a toga party. Tell me, Artema, what's a girl have to do to get invited to a wing-ding like this?"

"Gotta be nuts, I guess," I snipped, turning my back on him.

Grinch! I immediately castigated myself. Why so sour? I should have been celebrating. I was in Madagascar, land of amazing, supernatural eruptions. Slippery psychic phenomena. Astral rock and roll. I was the guest of honor at a party twelve years in the planning. I had it on astrological authority. Why have a heart like a stone?

I looked around at the joyous Malagasy. I didn't *want* to persevere. I didn't want to be solitary. I wanted to belong. I wanted to be a butterfly, not just someplace where the magic lands, refuels, and then flies off into the sunset to mate.

Mate..! Ha! Maybe that was why I was so testy. Maybe I wanted to mate.

I stole a glance at Jack out the corner of my eye. He was drinking rum and sharing my picnic with the guys in checked night-shirts shoveling dirt, trading jokes in crummy French with the grave-diggers. Buddies already.

Mooresby... Now *there* was a butterfly.

Someone had given him a white cloth which he'd tied around his head like a buccaneer, to protect him from the heat. With that mustache and those white teeth I had to admit, he had style. But... mate?

No way.

The *famadihana* blazed on. The band honked out foot-stomping tunes, lusty as ever, although their impeccable teamwork had unraveled somewhat. The cat had hopped the fence for greener pastures, laid down his sax and was locked in an embrace with a barefoot girl in tight braids and a pink washdress, and the four clarinets had gone wandering off, serenading some maidens in red.

The sun was very hot. My smile was starting to hurt. That's always a bad sign. It happens to me at parties mostly, when people start pairing off to dance. That's when the old lord-don't-let-me-be-a-wall-flower tape kicks in. I usually head for the rest room until the music stops. Come to think of it, that's how I met Raul—on the way to the Ladies. He had his eye on me. He grabbed my hand, twirled me around, and taught me to salsa right there between the *Damas y Hombres*, in the hallway reeking of Lysol and corn tortillas, dodging crates of Corona and waiters with slicked-back hair dressed in phony *charro* outfits glittering with silver ric-rac. He wouldn't let me go. He kept me dancing the whole set, pulling me hard against him at the end of the last song. "Let's go home, *querida*," he said. "I want to eat you." And then told me his name.

I started edging toward the tomb.

There was a great deal of activity near the entrance. Long rolls of pale yellow straw matting were being carried out and placed on the ground. People pushed and crowded for a look, singing and swaying in time to the music, drinking and talking without missing a beat. Some laughed and joked, others were overcome by emotion, their dusty faces streaked with tears. I tried to get a good look into the tomb itself, but all I could see were some stone slabs, like bunk beds, and more rolls.

"*Viens, vazaha-be. Viens!*" Hands tugged me forward, pulling me through the crowd to the edge of the action where women knelt, unrolling the mats.

Even though I'd shared a taxi with Uncle Rasolo, I wasn't prepared for the Ancestors quite so up close and personal. Dried bones or green flesh, it didn't seem to matter. All were tenderly being washed and sung to, cradled lovingly in the arms of relatives who whispered news, gossip, blessings, prayers and imprecations into their shrouds. Young women pinched pieces of dried skin from old bones and hid them between their breasts. Souvenir teeth were plucked out of skulls, and tufts of black hair snitched from scalps. I saw a gold ring being slipped off a withered grey finger, kissed, then placed on a calloused brown one.

Rasti wriggled through the kneeling women to reach my side. "It is because they fear them that they do this. They will do anything to appease the *razana,* to keep peace in the village. Without the Ancestors' blessings, they believe that crops will fail, babies will die, and angry ghosts will return night after night in dreams, to haunt them." He searched my face for a reaction. "You do not fear your Ancestors, mademoiselle Eva?"

Popi and Hermina? Those crazy Italians from Cleveland who dyed their hair, drove a Nash Rambler and carried licorice in their pockets? It was a startling thought.

"Italians are different," I said. "We'd rather dance than haunt."

No sooner than those words were out than a gang of dancing women dressed in matching floral print dresses—aqua orchids and orange tiger lilies rampant on a magenta ground—descended on me. They gathered me up into their collective, tropical bosoms as naturally as a Venus flytrap snaps up a thirsty bee, searching for rainwater in its sticky throat. A fat woman with teeth spaced like fence posts grabbed my hips, jiggling her broad flowery belly for me to imitate. A beautiful young girl wearing a house key on a string around her neck insinuated herself under and around my arms, weaving herself against me, her eyes shooting sexual sparks. Two matrons locked arms and executed a Rastafarian *schottische* accompanied by a brace of bleating coronets, then collapsed into giggles.

And another bottle went around.

Rum, sweat and sunshine. The carnival of death had become a manic Mardi Gras. The band—what was left of it—moved in next to the tomb where the Ancestors were being outfitted in new silken shrouds, and the music shifted to a simple, primitive rhythm. People crushed closer and closer to see and touch their loved ones, to say goodbye before they were rolled up into new straw mats and stitched into fresh cocoons. We women—yes, it was "we" now, thanks to the rum and the music—began threading our way around to the the back of the tomb where some dirt steps led to the roof.

The top of the tomb was flat. The wind blew strong and warm. Imerina curved around us, the horizon clear and crisp, untramelled as a painted diorama. Clouds plowed overhead like Dutch galleons looking for a port to plunder. Every now and then a mainsail or a poop deck would break apart and cruise off on a tour of its own, only to dissipate in the bright blue sky.

The women formed a circle around me, waving their arms in a curiously innocent, fluttering motion, while their grinding hips proclaimed a very different, lascivious message.

"Come, *vazaha*. It is the Dance of the Ancestors," a toothless old one hissed as she moved to the center of the circle, gripping and guiding my hips in time to the monotonous rhythm. The circling women in their brilliant dresses moved in and out, opening and closing like the petals of an enormous rose.

I whipped off my bandana bandage, watching M. Ratelifera's healing herbs floating off in the breeze like so many snippets of loose tobacco, and I gave in to the ancestors. Drowning in snare drums, horns and guitars, I closed my eyes, grooved and forgot. About being a solitary vazaha who's supposed to persevere. About James Artema, Ph.D About Raul, art and Macy's, about burn-out and scrap. About lemurs, monsoons and discovering species. I twirled like a Sufi, caught between heaven and earth. I even forgot about Jack.

Not for long.

"What are you doing?!"

It was Mooresby, bellowing up at me from the base of the tomb. "Get down, Artema! Get *down*!!"

"You blind?" I shouted back. "I am!!"

I snapped my bandana at him, fell to one knee, then sprang up into the air.

The crowd went wild.

Thump-a-thump. Thump-a-thump. The boogie side of my brain took command of my hips. Bump grind. Bump grind. Yah, hah! Shameless stuff. Step step step, spin, kick! Spin and KICK. Shake your grooveee thang... I slid to the ground, crouched momentarily like a dying swan, then exploded sideways in my best Madonna imitation.

More cheers. Shouts. Trumpets!

Spin, jump and kick. Jump, kick and dive. Feeling good. Stayin' alive, stayin' alive...

All I needed was some thigh-high boots and a gold chain or two...

I was on a roll. A pretty inspired one, too, if the hollering and the clapping meant anything.

Spin kick. Flex dip. Whip and dive. So what it's not the seventies? Who cares!? Nothing ever dies here. Not even disco. I swung my hips until they ached. What with the rum and the sun and the tunes, I hadn't felt this good since Raul and I tore it up at the El Cantador in Benicia four years ago. No partner needed today. My dance card was filled with the ancestors!

"*Kabary! Kabary!*"

"A speech, mademoiselle. They are wanting you to give them a speech."

I could barely hear Rasti's voice over the tumult.

"*Kabary!!*"

I could see Jack cringe, tugging at both ends of his mustache in despair. In fact, he almost yanked it off his face, probably wishing he had a lasso, or a rope—to hang me. He shook his head from side to side is if to say: *No! Don't do it!*

I'm not much of a public speaker to begin with, but seeing Jack writhe around, mortified like that... well, it kind of knocked the stuffing out of me. Sobered me up pretty fast. I looked for an escape route, but the dancers had closed ranks behind me, forming a solid hedgerow of orange and turquoise flowers.

Vamp, Eva. Vamp! Common sense told me that in a minute they'd change their minds, start dancing again and I'd be off the hook. I sashayed to the front of the tomb, concocting what I imagined would be a sweeping, grandiloquent, Shakespearean-yet-feminine *vazaha*-sort-of-a-rap.

It was an okay idea, but it lost something in translation for I tripped over a loose stone, lunged forward, and catapulted over the edge of the tomb, taking a header onto the mound of ancestral body-bags bundled below. I bounced across the slippery straw matting, skidding to a crash-landing in the dust at the feet of two hundred stunned Malagasy.

Some boogie. Some rap.

Jack hauled me up off the ground.

"Christ, Artema! You really blew it. What is it you want... a *riot?!*"

"No, I'm not hurt. And thank you for asking," I said.

I dusted myself off with considerable dignity, adjusted my jeans and tucked the crocodile tooth back into the neck of my blouse, anxiously fingering its sharp point.

The old *mpanandro* came to my rescue. He raised his staff overhead and magically the crowd fell silent.

"*Kabary!*" somebody suddenly shouted again, drunkenly. "*Kabary!!*"

All faces turned towards me, waiting expectantly for some *vazaha* pearls to drop in their laps. My mouth was dry and my ears rang with rum. What *do* you say at an exhumation?

I needn't have worried—Rangita knew.

At the outermost edge of the crowd, standing quietly apart from the milling throng, was a small, dark woman dressed entirely in white from head to toe. A *lamba* partially covered her head, but no matter, I'd have known her anywhere. Seated on her left shoulder like a tame cockateel, was a tiny figure clad in a white cape. Its face was hidden in the cloth, but a tell-tale radiance leaked out from between the folds.

The *kokolampo.*

No doubt about it.

18

I peered over the expectant Malagasy, fixing my eyes on Rangita's solitary, white-clothed figure. Unmoved and silent, she went unnoticed by the others who faced me. The *kokolampo's* cape floated out over her shoulders in the wind, casting off slender ribbons of light that, returning, encircled the two of them in a curious halo brighter than the sun.

Her lips didn't move, yet I heard her soft voice quite distinctly, saying: *Do not be afraid, my sister. There is a song, rising up inside you. Be still and trust. This is the truth you seek, speaking through you. Listen, and let it float through the lens of your mind's eye, permit it to seep into the valleys of your inmost ear, allow it to wash over you and fill your heart. Know and believe, Eva: your spirit has gone before you along all the by-ways that have led you to this place. It has levelled mountains, skimmed across burning wastes and skipped over the oceans like a pebble. Sing, sister. Sing!*

Sing? Me? Out of the question. Dancing I could handle. But, singing?" I prepared to bolt.

No! There was no mistaking her tone. It was regal, commanding.

I say "tone," yet no sounds were actually uttered. The communication between us was taking place on a mental or telepathic level by some kind of thought transference beamed into my unconscious mind and translated into words by my consciousness.

I tried to lift my arms—I could not! I tried to lift my feet, but they too were stuck, rooted in the dust. *My muscles had turned to stone.* I stood there, stupefied, like a toy doll stapled in a cardboard box.

Engage, brain cells! My face changed from pink to red as I struggled to commandeer my synapses.

Something was terribly wrong. Why in the hell wouldn't my frozen legs obey? March! One, two... Nikes, don't fail me now.

The song is in you, Eva. Rangita's low voice echoed in my head. *Ordinary speech will not suffice. You must open your mouth and sing.*

I zapped her with the blackest look I could manage. *Rangita, you and your illuminated elf are messing with the wrong vazaha.*

Tough words, but no action. No matter how I struggled, I couldn't break loose of her spell.

I squinted, trying to fire up some neurons.

Forget it. The hard disk had crashed. All terminals were down. Headquarters were in enemy hands. I remained stuck, a fly in amber. Rangita had nailed me with her mind.

I tried to focus my eyes. No dice. Even my pupils were being held hostage. The best I could conjure were blurred, pointillistic sensations of heat, light and color; splashes of red, umber, and deep ultramarine, daubed here and there on an uneven canvas of tan and white. The fuzzy colors reeked of rum, perspiration and sweet, rotting flesh. I would have toppled over, had I not felt an odd little *zetzz!*—an electric shock on the pinkie of my left hand. The moment I felt that touch, suddenly everything zoomed back into focus again.

I looked down. At my side, cuddled up to my kneecap, was a very small person, wrapped in ordinary white cotton. Flashing up at me from the depths of the cloth were two shimmering, perfectly round, silver eyes, brighter than daylight itself.

I shot a glance over at Rangita. Sure enough, she was alone now.

Okay, Queen R., I glowered at her, sending her a psychic telegram of my own. *You win...for now. But when this sideshow is over, you and I are going to sit down and have another kind of chat—a sisterly, little kabary. Just you and me. This is the last time you mess with my head.*

Hard talk. But it did a lot to boost my shattered ego. I straightened my blouse, smoothed back my hair, squeezed my croc tooth, took a deep breath and began to speak.

"Esteemed friends, mothers, fathers, sons and daughters of Madagascar," I nodded towards the wrapped bodies, "Honored Ancestors of Ambodivorondro..."

A communal sigh of anticipation rippled through my listeners. The *mpanandro* thumped his staff twice for silence, the dancing women placed their arms around each other's flowered waists and the coronet players tucked their horns into their waistbands.

"I beg your forgiveness, for I am but a poor and inexperienced stranger to your country, a visitor whose words and phrases are woefully inadequate to speak to your ancestors..." I paused and bowed low, palms pressed together on my chest, throwing in a mumbled *namaste* under my breath for good measure. "Thus may I humbly present myself. My name is Eva Victoria Artema, daughter of Lila and Carlo Artema, sister of Michael, Ernesto, Paul and James Artema, granddaughter of Carmine and Hermina Artema and Edwin and Muriel Anne Carlson."

Rasti translated my family tree carefully and solemnly, making appropriate, dramatic flourishes before introducing each new relative by name—after all, this was serious ancestor-talk.

"It is my deepest pleasure to have been invited to this joyous celebration..." I trailed off, recalling the chain of untoward events that had resulted in my "invitation."

I paused to regroup and saw Jack Mooresby lurking near the

mpanandro, legs firmly triangulated, his muscular arms crossed over his chest.

Jack's face was flushed from the sun. Wisps of black hair curled tightly on his temples and his hooked nose cast a curved shadow like an eagle's beak against his tanned cheek. His profile reminded me of an Assyrian warrior-king carved on a stone temple; severe, handsome, critical. I wanted not to care what he thought, but—I won't lie to you—I certainly did. I'd even go so far as to say that what I needed most right then, after being pulverized by Rangita's mental hammer-lock, was a good, strong dose of his arrogant, cowboy machismo. Vulnerability is a painful business. I've spent a lifetime avoiding it. A girl growing up with four brothers and no mother to protect her learns to hold her cards close to her chest. Very close. Maybe that was why I was so drawn to Jack. He was no sensitive New-Age guy. He wasn't afraid to be an old-fashioned, macho jerk.

I tugged down my shirt-tails and cleared my throat. Was it his toughness I wanted? Or, was it that I wanted *him* to be tough, so that I could be soft?

Back to center, Eva. You're drifting dangerously. James is your mission, your *raison d'être*. Not a surly pilot you've known less than a week.

Machisma, Eva! I resumed the *kabary* in a fierce, warrior tone of voice. "So it is that I join you and your Ancestors this morning, a stranger from a land far, far away, a land where the fog swirls, the sea lions bark, and the winds blow straight and cold from the shores of Asia. I have traveled halfway around the earth to honor your beloved grandmothers and grandfathers, the *razana*, the Ones who do not die. For them I have crossed three great oceans and two seas..."

"*Kai!*" The Malagasy were suitably impressed. It was an auspicious beginning.

I stopped to give Rasti a chance to catch up, then, "I have soared above canyons and mountains of ice riding in the belly of a giant steel bird..."

They shivered, tugging their *lambas* closer.

A poetical 747! Not bad...

"...flying high above deserts so spiny and brittle that a thousand zebus could not find their way among the dry, red stones."

They turned to one another, shaking their heads. "*Kai. Kai!*"

Dry red stones... I was warming up.

"I have survived eternal night in the Cave of the Blind White Worms..."

The floral ladies shuddered and clung to each other.

Blind, white worms... Oh, excellent!

"...I have ridden on the back of a crocodile queen."

At this, they gasped and clapped their hands over their mouths.

This *kabary* stuff was definitely okay.

There was no stopping me now. I don't know where they came from, but the words flowed into me, through me, and out of me, effortlessly and inexplicably, as if in a dream. They tumbled out, piling up in measured, poetic cadences, as artfully arranged as stacked fruit in the Zoma market. The strange thing was, I'd never thought much about poetry, although I do have a philosophical side. I think it came from Hermina, my grandmother, who used to tell me, "Life's like a blender. You've got all these speeds—mix, grind, chop blend and puree... they're like abilities. We never use half of them." Hermina was convinced I had abilities. All kinds. She encouraged them. "Remember, Eva, chop, mix and blend," she'd say, then wink, and slip me an extra brownie.

Grandmother Hermina, this song's for you. I lifted my eyes to the heavens above and sang.

> *Life is like the lightning between clouds*
> *a flash, then all is darkness.*
> *Only life in death endures.*

> *Life is like a dew drop on the bunch-grass*
> *shining, yet it dries by noon.*

Only life in death endures.

Life is like the moon's coin on the river
silver, yes, but spent before the dawn.
Only life in death endures.

Life is like the setting sun, strong and red
you turn and blink, and it is gone.
Only life in death endures.

Life is like a waterfall cascading, a big roar
once past the thunder, all is still.
Only life in death endures.

Life is like a beggar's bowl, full in the morning
by evening, just an empty cup.
Only life in death endures.

Life is like a lightning bug, blowing in the wind
Here! You can't catch it.
There! You can't catch it.
Only life in death endures.
Only life in death endures.

I chanted this song in a trance, singing the final chorus in a faint, small voice so weak and thready that the words shivered away, fading on the warm wind like so many ice cubes melting.

Only life in death endures... Did I really believe that?

No matter. What mattered was that my *kabary* was a smash hit with the rum-soaked groundlings. They burst into wild applause; clapped and stomped and cheered, enormously pleased with the entire performance.

Rasti surfaced at my elbow. "Bravo, mademoiselle. Bravo!" He took both my hands in his, smiling broadly. "You... *are* a magician."

I relaxed and basked in his praise.

The good-time feeling lasted for less than a second. Gazing past him into the near distance, I saw Jack's Land Rover begin slowly rolling down the hill, bouncing over potholes, picking up speed in an alarming fashion. Standing on the driver's seat, clutching the steering wheel, was a child wrapped in a white cloak, so tiny that it could hardly see over its rim.

My eyes bugged. I couldn't help it, I started to giggle.

"What's so funny?" asked Jack as he joined me.

I pointed past him at the careening vehicle.

"Hey, kid! *Arretez!* Stop! I say STOP!!" Jack's mustache quivered violently on his upper lip like a dark, angry butterfly. He sprinted after the truck, shouting over his shoulder at me, "Artema!! If anything happens, I'm holding you responsible. This is *all your fault!*"

He was right, of course. But it didn't keep me from laughing.

19

Mahery is Malagasy for chaos. That's what happened next. Sheer *mahery*.

Jack ran hollering down the slope toward the Land Rover with Rasti panting at his heels. They were followed closely by a posse of grave diggers who staggered drunkenly after them, checked *malabars* flapping in the breeze, lugging their freshly wrapped Ancestors on their shoulders like oversized sushi rolls. A couple of trumpeters took up the chase. Three maidens in red linked arms and raced after them, kicking away a pack of excited mutts who peeled off sideways, raising a balloon of red dust that completely obliterated the gang of caterwauling kids who were coming on strong, two steps behind.

Taking advantage of this diversion, Rangita broke loose, heading in the opposite direction of the crowd. Without hesitating I ran after her, determined to capture her and put my foot on her astral neck until she gave me some straight answers.

She moved swiftly along a narrow trail up a sharp slope,

angling towards a ridge. I followed quickly, losing sight of her as she crossed over the top, tracking her again when she doubled back over a rock bridge that led into a stand of eucalyptus trees growing in a steep draw. Her white garments flashed as she shunted here and there among the bare tree trunks.

I ran faster, hell-bent on catching up with her, following her darting shape down into the shadowy grove, my eyes glued to the flitting white form dashing through the forest. The lower I went, the thicker the brush became. It was now higher than the top of my head—so high, in fact, that it formed a green, leafy maze blocked on either side by prickly, impregnable walls. I could no longer see Rangita, but I kept on running, zig-zagging through the dense underbrush until the trail opened up at last at the edge of a round meadow full of tumbled stones and enclosed by a circle of tall eucalyptus. At the center of the meadow, like an elephant dozing in the noonday sun, was an imposing slab of upright granite about fifteen feet tall, pock-marked here and there with black smudges.

I stopped to catch my breath and get my bearings before continuing. From this red dirt hub many identical paths branched off, radiating outward in wildly different directions.

Which was the right one?

I knelt down and scanned the soft earth for Rangita's footprints. The ground before me was smooth and except for the faint rice-pattern of dried rain drops, completely unmarked. Not a hoof, paw, toe or claw dented the pristine, red clay.

It didn't track. There was no other path, I was certain of it. She must have passed by here.

I looked behind at the trail I had left in the dirt. The imprint of my tennis shoes had made a definite design of diamonds and circles that led up to the spot where I now stood.

Where were Rangita's footprints?

I back-tracked a short distance in the direction I'd just come, studying the ground carefully. Apart from my shoes, there were no footprints of any kind, anywhere. Nothing had recently passed this way. What then had I been following through the trees? A chimera?

Chasing chimeras again, Evie dear? Grandfather Edwin used to say that whenever he'd catch me daydreaming. He'd peer over the top of the Cleveland Plain Dealer, then snap the newspaper shut and launch into a lecture on Niobe, Inanna, or the cult of Cybele. Most of the time, I didn't have the foggiest idea what Grandfather Edwin was talking about. I remember looking chimera up in the dictionary to discover that it meant an illusion, a trick of the mind; something to do with mysterious methane flames that have been burning since time immemorial, leaking out of cracks on an obscure mountainside in Asia Minor. The ancient Greeks, according to Grandfather Edwin, had a myth about these fires, a tale of thwarted love and a fire-breathing monster with the head of a lion, the body of a goat and the tail of a snake. Odysseus used the flames as a beacon to guide him safely home from Troy. As a child, I had tried hard to imagine the chimera, conjuring up those eerie, sacred fires—flickering, malevolent, orange cat's eyes gleaming out of the dusky hills above Grandfather Edwin's Homeric sea.

I sat back on my heels and wiped my face with my bandanna when a notion struck me. Was not the *kokolampo* also a kind of beacon? A Malagasy beacon? As if recalling a dream, I saw once again that strange ball of light, carried so gently in the Old Queen's mouth, nestled between her jagged fangs, casting its comforting glow on the rock walls of the underground caves as we slid past. That beacon had been responsible for guiding us out into the drizzling rain, into the rice paddies where hidden frogs croaked their clammy hearts out. That same light had mysteriously transformed itself into the *kokolampo* who returned to me the *ody* I'd thrown into the roiling river.

I buried my face in my hands.

What was I doing crouched on this God-forsaken patch of red dirt, chasing after Malagasy ghosts, fabricating myths when I should have been on the road to Mananjary? Michel Rakotomana could not have stated it more clearly. *Kokolampo* are myths, legendary creatures, just like Vazimba queens and sacred crocodiles. Flaring quarks of racial memory illuminating the starry cosmos of the Malagasy unconscious. Pinpricks of unfathomable dreams that a *vazaha* will never begin to understand, let alone share.

Then why was I being plagued with these imaginary beings, whose disruptive presence demanded that I accept their reality, even though every fiber of my rational being rebelled?

I gazed up at the tremendous stone plinth looming above me, feeling abject and overwhelmed, like a supplicant at Stonehenge. The feathery tassels of the surrounding eucalyptus shuddered in a passing breeze, suffusing the air with their sharp, resiny scent. Drifting over the hills from far away, from another lifetime, came the faint, lonesome sound of dogs, barking, and a car horn, honking.

Jack...

The ribbon of sound carried on it the arrogant curve of his nose, the smooth bulk of his muscular, brown arms, his teasing, gold-flecked eyes, and the memory of his faded 501's that I'd mentally unzipped a few hours ago.

Damn!

I'd failed dismally at everything I'd undertaken since my arrival. I hadn't even been able to orchestrate a simple, Sunday picnic without rudely crashing an ancestral celebration and incurring the wrath of the only person in Madagascar I had met who actually had the means to help me find James. In one fell swoop I'd blown off a car, a helicopter and—this really hurt—a man who understood the erotic potential of ears.

Shit.

I rammed my hands into into my pockets. Way down at the bottom, among some gum wrappers I felt a familiar shape.

Okay, little pal, I thought. Here goes nothing.

I clenched the little bundle of sticks, beans and bristles in my fist, and shook it aloft three times, calling out the only incantation I knew, "Ro, sham, po. Ro, sham, po. Rock, scissors, paper. Which way to go?" I closed my eyes and squeezed the amulet again, grabbing the crocodile tooth with my other hand. "RO! SHAM! PO!" I shouted. "Yo, Vazimba! HO!!"

No sooner than the magic words were out than there was an incredible FLASH! like eight billion flashbulbs going off all at once. When I opened my eyes, I found myself ringed by dozens of balls of brilliant light, ping-ponging back and forth off the ground like grasshoppers on speed, shooting off showers of sparks every which way. "Hey!" I yelled, dodging the balls and shaking the *ody*, "*Bastante*. I got the message. Enough!"

The balls whirled around in a frenzy before coalescing into one, bright mass about the size of a grapefruit. It quivered, waist-high in the air in front of me. I reached for it, and it responded by zooming away, just beyond my grasp.

I knew the drill. It meant: follow me.

The sparkling grapefruit led the way. I hurried after it across the center of the meadow towards the upraised megalith, avoiding the rocks strewn about. At first I thought they were natural formations, but then realized that they had been arranged in a crude pattern. I stepped over a low, tumble-down wall and directly ahead I saw a tremendous, flat stone lying on its side, covered in fresh blood. The black granite glistened scarlet in the sun, like a slaughtered ox.

Mary, Mother of Jesus! Without thinking, I crossed myself, a superstitious habit I'd abandoned years ago. I turned around, sniffing the air, scanning the woods in every direction very slowly and very carefully, wary as a grizzly. High above, puffy clouds stretched out across the blue sky, thin and taut as a winding sheet. In the grove, eucalyptus leaves chittered like gossiping Ancestors.

I took one, cautious step forward.

The stone was an altar.

It was frosted with feathers. On a corner lay a pair of recently severed zebu horns and two hairy, roundish objects that could only have been testicles. Scattered across the pooling red were handfuls of blackened, silver coins. Encircling the altar on the ground below were small bowls filled with fresh rice, milk and honey.

I had interrupted someone at prayer.

I stared at the black granite slab buzzing with flies, feeling sick, puny and at sea, stranded in a Malagasy meadow under a towering stone phallus, barricaded on all sides by trees that whispered: *death, death…*

The altar shook me deeply. It was shocking, archaic, and strangely sexual. From somewhere in the depths of my childhood thundered the terrible sentences: *And Isaac said, "Look, the fire and the wood, but where is the lamb for a burnt offering?" And Abraham built an altar there and placed the wood in order; and he bound Isaac his son and laid him on the altar, upon the wood. And Abraham stretched out his hand and took the knife to slay his son…*

My chest tightened. No wonder there were no other footprints here. This disorderly tumult of stones must be a Vazimba tomb. I was trespassing on ancient, hallowed land—forbidden ground.

The pointed zebu horns stabbed defiantly at the sky. Bees grazed the lips of the honey bowls. A white feather twisted in the sticky blood. Abraham had been prepared to sacrifice his only son. But what about Isaac? There was no mention of what *he* thought about God's plan. And me? What about me, Eva Artema? Was I to be the Vazimba's sacrificial lamb?

Hell no!!

I turned tail and fled; ran scrambling over the wall, hop-scotching over fallen rocks and dodging around hummocks of brambles in my haste to leave that accursed place. When I reached the point where the meadow joined the path, I paused to catch my breath, taking one last look back at the grisly altar.

It was a dreadful error, for instantly something white landed on my left shoulder. It dug into my collar bones, dusting a smudge of sparkles across the sleeve of my denim jacket. The cotton cape disguised the tiny, fin-like appendages, but I felt them through the cloth, pinching onto my shoulder with a possessive, cartilaginous grip. At the same moment, I became acutely aware of Rangita's presence behind me. Her unseen body was palpable, and very close. There was a distinct odor of vanilla and cloves overlaid by an acrid, female musk. I could feel her breath too, warm and soft as cinnamon butter, stirring the tendrils of hair on the back of my neck.

My voice trembled in a rush of powerless rage and desperation. "Rangita, I know you're here. Isn't it time we stopped playing this tiresome game of hide-and-seek?"

She laughed softly. "Not yet, my sister. But, take heart. Life is a landscape with many paths. You have chosen an unmarked path, surrounded by invisible forces you do not comprehend. To catch hold of the invisible, you must first penetrate as deeply as possible into the visible. In order to succeed, you must give in to the greatest terror of all—terror of not knowing."

I began to turn my head, but she stopped me. "Do not turn around, Eva. Just listen. To walk upon this path, to move among *Les Invisibles*, requires above all faith and courage. I can help you, but in order to do so you must surrender and trust in me—completely."

Faith and courage.

I was no stranger to those two. Hadn't I clung to the Old Queen's back without flinching as she dove into the grim depths of the underground river. But, trust in a chimera?

"Surrender to *you*? Someone I can't even see, who reads my mind, freezes my muscles, and puts words in my mouth?"

I whirled around, addressing empty air behind me.

"First you're visible, then you're invisible! Here, there. Up, down. On, off." I exploded in righteous fury. "Trust? How can you expect me to trust someone who commands her caped crusader to play tricks on me, taunting me with balls of fire and flashing lights? Who hijacks cars and preys on people..." I twisted sideways, clawing at the thing perched on my shoulder, "...like some kind of... vulture?"

I tore at the white cape, trying to grab hold of the cloth, but the more I struggled, the harder the *kokolampo* held on, scrambling around onto my back out of arms' reach. The horrid little flippers, or whatever they were, dug into my flesh like a pair of steel fire tongs.

"Cut it out!" I writhed around in a wild St. Vitus dance, trying to dislodge the coin-eyed sprite. "You're supposed to be a beacon. A saviour. A goddamn *friend!*" I staggered across the empty clearing, flailing away, moving towards the altar with its dismembered zebu horns, flattened testicles and offerings of honey swarming with flies and bees.

Suddenly, I had an idea. Pretending to stumble, I fell to the ground, surreptitiously picking up a sharp, pointed stone from the ones scattered about. I wheeled towards the altar. Closer, closer... now!! With a mighty effort I turned and wrenched the *kokolampo* loose, throwing it down onto the bloody surface of the stone, flinging my full body weight on top of it.

"Aieeee..." The tiny creature squirmed furiously underneath me like a trapped sting-ray, uttering a horrible, high-pitched keening that pierced my heart.

I raised the pointed rock murderously over my head and thundered, "Rangita, you Vazimba coward! *Show yourself!!*"

I felt a strong hand close around my wrist like a manacle and squeeze, forcing me to release the stone. But I wasn't about to give up my hard-won bargaining chip so easily. Nauseated by the stench of blood and the whirring of flying insects beating around my face, nonetheless I held fast, flung full-length on top of the *kokolampo*, holding it hostage.

Rangita circled the perimeter of the stone until at last she faced me directly. With a haughty, royal gesture, she threw back the white *lamba* shrouding her face.

I was stunned.

She was magnificent. Her glossy black hair, always hidden from view under the blonde wig, was piled high in a virtual castle of intricately dressed braids. These were bent into astonishing, flying buttresses of plaited hair, affixed into glistening, blue-black bridges that twisted and dove under and into each other, reappearing again in complex crenellations ending in tassels of bright, shining silver beads that danced on her shoulders. The effect was spectacular, undisputably as elegant as any of Watteau's periwigged French ladies swinging in an old-fashioned garden.

Although Rangita was small and compact, now she exuded a powerful aura that made her seem much larger and far more imposing than I remembered. Her dark face radiated confidence. Around the edges of her brown irises glowed a curious blue light that seemed to emanate from somewhere deep inside her skull. Her mouth was dainty, yet full; the upper lip formed into two soft points just under small, well-shaped nostrils. Her cheekbones were high and slanted; her neck was surprisingly strong and muscular, a deep brown column rising out of the folds of her white, toga-like *lambas*. Around it she had fastened a necklace of silver coins and crocodile teeth set in silver filagree exactly like the one I now wore.

She frowned, looked deeply and gravely into my eyes, and leaned across the altar, pressing her palms on the black granite surface for emphasis.

"*Tiens*, Eva. *Moramora*. Calm down. Be still. Listen to me carefully." She spoke very slowly and deliberately. "Finding your brother James will be dangerous work..."

My heart stopped. My God. James! What if she knew how to find him!

"I cannot guarantee your safety if you undertake this journey. The *vazaha* oil men are powerful, but in the end my own people may prove the most dangerous adversaries of all. There are those among us who would prefer to see the entire island of Madagascar go up in flames rather than allow strangers to penetrate the Blue Rainforest. *Vraiment*, many *vazaha* have died or gone mad trying to do so." She sighed again and shook her head before continuing in a low voice. "And there is a good chance that your brother, James, may be one of them."

Rangita's chilling warning sailed right over my head. As soon as she uttered that one, magic word—James—my mind had begun to whirl ecstatically and I ceased to hear anything more.

Very big mistake.

Had I paid attention, I might had the presence of mind to ask her a couple of blunt, Yankee questions, such as: *Why are you helping me?* and *What do you want from me in return?* It would have saved me a lot of grief. Instead I blurted out, "All right. I surrender. Where do I—we—go from here?"

"To Mananjary," she said, and smiled for the first time. "But first, you will need to release Noro."

Noro! The wretched little demon had a name!

I stood up and immediately the *kokolampo* wriggled out from under me. Pushing off from the edge of the altar as lightly as a gull hops off a sea cliff, it spread its snowy cape and headed upwind directly into the eye of the sun, until—*plinkk!* like a bursting soap bubble—Noro blew apart into radiant shards of light.

I turned turned back towards Rangita, only to discover that she, too, was gone... vanished into thin air.

I stared down at myself. My jacket and jeans were soaked with sacrificial blood, my arms were festooned with chicken feathers, my shoes mired in honey and festered with bees.

"Are you listening, Jack?" I threw up my arms at the empty hills. "Hey! I'm confessing to you, Mooresby! D'you hear? You win. Call in the exorcist! Bring on the white coats! Eva Victoria Artema is certifiably... nuts!"

There are only two ways to live your life. One is as though nothing is a miracle. The other is as though everything is a miracle.

Einstein said that. He was a full-blown, raving mystic. The light bulb lit up for him one day as he stepped down off the bus. *Blam!* There it was, the Theory of Relativity, laid out in front of him on the cracked pavement, perfect and whole, fresh and pink as a squealing newborn. A miracle.

I slogged up the steep slope. At the rate I was going, I was going to need more than one miracle to get to Mananjary. In fact, just getting back to Tananarive without a car would probably require a crash Course in Miracles. I envisioned Jack Mooresby, kneeling somewhere in the dust beside his wrecked Land Rover overturned like a beetle in a ditch, its radiator rammed into a pile of sandstone boulders. My last glimpse of the truck, with puny, irascible Noro at the wheel, had doom written all over it. I hauled myself up the rocky slope trying to fantasize alternative modes of transport. The only image that came to mind was a rumbling, wooden-wheeled *charrette*, piloted by Mad Jack, whip in hand. It was not a satisfactory fantasy.

"Ar... te... maaa..."

He stood silhouetted on the brow of the hill, waving his arms, doing a crummy Sound-of-Music imitation. He still wore the pirate's rag wrapped around his head.

"Moores... beee..." I yodelled back and waved, breaking into a run.

It's funny. Sex is like air. You don't miss it until you don't have it. Then you realize you can't live without it. Everything else falls by the wayside. Seeing Jack on the top of the mountain, hearing him calling to me like that, fired up a lot of sleeping synapses in my medulla—not to mention my yoni. I must have made a pretty piratical vision myself, storming the summit, for when I hove into view, sweating and panting, my legs shaking from the exertion, Jack grabbed me first, then thrust me away, holding me stiffly at arm's length, caught between concern and revulsion.

"What in hell's happened to you *now*?!!"

"I'm okay. Really. This... I mean, it's just... animal blood. Chicken. Or zebu."

"Chicken or zebu!" He shook me like a bad, wet puppy, flaring his arrogant, Assyrian nostrils. "Holy shit, Artema. Next you'll be telling me you were down there in the bushes lighting fires and sacrificing wild pigs to Odin."

Close, but no cigar.

I opened my mouth to deliver a blazing retort, but he cut me off at the pass.

"Shut up and get in the goddamn car," he said gruffly. Then he pulled me against him, cupping my chin with both hands, and kissed me—hard. Teeth, tongue... the works. Whereupon I fainted. Dead away.

I know what you're thinking. She *swooned?* Omigod. How Jane Austen. But, don't sell me short. Consider those four years I lived alone after Raul walked. Was there ever a man when I needed him? Like... on Saturday night?

No.

So comes this bush pilot dressed like Captain Kidd—a guy who's *living* a Code Blue existence for crying out loud, on a forgotten island at the end of the Indian Ocean—and this guy wants to kiss *me*? For that kind of miracle, I can bend the rules and take a few orders.

I didn't have to. When I came to, Jack was lifting me into the back seat of the Land Rover and Rasti was solicitously rolling up his lab coat into a pillow, arranging it under my neck. The car motor was running. From what I could make out, miraculously there were no dents, no flat tires or broken windows.

Jack threw it into first gear and we were off. A crowd of urchins ran after us calling, "*Au revoir, mam'selle mpi kabary! Au revoir!*"

I closed my eyes.

Move over, Einstein.

I guess I needed to sleep, because that's what I did most of the way back to the capital. Slept and dreamed twisted sagas of drunken crocodiles and armies of caped *kokolampos*. I drifted in and out of slumber. When I finally awoke, I lay quietly, listening to Jack and Rasti, playing possum and keeping my eyes shut.

"*Fasambazimba* you say?"

"Sacred sites you are calling them. They are cemeteries. Tombs of the vanished Vazimba."

"So you think it's possible she stumbled onto one down in that canyon?"

"In Madagascar, anything is possible."

Rasti's voice dropped lower and I strained to listen.

"*Fasambazimba* are dangerous places, filled with evil spirits waiting to bring vengeance on the living. I did not have the heart to tell her that, when she insisted we visit one." *A Malagasy will do anything to avoid saying No...* "I am sure of one thing, however.

Mademoiselle Eva is very lucky to be alive."

Jack whistled, "There you go again, Rasti. Me, I just don't buy it. All this woo-woo stuff."

"Perhaps when you have lived here a few lifetimes, you will understand."

"One man, one lifetime. That's how I see it. You give it a whirl. Lift a few skirts. Hoist a few *Trois Cheveaux*. Then, *phfttt*, roll over Beethoven and it's lights out."

I didn't have to open my eyes. I heard Rasti's pen click and knew he was scribbling down Jack's latest batch of macho crudities.

"What d'you think about her brother, James? From what you've told me about Rakotomana, I'm betting there isn't a snowball's chance in hell he's still alive."

James! Rakotomana! My antennae shot up. It was all I could do to keep my eyes closed and control my breathing.

"Rumors, my friend. Rumors. Like malaria, they are a tropical affliction. Born of boredom and fueled by equal parts envy and greed. Even the *razana* are known to spread rumors."

"Nevertheless, if Rakotomana *is* trafficking in endangered species as you say, why doesn't someone blow the whistle on him?"

"*A hand filled with gold knows how to keep silent.*"

Gold. Silence. Trafficking in endangered species... I held my breath, trying to stay calm.

"I can't believe a few lemurs could bring all that much on the black market."

"Forgive me, my friend, but you are very much mistaken. For an *aye-aye*, it was rumored a German collector offered 125,000 American dollars last year. There were no takers." Rasti laughed sadly. "But then, perhaps nobody could find one. It is rumored there are only nine left in the world."

"There aren't any *aye-ayes* in the Blue Rainforest. My understanding's that they're only found on the island of Nosy Mangabe."

"Perhaps yes, perhaps no. Like so much else about the *aye-aye* and the Blue Rainforest, no one knows for sure. Myself, I cannot say. *Mais c'est le bruit court que...*"

"Spare me, Rasti. No more of your rumors."

"*Ecoutez*, Jack. One more. It is *très fantastique*. They say that somewhere in the Blue Rainforest, *Paleopropithecus* still walks!"

It was Jack's turn to laugh. "You don't say. Not ol' *Paleopropithecus*." He added sarcastically, "I thought he'd died and gone to heaven sometime B.C..."

Unperturbed, Rasti pressed on. "*Exactement*. That's what everybody else thought. Until last fall he was considered extinct. Dead as a dodo bird. Then started the rumors about a very dark, man-sized lemur with a rounded head and a man's face, with frizzy fur at the top, like hair. In Malagasy we are calling him *Tratratratra*."

"Come off it, Rasti. *Tratra* belongs in a glass case in Tzimbazaza Museum, along with the pygmy hippos and the aepyornis."

"Perhaps it is not *Tratra* we are talking about after all. Perhaps we are talking about a wholly different species. Something new. Something as yet... undiscovered."

"Who's starting these rumors anyhow?"

"Who knows?" Rasti sighed. "However I have heard Michel Rakotomana's name mentioned in connection..."

Rumors! I wanted to scream at him. Michel Rakotomana has never been *near* the Blue Rainforest.

"...and that of Ambassador Theron."

That bloated old smoothie?

"And," Rasti added slowly, "a certain Dr. James Artema."

Jack whistled in disbelief.

I almost levitated off the seat. My brother? A smuggler of extinct animals?

"Wherever one finds an empty green spot on a map that reads 'Unexplored'... there, you are finding trouble," Rasti said.

"Unexplored... Not for long. Jerome, you're my best friend and I trust you. CANTEX has secretly been given permission to begin exploratory drilling in the Blue Rainforest."

"In Zaohitra Reserve? *Mon Dieu! C'est impossible!* The nature

Reserves are strictly off-limits. It is Malagasy national policy."

"I'm telling you straight, Jerome. I haven't been down there yet, but I hear they've been airlifting equipment into the jungle for over a month."

A fatalistic resignation clouded Rasti's cheery countenance. "We have an old saying: *The impossible cannot be bought.* Clearly this is no longer the case." Rasti continued slowly, seriously, "Jack, if what you say is true, then the situation is far more tragic than you can imagine."

"C'mon, this isn't the first time someone's bent the law to fit his agenda. You said it yourself, wherever there's a green spot, there's trouble. Besides, don't worry about *Paleopropithecus.* He's a rumor, not a reality."

"It is not *Tratratratra* that is the problem," said Rasti. "It is Andrebabe, the invisible village."

Andrebabe!? So Rasti knew about Rangita's village, too!

"I fear we shall lose it, forever."

"There you go again. How can you lose something that doesn't exist? Who lives there anyhow? Ghosts!"

"Perhaps, and perhaps not. They say..."

"Spooks!" Jack interrupted in exasperation. "Nothing but spooks and rumors of spooks." He down-shifted and the Rover shook like a beggar's tin can as we lurched over a pothole. Through the slits of my closed eyelids, I saw Jack turn and look at me.

"She's so beautiful, isn't she? Those cheekbones. Those lips. That hair. Damn," he blew out a deep, frustrated breath. "I wish I'd never met her. The last thing I need in my life right now is another crazy, beautiful, green spot."

"But, my friend," Rasti made an effort to brighten up, "she can sing and she can dance."

"*Disco!*" Jack snorted. "I'd rather eat barbed wire than disco."

I knew right then I had a ways to go before I saddled up with this cowboy.

21

Two letters were waiting for me at Le Terrace. An oversized, ecru envelope and a thin yellow telegram stood stiffly side by side in slot Number 27 like blind dates at a formal dance.

"*La poste*," growled Madame Moreau. Her carefully penciled brows, obscured by a hanging miasma of cigarette smoke, teemed with questions.

I didn't bite. "*Merci*," I said without elaboration, and took the letters over to the window-seat near the bar. I turned over the larger one. The blue sealing wax stamped with the ornate letter "R" was still intact. I tore open the telegram first.

"EVITA STOP PAPA HEART ATTACK MAY 18 STOP NOT OUT OF WOODS YET STOP OUR LADY MERCY HOSPITAL STOP PAPA ASKING WHEN YOU JAMES COME HOME STOP MIKE ERNIE PAUL STOP"

When you James come home? Tears burned on my cheeks. My

father was dying. The father who had farmed me out and all but forgotten me was calling out for me at last. Why hadn't he said that years ago, when I needed him?

I leaned my wet cheek against the glass. Long rays of sunlight stroked Madame Moreau's cat, sleeping in a square of sun on the black and white parquet tiles near my feet. An old railroad clock ticked loudly over the door into the empty bar. It was Sunday afternoon. God's time. The time of *famiglia*. Through the window I could see Malagasy mothers, fathers, aunts uncles babies, strolling through the deserted Zoma market, starched and pressed for church, talking and laughing, sharing jokes and family stories. Even the beggars seemed happy for once, and the families dropped coins into their hands without being asked.

I folded the yellow paper and stared through the streaked glass. Somewhere in Cleveland, Carlo Giovanni Artema lay dying, listening to the squeak of nurses' shoes and the metallic clink of curtain rings as interns stopped by, flipped the chart, disappeared without speaking. Somewhere my father lay, listening, listening for the sound of his lost children, praying as each set of footsteps approaches that it will be us, his beloved *bambini*.

I stuffed the unopened envelope into my knapsack, wiped my face with the back of my hand, and returned to the front desk clutching the telegram.

"Madame, I must use the telephone immediately, to call America."

She shrugged and removed her cigarette, carefully pinching a bit of white paper off her lower lip between her thumb and forefinger. "I regret the phone lines are down. That is how it is all over Madagascar today. Often on Sunday this occurs." She exhaled a spume of pungent smoke, "We are quite used to it..." Bending down, she reached under the desk and held out a pink towel and a large bar of home-made brown soap. "Please, Mademoiselle Artema, in my private apartments I have a bath tub. Because it is Sunday, *le Volcano* is hot. There will be plenty of water for you." She thrust the soap and towel at me. "A gift, *pour le telephone*."

"Thank you," I mumbled. "Thank you very much," not even trying to hide my tears. It was Sunday in Madagascar, and Madame was the closest thing to family I had.

I floated around in the hot bath until my skin puckered and shriveled before opening Rangita's letter. I had propped the envelope up on the soapdish and watched it through wavering floods of salty tears.

I've never gotten used to crying alone, especially after Mama died. If there's someone sitting beside me, something happens— call it hope, if you will—but it makes it easier to let the tears flow. Rangita's letter, leaning against the cracked porcelain of Madame Moreau's soapdish, had the same effect on me, of a sister, or a mother, sitting quietly and patiently, listening to me weep.

When there were no more tears left to shed, I blew my nose and swung my legs over the side of the old tub, letting the hot water drip on Madame's polished floor, and cracked open the sealing wax.

"*Ma chere Eva Victoria,*" began the familiar blue handwriting:

> *Thinking of your father,*
> > *you cannot stop weeping.*
> *Trembling for your brother,*
> > *you are drowning in tears.*
> *Fearing the hand of Death,*
> > *you are making a big river.*
> *Do not fear the river.*
> > *Jump in and swim across.*
>
> *Even if you talk to it sweetly,*
> > *you cannot walk on this water.*
> *Even if you build a high wall,*
> > *you cannot staunch its flow.*
> *The river is mahery, with a will of its own.*

You cannot tame it.
Do not fear the river.
Jump in and swim across.

If you have magic powers, why not make a bridge?
If you have magic powers, why not build a pirogue?
If you have magic powers, why not fly?

When a woman wants to shoot an arrow,
she makes a bow.
When a woman wants the people in the
marketplace to look at her, she braids her hair
and wears ornaments.
When a woman wants a man, she must learn
how to say Yes.
Do not fear the river.
Jump in and swim across.

Rangita, Reine de Vazimba

At the bottom she had penned: *Beware the ferryman at the river's edge. He is not what he seems. R.* And in even smaller script, she had added in the margin: *Forgive Noro. She is willful, but useful.*

I swirled around in the soapy water. Noro wasn't the only one who deserved some forgiveness. I could think of a long list of candidates, beginning with Papa, Raul and Jack, including Rangita herself. I still held it against her for turning me into stone at the *famadihana*. Contemplating forgiveness, stretching my arms to the ceiling, I observed how quickly the abrasions on my left shoulder were healing. M. Ratelifera's herbs had actually worked. Sinking lower into the water, I eyed the pull chain on Madame Moreau's water closet, nervously wondering if she had her own resident roach hiding out behind the tank, ready to spring into action.

Steam clouded the small, barred window high on the wall. Over the top of my kneecaps I could see the heap of blood-soaked khaki I used to call clothes. I'd bought those pants and jacket at Banana Republic; fashionable threads to conquer the Developing World. Reaching over the tub's edge, I rolled them up in a ball and lobbed them into the trash basket under the sink.

Farewell, banana couture.

Hauling myself out of the water, I padded over to the wash basin and wiped off the damp mirror, peering at myself through the fog.

Who *was* that woman there, on the other side of the glass, her blonde hair sleeked back severely, her face stripped of makeup, of color, of artifice, her eyes dilated—two black holes squeezing the blue irises into thin, concentric rings of pale light? As I stared into those sad, confused, exhausted rabbit holes, I saw in them exactly what Rangita had tried to warn me about: the terror of not knowing. What I definitely did *not* see was trust in the river of life.

Love the river, stay by it, learn from it...

I'd first read those words in a hostel in Nepal, in a battered copy of Siddhartha abandoned by a hippie searching for nirvana in the Hindu Kush. Siddhartha believed he could understand himself by learning about the river; that if he understood the river and its secrets he would then understand all the secrets of life. *You cannot step twice in the same river, for new water is always flowing in.* He saw that the water continually flowed and flowed and yet the river was always there; it was always the same, and yet every moment it was new. If this was true, he asked, what then is this thing we call river, that it can forever be new and forever the same? Wherein lies its riverness?

By now I'd completely lost sight of myself in the steamy mirror. Our bodies are like the river, I thought. Cells reproducing, processing, dying constantly even as we live. "Who are you?" the caterpillar asked Alice in Wonderland. "I... I hardly know, Sir, just at present—at least I know who I was when I got up this morning, but I think I may have changed several times since then."

Memories of the caves, the *kabary*, the altar and Noro washed over me. I looked down at my damp, pink Eva-ness. I was Siddhartha's river, was I not? In the wake of time's passage—a year, a month, the week since arriving in Madagascar, in just the few hours since leaving the *famadihana*—thousands of cells that were me—my very own Eva-cells—had ceased to exist. I was not the same person that I was before, not even five miniscule minutes ago. New cellular life—new water, new salt, new minerals—were now flowing through me, in me, as me, forming and re-forming—transforming. Yet somehow I remained intact. I was changed, and at the same time changeless, the invisible made visible, and then dissolving again into nothing. Yet... through it all, I was me.

I wiped off the mirror with a corner of the towel, feeling like a dog going around and around in circles, trying to catch its own tail, when it struck me... *Only life in death endures...* The river! I'd been singing a song of the river this afternoon on top of a windswept mountain. Singing about how, if life and death are interchangeable and eternal, then they are both river, the river of life is One, and the world has no beginning and no end, amen and *moramora*. Einstein was right, time and the physical body are not only elastic, they don't even exist, except as a construct of our limited, finite minds, nothing more than mental devices to measure experience and the relative positions of perceived objects. Reality exists elsewhere, at another, spiritual—call it astral—level. And yes, by this reckoning, Queen Rangita and Uncle Rasolo do indeed live. Everywhere we turn we are always entertaining angels unaware. Dead uncles, Vazimba queens and bad-tempered, bug-eyed water sprites. Rasolo and the Ancestors... they *all* live.

Ho. Time out. What Rangita had suggested in her letter was something practical, not philosophical. Namely: *to jump in the river of life and swim across.*

I leaned forward, peering into the mirror through the damp steam.

What's holding you back, babe? a cowboy said. *No guts?*

Guts? I sucked in my cheeks and turned sideways in the mirror.

Eva Artema? No guts? I began twisting my hair into a tight, French braid.

So the river is *mahery*, is it? Has a will of its own? Well, so did I!

My fingers flew through my hair, pulling it so tight over my temples that my eyes folded into Asian slits.

I'm no wimp! Ain't no river deep enough for this disco queen. I pulled the plug on the tub, kicked the wastebasket once, and headed to my room.

Mahery, here I come!

At the end of the corridor, taped to the door of Number 27, I found the third communique of the day. It wasn't a telegram, but it might as well have been. Printed in bold, black pencil on a piece of scrap paper, it said:

FLYING CANTEX GEOLOGISTS TO RANOMAFANA TOMORROW 5:00 A.M. SHARP. ONE SEAT LEFT. YOURS? JACK.

As usual, he didn't mince words.

I hurried inside and got out my topo map. Ranomafana was a pinpoint in the mountainous southeast, three-quarters of the way to Mananjary. It was a green spot, all right. Very green. Indisputably jungle. Not the Blue Rainforest, but close.

I let the towel drop to the floor and began throwing things into the duffel. It had been a hell of a Sunday. As I packed, I had a field day forgiving everyone who had ever crossed me—even foul-tempered Noro—happily humming a little work song to myself. *If you have magic powers... why not fly, fly, fly? Uh huh, uh huh huh...*

Suddenly I was jolted by an awful realization. The magic *ody*! It was in the pocket of my jacket!

I whipped the towel around me, dashed back down the hall to Madame's apartment and flung open the door to the bathroom.

The trash basket was empty.

I rushed over and pulled it out from the shadows under the sink, hoping against hope...

Yes! There *was* something down there! Something brown and untidy, with twigs sticking out the sides.

I reached in and grabbed it.

Hiissssssssst!!! The *"ody"* spit out a loud, angry warning and flew directly at my face, hitting my Third Eye with kamikaze accuracy, all six legs and reticulated antennae of the monster cockroach pinwheeling around to beat the band.

I almost fainted, but two times in one afternoon was not only ridiculous; it was pathetic. Instead, I bolted out the door, slamming it safely behind me just in time to see Noro sliding down the wide walnut banister, legs akimbo, sporting a turban of blood-stained khaki.

Useful? This *kokolampo* was diabolical. She'd stolen my *ody*! And to think I'd just forgiven her!!

I sprinted down the corridor, taking the stairs two at a time, hanging onto the scrap of pink terry cloth with one hand and clutching the railing with the other. I hit the mezzanine landing at the same time Noro hit the first floor. She shot off the end of the polished banister like a ski-jumper, was airborne for about ten seconds, and landed *ploomph!* in a large, raffia laundry basket full of rumpled bed linen that was standing open at the foot of the stairs. As if on cue, Maurice, who had been standing guard below, dumped the lid on the hamper and began dragging it towards the kitchen.

"No! Wait, Maurice..."

I descended three steps, then halted. In the foyer at the bottom of the stairs stood three men with their backs to me. At the sound of my voice, Paul Cummins, Eli Mazan and Jack Mooresby turned around.

"Well, well, if it ain't little Miss Eva, come in out of the rain," leered Paul, tipping his Stetson in the direction of my naked thighs.

"Howdy, ma'am." Eli gulped, going red.

Jack said nothing. He just slid those mirrored glasses off, real slow. "Five o'clock sharp," he finally said. "Dress warm, Artema. It can get cold in a bird at a thousand feet."

"Roger," I said. "Ten-four. Over and out."

I had to hand it to him. The guy didn't flinch. And he didn't put his glasses back on, either. Making me think that there was an outside chance that someday we might ride the old hoot-owl trail together after all.

22

I was waiting in the lobby at 5:00 a.m. with my gear packed when Jack knocked on the glass doors. A sleepy Maurice put his *panga* aside in order to let him in.

"Good timing, Artema." Noting my down vest, he grinned and made a thumbs-up sign as he slung my duffel into the back of the Rover. "You got good ears," he grinned.

I blushed, pulled down my woolen watch cap and climbed in.

There were scarcely any cars on the road out to the airport, but despite the early hour there were hundreds of pedestrians streaming along the dirt shoulders, pouring into Tananarive to begin another Monday. Women were already spreading wet laundry to dry on the hedges and bushes that lined the highway. Here and there the rising sun grazed the edge of a brilliantly colored *lamba* and it caught fire, blazing up in a frenzied patterning of orange and scarlet paisley drawn taut over dark green leaves still damp with night dew. Small roadside shacks puffed woodsmoke, their owners dispensing hot coffee, tea and greasy rice-cakes to the rushing hordes. Zebu carts loaded with charcoal, bananas, manioc, coffee beans and rice clogged the road, hogging the center with equanimity, expecting cars and buses to make way for them.

I scoured the outskirts of Tana, trying to recognize any streets or houses from my nocturnal adventures. In the uncompromising light of dawn, it seemed inconceivable that any of them had actually happened. My mind was filled with a welter of overlapping memories, each successive image more improbable than the one that went before—the tiny blue door of the Hotel Kokolampo, the twisting subterranean tunnels, the albino crocs, the Old Queen, even Dr. Rabansoro, his face glowing like a transcendent, spiritual pumpkin, humming songs about invisible villages over a clothesline full of rain-soaked laundry—it all seemed a fantastic dream. Snug in the speeding Land Rover, tucked up between a pilot, an engineer and a geologist, the tables had suddenly turned. I had become a First World acronym: S A F E and S A N E. Zipped into my down vest, I clung to this cosy, protected feeling the way a baby lemur clings to its mother's furry chest. At that moment, if you'd have questioned me, I would have laughed and dismissed everything that had happened since my arrival in Tana as mere hallucinations, a very bad dream.

But... I would have been lying.

For every time my fingertips touched the scabby abrasions on my left shoulder, they awoke me to a deeper and more disturbing reality, one that it was pointless to deny. Every time I felt the outline of Rangita's silver filagree crocodile tooth, resting cool and sharp on its chain between my breasts, I was drawn down into the darkness, into the vortex of an unravelling mystery over which I had no control.

There is a dream, dreaming us...

Yes, a dream *was* dreaming itself through me. It was dreaming itself whether I liked it or not—whether I understood it or not—and my brother James was somehow at the shadowy center of this dream. What was maddeningly, terrifyingly unclear, however, was whose dream it was, and in what way my own psyche was

171

responsible for its unfolding.

Three CANTEX 500D helicopters were grouped in a far corner of Ivato Airport, huddled forlornly together like malarial mosquitoes on small landing pads near a chain link fence. My fellow passengers ambled around aimlessly on the tarmac, smoking cigarettes and kicking pebbles while Jack checked over the engine. Paul Cummins I already knew. Dr. Fred Pearson introduced himself as a CANTEX geologist. He was a tense, grey-haired man with darting eyes and a clipped Midwestern accent. He stopped often to clean his glasses with chemically treated papers that he took out of the pocket of his vest. Blind and blinking, he looked more like a low-ranking, bureaucratic mole than a savvy, bush-wise scientist. Not that he didn't have the requisite geologist's lantern-jaw—he did. But there was something about him—a self-serving, rat-like nerdiness—that rankled me, stirring up my stomach acids, already churning from the burnt coffee bought at a stall along the roadway.

Jack started the engine and the rotors roared into life. We clambered into the cockpit, ducking through a whirlwind of dust. Fred and I shared the bench seat across the back with our luggage. Between us stood an enormous secondary fuel tank which was very reassuring, although it made the seating cramped. We adjusted our headsets and after a brief conversation with the control tower, we were airborne.

Within minutes after we left the capitol, I immediately understood what James meant about the spidery red footpaths criss-crossing the island. The apparently desolate hills and forested valleys were laced with a fine network of brick-red arteries, converging on villages, wriggling off again into the hinterlands, reconnecting at clusters of sturdy brick houses with thatched straw roofs. They became fewer and fainter, but were still clearly visible, as we left the shimmering paddies of the *haute plateau* and flew south towards open country.

"*Savoka.*"

I strained to hear Fred Pearson over the throbbing roar of the helicopter's engine.

He tipped his head towards the view through the plexiglass bubble. "Grasslands. Veldt. Savannah."

"Big time cow country," Jack said over his shoulder.

The landscape had changed dramatically. Mountainous, heavily cultivated farmlands had flattened out into barren, burned-over, brick-hard laterite hills, deeply gashed by erosion ravines. It was a depressing sight, as if an ax murderer had taken a hatchet to a human body. Everywhere I looked I saw rivers, running red; the island was literally bleeding to death.

Fred Pearson leaned towards me and tapped my knee, speaking into his mouthpiece through thin lips. "See those fissures? They've got a special name for them in Malagasy—*lavaka*. Madagascar's digging its own grave. Been going on since men first settled here. This island was a paradise once. Now it's on its way to becoming a gigantic, red sand dune inhabited by desperate, hungry ants. Overpopulation, deforestation, burning... followed by torrential cyclones. You can see it clearly from up here: all that's left is thin clay over sedimentary layers. Every year the cycle repeats itself and more topsoil is lost, swept out to sea. But the Malagasy continue to sacrifice their future..."

"...in order to survive in the present." I finished his sentence for him.

Fred ignored me. "That's not the worst of it. Roughly 80 per cent of the country's GNP is plowed back into the ground to service this... this useless cult of the Ancestors." He spat out the words. "When someone dies, the family's entire resources go to pay for the funeral. Enormous herds of zebu are slaughtered. Tens of thousands of head! For what? To propitiate the damned *razana*!"

I started to reply, but he shut me down.

"Name me one modern nation where ghosts run the show? No wonder their economy's a disaster! Progress? Forget it. There'll never be any progress here."

I took a deep breath. "Maybe the Malagasy don't believe in it," I said.

"Say *what?*"

"I said... maybe the Malagasy don't believe in progress. At least not the way we do. After all, if you believe that time is a circle..."

For a geologist supposedly trained to take the long view, Dr. Fred Pearson didn't cut me, or Heraclitus, much slack. "Time?" he snapped. "Time is *all* we humans have. The Malagasy better start believing in it because it's running out for them. And when it does, they're going to wake up starving and find they've created an ecological nightmare they can't escape."

As he said that, I had a vision of Rangita the hustler, cheerfully cruising the bar at Le Terrace in her frizzy blonde wig, loaded down with an armful of broken watches, each one telling a different time, followed by another vision of Rangita, the Vazimba queen, as she stood proudly beside the sacrificial stone—strong, glossy and uncompromisingly regal, draped in a ceremonial *lamba*, arms and neck loaded with chinking silver coins and tiny crocodiles.

A terrible pang seared me. Mysterious sister, Vazimba queen, where are you now? On the banks of what eternal river are you standing, as the red waters race to the sea?

"*The zebu will lick bare stone, and die in the earth of the place he loves.*" Jack looked sheepishly over his shoulder when he said that, embarrassed to be caught out quoting poetry. "Old proverb," he hastily added. "One of Rasti's favorites."

"Sounds more like a grim prophecy than a proverb to me," Paul Cummins introjected. "In my experience, wherever you've got your natives, you've got a guaranteed punch-up on your hands. It's the same everywhere, back home in Navajo-land or over here in the Third World. You gotta fight for every inch of progress, and then some. Take Borneo," he twisted around to face Fred and me. "Back in 1997 CANTEX is invited to come over and take a look around for oil. In less than a month, all hell's broken loose. People falling over themselves trying to get a little piece of the filet.

Politicians, farmers, road-builders, head-hunters, whores—you name it. To them, forest is forest. What they want is motor-bikes and television sets. Can't get enough of 'em. Parents are selling their daughters to flophouses downstream for refrigerators and *tennis shoes*, for chrissakes. And the girls are glad to go. For a while you've got a win-win situation. Everybody's happy. Then they discover a bunch of stone age Indians living naked in some caves eating roots and beetles. Somebody gets 'em riled up, and before you know it the Indians are shooting poisoned arrows at our engineers and throwing themselves in front of our d'ozers—just like those little bastards from Greenpeace. There's an international uproar and boom! we're canned. Booted out of the country!"

The cords stood out in Paul's neck. Crescents of sweat darkened the armpits of his cowboy shirt. "You were there, Jack. Remember? We had the Japs lining up for the logging rights, only too happy to take down them trees for us free of charge, shipping 'em back home to make into chopsticks and bowling alleys. I'm telling you, Fred, it was one helluva sweet deal until the natives went and got up on their hind legs. Best damn shot CANTEX had to hit paydirt since the scramble for the North Slope, and we let some uppity bare-ass Indians fuck it up!"

Uppity bare-ass Indians...?!!

I leaned forward, trying to get Jack's reaction, but he went sapphire on me, staring straight ahead, conveniently hiding out behind his mirrored shades. Disgusted, I tore off my headphones, abandoning myself to the deafening thump of the rotor blades.

We whirled on through the early morning sky, traveling south, skirting the central, mountainous spine of the subcontinent. Far off, silhouetted against the breaking dawn, rose the cloud-covered heights of the eastern escarpment where the remaining fringes of primeval rain forest lay. The contrast between the dusty, arid *savoka* to the west and the lush green of the eastern mountains could not have been more profound. In the low hills directly below us the sun glinted off an intricate patchwork of irrigated terraces. Jack pushed the throttle forward and we made a swooping dive down towards a paddy where a group of men and boys were chasing a pair of zebu through the sticky, knee-deep mud, thrashing at their scrawny flanks with long sticks and laughing. They stopped when they heard us and jumped around in the ooze, waving and hooting wildly as we circled overhead.

"Betsileo plowing party." Jack waved back at them. "Of the eighteen Malagasy tribes, the Betsileo are probably the best rice farmers. They know how to use every inch of land. Must be their Indonesian blood."

"Don't all Malagasy have Indonesian blood?" I asked.

"I hear tell." He pulled back on the stick, working the foot pedals, slamming me against the back seat as we zoomed skyward. "All except... the Vazimba."

It was a stinger, and it stung. I did an abrupt right face and went diamond on him, turning to Fred. "Tell me, Dr. Pearson, you're a scientist familiar with Madagascar. What's your opinion of these mysterious Vazimba?"

Fred fixed me with a long, grey, geological stare. "Bullcrap," he said. "If you'll pardon my French."

"Vazimbas?" Paul Cummins butted in. "I've heard of them. What're they, anyhow? Some kinda tribe?"

"You could say that," Jack said. "You might call them the *original* tribe."

"Say," Paul said, suddenly anxious, "these Vazimbas... they wouldn't live any place near to where we're planning to drill now, would they?"

Jack laughed. "Don't worry. They've been gone for a century or two. Or three. Extinctified. Dead and buried along with the Aepyornis, and the giant crocs."

"Crocs?" Paul snapped his fingers. "That reminds me. You guys remember that big lunger they shot out at Lake Anosy a couple of nights ago? Well, get a load of this. After they skinned it, they gutted it and hung it up to bleed. Hired four Antandroy guards with spears to look after it. Comes the morning... what do they find? *All the teeth are missing!* And the claws, too. Picked cleaner'n a whistle. Funny thing was, there were no knife marks. And no blood. Nothing but silver sparkles smeared all over its jaws and feet. Weird stuff, that silver. Like ground up mica, or snow. Disappeared as soon as you touched it." Paul shook his head slowly back and forth like a retarded brontosaurus, "Now how... in... the... hell... d'you... figure... *that?*"

"Beats the shit out of me," I said, and burst out laughing hysterically.

Dr. Fred Pearson was appalled. Cummins, stunned. Jack Mooresby didn't even break stride. "Ranomafana. Dead ahead." He cut the throttle, mock-saluting me over his shoulder. "No pun intended, mademoiselle."

It was an attempt to connect—a pretty lame one. But I'd have been cruel not to honor the intention. I squinted out through the bubble towards the heavily-wooded eastern mountains, shielding my eyes from the sun's glare. "Ranomafana, huh? Sure looks like a wild and crazy beautiful green spot from here."

Jack Mooresby didn't turn around, but I could tell from the way his mustache twitched that he was smiling. "Not half as crazy as some green spots I know."

"Damn," I said. "I thought for a minute you were going to say... *beautiful* green spots."

"Artema," he was chuckling. "You're pushing it..."

The river is mahery, with a will of its own...

"Who, me? Do *I* walk on water? Or fly? I leave that to magicians like you."

When a woman wants to shoot an arrow, she makes a bow...

"All I know is how to do is sing. And disco..."

When a woman wants a man, she must learn how to say Yes...

"You'd never catch *me* dining on barbed wire."

Paul Cummins grabbed his headphones and shook them. "What's goin' on here? Who in the hell's eatin' barbed wire?"

"Our pilot," I said. "It tastes better than crow."

"Crazy, goddamn green spot," Jack shook his head, laughing.

"You bet," I said.

It wasn't a bona fide *Yes*, but it was in the ball park. I was learning.

23

Ranomafana was a crazy green spot all right.

We blew down onto a patch of lawn directly in front of the Thermal Springs in a swirl of damp red dust and bent saplings. A collection of woven raffia and wood houses huddled around several pastel cement buildings backed up against a solid wall of vegetation. After the cool, crisp air of the high plateau, dropping into Ranomafana was like stepping into a locker room. Everywhere steam rose in plumes from wet, corrugated tin roofs as last night's rain evaporated in the morning sun.

The Hotel Thermal hovered over a natural hot springs, anchoring the town like a grand dowager presiding over a tea party for poor relatives. It consisted of sprawling buildings of ochre stones flanking a terraced veranda bordered by neat flower beds in which spindly poinsettias and a clutch of weak, black-spotted roses did their best to make a civilized show. Defying such attempts at cultivation, masses of wild, spiky bromeliads swarmed on nearby trees, the spiky, miniature orchids perching on thin, stiff stems like handfuls of frothy tropical popcorn. The drive encircling the lawn was teeming with people as we landed. It seemed everyone in town had turned out to welcome us. I was impressed, but not surprised. After all, how often does a helicopter land in your front yard, particularly in an outpost like Ranomafana?

It took me a moment to catch on: except for a few children, nobody was paying the slightest attention to us. Instead, they were fixated on something lying on the flagstone verandah. As soon as Jack cut the engine and the rotors skimmed to a stop, I understood why.

Strapped into a makeshift litter of stripped bamboo and woven raffia was a long, thin, very dirty, very angry white man. He was raving, thrashing back and forth underneath a woven netting that had been rigged to keep him from tumbling off the stretcher, but now doubled as a restraint to prevent him from attacking his rescuers. He had several gashes in his head and a score of infected wounds on his pale calves. He reared up as we approached, lurching sideways off the stretcher.

"Rexworthy, Sir. Curtis T. Rexworthy II." He wrenched out the words, then fell back onto the cot deliriously. "Aaach! Wogs! Nothing in this country but wogs and frogs! Tell 'em all to go to bloody 'ell and God save the Queen." He made a feeble attempt to salute, but his arm caught in the netting and he exploded in a stream of curses before collapsing back onto the straw matting.

The Malagasy formed a polite circle around him, at pains to keep a safe distance. They peered down at him, mesmerized by the flailing apparition as if he were a gigantic, noxious insect.

"C'mon, let's get him inside," Jack said. As he stooped to pick up the poles at the head of the litter Rexworthy suddenly twisted sideways, his rage-filled eyes bloodshot and flaring. "You'll never find 'em! They're *ours*, d'you hear me. Ours!! *Hapalemur erectus*. Bloody great giants. Flat faces, hands like a man. Ran through the forest on foot like it was nothing, I tell you. *Nothing!*" His eyes as rolled as wildly as gumballs trapped in a vending machine. His black hair was matted with mud, nettles and dried blood. I noticed that his boots were rimmed with grey-green mildew. No telling how many weeks since his feet had seen daylight.

Jack moved in swiftly. "Paul, give me a hand carrying him."

Paul Cummins went around and cautiously picked up the poles at the foot of the litter, grumbling, "Now you don't go expectoratin' at me, lil' buddy. No surprises now, y'hear?"

Together they lifted the stretcher and carried it into the cool, shadowy lobby of the hotel. The crowd of inquisitive Malagasy swarmed after them, pressing close at the doorway, jostling for a good view.

Jack turned to face them. "Which of you brought this man here?"

Eyes widened, but no one stepped forward.

"Who found this man?"

Silence.

He tried to keep the exasperation out of his voice. "Is there anyone who might be able to tell me something about this man?"

The silence deepened. Jack waited. He seemed to have forgotten his advice about direct confrontation. Only the drone of shiny black hornets scumbling in the scarlet trumpet vines outside the windows broke the stillness. From the kitchen came the clash of metal dishes and a surge of girlish laughter.

Rexworthy suddenly awoke, calling out pitifully, "Oh, oh my love..."

Perhaps spurred by his moans, a barefoot man took one, tentative step over the doorsill. He wore a ragged navy blue t-shirt and a tightly woven straw derby. "You must forgive me... I cannot be sure of any of this..." he hedged. "However it is rumored that he is a scientist from the U.K. He may have been in the forest for three months, or more, I cannot say." He looked around for support before continuing. A few nodded their heads in agreement, but most remained closed and silent, not wanting to be attached to such bad news.

His voice fell to an inaudible whisper, "Some people have been heard... from time to time... he is known by some as...

Monsieur *Maki-be Le Blanc."*

At this, several children giggled but were quickly hushed by their elders. I saw the corners of Jack's mustache quiver, but he deftly saved face by tugging on the ends, restoring his respectful demeanor.

It was true. With his pale, foxy snout and scrawny limbs, Rexworthy *was* a dead-ringer for a big, white lemur. Yet, despite his gangly awkwardness and pointy features, he was not an unattractive man. Through the dirt and the netting, I could see his translucent, slender hands; they would not have been out of place fluttering over a Steinway.

Jack took command. "He needs a bed, a bath, water and food, not to mention antibiotics for these leech bites and Fansidar for malaria. Fred, get my first aid kit in the cockpit. Artema, you speak French. See if you can't scare up the manager and find him a private room. He'll be starring in a Malagasy three-ring circus if we leave him out here any longer."

I didn't have to search far; the manager materialized at my elbow, introducing himself as Monsieur Zoty, pumping my hand up and down vigorously many times. "*Bonjour, bonjour, bonjour.* You are mademoiselle...?"

"Artema." For a second I thought I saw his eyes light up when I said that, but as he didn't respond I dismissed it as wishful thinking.

"Ah, yes, yes. Very good. Yes, well, you see, Mademoiselle Artema, The Monsieur, er..." he sucked in his breath, "I regret to inform you but at the present time the hotel is fully booked."

"But surely... Can't you see? The man is ill. He needs rest and medical attention immediately."

Zoty shrugged helplessly, grimacing and smoothing his hands in a downwards motion over his stomach as if he had a bad case of heartburn. I looked around but Jack and Paul had already disappeared down the corridor with Rexworthy. This called for an end run. Nothing major. Just a small but effective display of flexed muscle.

"How many rooms do you have reserved for CANTEX?"

"Excuse me, I will need to consult the book"

I dogged Zoty to a desk where a crumbling ledger stood open. He rifled through a bunch of blank pages, then slammed it shut and announced, "Three rooms have been reserved."

"Excellent." I drew myself up imperiously. "We will release one of them to Monsieur Rexworthy." I put out my hand for the key.

Zoty balked, wringing his hands and looking extremely pained. "Mademoiselle, this is most awkward..." his voice sank to an embarrassed whistle. "This man Rexworthy, he cannot stay here."

"But... I don't understand."

"My employees will desert me. Cooks, maids, gardeners—they will all quit."

"Why would they do that?"

M. Zoty lowered his eyes, studying the wood floor intently before replying.

"Because... *he has been to the mountain.*"

"Artema!!" It was Jack, calling from an interior corridor. "Bring three or four bottles of Eau Vive, will you? This guy's as dry as a Texas armadillo."

I locked into Zoty's pleading, brown face. "Been to *what* mountain?"

The manager looked over his shoulder fearfully before replying. "Ambondrombe," he said. "The Mountain of Spirits. No one has ever returned from Abondrombe... *alive.*" His terror was real.

"Ar... te... ma...!" Jack's voice echoed down the hall.

This was not the time to debate the travel advisories currently in effect on Mt. Ambondrombe. "Well," I said firmly, "With all due respect, it seems that the ghost of Monsieur Rexworthy has returned to Ranomafana. Therefore, I shall give him my room. May I have the key, please." I put out my hand under his nose.

Poor Zoty. If a truck had run over him going backwards he

could not have been more crushed. You couldn't help feeling sorry for him. At the mere mention of the word "ghost" he'd shriveled up. It was like throwing a bucket of water on a witch. Bushwacked and miserable, the manager handed over my room key with a trembling hand and pointed the way.

"*Merci,*" I said, and had started down the hall when Zoty reappeared at my side, determined to make one last emotional appeal. His sincerity was touchingly real.

"Mademoiselle, I implore you. Be careful. Whatever you do, you must not touch *Maki-be!*" He stopped and put both hands out, blocking my way, beseeching, "To touch a ghost... *is to die!*"

Ghosts—again!

I backed away from him and continued down the hall. After what I'd been through in the last few days, I felt recklessly cavalier--if not completely immunized—about supernatural beings, particularly ones as mundane as Curtis Rexworthy II. In fact, in a perverse way, I was actually looking forward to playing *Maki-be's* Nightingale.

As soon as they transferred Rexworthy from the stretcher to the bed ,Paul and Fred took off, mumbling something about pre-Pleistocene carboniferous strata and breakfast, leaving Jack Mooresby and me to deal with an extremely uncooperative patient.

The first thing we did was to strip him and gently sponge off his body. The *rano-mafana*—hot water—for which the hotel was named, did not seem to exist, and we had to make do with rusty, lukewarm liquid carried in plastic buckets from the lavatory. We tried to counteract these dubious ablutions by slathering his insect bites and scratches with antibiotic creams from Jack's kit.

As protection from the mid-morning sun, Jack had drawn the heavy, chintz drapes, shrouding us in an unnatural, overheated gloom, shutting out any view of the garden or the rainforest beyond. He worked quietly and efficiently, speaking very little, tending to Rexworthy with the rough tenderness of an experienced battlefield surgeon. I hovered around the edges, daubing at the incoherent scientist with scraps of clean linen, making comforting sounds and trying not to get in his way. When Jack was finished, he took the corner of a towel and wiped his face and neck, then sat back on his heels beside the bed.

"It's time to stop playing doctor and find a real one. It may be like looking for a needle in a haystack in this town, but I have to try."

He stood up, reached over and brushed a strand of hair off my damp cheek, tugging it tenderly around my earlobe. "Hang in there, Hot Lips," he said softly. "I'll be back as soon as I can." Then he moved to the door, pausing with his hand on the knob to stare at me for along moment. "As green spots go, Artema," he whispered in a husky voice, "you're a winner."

For the next several hours, I alternately mopped the perspiration from Rexworthy's wracked body and bundled him up in woolen blankets. During that time I gathered from his feverish rantings that he was a variously a viscount, a biologist and, more than that, quite possibly, mad.

It was a savage irony; I'd traveled halfway around the world on a mission to rescue James from just such a fate, only to land up in a dank, claustrophobic hole, nursing a total stranger, while outside, not more than six feet away, the brilliant emerald edge of a teeming, primeval wilderness unfurled, stretched, clambered with jubilant abandon up and over steep, misted hillsides in a tanglement of impenetrable jungle vibrating with unseen life, culminating somewhere high in the clouds as a mysterious Spirit Mountain named Abondrombe. And beyond this still further, across unnamed mountains to the east, lay my goal—the unexplored fastness of the Blue Rainforest, mythic and unattainable as the fragment of a dream. A chimera, floating just out of reach.

I folded the cloth and dampened it again, pressing it against Rexworthy's burning forehead. Then, to rest my eyes, I laid my perspiring forehead against the cool flesh inside the crook of my elbow and heard the regular, reassuring noises of my pumping heart. At once, I became flooded with thoughts of Papa, trapped in Our Lady of Mercy hospital, imprisoned by his own faltering heart, dependent on tubes, machines and his children's safe return to sustain life.

Fathers, sister, brothers. Ghosts, spirits and ancestors. Caves, mountains and altars. Razana, kokolampo, Vazimba, Rangita. Mahery... mahery... malaria. The words spun wildly, beating with the rhythm of my blood. *corazón,* I prayed. Lord, please give me *corazón.*

Rexworthy stirred and tried to speak. His breathing was labored and he exhaled the rank, brown odor of illness. I pulled the sheet up over his bare chest, tucking it in behind his slender shoulders. There was a terrible innocence about his milk-white flesh, gouged at random by maroon sores, bites and slashes; a marble-like purity that reminded me of Michelangelo's *Pieta* and the dying Christ, draped and languishing in his mother's lap.

"Hapelemur..." Reworthy's thick, dry tongue, bent at an angle in his throat like a parrot's, worked from side to side as he struggled to articulate the Latin. *"...erectus..."* A numbed opacity blanked his roving eyes; the colorful irises had shrunk to the slimmest thumbnails of green, overtaken by metastasizing black pupils that sucked in the shadows gathered in the corners of the room, eating up that darkness and reflecting nothing back, not even his pain.

If thine eye be single, thy whole body will be filled with light. But if thine eye be filled with darkness, thy whole body shall be filled with darkness also...

I slumped down, my head cradled on my arm, leaning on the outermost edge of Rexworthy's bed. This was what suffering meant. Blinding plains of pain. Imploding fields of darkness. World without end.

Somewhere in the forest a bird screamed. In the distance, a truck braked, gearing down for a curve. Downstairs, a toilet flushed, shaking ancient pipes. Out by the kitchen, someone was beating rice. Alone, in the darkened room, bending over this strange man, I was overcome once again by the same feeling of helplessness and disconnection from reality I had experienced since my arrival—the sense that I was being held underwater against my will, and that whatever was happening, nothing—none of it—was real.

"Run!" Rexworthy suddenly flung himself bolt upright, his eyes flat and feral in his angular face. "Run! Don't let the bastards catch you! The nets! Watch out for the nets!!" He threw himself backwards, then shot up again, shaken with fits of trembling. Legs akimbo under the blankets, long, skinny feet banging spasmodically against the wooden bedstead, his clumped Rastafarian hair streaming back from his temples, he was being tortured by a horror movie unreeling in the hallucinating theater of his mind.

Reaching out, he grasped my shoulders, smearing me with his sightless, unseeing eyes. "GET AWAY NOW!! Forget the lemurs! It's too late to save them. Save yourself!" Then, astonishingly, he buried his face in his hands and, curling into a fetal position, began to sob loudly, "Bibi. Oh, Bibi, my darling..."

It was then that I understood: *More than one man had gone to the mountain.*

Bibi was my brother James' nickname.

24

I sat rigidly, listening to Rexworthy call out my brother's secret childhood name, trying to absorb the shock of the words.

James... gay?

If this were true, why hadn't he confided it to me, his sister? I fought for calm. Stay focused, Eva. You're on a mission. Remember Rangita: *The essential qualities of a warrior are sustained effort and unbending intent.* And don't forget love. You traveled 10,000 miles around the world because you love James. Only one thing counts: Where is Bibi now? Curtis Rexworthy had some, if not all, of the answers, but it was no use trying to question him. He'd lapsed into a deep slumber before the tears had dried on his unshaven cheeks.

Just then a girl poked her head into the room and asked softly, "Excuse me, mademoiselle, you will be taking lunch with the others?"

Lunch? The word had a strange, foreign sound, as if describing an exotic ritual in a foreign land. How could I possibly eat when James was out there, wounded or dying—maybe even dead?

Mangia, bambina, I heard Grandmother Hermina's familiar accent, cajoling me. If you gonna dance, Evie, you gotta eat.

I looked down at Rexworthy, rolled on his side, curled up under the sheet, like a sleeping chrysalis and felt an unexpected rush of wild anger—at him, *and* my older brother.

"They are waiting for you downstairs," the girl said quietly from the doorway.

"So, let them wait," I muttered, shutting the door on her.

I stared at the inert scientist, and in the gloom of that spartan room I vibed him with the blackest, bitterest, most un-Christian thoughts I could muster. I slaughtered him mentally. Saw him hanged, drawn and quartered. Burnt at the stake. It was a vile thing to do, but I'll confess, it felt great. I can vouch for it—murder's an exhausting business when it takes place in your imagination, but it has a salutary effect on your psyche—like a whiff of mineral spirits. After a couple of minutes of slicing and dicing poor Rexworthy, I felt completely cleansed, rejuvenated. Reborn would not be stretching it.

As I felt the unmistakable, treacly warmth of forgiveness seeping into the corners of my heart, I surprised myself by what I did next—I leaned over and gave the great white lemur a kiss on his chapped lips.

He sighed, and smiled in his sleep.

I couldn't help it; I found myself smiling, too.

Rexworthy was a kook. But was I any less—I who rode crocodiles and hung out with *kokolampos*? If James had cared enough about this guy to let him call him Bibi, a peck from me was hardly out of line. After all, I was James' sister and that made the three of us *tutti familgia,* didn't it?

"*Ciao,* Rex," I whispered in his sleeping ear. "Lunchtime."

The dining room was crowded. I had to squeeze past a long table of tourists to get to my seat between Fred Pearson and Paul Cummins.

"Twitchers," said Fred, cocking his head at the neighboring table. "Brit birdwatchers. See those binoculars around their necks. Dead giveaway. " He handed me a basket of bread. "We saved you some. How's the patient?"

"Thanks. He's sleeping, but I'm worried." I tore off a hunk of the crusty, warm stuff and looked around the room anxiously. "Is Jack back?"

"Haven't seen him," said Fred.

"Been gone all morning," added Paul.

A waiter brought three steaming bowls of vegetable soup and another basket of bread. Paul and Fred tucked into their lunch with a vengeance, leaving me free to gather my wits and observe my surroundings without interruption.

The dining room was large and airy, with many french doors opening onto the verandah and the gardens at the back. Shafts of sunlight slanted in, lighting up the planked floors. White plastered walls and a beamed ceiling, flowered cloths on the tables, and a monolithic philodendron lent the place a rustic congeniality. Except for the Malagasy spears, woodcarvings and raffia weavings, we could have been in Provence.

The birdwatchers were a noisy bunch. They attacked their lunches like a flock of purple grackles on a lawn at daybreak, talking non-stop as they chopped, clinked and swilled. A row of empty Three Horse beer bottles lined the center of the trestle table, no doubt accounting for the conviviality of the silver-haired group, who peered through bi-focals over sunburned noses, comparing notes on the morning's sightings. Their leader, a young, cherry-cheeked naturalist in a blond goatee and Harris tweed driver's cap, struggled manfully to eat and answer the barrage of questions directed at him.

"Now George, about those supposedly extinct golden bamboo lemurs that woman from Duke University and that German fellow, Meier, discovered around here. Any chance we'll catch a glimpse of them this afternoon?"

George cleared his throat pompously.

"My guess is no, Mr. Stiegwald. *Hapelemur simus* are a shy lot. They're the bloody devil to spot; their camo's almost perfect. The way Patricia Wright found them was by listening for the noises of crunched bamboo stems."

The twitchers looked crestfallen.

"Buck up," he added heartily. "That doesn't mean you folks won't have a good chance of seeing some lemurs. Over eleven species have been sighted near here."

"Don't the Malagasy hunt them for food?"

"Not in Ranomafana. In this part of Madagascar it's considered *fady*—taboo—to eat lemurs. The locals believe they're the spirits of their ancestors."

Lemurs... Ancestors? Hadn't Rasti told me the same thing?

"Unfortunately, that's not the case in other parts of the island where lemurs are fair game for spears, sling-shots and traps. But the real danger is de-forestation. Logging and slash-and-burn are squeezing highly specialized species like the goldens out of existence."

"What about the *b..b..b..babakoto*?" stammered a wafer-thin septuagenarian with shaking hands who was lashed into a green plastic poncho and a rain hat.

Babokoto? My eavesdropping ears tingled. Where had I heard that word?

"*Babokoto*," their leader pronounced, "is Malagasy for 'grandfather' and translates as *indri-indri*, the largest living lemurs. Startling black and white fellows these *indri*—like leggy pandas, really—with round, piercing, amber eyes and a keening wail. Sound completely human, they do. No wonder the natives are too frightened to hunt them. They believe that they've got magic powers, that if you throw a spear at an *indri* it will grab it and throw it right back at you! Believe they're their Ancestors, come back to haunt them."

I tore off another hunk of bread. Was *that* what Rexworthy had been shouting about? *Great giants... flat faces... hands like a man...*

"Hauntings, sorcery, taboos... there's far too much black magic out here for my taste," huffed a fat, balding Friar Tuck. "Country's a bloody thicket of fear and superstition. If you don't believe me, take a look in their eyes."

I leaned back against the hard wooden chair, feeling the heat of the noonday sun beating down on the white umbrellas of the Zoma market, hearing the melodious hubble of Malagasy drifting up to the balcony of the Terrace where Rangita and I had leaned together, observing the peaceful comings and goings below, remembering her promise: *Sister, I can help you, but you must surrender and trust me completely.*

"Quite right, dear," sniffed a wrinkled grey wren who must have been Friar Tuck's wife. "Fear is always a bad advisor. It quickly turns to madness under the tropical sun. We saw it happen out in Rangoon, remember Scotty, the Brig?" She turned to include the group. "Went quite round the bend, Scotty did. Ended up on a banyan tree stark naked singing 'It's a Long Way to Tipperary.'"

"Bloody well deserved to end up in a tree, too," harrumphed Tuck. "Wasn't sun but drink did in the Brig."

"White man's got no business in the tropics," a booming voice interrupted. The speaker was a huge man slouched at the end of the table smoking a green cigar.

"Aw, climb off it, Manchester," said a swarthy little trencherman at the other end of the table. "It's common knowledge your firm made a bloody great pile off the rubber tappers in Sulawesi. I hear after you boys pulled the plug on your operation the natives went on a spree and raped the environment for good—murdering female orangs and selling the infants for a farthing to the Taiwanese. Hacking up rhinos for horn." He shouted, "We're talking about *extinction* here, man. White man's got to take *some* responsibility for extinction."

The leaf-thin man spoke up timidly, "H... how do you draw the line between r..responsibility, interference and f..f..folly? I'll wager the natives don't lie awake nights crying about every f..f..fallen tree and d..dead beetle, calling *them* 'Ancestors,' now do they?"

"You implying that's *our* job, Maxwell?"roared Manchester, aiming the tip of his smoldering cigar at the trembling man. *"Ancestors suck eggs!!"*

The leader, George, and I stood up at the same time. Our eyes met, then caromed away in embarrassment. I saw Zoty raise a hand in front of his face, as if to ward off a blow. Even Paul Cummins and Fred Pearson had the grace to look shocked.

Eager to make my escape, I began stuffing a fistful of ripe bananas and French bread into my knapsack to take to Rexworthy.

"Eva, your soup's getting cold," said Fred.

"I know. But I'd better check on the patient. I've been gone quite a while."

Paul stood up awkwardly, "We, er, Fred and I, we thought..."

"Sit down for a minute, won't you, Miss Artema."

Miss Artema?

Fred was falling all over himself to be amiable. Flapping. Like a red flag. I hesitated, then zipped my pack and sat.

"Jack told me a little something about your brother..." Fred began.

"We're all real sorry about him, but here... take a look." Paul pushed his soup bowl to one side and began unrolling a battered topo map, pinning down the corners with cutlery and coffee cups. "Here's us..." He pointed to a wiggly road and greasy dot.

"...and this here's Zaohitra Reserve," Fred Pearson reached over and traced a line along a ridge to the east. "What you call the Blue Rainforest."

I glanced up just in time to see Paul and Fred exchange glances. Paul was sweating heavily.

The back of my neck bristled. What in the hell was going on?

"Show me Mananjary," I vamped, knowing perfectly well where it was. I had the same map in my pack. I'd memorized every wriggle, dot and green spot.

"Here, on the coast." Fred pointed to a point about seventy-five miles to the southeast of Ranomafana.

"And Mt. Abondrombe?"

They looked at each other again.

"Spirit Mountain," I clarified.

"Never heard of it," said Paul.

"Me neither," said Fred. "Now Eva, getting back to the Blue Rainforest... Nobody's ever... People don't..."

"Go on. Tell her the truth, Fred." Paul Cummins spoke with a grim, unsmiling face.

Fred tapped the map with a pen. "Smart people steer clear of Zaohitra. Kind of a dead man's zone, you might say."

Paul laughed. It was a pithy, ugly sort of chuff. Coupled with his ghoulish smile, the effect seemed calculated to frighten me. "What we're trying to say is: You seem like a nice girl. Don't go there. Plain and simple."

Paul couldn't have made it more plain. Or simple. Rakotomana had issued the same warning in his office a few days ago.

"Gentlemen," I stood up. "Thank you for sharing." And I turned on my heel and left the dining room. *Corazón.* I might not have had it when I arrived, but I was sure getting a feel for it now.

My legs shook more than I expected as I hurried down the hallway towards Rexworthy's room. I rounded the corner with anticipation, breaking into a run, hoping he'd be awake when I returned.

Curtis Rexworthy and I had a lot to talk about.

The room seemed much darker than I'd remembered. Rexworthy lay on his back with both hands extending outward, exposed and dangling over the sides. The sheets and blankets were pulled up in a great disarray covering most of his face. He must have grabbed them up during a bout of malarial shivering. The room was very hot and stuffy. Rexworthy seemed unnaturally quiet. I crept closer and bent down to listen, putting my face next to the sheets, expecting to hear his labored breathing under the cloth.

The stillness was profound.

It was a moment before it sank in: he *wasn't* breathing.

I gingerly pulled back a corner of the bed-covers. Rexworthy's smiling, alabaster face was frozen into a mask of agony and terror. A trail of vomit bled out of his mouth and onto his chest.

The great white lemur was dead.

My knees really started to shake then. I crossed myself. Father forgive him... Ancient corpses stacked up in a cave are one thing, but this was a real, live, *dead* person. Somebody I knew. Someone who knew my brother, and loved him. *Famiglia.*

I reached out to touch his hand.

It was still warm.

I jerked my own back as a dizzying shock of recrimination and guilt swept through me. It was all my fault! I could have saved him. I should never have left him alone. Oh Father, forgive me. Forgive me... I sank to my knees beside the bed. Outside in the driveway the chattering birders trooped across the gravel driveway, heading for an afternoon in the forest. Manchester and Maxwell were still arguing about the white man's burden and the fate of the *Hapelemurs.* Kneeling beside the body, I noticed that one of the dead man's eyes was slightly open. A wedge of translucent, glassy green still sparkled under the fringe of dark lashes. The point of his pink tongue stuck out of his mouth. There was something peculiar clinging to it—something grizzled, like a piece of undigested skin. It was piteous. And creepy. I reached over and lifted the covers, preparing to draw them over his head.

It was then I saw them—two more pieces of grisly chicken skin, tangled in the vomit of gruel drying upon his chest.

It hit me in a blast: *Tangena!* Rexworthy hadn't just... died. He'd been poisoned.

It wasn't malaria—it was murder.

25

As I stared at the inert mound of bedding that once was Curtis Rexworthy II, something socked me hard in the gut. A shooting blast of energy, uncoiling in my toes, spiralled upward through my body, surging against the inside of my skull like a tidal bore, flowing back down across my face and shoulders, flooding my chest. My hands and feet tingled, my ears rang. I'm no New Age groupie, but I guessed right away what it was: Kundalini was kicking my ass.

I'd read that kundalini energy had something to do with sex and transcendence, but nobody ever mentioned *death*. If I hadn't had a name to pin on it, I'd've been certain I was dying. As it was, I wrapped my arms around my shivering body and hung on for dear life, praying that it wouldn't take me out, too.

The shaking slowly diminished and in its wake I noticed that something very odd was happening to my skin. It seemed to be on fire, yet I did not burn. A shimmering nimbus radiated outward from my body for a distance of about a foot. This gentle light appeared not to be emanating directly from my physical being, but remained separated from my skin and clothes by a space of several inches. I'd turned into a glowing yogi! Just like Dr. Rabansoro.

I glanced over my shoulder, morbidly fearful that Rexworthy's silent, shrouded corpse would rise up and shake an accusatory finger at me. And why not? By all rights Rexworthy had joined the *razana* now, hadn't he?

An Ancestor he may have been, but Lazarus he was not. He lay quietly unmoving, wrapped in his swaddling clothes, deader than dead. Whatever secrets he and James had shared would remain secret, forever. *Maki-be* was just another anonymous *vazaha*, an untagged, foreign corpse in an obscure jungle with nothing to identify him but the faint outline of a pointed nose, poking up into the sheet like a tent-pole, and two long thin bare feet, their pale, prehensile toes clenched, as if grabbing for a tree branch and finding instead nothing but the impartial air of eternity.

Skrettchh, skrettchh. There was some shuffling back and forth outside in the corridor. A woman's voice began singing a Malagasy song, followed by the sound of a broom whiskering around close to the door, which I had left standing ajar.

Quick! Heart pounding, I moved swiftly to secure the lock, snapping the bolt decisively. Then I turned and caught a glimpse of myself in the mirrored armoire.

I was... radioactive.

Like a sparkler on the Fourth of July, every square inch of me was lit up with a blueish-silver light. My blonde hair shone like a Viking's helmet, my nose and cheeks were etched and luminous. The curves of my breasts and hips were lunar. I was an original, barium Barbie! Peeking out from under my collar, the necklace of silver crocodiles blazed with the light of forty million fissionable roentgens. I tugged the gnarled, yellow croc tooth out from its hiding place between my breasts. Maybe it could save me!

"Ro Sham Po. Old Queen, go!"

I'm not sure what kind of fireworks I expected from the thing, but it was no magic *ody*. Nothing changed. The halogenic voltage around my body didn't diminish. If anything, it grew brighter. I was about to tuck the tooth back into my shirt when I smelled the distinctive odor of cloves and vanilla seeping from the armoire. I pressed my forehead against the cabinet and tapped on the silvered glass lightly with the tip of the tooth.

"Rangita," I whispered. "Are you in there?"

There was no answer.

I groaned. Was I bonkers? Had Rexworthy's murder so completely unhinged me that I'd started talking to a closet doors, expecting them to answer me? Had kundalini kayoed my senses entirely? I squinted intensely into the mirror, but no matter how hard I tried I couldn't make out anything at all inside.

I leaned against the glass. "Sister, come closer. I can't see you."

Very slowly, something moved within. My reflection began to change, drift, become wobbly, as if I were dipping my hand into a crystal pool. I blinked. There, mirrored in the armoire, was another hand clutching a crocodile tooth on a silver chain exactly like mine. It was a small, dark brown hand, and didn't glow at all, but sparkled instead with rococo silver rings of twisted filagree, encrusted with garnets, amethysts and coral. It hovered just inside the glass the way a wild, brown trout hovers in a mountain stream, submerged just beneath the surface of the clear water, rising and falling in the crystal shallows, shuddering, yet holding form, tantalizingly near, yet as unattainable as a distant star. The jewelled fingers clutching the talisman exactly mimicked my own, phosphorescent fingers. It was as if we were two magnets, charged positive and negative, drawn together by an electrical force field.

"Rangita, please answer me. I'm scared. What happened to Rexworthy?"

Still, no answer.

The overheated room was saturated with the sweet reek of vanilla and the melancholy presence of the dead man. Dusky shadows swung heavily from the ceiling and the corners like webs spun from the abdomens of giant spiders. No sunlight penetrated the drawn curtains. The room had become a tomb, a dwelling place fit for an Ancestor. Suddenly, I wanted Jack Mooresby. Now. And badly.

"Speak to me," I begged. "What's happening to me?"

I squashed my nose against the glass, remembering her intimidating *son et lumière* show in the meadow of the Vazimba altar. She certainly hadn't been shy about flashing her queenly powers then. Why was she hiding from me now?

My mind raced, inventing scenarios. Maybe *she* had killed Rexworthy. Or sent her *kokolampo*, Noro, to do the dirty work. It was not impossible. Or—this thought sent a genuine shiver of terror through me—perhaps she was somehow trapped and in danger herself?

"Eva... *ma chere*..." Rangita's voice wavered unsteadily, insubstantial as a drift of woodsmoke, floating up from faraway, deep inside the earth. I had to lean very close to the glass in order to hear her.

"There is no time to explain. They are coming for you with hearts that are hard and ugly. Do not let them catch you, for they will curse you with blame and confusion and prevent you from reaching the Blue Rainforest. *Ecoutez*. Go to the Bobo. You will find a *taxi-brousse* to take you to Mananjary. *Vite!*"

"The Bobo? Wait... What about *him*?" I pointed to the lump that was Rexworthy. Those feet! Those still, sad, white feet. "He... I... I can't just abandon him."

I felt a piercing grief. *Famiglia*. He was *famiglia*. And wherever Curtis Rexworthy II's family tomb was, he deserved to be buried in it. That much I could do for him. In my brother's absence, he was my responsibility.

"Let him go," said Rangita. "Those who sicken from eating what they love and die from what they desire, say nothing, and are not distressed. They are content, free from regret. For they are like young crocodiles swallowed by their mother, consumed by the belly that bore them, so it is they die for what they love."

"But..." I remonstrated.

"Let him go," she repeated. "The hairs on your head cannot

bind death—loose them. Your tears cannot restrain it—dry them. You must let him go. There is nothing you can do for him now."

"Yes, there is," I said. "I can bury him."

"Others will bury him. Others will weep for him. It was his time to die."

"His *time*?" I flashed on the pieces of chicken skin, the vomit. "What do you mean? He had no choice!"

"There are those who would prefer being pierced by a spear or forced to drink *tangena,* than to lead a lifetime of sorrow."

Tangena? So, my guess had been correct.

"He *was* poisoned, wasn't he?" My anger leapt at her. "You knew about it, and you let it happen! Why?" I was becoming extremely agitated. The outer edge of my halo was quivering and jumping all over the place.

"There is a time for good, and a time for evil. And a time for death. You waste time by asking too many questions, sister," she said peevishly.

I was formulating a retort when I heard a great uproar in the hall outside; shouting and clumping boots. Someone rattled the door handle, then began pounding on it.

"Eva! You in there? You okay? Hey, open up. It's me."

Jack! Thank God!

I opened my mouth to yell to him.

Faster than a snake's tongue, Rangita's hand shot through the mirror and grabbed my throat, choking off any response.

"No!! You must not!"

"But, I need him," I managed to croak.

I tried to yank myself away, but her fierce grip tightened. Little warning stars began to twinkle at the back of my eyeballs.

"What? Have you forgotten your mission so soon? *James* needs you."

"Aaaahhh... You're hurting me!" I gasped, flailing absurdly against the mirrored armoire. This was a lot worse than being turned to concrete up on the mountain top.

"Listen to me, little sister!" Her sharp nails dug into my

windpipe. "*We* need you. Andrebabe needs you."

A roaring filled my ears. I twisted sideways but the twinkling stars multiplied and then the sky started going black.

"Hey, Artema! I know you're in there. Answer up!" Jack Mooresby drummed furiously on the wooden door with his fists, then kicked it once or twice for good measure before storming off towards the lobby hollering loudly for Zoty, the manager.

As his footsteps died away, Rangita's grip relaxed. A second hand joined the first around my neck. This time they encircled my throat with astonishing gentleness. A soothing warmth poured from them, healing the bruised flesh that only a moment before they had seemed intent on crushing.

"Oh sister, mirror of myself, forgive me. It is your stubbornness that has forced me to hurt you." Her warm hands remained around my neck as she added, "Go to the Bobo. Now, while you have the chance. Believe me, do not let them find you with this dead man. They will take you back to Tananarive and torture you with endless questions. You will never find your brother."

She was right. Things had become far too complicated. I'd never talk my way out of this pickle. The thought of being embroiled in endless Malagasy litigation, or worse—jailed or deported for no cause, with no possible defense—struck terror into my *vazaha* heart. Better to flee and take my chances alone on the road.

A solitary vazaha perseveres...

My knapsack lay where I'd dropped it next to Rexworthy's bed. When I stooped to pick it up I noticed a dirty piece of orange nylon climbing cord lying on the floor near his heaped clothing. Curious, I tugged on it, dragging a small waterproof ditty bag out from under the bed. Without stopping to examine it, I dumped it in my pack next to the bananas, French bread and James' bundled letters, snaffled the lock, and turned for one last look at the shrouded corpse of the man who had been my brother's lover.

"*Adio, fratello,*" I said softly, touching his cold toes.

Across the room I saw myself reflected again in the armoire. The glow was gone, and so was any trace of Queen Rangita. Slipping my pack over my shoulder, I unbolted the door and turned to salute Rexworthy and Rangita, imagining their Ancestral souls flying out to meet each other across death's eternal night.

I glanced up and down the hall, suddenly panicked.

Where on earth *was* this... Bobo?

A whiffle of vanilla singed my nostrils and I heard a low voice whisper, "Look for Mickey Mouse."

Mickey Mouse? Was she kidding?

2b

I scuttled down the empty corridor and escaped out into the brilliant tropical sunshine, dashing alongside a honeysuckle hedge alive with humming birds, checking to make sure that no one was following me before I crossed the wide driveway.

Jack's helicopter was perched just as we had left it. The sun's rays bounced off the Cyclopean windshield of the aircraft in blinding rainbows; underneath, a rabble of boys turned antic cartwheels in the thin shadow of the tail, entertaining a row of girls lined up a short distance away.

Sayonara, cowboy, I thought as I ran past, darting out onto the main road. Mooresby, I think I could have loved you but for a couple of small, messy wrinkles in life's bathmat—a missing brother and a murdered man.

This *vazaha* heart was taking a big beating—a mighty big beating. The whole Rexworthy horror show, and now having to flee without saying goodbye to Jack; I was hurting real bad. But I didn't cave in. Four years in Amoroso Boot Camp with a *chorizo* named Raul Pedregoza, you can believe I was trained to hang tough during times like this. By now I was a goddamn Green Beret of love.

Boot Camp Lesson Number 1: Anyone walks, make sure it's you. Don't let *anybody* out the door in front of you.

Lesson Number 2: Whatever you do, don't look back.

Lesson Number 3: Stow the kleenex. Big girls don't cry. They look down and see their heart splintered into a zillion pieces, broken shards piled up around their ankles like heaps of busted crockery, why they just laugh and say: Call for the dustpan, I wanna dance.

As soon as I was out of sight of the Hotel Thermal I cut loose, jumping over red rain puddles, leap-frogging over crumbling, muddy fissures, hopping over invisible *corazonitas*, trying not to let the aching hole in my chest slow me down. It felt good to run. On porches bordering barren storefronts, groups of men had gathered, smoking and talking, or just staring off into the steaming jungle beyond the road's edge. They turned and looked at me curiously; a mutant lemur in khaki, coughed up after a rainstorm. There wasn't much to the town of Ranomafana. A few more hops and it was over and I was staring down the rainforest and wondering where Mickey Mouse hung out.

No worries. There he was. Directly across the street, on a faded signboard of a vendor's stall, The Mouse saluted visitors with a skinny, painted pastel arm. *LE BOBO A VOTRE SERVICE.*

Mired in front of the Bobo, doors and windows hanging open, was a battered tile-red Mercedes bush-taxi. The big bus was jacked up at one corner and I could see a man's legs extruding from under the chassis. He was banging on the transmission with what must have been a lead pipe filled with concrete. The sagging bus was a wreck. Vehicular mickey-mouse raised to high art. I'd seen more luxurious cars at demolition derbies. But I was on the lam in Ranomafana; a fugitive fleeing from a murder investigation en route to a green spot on a blank map, praying that by some miracle a brother would be waiting for me at the end of the trail. I needed all the help I could get. So I hunkered down in the sticky mud and tried to make contact.

"Mananjary?" I said in what I hoped was an encouragingly *simpático* tone of voice.

The driver responded with unintelligible grunting and a spasm of muddy, polyester legs, escalating his pounding.

"Mananjary, *aujourd'hui*?" I yelled this time, squirming closer to him until I was virtually underneath the bus. "I must go... please, are you leaving for Mananjary today?"

Ignoring me, he hauled off and attacked again, bent on destroying whatever remained of the motor.

Above us people clambered optimistically aboard. The van rocked back and forth like a creaking, red Dumbo as travellers greeted one another, paying no attention to the fact that the bus was jacked up for repair, clearly going nowhere, or that it was balanced perilously on one, skinny rod and might very well crash to the ground at any moment. In the midst of it all, a little dog started barking insistently: *arkkk, arkkk, arkkk.*

A dog? I thought. Who on earth would bother to take one of these scrofulous Malagasy hounds travelling with them?

Arkkk, arkkk, arkkk... the dog carried on in the ratchety chirruping of a newly hatched bird.

Food. That was it. They were planning to eat it. Hi honey, I'm home. Throw another mutt on the barbie.

I was contemplating roasted pet when from behind one bald tire I saw an alarming sight. Tearing around the honeysuckle hedge, steaming full speed ahead towards the Bobo, was a firestorm of irate males. Monsieur Zoty and a constipated-looking *gendarme* in a brown uniform were leading the charge, closely followed by Fred Pearson, Paul Cummins and Jack Mooresby. From the looks on their storm-trooper faces I heard my cell door slam shut. It was obvious that the combo of a dead *vazaha* and three pieces of chicken skin spelled curtains for Hot-Lips Artema. I shrank deeper into the greasy shadows, wriggling closer to the source of the metallic detonations, all the while keeping my eye on the approaching posse.

"Mananjary... How much will it take?" I pled between hammer blows.

The driver didn't respond. In addition to being deeply offended by direct confrontations it was becoming obvious that Malagasy enjoyed pitting their cool self-possession against foreign impatience and agitation.

"*S'il vous plaît..*" I tried again in my most mendicant French, throwing in as many conditionals and subjunctives as I could.

The pounding continued, drowning out my words.

Stymied and desperate, I did what every conscientious, politically-correct traveler vows never to do—I expedited. I reached into my pocket and took out a fat wad of francs and waved them around in the darkness where the greatest amount of noise seemed to be coming from.

Magically, the noise stopped.

Leaping through this window of opportunity, I squirmed closer, gripping the bribe tightly until I was *mano a mano* with the driver, who was stretched out flat on his back on the ground.

To say he was blown away to see me would be an understatement. His eyeballs shifted frantically from the money to me and back again. He opened his mouth, but I quickly silenced him by pressing the handful of bills across it, pointing up the street to the posse thundering down upon us, trying to look as terrorized and helpless as possible—which wasn't all that difficult. I wasn't the only one who was afraid. Being pinioned in the prone position next to a mad *vazaha* under a broken-down basher dangerously listing to port and rapidly filling with tumultuous travellers and their livestock had a similar effect on the driver. Terror was something he definitely related to.

So were the francs. My freedom depended on it. "Shhhhh! *Je vous en prie!*" I pressed the Fan of Ten Thousand against his open mouth, begging for silence.

Twelve legs and twelve shuffling feet surrounded the bus. From where I lay, I could see Jack's old boots and about eighteen inches of familiar, worn 501's. Oh, he was so close I could have reached out and kissed his scuffed, cowboy toes.

"Where'n hell's the driver of this here rig?" Paul Cummins was stomping around in his expensive Tony Lamas, making a mess in the mud, blowing smoke and talking tough.

I took a deep breath. Showtime, Einstein. I boldly thrust the thick packet of francs into the neck of the driver's open-collar shirt, laid my other hand on top of them, pressing them against his heart, smiled and blew him a kiss to seal our bargain. Without saying another word, he took them and slipped away from me, up and out into the sunshine.

I wish I could tell you what all they said, but it was in rapid-fire Malagasy. Me, I kept my eyes on those boots and those 501's, curled up like a broken-hearted chameleon in the sheltering shadow of the thrashed bus. The *kabary* went on for a very long time. Finally the posse and the driver shook hands all around and I saw twelve feet begin clumping slowly back up the road towards the Hotel Thermal.

"You don't think she'd've lit out cross-country, do you?" I heard Fred ask. "We showed her the map. Maybe she thought she could make it over the top of Ambondrombe and into the Blue Rainforest that way."

"She'd have to be crazy," said Paul.

"Sure as hell," Jack sighed. "But there's no telling. That Artema, it'd be just like her to tackle a big green spot like that all by her lonesome."

"Big green *what?*" said Fred.

"Forget it." Jack cut him off irritably. "She's probably hiding somewhere around here in Ranomafana, scared shitless."

Scared shitless!

I started to get mad, until I realized... Jack Mooresby had

actually sounded bereft.

"C'mon. She can't be far. Let's spread out. I'll go north. Paul, you go with Zoty. Fred, you get with Captain Rebasandromandra and start grilling those villagers again."

"What I don't understand," Fred's voice was fading as they walked off, is how come everybody's so certain it wasn't malaria."

"Sir," said Captain Rebasandromandra in a low, doomsday tone, "everyone knows. Monsieur Rexworthy had been to the mountain."

"Ambondrombe? What the hell difference does that make? There's nothing up there but fog and lemurs."

I strained to hear.

"On the contrary, Sir," the Captain spoke haltingly. "Perhaps you have heard of... Andrebabe?"

"The invisible village? Get *real*." Jack's irritated retort was tinged with a gruff bravado.

"Yes indeed," Zoty spoke up timidly. "Many have gone to the mountain in the hopes of finding Andrebabe. They never return."

I felt a schizophrenic surge of hope and fear.

So I wasn't nuts... but I didn't want to die. That thought was followed by a dreadful, sinking certainty that James was already dead, and this entire, spiralling nightmare had only one possible conclusion—my own ignominious and unsung death in a rainforest at the end of the earth. That would kill Papa for sure, the two of us—James and me—lost and gone forever, *au bout du monde*.

What jerked me back to business was the look that Paul and Fred gave each other. It was the same look they had shared earlier at lunch. It was nasty and evil and real. It had nothing to do with ghosts. The look gave me the willies all over again and I wanted to yell: Watch out, Jack. Be careful! But all I could do was lie there on the mud, watching the men recede into the distance, grateful to be alive, praying that Jack would figure things out for himself.

I felt a tug on my left foot and the grinning face of the driver appeared upside-down, a foot away from mine.

"No problem, mademoiselle," he said. "We go!" And extended

a long arm to pull me up and out into the light.

It took more than a few anxious minutes and several serious whacks before the motor came alive. I squished inside at the last moment, taking my seat—if you could call it that—balanced in mid-air between two nursing mothers. The bus was full of enthusiastic Malagasy and selected companions from the animal kingdom. These included two tom turkeys strapped into a wicker basket on the roof and several chickens that roamed freely inside the bush-taxi's interior, scrabbling over the voyagers, who brushed them aside like outsized, feathered house flies. A little boy wearing a raffia hat and cloak and a bent pair of wire-rimmed glasses clutched a bamboo cage full of damp, green craw-dads against his woven, straw chest. Next to him an old man cradled a slab of freshly butchered zebu meat packaged loosely in palm leaves that leaked onto the lap of a pretty Chinese girl tarted up for the journey in a lavender lace blouse, chartreuse skirt and orange plastic sandals. She appeared not to notice the dripping, leaf-wrapped steaks, but kept her nose stuck in a pulp paperback that bore on its cover the garish image of a bearded, crucified *vazaha* and the hallelujah title: YES! HE IS RISE! As we rumbled out of town somebody pulled out a bottle of cloudy homebrew and a motley cheer went up. I took a swig as it was passed around and my spirits rose considerably. It gave me the courage to study our chariot at closer range.

Big Red wasn't your four-star Michelin *pneumatique*, but it was a big improvement over a zebu cart. The seats facing each other were broken, several large stretches of floorboards were missing— no doubt the result, or perhaps the cause, of the Neolithic bashing—and one of the side windows had been reduced to a collection of hanging glass shards taped weakly together with transparent scotch tape.

"Mananjary?" I smiled broadly at the mothers, subtly adjusting my cheeks over the air space between them and at the same time trying to find a comfortable place on my lap for my knapsack.

"*Oui*, Mananjary. Pour *sambatra*," they answered simultaneously as their two babies smacked and snuggled contentedly at their breasts. The mothers were dressed in tatters, but their white teeth and smooth skin were extraordinary and perfect, like their children.

I settled back. Scared shitless? Not me, Jack. I'm on my way to the mountain! Nothing can stop me now. How many times had I said that since leaving San Francisco? I'd lost count. But it didn't matter. This was still now, and I was still on my way. I had my freedom; I was unstoppable.

I gazed out the broken window in a rum-soaked haze, staring at the rainforest unfolding, remembering Rangita's words. *Time is a circle, we are always at its center. There is no outside. We are ever inside. The outer rim of reality is exactly at the center of itself, and wherever that eternal is, we are.*

And the Now where I am is here, I thought. In an old red bus rumbling downhill to the Indian Ocean, surrounded by the sweet sound of babies gurgling and chickens flapping, sharing a broken seat with a solemn little boy clinging to a cage of crayfish dipped from a waterfall at dawn. I am here at the center of Now, alive and free. There was no place else to be.

"*Arkkkk, arkkkk...*"

I'd almost forgotten about the dog. As I swivelled around to check it out, something warm and grey and incredibly soft attacked me from behind, wrapping itself around my neck, chittering and squeaking.

The "dog" was a young ringtail lemur. Its miniature black hands patted me curiously, messing up my hair, tugging on my zircon studs. It reached down into my shirt and yanked the crocodile necklace out of its hiding place, shaking the tiny silver crocs till they chimed. Then it bit the old fang ferociously, as if it were a piece of fruit, before zeroing in on my knapsack, digging frantically with both hands on the canvas sides before giving up and settling down with its pointed snout resting on the pocket where I'd stashed the bananas and French bread intended for Rexworthy. Its intelligent, amber eyes gleamed in expectation of the feast to come.

"*Maki,*" said the Chinese girl, dropping her book and clapping her hands together. "*Maki* love *vazaha.*"

I kept smiling and nodding.

I didn't have the heart to tell her about the hidden bananas. And I certainly wasn't going to tell her about *Maki-be.*

27

Slowly, slowly we descended to the coast. The road was narrow and skiddy, with drop-offs from the verge into lethal depths. We plunged in and out of deep mist, accompanied always by the roar of unseen, rushing rivers, deeply hidden in gorges rampant with orchids and creeping lianas. It didn't take long to figure out that our driver, whose name was Rosy, was suffering from a severe career maladaption. Every time we approached a blind curve he tromped on the gas pedal and leaned his full weight on the horn and Big Red would swerve towards the cliff edge balanced precipitously on its two outermost wheels, giving twenty-three Malagasy and one *vazaha* an opportunity to see their lives passing in review as Rosy struggled to regain control. Recovering from the brink, he'd blast straight through the thick mist, horn blaring, turkeys gobbling, Big Red hogging the center of the road, churlishly defying any oncoming vehicles that dared to challenge our right-of-way.

It was impossible to keep my balance in the swaying vehicle, and I soon grew tired of apologizing to the mothers for sitting on their babies' faces and concentrated on not losing my lunch. This required fresh air—a commodity in short supply in the overcrowded vehicle—and I was relieved when Rosy pulled off the road and crawled underneath to bang on the motor a few more times. As the others drifted off, I found a flat rock to lie down on and tried to talk my queasy stomach into obedience.

Maybe it needed a banana.

I opened the small pocket on the front of my pack. The ringtail, which Rosy had tethered to the roof rack, saw me and let out a loud, lemurian *arkkkk* of greed and outrage and began to jump up and down on the two toms, which responded by viciously pecking at its long, fluffy tail through the reed basket.

Rexworthy's orange stuff sack lay on top of the bread and fruit. I sat quietly, stroking the rough texture of the fabric, feeling the shape of it the way you'd feel the outside of a Christmas stocking; excited and apprehensive, afraid you'd find that proverbial lump of coal, or something equally grim, way down at the toe.

What was there to be afraid of? I asked myself.

The answer was... Nothing. Except the truth.

I undid the strings and dumped the contents of the sack onto the rock. Out tumbled a can of film, a weathered spiral notebook, a Swiss Army knife with the scissors missing, a mechanical pencil, mosquito repellent, three hanks of thin, nylon cording, a sealed letter, a small halogen flashlight, a bottle of malaria pills and an unlabeled tape cassette.

I was about to drop the sack as empty when I felt something else stuck way down in the corner. I gave the bag a couple of rough shakes, and out popped... a miserable little bundle of beans, mud and sticks.

Santa baby! My old pal, the magic *ody*!

I picked it up and inspected it carefully. Maybe it was a different *ody*, Rexworthy's personal talisman.

Nope. No doubt about it. It was the very same *ody* I'd found in the ditch after the Ambassador's party; the one I'd thrown away in the pocket of my jacket in Madame Moreau's bathroom. It was mine, all right. So ugly only a sorcerer could love it. But what was it doing in Rexworthy's sack?

It could only have been put there by Noro. Or Rangita, herself.

The notion was so perplexing that I dismissed it, placing the amulet on the warm granite next to the rest of Rexworthy's things, and began to sort through the intimate bonanza spread out in front of me. I put the film, the letter, the notebook and the tape to one side. The film was useless at the moment, but might prove valuable later, so I tucked it into the deepest part of my bag for safekeeping. Then I leafed through his notebook. It was a mass of densely packed squiggles and scientific shorthand that would require careful study and possibly a dictionary to decipher. The letter was next, addressed in precise printing to: Dr. Emmett Sandringham, Department of Biology, University of Bristol, Wilton Hall, Bristol, WE7-6AA, Great Britain.

I got comfortable, lying flat on my stomach across the stone, and slit open the envelope.

"*Dear Em, My research team has disbanded prematurely in a depressing display of temper, testosterone and territoriality. Digby and Howell have headed off to Manongarivo Special Reserve where it is rumored there is a subspecies of salamander in which the male has a dildo on its back. Histochemical work conducted in Germany on an embalmed specimen suggests that this dildo provides not only tactile stimulation, but also when rubbed into the female's cloaca, releases pheromones— amphibious aphrodisiacs! But these are guesses, nobody's actually seen them at it. The chance to observe these randy sallys getting down and doing it* in situ *proved irresistibly intoxicating to D & H, who decided that a paper on morphogenic sexuality would make a far glitzier scientific debut than chasing pro-simians about in the rain, and they decamped.*

"*Our team could have survived their desertion had not Herr Frankel and Phoebe Swalls packed it in also, abandoning our base camp during a lull between downpours. 'What can't be seen, can't be hunted. We're off to Nosy Mangabe to look for aye-ayes!' was Phoebe's parting thrust. The bitch hurled it at me as I squatted under a bit of plastic tarp in a driving rainstorm, hoping for a glimpse of our elusive quarry. I can't say as I blame Swalls for deserting. The rainforest isn't exactly Hampstead Heath, and Herr Frankel was pretty deep in her knickers by then. He wasn't the only one. Our infamous Ranomafana flying leeches had developed a touching affinity for Swalls also. Every time she retired to the forest to relieve herself she'd return to camp with a dozen of the little buggers plastered to her butt. She never quite got the knack of backing them off with a lighted cigarette——the spurt of blood does take some getting used to—and she came to rely on Herr Frankel's assistance for this task, no doubt inflaming his already considerable Teutonic lust for her big, pink posterior.*

"If it weren't for James Artema—a gorgeous Yank from Cornell out here on a sabbat. and a jolly good primatologist into the bargain—I'd have tossed in the towel myself and to hell with bloody Bristol Biological and the advancement of science. But we're on to something, Em. Something really big. At first we thought we'd re-discovered Paleopropithecus (extinct), but this is a new species—we're sure of it! Hapelemur erectus is what we're calling it for now. Picture if you will a lemur the size of a child, perhaps a meter and a half tall, with a flat, dark face shaped exactly like a man's. We hear groups of them moving through the jungle, but we've never spotted more than one individual at a time, and those only fleetingly. They seem to travel in troops on the ground like humans, which by all rights should make them much easier to track than your ordinary sifaka and bamboo lemurs. The curious thing is, as soon as we approach them, a peculiar blueish fog descends, and by the time it lifts, they're gone, vanished into thin air. Another odd bit—Artema will corroborate this—we sometimes hear them deep in the forest, singing. Not your usual lachrymose Indri-indri death howls, but angelic harmonies, like a C of E choir! It's most unsettling.

"More distressing yet, Artema's visa has run out and he's received no answer from Michel Rakotomana at International Wildlife in Tana about extending it. He claims he has sent dozens of letters to Rak. telling him about erectus and pleading for an extension, but there's been zero response to date. I can only surmise a failure of la poste, but Artema has darker fears—professional jealousy for starters. Rakotomana is a French-trained

taxonomist, and a very ambitious one—remember how he sucked up to Prince Philip at the World Wildlife conference in Strasbourg last fall? A major discovery like Hapelemur erectus would put him on the map in a big way, and funnel off some major funding from WWF for his own group, the IWC. While I don't subscribe to Artema's conspiracy theories, he has a point. It's a murky business..."

Murky? I thought, snapping the letter angrily. How about homicidal?

"Nevertheless Artema and I have decided to join forces and mount a small expedition to track Hape over Mt. Ambondrombe and into Zaohitra Reserve. The villagers on this side of the mountain are being most uncooperative. In fact we've been completely unsuccessful in trying to hire a guide to take us in—taboos, spirits, ancestors, hair-raising tales and dire warnings—they'll scumble up anything as an excuse. If we must, we'll go it alone, and if we don't succumb to malaria or the usual host of scorpions, spiders and giant centipedes—what the Malagasy call Hazo and Tazo—jungle and fever—I promise you we'll return with news that will set science on its ear!

"It goes without saying, funds are low. PLEASE SEND MONEY SOON. Poste Restante, Ranomafana. Pounds Sterling only. Cheques are quite useless. Wrap the bills well, label them 'Printed Matter,' light a candle and say a prayer. The mails are notoriously subject to tampering. God bless you, Em. Bibi and I will be heroes, or die trying. Count on it. Rex."

"We must go now, mademoiselle."

Rosy had crept up silently behind me. He was holding a greasy wrench in his hand and was staring at Rexworthy's little collection of gear spread out like offerings on the stone. His mouth dropped, his eyes grew very round and he swallowed hard when he saw the *ody*.

"Excuse me..." I quickly swept everything up and stuffed it back into the nylon bag.

There was a long pause while Rosy gathered his wits. He appeared shaken and indecisive. Finally, reaching into his pants, he drew forth the roll of bills I had pressed on him earlier.

"*Mahamenatra izany*," he said, looking defensive, and deeply ashamed. "Please... take them. They are yours." He indicated my backpack with a nod of his head. "The *razana* would be angry if one refused hospitality to a *vazaha* who must drag her house about on her back like a snail, sleeping upon the ground among ghosts and wild boars."

It was my turn to be defensive and ashamed.

I took back the money solemnly. "Perhaps... you'd find this useful?" I handed him the shining red knife with the silver cross embedded on its flank.

Rosy picked it up, inspecting it very, very slowly. Touching the tip of it to his forehead and his lips, he said simply, "*Merci*. May we arrive safely at Mananjary."

I had a vision of Rexworthy's long, thin feet poking out from under the sheet and was suddenly swamped by a *tsunami* of fear and longing for my brother. Had James died trying? Was that the real truth; the unthinkable, unacceptable, unalterable truth that had been lurking in Rexworthy's sack? The unspeakable lump in the toe of the Christmas stocking?

Rosy put out his hand.

"Let me help you. There is room for you next to me on the front seat," he said. "From there you will have a better view of our beautiful country."

28

Sadly, if beauty there was, it was only in the eye of the beholder.

What I saw that afternoon as we lurched over the eastern escarpment winding down to the coast was more like rape, pillage, fire and brimstone. Great swaths of steeply forested hillsides were burning out of control. Wherever they weren't engulfed in crackling orange flames, the remaining trees were being hacked to death. Everywhere I looked, axed stumps stood like rotten teeth in a blackened wasteland. Here and there in a few inaccessible canyons and on high ridges, dense patches of ancient trees remained untouched by fire and loggers' hatchets. They towered above the smoking ruins, innocent, green birthmarks on a red-earth corpse, lush memories of a fast-disappearing Eden, now primeval hostages in the ongoing battle for food and fuel.

Rosy waved at the dense smoke soaring up over the savage landscape. "It is *tavy*," he said. "We light the fires to call forth the rains and soon the planting will begin."

He's got it all mixed up, I thought. Fires don't bring rain. If anything, the smoke should drive *off* the rain clouds.

"Rosy, all this destruction... The animals, the birds, the insects. These huge trees, once they're gone... "

"*Fa fomba vao*," he said, shrugging. "It is the custom. The Ancestors have decreed *tavy* and we must burn. Besides, there have been fires in Madagascar since the beginning of time. One thousand years ago there was a Great Fire, the greatest fire of all. It burned everywhere, destroying the entire *tanindrazana*, and yet, as you can see..." he pointed at a green ridge, "still we have forest." Reacting to my expression, he reached over and patted my knee, "Don't worry, mademoiselle. The *razana* will never allow Madagascar to be destroyed."

We rounded a sharp curve and plunged into a stinging pall of smoke. In the instant before I squeezed my eyes shut I saw something white streaking wildly back and forth in the branches of a tall tree. It was a lemur, an exact twin of the sad-eyed mother in the Tzimbazaza zoo. As I watched, the flames leapt to the treetops, billowing through the dense foliage, chasing the animal higher and ever higher, where it clung, grasping desperately for the last, shivering twigs of the uppermost branches. There was, literally, nowhere left for it to go. The surrounding forest had been destroyed, clear-cut to the ground. All that was left was a seething mass of burning coals and scorched earth. Through the broken windows of Big Red, over the roar of the diesel motor, I could hear the agonized shrieks of the wild, white lemur mixed with the answering *arackkks* of the baby ringtail chained on top of the bus; species calling to species, heart-rending dirges of entrapment and death, echoing across a chasm of fire, from one who had lost its freedom to one who was losing its life, whose padded, black feet hadn't a snowball's chance of making it across that burning land to the small section of forest still standing in the valley below.

In that blink of an eye, I understood: *This was extinction.*

A lone lemur, silhouetted against a saffron sky full of fire, plunges to its death. So simple. And final. With the snap of a burning twig, a unique arrangement of genes that took millions and millions of years to evolve, goes up in smoke. *Kaput*. It's over. Another notch erased from God's belt. In that twinkling of an eye, I saw suffering and death and extinction. I saw one of God's infinitely marvellous and various creations catch fire, lose its grip, and fall through the sooty air, arms outspread like a charred angel, and in the wake of its small, unsung passage the world was diminished; with that free-falling lemur, some of the wonder went out of the world.

I felt a lump in my throat, tears rising.

Hold on, Artema, I thought. Nature's wild beauty has no room for sentiment. Like Einstein's tree, the lemur would have fallen to its death in the forest making a noise, whether anyone heard it or not. The rose on the mountain blooms, whether anyone sees it or not. Unlike the dream of culture and civilization, nature simply exists, in all of its infinite majesty, saying I AM, I AM, constantly destroying and resurrecting itself, intemperate, unyielding, indifferent.

Indifferent to everything, except human intervention, I thought bitterly. I poked through my pack for my sunglasses, jammed them on my face, ashamed of my species.

The earth absorbs death to produce life. It had been one of Grandfather Edwin's favorite themes. "Death is essential," he lectured me on Sunday mornings over scrambled eggs and cinnamon buns. "It's what keeps evolution going, recycling matter, ideas, species, civilizations. No matter how fine and beautiful things are, they have to get cleared away to make room for the next step. Death creates room on the planet for new masterpieces. In nature, as in art."

But what, then, of the *razana*, who supposedly lived forever? Rangita and Uncle Rasolo, where did they fit in? What about the astral, ancestral world of the Malagasy, those endlessly interfering grandmothers and grandfathers who make daily contact with the living, without whose ghostly intervention nothing can be brought to fruition in the everyday lives of their children? Didn't they give the lie to extinction?

And what of the terrible spectre, Death?

Maybe the Malagasy *were* right. What if death were nothing at all, a mere shadow, a dream, dreaming itself, as fleeting and insubstantial as life. If so, then extinction was just another dream. A First World chimera. Something for politicians to rally around and scientists to lose sleep over. If the Malagasy were to be believed, there was nothing to worry about—not the death of a solitary lemur, nor the death of an entire civilization. Forget the sack-cloth and ashes. Up with Uncle Rasolo! It was the duty of the living to celebrate. Our job was to kick back and party on down in Death's honor, like the merry-makers up on the hill at yesterday's *famadihana*, getting wasted on homemade rum, pinching powdered flesh from the dry bones of aunties, turning their lives over to the ancestors for safekeeping.

Big Red shuddered as Rosy maneuvered around a slow-moving zebu-cart hauling charcoal from the dying forest down to the coast.

No. They were wrong. I looked back at the charred forest. Extinction *was* real. That white lemur *was* gone forever. How many more were there left of its kind, hiding out in the tiny islands of rain forest still standing? A dozen? Six? Two? It was curtains for them. The final act. The end of the trail. An entire gene pool hung out to dry in the hereafter. No amount of ecological bombast or statistical flagellation could have driven extinction's reality home more clearly than the vision of that single, blackened lemur. It had laid waste my heart like a blast from a thirty-ought-six. I buried my face in my hands, hearing Rangita's soft, teasing voice: *The Vazimba? Why... we live. As always.*

I needed more than an Einstein to solve this. I needed a Boddhisattva.

I got Noro and Jesus instead.

29

Michel Rakotomana had warned me that the roads leading to Mananjary would be filled with people travelling south for *sambatra*.

Sure enough, once we left the burning forest and reached the flatlands near the coast, we entered a seething mass of humanity on the move. Whole families streamed along the sides of the highway, carrying belongings in baskets on their heads and babies strapped to their backs. The number of zebu carts, *taxi-brousses* and dusty Citroen 405's had mushroomed until now, late in the afternoon, the narrow, two-lane highway was choked with celebrants. Bouncing along on the front seat of Big Red next to Rosy, I felt like the proverbial *vazaha*-in-the-window. Even with my watch cap pulled down over the top of my Ray-Bans, I was unmistakably a loaf of white bread on parade. Kids would catch sight of me and dance alongside in the dust, waving and shouting "*Bejour, bezjaha*," then detonate, holding their sides, collapsing into giggles.

I slid down on the seat and pulled the collar of my shirt up, trying to hide my pale skin. There might not be many computers in Madagascar, but for sure there were telexes, and a working telephone or two. No doubt the *gendarme* in brown had notified Mananjary by now, alerting the authorities to be on the lookout for an escaped murderess.

"You are ill, mademoiselle?"

"No, Rosy, just a little tired. It's been a... heavy day."

That was an understatement. Every inch of my body screamed from being wrenched this way and that way as Big Red squealed down the mountain. And my soul was a shambles. I longed for Papa, feared for James, and grieved for Curtis Rexworthy, as piteous in death as the white *sifaka*, leaping to take its place in the pantheon of extinction. Feeling confused, weak and very lonely, an infinitesimally small green blip on a monster topo, I surrendered to another kind of ache; a passionate, sexual ache that came at me out of nowhere like a line drive off a fast pitch. A kundalini kind of yearning. A shameless, scratching itch for Jack Mooresby.

Big Red slowed to a complete halt in the milling crowd. Just ahead, a makeshift roadblock of palm trunks had been thrown up across the highway and uniformed men were stopping traffic, searching every wagon and vehicle, pulling out passengers, opening bags, poking through baskets.

Rosy shook his head, looking grim. He inched the bus into the center of the road trying to squeeze past an overloaded wagon. Panicked, I scrunched down even lower on the front seat and let out a groan. There was no way I could slip through this crowd unnoticed.

That's when I saw Noro, on the back of a truck next to us, tucked in between two jute bags lumpy with manioc. Her legs— legs, feet, fins, whatever they were—dangled over the slatted, wooden sides, her little white cloak demurely covering her. In fact, I might not have noticed the tiny *kokolampo* at all, mistaking her for a sack of laundry, if it hadn't been been for those glowing eyes. They were heart-stoppers, swaying in the hollowy shadows under her hood, flashing on and off, blinking tail-lights from Hades. We shouldered so close to the zebu cart I could've reached out the window and touched her. I was terrified that Rosy or one of the passengers would notice her, but the instant we came alongside, Noro blinked furiously, then curled up into a bland ball, inconspicuous among the mound of laundry bags.

"*Mon Dieu!* I am suddenly having a mad idea," Rosy exploded in a most un-Malagasy outburst, slapping the steering wheel. He wheeled abruptly off the main road, scattering kids and dogs, and roared across a cultivated field, dodging cornstalks and patches of manioc, diving into a thick canebrake, emerging finally onto an unmarked, rutted earth track, leaving the *gendarmes* and the roadblock in the dust.

There was a brief ruckus among my fellow passengers, but after some tart, verbal skirmishing everyone settled down and seemed to accept the detour as somehow providential. The exception was the Chinese girl. She shot me punishing looks from time to time over the pulp pages of HE IS RISE, but I chose to ignore her, telling myself that a *gendarme* is a *gendarme* is trouble, whatever color his uniform, and that it never pays to tango with the law, especially in the bush *au bout du monde.*

"In an hour it will be dark and the snail will have only its shell and the moon for company." Rosy winked at me. "I think it is better to sleep with Jesus than on the ground with wild beasts, is it not?"

"Why, yes," I said, "of course." It seemed more than reasonable, under the circumstances.

Yes... Maybe it was my crazy imagination, but each time I surrendered and said that word, things seemed to get a little easier; I felt a little less lost, and a lot closer to James. It wasn't a fantasy. Things *were* turning around. Going my way... for once.

Night had nearly overtaken us by the time we reached our destination: a rambling, two-story building, girded on all sides by a high, whitewashed wall and topped by a weathervane in the shape of a Roman cross. Slightly elevated on a small knoll in the middle of a spreading sisal plantation and guarded by two tall traveller's palms, the mission glowered over the landscape. It reminded me of a malevolent blimp, the way it hovered in the low sky just above the horizon line. I stuck my head out the side window, half expecting to hear the growling hum of a dirigible motor above us in the gathering darkness, but there was no sound except the dry, clacking fronds of the two sentinel palms and the hungry *awrrrckkk* of the little lemur tethered on the roof of the bus. There were no lights in the building; not a single flickering kerosene lamp enlivened its tense, brooding outline. Stretching away in straight lines in all directions were row upon row of pointed agaves whose hemp fibers would be stripped and fashioned into rope and sisal matting. There was just enough light to make out the muscular, saw-tooth edges of the thorned cacti, thrusting upward out of the orange-red earth, jabbing rhythmically into the purple twilight at regular intervals, like the uplifted arms of dervish dancers.

Leaving the motor running, Rosy jumped out and pounded on the door of a flimsy shack that cringed against the wall encircling the house.

"*Gardien! Gardien!* Open up. Pere Soren's guest has arrived!"

A flap of wood creaked open and one bloodshot eye gleamed in the light from Big Red's headlamps. There was a muffled convo, then the shutter snapped shut and Rosy returned to the bus. He was frowning.

"He wants to see your documentation."

"Documentation?"

"Your permissions. The priest is not here just now. The guard, he must see a stamp before he can let you in."

My fellow travellers had turned to stone awaiting my next move. Even the chickens and the turkeys quit their gabbling and leaned towards me.

A solitary vazaha perseveres...

I rifled through my pack, while covertly trying to assess the guard's reading skills on the basis of his one, red eyeball.

"I trust this will suffice," I said stiffly, trying to appear deeply affronted. I handed Rosy a telegram from Cornell University to Dr. James Artema in Tananarive, demanding his immediate return. It had been mis-directed to the U. S. Embassy in Washington, D.C., then bounced to Oman, Somalia, Kenya, and finally Madagascar. It was plastered with a blitzkrieg of highly official rubber stampings in purple, red and green. At the bottom was a fat, round stamp from the Antananarivo Post Office which read:

DECEASED / RETURN TO SENDER. USAPO.

I held my breath.

One-eyed Cerberus studied it for a long time, turning it this way and that in Big Red's headlights, grunting and mumbling and shaking his head *non, non, non.*

"*Monsieur le gardien*, it is already dark. If you will, mademoiselle is a *Christian*," Rosy spoke loudly and ominously, greatly exasperated. It was the second time I'd heard him raise his voice today.

Maybe it was the word Christian that clinched it, but the guard slowly shuffled out of his shack and unlocked the gate. Rosy lifted my pack, placing it inside, then hopped back into Big Red and gunned the motor.

"Wait! Rosy! Don't leave me like this! Where am I? How far is Mananjary?"

"Very close, mademoiselle. I promise you. No problem. Tomorrow you will arrive." He threw the bus into reverse and began backing up.

"Tomorrow? But... how will I get there?" I hung onto his door handle like a leech. "They're looking for me. You can't leave me alone like this."

"You are right," Rosy said, after a moment's deliberation. Dropping the clutch into neutral, he sprang out and hauled himself up onto the roof, untied the captive ringtail and handed him to me. The lemur flew into my arms with the hearty effusion of a freed slave, clasping my shoulders and licking my face as if I were his long-lost ancestor. "Please accept him, with my compliments.

He will be good company for you on your journey." Rosy gunned the motor and leaned out the window, passing a hand gently over the lemur's furry shoulders. "I'm almost forgetting, *Mademoiselle Escargot*. His name is Maki."

Thus spoken, Rosy peeled out, abandoning me to my fate somewhere on the Tropic of Capricorn.

30

One-Eye marched up the broad flight of stairs, stopping every second or third step to grunt and whisper something into his sleeve in Malagasy—a curse, a blessing, or simply irritation at my unannounced arrival, I couldn't tell. He set down his kerosene lantern and fumbled with a hoop of keys, produced a large, iron twister and unlocked the front door, motioning me inside with a curt gesture.

The lantern shone on a library crowded with Victorian furniture and bric-a-brac. I inhaled the odor of every priest's room I'd ever been in—a celibate sort of smell—of repressed spunk, fustian and resin, carnuba wax, hair oil and stale cigarettes. The book-lined walls ended a full two stories above in a cupola where a circle of clerestory windows created an amethyst bracelet, reflecting the waning purple of evening.

The *gardien* chugged across the room, lamp in hand, like a character on a Chinese scroll. I followed him up more stairs, hanging onto Maki's leg cord to prevent him from disappearing into a series of ghostly bedrooms with furniture draped in protective muslin. One room looked particularly inviting. In it I glimpsed a four-poster bed covered by a wedding ring quilt stitched in faded pastel patches. A stern, black crucifix was mounted on the wall over the head of the bed, but the mattress looked thick and flat and two plump pillows nestled cozily side by side under the comforter as if expecting lovers.

Sadly, the honeymoon suite was not what One-Eye had in mind for me. He hustled to the end of the hall, reached up, unlocked a padlock and pulled an iron handle hanging above his head. There was an unearthly shriek of metal rubbing against metal and another set of narrow stairs, like a fire-escape, unfolded from a trap door in the ceiling. He handed me the lantern. "*La-haut.*" He jerked his head upwards.

"What? Up there? Me?"

"*Eny ary,*" he said, then set the lamp down and folded his arms, standing his ground. His single eye glittered defiantly, more than making up for the missing one.

I peered at the trap door and the void beyond. "Maybe I could just... you know... check around on this floor. There's probably a guest room somewhere with a bed just my size."

One-Eye glared.

I looked up again. Maybe that *was* the guest room. How bad could it be? It was only an attic and if the bed was too hard, I could always sneak downstairs later and crawl under the wedding ring quilt after One-Eye went to sleep. This was the house of the Lord. It should be safe to sleep with Jesus.

I shouldered my pack, grabbed the lantern, and started up the shaky steps. When I got to the top, I called down, "See you at breakfast. Don't forget the croissants and fresh-squeezed O.J."

This witty knee-slapper was lost on the *gardien,* who let go of the handle and pushed—hard. The stairs folded up immediately, slamming against the floor of the attic with a decisive *clanggg,* trapping me in the darkness. I was so startled that I let go of Maki's cord, and he ran off *awrackking* into the shadows. I could hear my jailer below, cackling and rattling his hoop of keys.

"Up your sleeve, One-Eye!" I fired at him in English through a crack in the trap door. "You don't know what kind of Jesus freak you're toying with!" Then I knelt down and hissed in French, making sure he heard me, "Be careful, old man. I've got God and an *ody* on my side. And a *kokolampo* for a buddy. I've got a goddamn hot-line to the Vazimba!" I paused to let that sink in. "Watch your step or I'll cut your bloody heart out and eat it as a midnight snack!" I rocked back on my heels, wishing I could see his face, when I suddenly became aware that...

...I was surrounded by angels.

That's what I thought they were at first. Then I realized they weren't angels at all... they were nuns.

Silhouetted in the lantern's light, ranged around the attic walls, were a dozen or so nun's habits hanging from pegs. My worst childhood nightmare had come true. I'd been locked in a Catholic cloakroom! I recognized Saint Valerian's deep, starched wimples, curving like gull's wings. They hung next to the plain grey hoods of Saint Catherine. Saint Agnes' navy blue serge gowns and surplices weighed in heavily next to the gossamer shawls and creamy cotton pleats of Saint Theresa. Nurses from all over the world must have come to this mission to do service, for in the corner, neatly folded on an army cot, were stacks of white armbands with red crosses embroidered on them.

I groaned and scratched futilely at the trapdoor where wood joined wood.

It goes to show, I thought. Sinners have no business in God's house. I should've jumped ship back at the roadblock. Taken my chances with the locals. Trusted my luck. I would have been in Mananjary tonight. Days were fleeting, time was wasting and I was on the lam. Any sense of optimism I once entertained fled quicker than Raul Pedregoza.

I slid into the dumper.

This misguided rescue mission was a cosmic joke, a game of Snakes and Ladders played by an inept fool ready to climb every improbable rung, only to be flung backwards again and again. Attempting to find a lone man in an uncharted jungle was a ridiculous proposition in the best of circumstances. It took Henry Morton Stanley more than two years, 450 bearers, 999 days and the mighty Herald Tribune picking up his tab before he found Dr. Livingstone on the beach at Ujiji. I'd begun my journey hoping to find James with little more than love, blind faith, a small stack of travellers checks and a beat-up topo map.

I pounded my fists on my thighs. Madness! *Madness!!*

It was my own fault! I deserved to take the big slide back to Square One. To be closeted in a stuffy attic with the discarded robes of pious virgins when I should have been hacking my way boldly through virgin rainforest, blazing a trail to my brother. I'd proved it again: I was a leech on the fecund flanks of life, sucking blood from other people's lives, pretending to be some kind of New Age adventuress on fantasy island, hallucinating about demons and invisible queens. Loony, that's what I was, a useless loony with about as much *corazón* as a Dilbert cartoon. Crazy green spot? More like a grass stain on life's *derrière*. Throw the bum out! I'd dropped the ball. I didn't rate another inning.

I took it out on my captor. "One-Eye, I warn you," I shouted at the top of my lungs. "You do not frighten me. I have looked death in the eye twice already this day. I have *been to the mountain*! And I have seen terrible things: a *vazaha* poisoned by *tangena*, and an ancestor falling from the sky, consumed by fire."

I pressed my ear to the crack.

He was down there, all right, breathing heavily.

From somewhere among the robes behind me came the sound of a muffled sigh.

I wheeled around.

The nuns' habits swayed gently back and forth on their pegs. A warm breeze moved through the attic, lifting the veils, twirling the hems of the garments in an impromptu dance. The kerosene flame guttered sideways at right angles to the floor; the attic was suffused with the scent of vanilla, cloves and tarnished silver.

I felt weak and dizzy. Every hair follicle tingled.

No!

I knew what was coming, trying to steel myself against the gripping *ennui* that began to envelop me, bending me to its will.

It was no use. I began to move in slow motion, as if in a dream. Opening the front flap of my pack, I pulled the *ody* from Rexworthy's ditty bag, holding it out in front of me. I felt the bristles prickling the fleshy cove of my palm, strangely warm, almost electric.

I knelt at the top of the stairs, lips pressed to the crack. Smoothly, without any preamble, my mouth started moving, words forming. I heard them dimly, through ringing ears, as if underwater. Regal commandments. Poetic directives, echoing from an unknown, invisible world, shaped in the language of another time.

> *Lower these stairs, gate-keeper, or—*
> *I swear upon this ody I hold in my hand—*
> *as the moon rises tonight I shall sharpen my teeth*
> *and dance naked in its silvery light*
> *on your grandfather's tomb.*
> *I shall make your children ugly,*
> *like little dogs that are satisfied*
> *with burnt food.*
> *They will drag along like inedible geese,*
> *useless as moths that guard a ford*
> *ruled by hungry crocodiles.*
> *No longer will you rejoice*
> *in the resounding tread of the moon.*
> *No longer will you awake*
> *to the booming gallop of the sun.*
> *No, you will be like the little crab,*
> *and I will eat you, before dawn,*
> *together with your shell.*

There was a long pause, then a hissing uptake of air, a throaty moan, and with a tremendous crash the stairs unfolded, followed by the sound of running feet and a door slamming. It happened so quickly it shocked me out of my trance. I almost fell head-first through the open trap door. It took a minute before I understood what had happened: the *gardien* had fled. I was free!

"*Awwarackk!*"

Under the cot, a black and white striped tail whisked wildly back and forth, dusting a line-up of clumpy nun's brogans.

"Hey, Maki," I scratched on the floor. "C'mon out, little fella. Don't be scared."

Whimpering softly, the lemur hesitated, poking its nose between the shoes to test the air, then bounded towards me, patting his cool black hands over my cheeks, licking them.

I held up one of Maki's skinny arms and waved it at the empty habits. "Round one for Artema. Listen to me, sisters. Go tell it on the mountain. Carry the word to Carlo Artema in Our Lady of Mercy Hospital in Cleveland. Tell him his daughter, Eva Victoria, finally won one."

Then I began a careful retreat, picking my way slowly down the ladder, balancing Maki, the lamp and my pack. It's true, I wasn't exactly forging ahead. But neither was I sliding downhill. You could say I was holding form. Vanquishing the guard had been a small, important victory. But, an inner voice nagged me. Who—or what—was *really* responsible for the victory? Rangita, the *ody*, or me?

It was a sobering question.

Father Soren's larder was a poor thing but I managed to scratch together a meager supper for my companion and myself: two tomatoes, a handful of small, red onions, a tin of boiled zebu and a can of brisling sardines in mustard. I added half a French roll from the Hotel Thermal and a banana for Maki, spreading everything out on a sticky oilcloth table in the kitchen under a calendar dated 1959. On it was a photograph of a village in the snowy Alps. A faint penciled arrow pointed to a Tyrolean house with a smoking chimney—possibly Pere Soren's childhood home.

After dinner I took up the lantern and explored.

The place was a combination hospital, monastery, business and private residence. I wondered if it were typical of all missions in Madagascar—Catholic or Protestant. Wondering, too, if the various denominations had succeeded in dividing up the country peacefully, as Paul Cummins had suggested, or if they still squabbled among themselves for territory and converts. It was built on such a grand scale and filled with such an abundance of treasures—handicrafts, photographs, musical instruments, leather-bound volumes of science and poetry, letters, church documents, business and medical records—that I concluded it must be a star in the papal crown, dispensing religion and medicine with equal authority, with the sisal plantation keeping the whole operation afloat.

I nosed around, keeping the kerosene flame very low, anxious not to arouse the *gardien's* suspicion. Eerie shadows crept behind the chairs and tables; as I swung the lantern to and fro, they would expand without warning, zooming up the walls only to expire in the tonsure of the darkened cupola.

A collection of indigenous insects framed under glass drew my curiosity. I noted with some surprise that Father Soren was a well-schooled entomologist, for his specimens were meticulously stretched, mounted and labeled. Most were unknown to me. One, however, I recognized. Alone in its own frame, floating over a cork background on a long, black, mounting pin, was an old friend from my days as James' artistic batman: *Actia cometes*, the giant comet moth. It was a superb *Saturnidae*, much larger than any I'd ever seen. The wings, big as a man's hand, yellowish as ancient parchment, extruded downward ending in two, languorous, trailing tails. Longer than the moth's body, longer than both of the moth's wings put together, these tails were fantastic, impudent and breathtaking. In the center of each of the four wings, was a brown "eye"—a magical spyhole for God to keep watch on the world's wilderness. In another country, this sleek, creamy creature might have been a bird of paradise. Here, in Madagascar, the bird had adopted the shape of a moth—a moth of paradise.

I sank into a red velvet chair, admiring the perfection of the insect, comforted to share this priestly, male domain, half-expecting Grandfather Edwin to step around the corner of a bookcase, one finger marking his place in an opened tome, the other raised to impart some bit of arcane lore.

Once, long ago, James and I had sent off to a nature magazine for a *Hyalophora* cecropia moth cocoon. It arrived months later, a brown bag of spun substance attached to a broken twig. We had put it in a carton box covered in plastic wrap with holes punched for air, worried that if it hatched while we were at school it would fly off over Cleveland and disappear, like a birthday balloon. We waited almost a year but it never hatched. "Open it," I'd begged him over and over, desperate to know what went on inside a cocoon, to know what the insect looked like at the halfway point between caterpillar and butterfly. Finally, James agreed. I watched breathlessly as he slit open the cocoon with a razor. It was empty. I was devastated. "There's nothing there! They cheated us," I sobbed. "No they didn't," said James. "It's in there. It just doesn't have a shape right now. The living, organic material is spun right into the cocoon. The caterpillar is gone, the moth is yet to come." He wiped away my tears. "Transformation means giving up one form before you have another. You have to be willing to be nothing for a while."

The willingness to be nothing...

Was that what Rangita had meant when she'd warned me that in order to succeed I must surrender to the terror of not knowing?

I was trying hard to remain in that place of not knowing, but there was so much I didn't understand on this island. Every time I turned around, reality took a hike down another rabbit hole and I ended upside-down, too big or too little, locked in or locked out, like Alice, wondering what was real. Take Noro, for instance. Michel Rakotomana had dismissed the possibility of a *kokolampo* out of hand, saying that since no one had ever captured one and dissected it, therefore they had no reality.

I knew better, and I didn't need a taxonomist to confirm it: Noro was real; but hers was the reality of a cocoon, of a secretive, midnight shape-shifter. Each time I had encountered her, she'd been so diabolically... present. I could still hear her terrible, keening wail, feel the little fins pinching onto my shoulder. Yet, capturing her—laying hands on her—had proved next to impossible, like trying to capture a dream, or a nightmare. As for dissecting her... Outrageous notion! What could I conceivably hope to find inside that little cloak? A monstrous, misshapen child? A withered Malagasy troll? Then again perhaps, as Rakotomana had suggested, there was nothing there—nothing at all. A handful of white cloth and some silver sparkles.

But, her eyes? Those flashing, glowing eyes? They belonged— I mean, they *had* to be attached to something, didn't they?

Once again, as I tried to unravel the events of the past few days, logic fell prey to magic. I rubbed my hand hard across the velvet arm of the chair, feeling the silken nap heat up under my palm, thankful for sensation itself. Grateful to be alive.

"I am here," I repeated softly aloud. "I am here, I am Eva, I am real."

No wonder Madagascar had sent Rexworthy around the bend. Everything about this island demanded a suspension of disbelief. I was finally beginning to grasp what James had been trying to tell me when he had written:

"Nature has created a surrealistic world, a sumptuous world in which everything is like a fairy tale, a fairy tale that becomes a reality..."

I closed my eyes. Madagascar was a fantastical game played by a quixotic God on a red-dirt gameboard afloat in a turquoise sea. Men with the bodies of animals, animals with the souls of men. Crocodile queens and caped *kokolampo*... all interchangeable pebbles in a game of cosmic draughts. I would've drifted off had it not been for Maki. He was scrummaging around in the shadows as if the drawing room were a jungle-gym. In trying to execute a snappy segue he leapt from the back of my chair to a nearby bureau and missed, knocking a flock of photographs to the floor. I moved to retrieve them, and began to stand them up, one by one, only to find myself face to face with...

...Bibi!!

I held the picture directly under the hissing kerosene flame.

There he was; standing at the edge of a jungle wearing grubby camouflage pants and a sweat-stained Cornell football shirt. On his left, one arm draped over his shoulders, was Curtis Rexworthy. On his right stood Michel Rakotomana, thick and unsmiling. Off to one side was a Malagasy nun. Her small, dark face was blurred, slightly out of focus, as if the camera had tried to capture a soul in flight and just missed. Scribbled across her wide, white wimple in a familiar, spidery, blue hand were three words:

Courage. Andrebabe. Rangita.

"Jesus..." I whispered aloud.

I traced my finger over the writing, and was startled to see the ink smear, leaving a cobalt smudge across a corner of the sky.

It was still wet.

31

I was awake when the first cock crowed. The stars of the Southern Cross were sliding south over Antarctica and the sky was as dark as the inside of a cooking pot. In the east a thin, vermillion line hugged the horizon, tucked under a jade band and a violet streak.

I'd slept in my clothes; I was ready.

You can throw a nun's habit over anything, even a backpack. To make my getaway I'd chosen the order of St. Valeria—the same habit Rangita was wearing in the photo. That way if anybody saw me driving, I would look normal—that is if Malagasy nuns normally drove ambulances.

It was a chance I'd have to take.

I grabbed the keys I'd found in a bureau drawer I'd jimmied open. It had taken me until 2:00 a.m. to find those keys. I knew that if they weren't in Father Soren's pocket they had to be somewhere in the mission. At midnight I'd made the definitive discovery: a battered Land Rover out back in a shed. The paint was flaking off the scarlet cross on the side door and the tires were different sizes. I prayed it was driveable and had gas.

Finding the photo really lit a fire under me. That and the arrival of three policemen. I'd turned off the lamp and spied on them through the lace curtains as they milled around the main gate under the sentinel palms, waving their torches at One-Eye. You didn't have to be a brain surgeon to get the drift; they were on a witch hunt.

I calculated—correctly—that they wouldn't come for me until dawn; not after the cannibal *kabary* I'd laid on One-eye through the trap door. Witches *own* the Malagasy night. No sane man— even a lawman—would dare challenge a witch after dark, especially a *vazaha* witch. It was my plan, hatched during the long, sleepless hours, to make a pre-dawn dash to Mananjary and ditch the truck at a hospital or a mission. Okay, G.T.A. isn't the most hospitable way for an uninvited guest to repay her host, but after seeing the padre, James, Rex and Rangita, ganged up together in that snapshot, I figured the Pope would forgive me, us being *tutti famiglia* and all.

Moving quickly, I slipped on a nurse's armband, adjusted my head covering, and ran downstairs with Maki squeaking at my ankle. One-Eye's keys were rattling in the front door the moment I set foot on the ground floor.

I froze.

Feet stomped around in the entry. Rumble of baritone voices. Then silence. Hoarse whispering. Tentative shufflings. Coughing. A joining of voices. Swelling confusion.

Hitching up my skirts, I broke left, bolting for the kitchen, shoving through the pantry and then outside, running across the hard-packed earth towards the shed. I flung open the driver's door, preparing to leap in.

There was already a nun at the wheel. She said, "*En fin, ma soeur.* What took you so long?" and put out her hand for the keys.

Rangita.

The costume was new, but the regal voice that shook the starched edge of her wimple was not. In the early morning light her high cheekbones stood out against the white cotton like unsheathed weapons. Gone was the sweet warmth of those first friendly meetings. She oozed *soberbia*. Raul had it too; a Spanish quality, meaning vanity and pride and more—a towering arrogance that cut no slack.

"Get in the back," she ordered. "On the stretcher. Lie down."

I started to argue, but... why?

Call it a character defect, but I'm easily seduced by the obvious, and Rangita obviously knew a few Vazimba tricks I didn't—like how to appear and disappear at will, and in costume. It was obvious with skills like hers she didn't need a topo to find Mananjary. I did. She knew how to find a dugout canoe and I didn't. Moreover, the Blue Rainforest was her home turf.

Nolo contendere. I lay down and pulled the shawl over my face. "Be my guide," I said.

She jammed it into first, and we rolled through the back yard and down a slope to the gate where we were accosted by One-Eye and the *gendarmes*.

"Close your eyes and play dead, Eva. If you want to live."

I did what she said. Not to be morbid, but I had gained some expertise in dying during the last week.

"Let us pass," she demanded. "Our dear sister is mortally ill. If God wills it—and you open that gate—I shall reach the hospital in time to save her."

Even with my eyes tightly shut I could sense the policemen's flashlights scoping my veil, riveted on my disguise, sussing me out right down to the tips of my stout, black nun's shoes.

Someone cranked a handle.

"*Non!* Stay back! Do not open the door. No one must touch her. She is very dangerous." Rangita's voice rasped, "*Pauvre soeur.* She is infected with... *la peste noire!*"

The Black Plague! I had to hand it to Rangita. She was inventive.

There was a nervous jostling and a lot of fast, whispered talk. One-Eye threw the bolt and the mission gate swung out onto the open road. I didn't blame him. Capturing a witch certainly wasn't worth a face-off with the one of the Four Horsemen of the Apocalypse.

I was completely unprepared for the succulent, earthy dampness in the coastal air against my cheeks as we sped along, but not for the upwelling of unanswered questions aroused by Rangita's reappearance.

Was James alive? Where was he? Was I getting closer? Could I save him? Had Rexworthy been murdered? *Hapelemur erectus*, the upright lemurs? What were they all about? How did Rakotomana and the oilmen fit in? Who were the Vazimba? So many questions...

"Sister," I said, arising from the dead and crawling into the front seat after we'd bounced through the sisal plantation for a decent interval, "What in the hell is going on?"

"Life," she said. "Going on. As always."

Maki was in my lap, hanging out the window, gulping air like a spaniel. Coconut palms flashed past, dark x'es leaning this way and that, their rustling silhouettes criss-crossed against the rising sun. The dawn was more beautiful than any sunset I'd ever seen. A golden light pounced, tigerlike, out of the east, backlighting every tiny hamlet of palm-thatched huts we passed with a shimmery aura.

"How do you do it?" I dove in, starting with the most obvious question first. "How do you... manifest, like this?"

She smiled, steering deftly around a pot-hole. "Time is a circle. We are always at its center."

"Time... We need to start at the beginning."

She interrupted sharply. "You weren't listening. There *is* no beginning."

I sighed, "Okay. Time is a circle, we're at its center. I buy that. But, so what? I can't appear and disappear whenever I want. I'm human. Solid. Visible flesh. I... don't... melt." I pinched my arm to prove it.

"Eva," she said gently, "*buying* something is not the same as *knowing* something. Buying is thinking, knowing is being. You have bought a certain idea of reality—a dream, if you will—believing it to be a time-bound thing, neatly divided into hours and days, beginnings and endings. Having bought that idea, it has become your reality. There are others."

I had a sudden vision of Rangita the whore, playfully working the Terrace bar in her leopard-skin jumpsuit adorned by an armful of broken watches, a timeless dispenser of sexual bliss. And of Rangita, the imperial queen, glowing beside the sacrificial stone.

"Are you saying," I took a deep breath to steady myself, "that because time doesn't count, matter doesn't matter?"

She chuckled. "*Precisement.*"

"Then, all life is merely an illusion..."

"It is... as you believe."

Her musical laughter filled the air, mixing with the sunny, salt-smelling wind blowing in from the Indian Ocean. We were heading directly into the rising sun. Her small hands on the wheel were strong and uncompromising. She seemed as comfortable driving a Land Rover ambulance dressed as a nun as she had been sitting on a Russian engineer's lap, flirting in a frizzy blonde wig, her full breasts spilling out of spotted spandex. We drove east into morning, the humid wind whipping our starched wimples until they beat about our ears like frantic doves. Maki dozed in the sun, curled up in the pleats of my virginal lap, his bushy black and white tail wrapped around his pointed nose.

I reached across and put my hand over Rangita's for an instant... just checking.

Yes. Her flesh and bones were as warm and firm as my own.

"So, my sister, if you can become visible, can I not become invisible?"

Her nostrils flared. "You... are human. *We* are Vazimba."

I flushed defensively and struck back. "They say the Vazimba no longer exist."

"They...?"

"One hears... rumors." I hesitated, then plunged on. "In fact,

Ambassador Theron himself told me that you... I mean, the Vazimba, have been dead for over four hundred years." I had the presence of mind to bite my tongue before I finished the rest of Theron's scathing remark, "*if* they ever existed."

"*Vazaha* fool!" she twisted her head, dismissing him with a small, spitting gesture. "Try and understand, Eva. Matter is spirit perceived in time. When your time-blinded eyes cease to see spirit in matter, you weep, and call it death. For us, death is only one of many doors, opening onto an infinitude of planes. Invisibility is one of those planes; the one you call astral."

"Rangita, where *is* James?" I blurted it out.

She frowned. Her brow and upper lip were beaded with a fine sweat.

"He's why you're hiding in armoires and stealing ambulances, isn't he? He's the reason you call me sister and send Noro to tease me and tail me everywhere. He's the reason you dropped the *ody* in the ditch, and why you gave me this..." I wrestled out the silver necklace out from the neck of my habit, brandishing the crocodile tooth at her. "Let's stop going around in circles. Forget all this wafty talk. Only one thing matters: where is James?"

"*Il est perdu...*" she whispered.

"Lost?" I grabbed her and shook her violently. "I know he's lost. But *where!?*"

She braked and the ambulance slewed to a stop in the middle of the red dirt road.

"He is lost in the invisible village," she said. "Trapped in Andrebabe, on the astral plane."

32

"Do you believe in dreams?" Rangita asked.

Dreams? She'd just dropped a bomb that my brother was lost in the ether!

"You have a dream of saving your brother," she continued. "And that is why you are here. I have a dream of saving my village. That is why I am here. Our dreams intersect in James. Have I not already sworn that I will try to help you find him?"

"Yes, but you haven't explained why..."

She turned towards me imperiously. "In return for James' life, you must swear to help me." She started the engine and the ambulance lurched forward.

I should have jumped ship or refused on the spot. Instead, I waffled. "Help you... How?"

It was more than mere curiosity and desperation that sucked me in; I had a sickening suspicion that she was telling the truth about James being... astralized. I'd already had some serious acquaintance with Malagasy rabbit holes.

"We need you..." she raised her voice over the engine noise, "to save *us*."

"Us? You mean... the Vazimba?" I shook my head in disbelief, flapping the white wings of my wimple.

"Precisely."

"You're asking me to help save an invisible village that nobody's ever seen and most people don't even believe exists?" She was barking up the wrong tree. I was no New-Age Faust, ready to tumble to her devilish schemes. "No. It's absurd. It's insane!" I dug in my heels. "I can't... I *won't*."

Rangita smiled and continued, paying no attention to my sputtering. "You have already begun. Ever since your arrival, I have been testing you, preparing you to enter our reality."

Come in, come in. You have my blessing... The innocence of that greeting, with its sly promise of friendship.

"From now on," Rangita continued smoothly, "the path narrows, the journey becomes more dangerous. If we are to succeed, we must dream the same dream, hour by hour, moment by moment. It is the only way."

"I... how do we do that?" I should have kept my mouth shut, but I'd let curiosity and desperation out of the bag and all I could do was stand back and watch them plow up the fields of reason.

"Think of it as a dance," Rangita said. "I lead, you follow."

Time out. I'd tried that gig more than once, beginning with that first night when Jack Mooresby had pulled me onto the Embassy dance floor. I'd ended up twenty-four hours later discoing off the roof of a tomb.

"I'm not a good follower," I stated flatly.

"You must learn," she said "if you hope to pierce the veil."

Pierce the veil! A flotilla of red flags shot up.

"Thanks, but I'm not into veil-piercing."

"You have no choice. If you are to find James." Rangita's mood had suddenly shifted, becoming somber and threatening. "Do not try to resist, Eva. It is your *vintana*—your destiny."

I made the mistake of meeting her eyes. A chill wind shot

through me. Her penetrating gaze saw everything—my entire life, backwards and forwards. I knew it, and she knew it. She looked through me exactly like Ratelifera, the herb seller in the Zoma Market. She pinned my soul with her knowingness the way you'd pin a moth on a mounting board. There was no dissembling, or escaping.

"You see, I cast your horoscope the moment your brother entered the Blue Rainforest. You were born under the sign of *Alakarabo*, the scorpion, with a rising moon and your sun in *Adijody*, the stone buck. You were born on Thursday morning. Venus in *Adaoro*, the bull, has meant struggles and no peace with men. Mercury in *Alamady* means you are talented but poor, Mars in *Adalo*, the water-carrier, foretold that you would be childless. Pluto passing through *Alohotsy* determined that you would lose your mother at a young age..."

"Stop, stop, stop it!" I clapped my hands over my wimpled ears. No Vazimba queen was going to X-ray *my* life, even if she did happen to hit the bull's-eye about me being an impoverished, sex-starved Scorpio orphan.

"*Malemy, malemy*," Rangita whispered. "Be gentle. Be soft." It was her turn to place a hand over mine. "After all, sister, we both want the same thing, do we not?"

Did we? I was still mulling over her proposition and she was making it sound like a done deal.

"That is why I have given you an *ody*, and this..." She jangled the tiny silver crocodiles on her matching necklace with the crocodile tooth. "To protect you."

"And Noro?" I snorted. "Is she part of your insurance plan, too?"

Rangita sighed and frowned. "The Old Ones have minds of their own. In ancient times, before the time of the Vazimba, *kokolampos* roamed the island in the company of giant lemurs, sharing the Spiny Desert with the Aepyornis and the swamps of Tsaratanana with pygmy hippos. *Kokolampos* are *mahery*—creatures of chaos. Tricksters. Able to shape-shift into any animal—or human—at will. We were able to tame a few of them, like Noro. As for the rest, they continue to inhabit the wild, untamed places, creating mischief wherever they go."

"What... sort of mischief?"

She seemed very uncomfortable at my pressing her and answered slowly, choosing her words with care. "*Kokolampos...* have been known to possess people, entering their bodies, manifesting their power through them. Enslaving them. When they become angry, they will sometimes persecute these innocents, forcing them to roll upon the ground, threatening to kill them if they don't obey."

"I'd hardly call that protection."

"*Au contraire.* It is their wildness that makes them such excellent protection—for us. As you have seen, Noro often goes before me, sowing fear and confusion, allowing me to move about, appearing and disappearing, unnoticed."

"*Succubus.*" I said it under my breath, but she heard.

She scrutinized me. "Some frightened and superstitious Christians call them that. Surely you're not one of those?"

"Who me? Never," I said defensively, thinking of Father Michael's lurid descriptions of the devil, whispered through the grilled window of the wooden confessional; words purposefully calculated to inspire celibacy and filial piety in young penitents possessed by *mahery* hormones. I'd outgrown all that Satan stuff years ago...

Or had I...? I glanced uneasily over at Queen Rangita. She didn't *look* like the devil, and yet...

We'd reached the juncture where the dirt road met the main highway. Pilgrims on the way to *Sambatra* waved and made way for our ambulance, wishing us a *tres bonjour*. We waved back, two women of God heading east on a mission of mercy.

"You must be hungry," Rangita said. She pulled a large leaf tied into a square packet with straw twine from under the seat. "Please, go ahead. Unwrap it."

I did as she suggested. Inside were four, fat rolls of rice and a small wooden bowl containing a sauce made of green leaves.

She pinched off a ball of rice, tossed a few grains over her left shoulder, then dipped it into the sauce and handed it to me. "We call it *ro*."

I hesitated, studying the rice ball with a sudden shiver of fear and trepidation, engulfed by a wave of nausea and old-fashioned superstition. This wasn't a eucharist, it was a bribe, meant to cement my compliance, sealing my fate and making me hers. Such a simple act—eating a pinch of rice. Why did it feel as if I were making a pact with the devil, sure as cutting my wrist and swearing a blood oath? *Spooks. Nothing but spooks and rumors of spooks...* Jack Mooresby wouldn't have given this devilish claptrap the time of day.

"Eat, Eva. It is good. You will not regret it." Rangita's smile was gentle, her voice soft, her glance encouraging.

Jack, Jack... I cried out for him silently. Save me from this Vazimba madness! Make it all go away. Say it's only a bad dream.

I looked at the sticky rice drenched in *ro*. It reminded me of the livid moss dripping from the Old Queen's snout as she slithered out of the depths of Lake Anosy in Tananarive. *Voici la reine de Vazimba*, the old hag had whispered in my ear. *She is here.*

The green sauce dribbled onto the skirt of my habit. I watched the spreading stain slowly bleed out into the fabric. Untamed. Unchecked. Another crazy, green spot. Out of control. *Mahery.*

Dear God. A rush of fear churned up my stomach. I wanted to bolt, to run, to grab the next *taxi-brousse* back to Tananarive. I yearned for the safety of my studio and its orderly rows of pens and brushes and T-squares neatly tucked into enameled mugs, the pad of clean white drawing paper I'd left ready in the center of my table. I wanted my San Francisco artist's life very badly just then. Lonely? Single? Sure. But, so what? At least I was the one calling the shots.

I stared glumly at the rice.

My life... Who was I kidding? My life was dull, dry, barren, puny and insignificant. I wasn't some mad-dog bohemian genius living in chaos on the creative fringe, pushing the edges of the conceptual envelope. I was a skinny spinster with a short temper who earned her living mocking-up ads for supermarkets and used car agencies. The stack of watercolors I'd proudly completed still sat mouldering on the shelf, waiting to be discovered—like me. *What* life? A life surrounded by piles of scrap, with nobody to talk to but Arlo, my cat.

I suddenly saw Rexworthy's dead, white feet sticking out from under the bedsheet. They whirled around in my head, kaleidoscoping into the outstretched arms of a dead white lemur, falling through a sky full of fire. Those two had no life. They'd never go home, lying forever where they'd fallen, alone and forgotten, far from the family tomb or the green peace of the forest floor.

Yes. I'd said it a hundred times in the past week, but this was it! Yes, I was here. And James was here too, on the other side of the veil—wherever that was. And yes, I was going to pierce it and take him home to Papa if it killed me. *Familgia!* For the love of *familgia*, a person will do many strange and terrible things. I took a deep breath, grabbed the rice cake and stuffed it into my mouth.

Rangita's eyes lit up as she watched me chew. Then she took a bite, too. "We have a saying, *When people eat from the same plate, they may no longer struggle with each other.*" She looked so delighted it almost wiped out the feeling of doom in the pit of my stomach.

...almost.

"Now you must throw some rice over your shoulder. For the ancestors."

"But, you *are* an ancestor."

"That is true," she laughed. "And now, my dear sister, so... are you."

I looked down at my hands in stark terror. They were glowing. Brilliant. Radioactive. Then, in a blink, they were gone. And so was I.

I had... *disappeared.*

33

Invisible!

The sun burned through the window of the ambulance, falling onto the sleeping ringtail lemur that a moment ago had been curled up in my lap. Now it lay panting on the bare, plastic seat cushion, like a discarded grey and white fur boa.

I reached out to move Maki and realized with horror...

...the "I" that was me could no longer reach out! I was here. But where was here?

Nowhere.

I had no hands, no arms, no legs. I was isolated in a prison of invisibility. I saw, heard and felt; I was aware, and yet... I was not. I couldn't feel the morning sun, or smell the rich, salty, ocean wind, or taste the spicy rice I had eaten mere seconds ago.

What a fool I'd been! Rangita had taken me down, big time. For the price of a promise and a rice cake I'd surrendered my will, thrown away my body and sold my soul. I hung suspended in time and space, praying for help, immobilized by fear.

Help me, Father! I beseeched. Surely You can see I'm on my knees—even though my knees have disappeared. Whatever I've done, I'll make it up to you. Get me out of this pickle and I'm yours. I'll peel potatoes in a convent till my knuckles bleed and I go blind. I'll renounce men forever. Take up a begging bowl and wander the world in a gunny-sack praising Your name. You name it, Lord, I'm yours.

Prayer cannot help you now, beamed Rangita. *You have pierced the veil.*

Pierced the what!?

Give me back my body! I screamed silently at her, teeming with rage. *I want me!*

Let go of your anger, sister, she said quietly. *It does not serve you.*

Rangita's face, framed in starched white cotton, was calm and concentrated as she downshifted the ambulance to avoid clusters of Malagasy walking along the shoulder of the highway. I had to hand it to her, for a four-hundred-year-old queen who was born before the wheel was introduced to this island, she commandeered our ambulance like a Teamster. All good cheer and *noblesse oblige*, she waved and nodded to her countrymen as we rolled past.

No!! My soul howled. *I want arms, legs, fingers! I want my flat feet and my flat chest!*

Eva, stop and reflect. You <u>are</u> you, are you not? She paused for that to sink in. *In order to manifest your body again, you must deliver yourself from anger and master your fear. Fear gone out of control is the only emotion that can deter your ability to pass back through the veil.*

Darn right I'm out of control, I shot back. *I'm a human being. I'm used to being alive.*

Did I just say that? Oh, crazy green spotted madness! Thank God Jack Mooresby wasn't here to witness this Code Blue psychodrama.

What're you smoking, Artema? I countered. Even if Jack were here, there'd be nothing for him to see except a couple of mismatched roadies—a Malagasy nun and a sunbaked lemur. The crazy green spot had taken a powder. Popped a rice ball from hell and checked out of her body into Hotel Astral.

If you resist, Eva, Rangita continued, *you will remain stuck for as long as it takes you to face your fears.*

But, I shot back, *that could take a lifetime, or longer. You're talking about an eternity of invisibility!*

She looked over at me—or rather, at the place where I used to be. *If that is your wish. It is your choice.*

Her eyes had grown enormously large. They overwhelmed her tiny face, like the eyes of a wild sphinx moth. The outer edges of the brown irises were ringed with an eerie, blueish glow. I knew then, beyond the shadow of a doubt, that she was able to see me, even though my body was no longer there, just as she'd been able to see through me, when my body was there.

Seeing isn't the right word to describe it; rather, she apprehended me with her awareness. And as she did so, weaving its way through my consciousness, I heard a ghostly keening, a heart-rending, homesick moaning, like the wind soughing through pine trees before a storm or the cries of dolphins, dying in nets.

Listen, Rangita whispered. *It is the song of the Vazimba. Be still, and listen with your inner ear to the sound of our people. Put your ear to your heart and hear our music. It is the music of the universe itself, before the birth of men, before the creation of time.*

I grew still and listened.

It wasn't really music, it was more like a rushing of raw, primordial streamings from deep in the belly of the earth. The sound you'd imagine lava, red clay, and granite would make, if stones and dirt could sing. The shushing song of the ocean that hides in the pink curve of a shell when you hold it against your ear. The song of ferns, uncurling. The sound a snake makes, shedding its skin. Or a butterfly, pumping up its wet, newborn wings. Weaving in and out in a transparent ribbon was the song of the Vazimba, the Little People. I heard them singing to me from far, far away, from the edge of time. The music was hypnotic—wordlessly beautiful—and I gave myself over to it, letting my awareness be carried like a leaf, sailing here and there in its current, allowing it to carry me back, back to the beginning.

Traveller, there is no path. The path is made by walking...

It was only then I began to comprehend the meaning of time. I understood that although it flows endlessly, like the river, its endlessness is so immense that it appears to be fixed and still. We––men and animals—move about cutting paths, like the spidery red footpaths webbing Madagascar. These paths separate and converge, meet and vanish again, succeeding to join, failing to meet, advancing, returning, tracking, re-crossing. Time flows and passes, yet is always the same. Our lives are paths exploring that passage. My journey to Madagascar was such a path, my own, personal path, winding into the bush and out of the bush, arriving from nowhere, going somewhere I could not imagine but only dream of.

The enigmatic singing softened, shifting to a low, harmonic humming, a melodious, wordless hymn. Rangita's voice insinuated itself into my musings.

Long, long ago there was a time when the Vazimba carried clay spears and were governed by powerful queens. In vain these warrior queens battled invading men. The first came from the East in long double-hulled pirogues, bearing spears of iron that easily overcame our clay weapons. Then other vazaha men arrived from the West. They carried double-barreled muskets that rained steel balls of death upon the Malagasy.

By then there were only a few Vazimba left. Yet still they pursued us, driving us deeper and deeper into the forest, capturing and enslaving whomsoever they could catch until finally we were reduced to a handful of Little People hiding in the forest, darting from tree to tree, haunted by fear, hunted like lemurs.

I was a suckling baby when Queen Ranoro, my mother, ordered our homes to be burnt. She led us to an island in the center of Lake Marovoay, the Lake of Great Crocodiles. There, in the midst of the Blue Rainforest under the shadow of Mt. Ambondrombe, we built a new village, safe from attack.

That village, Andrebabe, is our fortress; Lake Marovoay is our moat. Its waters, and all the creatures living within it, are sacred, for when Ranoro died she was buried in the lake, and with her immersion she rendered its waters and the river flowing out of it, holy. Since then, every seven years, the people come to take the mahery water for their circumcision rites. Without the blessing of this powerful Vazimba water dipped from the lake, a Malagasy boy cannot truly be called a man, and he cannot be buried in the family tomb.

Sadness clouded her face.

Until now, Andrebabe has been our refuge, and the Blue Rainforest our garden. Living undisturbed in peaceful isolation we have been able to develop great spiritual clarity and power. Within the thickets of its green walls we have explored many mysteries. We have learned how to exist on alternate planes, including the plane of invisibility—the astral plane. We have learned how to live in eternity.

Powerful and ancient as crocodiles, we patrol the River of Time, guarding the world of the Ancestors, tending the veil that divides the living from the dead, the visible from the invisible, the mortal from the immortal— —the veil you call death.

Many people—those who do not refute our existence entirely—call us sorceresses, and tremble in fear of our power, accusing us of manipulating "hery" to work magic. They are not wrong, merely ignorant. It is true, we are powerful magicians. However we are neither witches nor witch-doctors. Our magic is of a higher order. We no longer have need to carry spears and make war. We have become, instead, spiritual warriors. You, Eva, are such a warrior. If you were not, you would not have undertaken this journey to Madagascar to find your beloved brother. If you were not, you would have lost heart and wandered forever in the Cave of the Great White Worms. You would have fled from our sacrificial altar. You would have given yourself up to the authorities in Ranomafana. You would have turned back in defeat at Pere Soren's mission. But, you did none of these things. You persevered. Now you must claim the river. Have no fear, jump in and swim across. For although you do not know it, you already own its waters. Do not falter. In order to pass through the veil you must release all fear and proclaim your Vazimba power. Without it, you have no chance of saving James, or Andrebabe.

I... Eva Artema... I began. I had utterly lost my will. I was being swept away. The truth was—I see it so clearly now—the truth was

I wanted to be swept away. I was seduced, enchanted by the dream of being a spiritual warrior.

There is a dream, dreaming us...

My dream had become Rangita's dream, Rangita's dream was becoming mine. True, it went beyond reason. But where was reason now? Reason had fled. Hung out a sign: Gone fishing. So there was no reason to ask how I was going to rescue James, or how I, a solitary *vazaha,* could possibly save an invisible village. Reason did not care. Nor did I. No, I was falling, falling... disappearing, bewitched under the spell of the dream.

Je suis... une reine...Vazimba. I am... a Vazimba... queen. I am a Vazim—

Hearing me speak thus, Rangita's dark eyes flamed with a brilliant cobalt blue light. Despite the bright morning sun, an even brighter, sizzling, halogenic glow quivered around her, sealing her body in a radioactive halo.

Come home, my sister, my queen, she crooned. *You have heard our music. It is time to come home.*

The instant she said *home,* I experienced an extraordinary rush of sense-memories. The pressure of warm, red water against leathery skin. Bullrushes, bending low, lazily scratching my back. Water hyacinths, tickling my snout. Through slitted eyes I saw dark clouds and wind rise up in the west. Thunder rolled along the edge of the mountains and rain spread silver across the river where I swam. The water flowing past my thrusting tail carried in its dark warmth the memory of echoing caverns and winding, underground rivers.

I felt... I can only tell you that it was—insane imagining!— what the Old Queen must have felt when she delivered me from the darkness of the caves that drizzly night in Tananarive. I felt exactly what a crocodile would feel... if crocodiles felt.

I AM A VAZIMBA QUEEN

I printed those five words in my journal on the Pangalanes

Canal halfway to Ambohitsara, balancing my notebook on my knees as Salim pointed the slender pirogue north towards the Blue Rainforest. Reading the square, black capital letters now, almost a year later, they are most assuredly the words of a mad, mad woman. Yet at the time, I promise you, I had no doubt at all of their truth. I had surrendered my body and entered Rangita's reality; I was dreaming her dream; we were one. Call it possession if you like— I won't debate you. But try, I beg you. Try to understand. The moment I wrote those five words everything shifted. In that moment I accepted my *vintana*. I became a Vazimba queen.

Thus Rangita and I travelled east, our fates and our futures inextricably tangled. Palms, farms, villages, cattle, men, women, children, flashed past, insubstantial and unreal as shadows. My anger and fear faded into nothingness. Content with invisibility, I had no use for my body, and forgot about it entirely until we reached Mananjary.

That all changed when we turned onto a broad avenue lined with drifting pepper trees and passed a nondescript building flying a tattered flag with a red cross on it. Parked in an adjacent field was a Bell 500 helicopter with CANTEX USA stencilled on the tail. There was an empty rescue stretcher strapped underneath. Lengths of black webbing—the kind used to lash a body in place— fluttered like funereal bandages in the morning breeze.

Mooresby!!

When I saw that helicopter, my invisible heart shattered into a thousand invisible shards. I forgot the Vazimba. I forgot James. I forgot my promise to God. All I wanted to do was bury myself in Jack's strong arms.

Soon enough, sister. Rangita burst into ribald laughter.

She flashed a wide smile and pushed the left sleeve of her habit up to her elbow, shoving her arm forward into the sunshine. A brand new watch gleamed on her wrist. I saw that it was a heavy, gold Rolex. Top of the line. *Le grand montre.*

With patience, perseverance and courage, one can achieve a great deal. But, avec l'amour, ahh... When one is in love and jumps in the river, then one achieves... miracles.

If I'd had a face, it would have been blushing. As it was, I had to admit there was probably nothing I could dream up that would make Rangita blush. She had a lot more than that Rolex up her sleeve. In fact, a smart *vazaha* could probably learn quite a few tricks about love from a sister like her.

I'm ready. I said. *When do I jump?*

She didn't respond, but just kept laughing until we reached the center of town, where I found the answer drinking beer in an open-air cafe, with a boa constrictor wrapped around his shoulders.

34

Rangita's sudden appearance galvanized my cowboy. He jumped up, overturning the small table where he had been sitting, and rushed out into the crowded avenue, savagely pushing pedestrians and zebu carts aside, throwing himself across the hood of the car.

"Where is she?" he shouted.

Rangita raised her haughty Vazimba eyebrows but made no effort to stop. Jack clung to the bonnet of the ambulance. Between the sombrero and the snake, he made one heck of a hood ornament.

"Slow down, Sister! Pull over. I want to talk to you."

Rangita nosed the ambulance through the throngs of pedestrians into the shade of a pepper tree. Jack slipped down off the hood and came around to my side and opened the passenger door. Maki opened one amber eye, took a look at the snake and rocketed into the rear, chittering in terror. Rangita didn't look exactly thrilled, but she didn't cringe.

"Name's Mooresby." He looked straight through me and stuck

out his hand. "Say, snakes don't bother you, do they, Sister?"

I couldn't speak for Rangita, but snakes scare the living daylights out of me. I've had an uncontrollable fear of them ever since I was six and saw one devour a baby blue jay that fell out of a nest on the back lawn.

Not Jack. He held the boa gently just behind its head. The serpent was steel grey, but the crafty hand of some forest demon had inscribed on its sides a row of dark lozenges ringed by dazzling, blow-torch blue borders that seemed to hover in the air slightly above its skin. You could see the muscles moving under its shiny flanks in a primeval peristalsis.

"See?" Jack said quietly. "A Malagasy *do*'s nothing to fear. It's a constrictor. Got no poison, no fangs. Nothing like our rattlers back in the States. I found this one crossing the road in front of the hospital. Bunch of kids were throwing stones at it, looking to kill it."

"I do not think they were trying to kill it," Rangita said stiffly. "This snake is *fady*. Taboo. They were probably trying to drive it back into the bushes. The people believe the *do* is an ancestor. You must return it to the forest from which it came."

The snake opened its yellow eyes, too small by far in proportion to its thick body. Rangita stared at the thing for a long moment, then whispered very softly in a voice that sent chills down my invisible spine, "There will be a storm at midnight..."

Oblivious, Jack blew past her. "Look, I'm a pilot. I fly for CANTEX Oil. I flew down from Ranomafana this morning on a... you might say... errand of mercy. A British scientist died yesterday under..." He tugged his thick mustache pensively, "...in somewhat... peculiar circumstances. There was a woman with him at the time of his death. She was a close personal..." Jack's mouth twisted oddly and he put both hands up and covered his face. I thought he was going to break down and cry.

I'm right here, Mooresby, I bleeped at him miserably. *Right under your nose.* He was so close I could have been sitting in his lap. I could count every tangled eyelash and golden fleck floating in those green eyes. I didn't have a nose, but I knew what he'd smell like: hot cotton, buttered toast and leather. It was torture. Finally, a guy who wasn't a flake or a nerd, who sincerely cared about me— and where was I? Etherized. Signed on with the Astrals and the playing field had vanished, along with the player.

"My friend, Mademoiselle Artema, is wanted for questioning in connection with this man's..."

Rangita interrupted loftily. "You will excuse me, sir, but I am a woman of God. Worldly matters are of no concern to me."

Jack's handsome face flushed deep red. He clenched and unclenched his fists, cracking his knuckles. "Please, at least allow me to finish. When I landed this morning I was informed that a woman—*a vazaha*—spent last night at Father Soren's mission. I guess she caused some trouble..."

Not *nearly* enough, I thought.

"From what I can figure out, two nuns left the mission before dawn in a stolen ambulance. They say one was extremely ill, suffering from plague. Obviously, Sister, that one is not you." His voice toughened. "Who was that other nun? I've got to find her."

"Ahhh..." Sister Rangita bowed her head and crossed herself, fingering her rosary. "Our beloved sister is... gone."

"Gone? Are you telling me she's... dead?"

The look of anguish on his face nearly tore me apart.

"*Non,* she is not dead. She is... *disparu.*"

"Disappeared?" He leaned over the seat, the heels of his hands pressing into the warm plastic, "Begging your pardon, Sister. You're a legit nurse, right? People dying of plague don't just... disappear on the way to the hospital."

"*Monsieur!*" Queen Rangita exploded. Her dark face became even darker and her nostrils flared dangerously. "You insult me, and my order. And—you are wrong. In Madagascar, people disappear all the time. She was my sister, she is gone. That is all you need to know. Further speculations are of no consequence. There is nothing more to discuss. If you will excuse me, I have business in town."

She turned her enormous, blazing, blue-rimmed eyes on Jack, but I knew that I was the one she was really looking at, because her message came at me hard and fast. *Make haste to the estuary of the River Mananjary. Salim is waiting with the pirogue. The tide changes at three. You must leave no later than that or the entrance of the canal will turn into flats of mud. Find Father Soren. He knows the way.* Gathering her skirts around her, she flung open the door dramatically and jumped to the ground. *Prenez garde, Eva. To surrender to love and persevere unswervingly. That is your challenge. Adieu.* She stormed off into the sunshine, a little brown woman in a nun's habit billowing out behind her like a spinnaker.

"Not so fast, Sister," Jack growled. "I'm not finished with you."

Too late. Rangita was gone, weaving upstream through traffic, leading him away from me the way a plover feigning a broken wing leads a bobcat away from her nestlings. Jack took the bait and started after her, waving his cowboy hat above the crowds, the boa constrictor wound tightly around his right arm like a layer of extra muscles. I saw people dropping away on either side of him, wide-eyed, whispering *fady, fady*, trying to avoid the taboo reptile.

Jack! I called after him silently. *Don't go! Don't leave me!*

Salim is waiting. The tide changes at three…

Automatically, I reached over and touched my left wrist to check the time and saw—not a gold Rolex, but something infinitely more welcome—my trusty old Timex. It read: 11:43 a.m. The metal strap felt warm on my arm. In the same instant I was engulfed by a delicious rush of earthy odors—wet plaster, gasoline, over-ripe bananas, woodsmoke, salt air and clove cigarettes.

Smells! I grabbed a hunk of cloth and rubbed it against my cheek until it hurt.

Hurt! I was alive! I was back!

"Jack! Wait up! Wait for me!" I hurled myself out of the ambulance. I'd gone about twenty feet from the car when I heard a shivery *awrrrack* behind me. Maki had climbed onto the roof of the car, which was now surrounded by Malagasy, laughing and lunging at him, trying to capture him. He ran back and forth across the burning metal, anxiously calling out to me from a sea of waving, brown arms. I couldn't abandon him; maybe they ate lemurs in Mananjary. Turning my back on Jack, I raised my hands. With a mighty leap, Maki was on my shoulder, both arms curled tightly around my head, his furry elbows in my ears. I stumbled around clumsily in my stolen brogues, all tangled up in the leash.

"*Pousse-pousse, ma soeur?*"

Whirling around, I faced a panting man, dripping with perspiration. He was tiny in stature and leathery as a twist of jerky. Around his loins he had wound a flowered *lamba*. His dusty feet were bare and he was pulling a wooden rickshaw painted in garish, primary colors: Chinese blue, parrot yellow, tangerine red. He smiled broadly, "Wherever you are going, mademoiselle, there is my happy destination."

I gazed ahead down the wide, tree-lined avenue, across the milling *sambatra* crowds but there was no sign of Jack or the fleeing nun.

"Take me to the river," I said, fighting back tears.

"*Avec plaisir.*"

The *pousse-pousse* man grasped the rickshaw poles and sprinted off down a broad seafront avenue lined with peeling, two-story houses. A hot wind blew directly at us from the reefs offshore filling the air with the steady roar of breaking waves. The driver ran along the edge of the seashore into the wind. From time to time droplets of his sweat blew backwards, splattering on my cheeks. Blooming jacarandas showered us in drifts of petals like lavender snow. Pepper balls snapped under our wheels. From outside the reef, beyond the foaming surfline, came the mournful hooting of a rusted tanker, lying to leeward on a turquoise sea.

I wriggled my knapsack off underneath my habit, pulled out a rock-hard piece of bread and gnawed on it. It was the first food I'd tasted since that fateful breakfast of rice and *ro*.

So, I mused bitterly. I'd pierced the veil. Big deal and so what? I didn't have Jack. I didn't have James. I didn't have Rangita. I'd even lost track of what day it was. I was starting to slide into my usual self-pitying mode, when something up ahead brought me up short. In the middle of the road was a knot of Malagasy on their way to a circumcision. The men wore long red robes and carried green pointed sticks that had been cut from the ribs of palm fronds. Among them surged a number of young boys in red and white smocks and tasselled caps. They'd smeared white marks on their cheeks. Some of them were beating on oval, wooden shields with the sticks. Many were chanting. At the center of this hullabaloo was a man in a cowboy hat with a snake wound tightly around his neck. His face was bright red and his green eyes bulged. I watched, horrified, as he fell to his knees, scrabbling and scratching at the serpent's coils.

"Jack!!" I flew out of the rickshaw like a blue serge bat, muscling my way through spear-chuckers and the about-to-be-men. Seared by an adrenaline rush of epic proportions, I charged into their midst where Jack lay, writhing, took hold of the big boa behind its head, and squeezed and squeezed with all my strength until my own face turned scarlet.

Forget the *fady*. This was my man!

It was awesome—*I* was awesome. I'd never even dreamt about touching a snake and there I was, wrestling with a monster. If you've never fooled around with a constrictor you can't imagine how strong they are. The last thing you'd ever want is to have one of them as a necktie. For what seemed like endless minutes I stared directly into the *do's* cold, yellow eyes, watching its shiny tongue dart in and out of its mouth, squeezing and pulling, pulling and squeezing. I hung onto that snake with all my power, sending it a silent message, *Let go, and I will let you go. Let go, and I will let you go*, until—unbelievably—I felt the great beast shudder and relax its grip.

Jack rolled sideways, rubbing his neck, his breath coming in huge, gulping gasps.

I raised the boa aloft triumphantly in both hands. It lashed about, so heavy that my arms shook from the effort. The men and boys erupted in a turmoil, beating their staves upon the ground and drumming wildly. I wasn't sure if they were grateful, or about to attack.

"Artema, you crazy fool!" Jack lunged upright and tore the creature from my grasp. He hurled it to the ground, pulling a knife from a leather scabbard on his hip, ready to slit its soft, white underbelly.

"No!" I knocked him aside and knelt beside the snake, my habit widespread over it, protecting it from harm.

"Go," I whispered to it. "Go home."

The serpent raised its head off the pavement, flicking its tongue towards me, and at once slung itself towards a thicket of salt bushes in a series of majestic, sinuous moves.

"P... Please, don't everybody th... thank me all at once." I tried to joke as I stood up, but my legs had suddenly turned to rubber.

"Why the hell not?" said Jack, sweeping me into his arms, crushing my wimple, planting kisses one after the other all over my face.

I didn't swoon this time. I matched him, kiss for kiss. But I had to call it quits when he slid his hands down over my breasts. It would never do for uncircumcised boys to see a daughter of God being deflowered in broad daylight.

When the kissing stopped, the questions began. I don't know who had more of them, Jack Mooresby or me. The *pousse-pousse* man had remained steadfast in spite of the snake-wrangling and when I pulled Jack on board he took off at top speed, leaving the boys and their fathers to shake their sticks and heads at the incomprehensible vagaries of *vazha* sexual mores.

Jack leaned back and assessed me. "So, Artema," he said drily "when'd you decide to take up the veil?"

"Mmmmm... Let's just say I had a message. From the Beyond."

He laughed, "Right. And my name's Houdini. What about the ambulance? Whose bright idea was that, yours or hers?"

"Ours."

It was true. Sort of.

"Well, your buddy disappeared." He snapped his fingers. "Just like that. She high-tailed it into an open market, I had her pinned in a butcher's stall—not a chance she could escape—and... I'm not sure what happened. There was some kind of flash behind me, I turned around, and when I looked back, damned if she wasn't gone."

I made an effort to seem surprised.

"Sonofabitch. Get a little more excited, why don't you. First you disappear, then reappear, then disappear. And now your girlfriend, same trick... Then all of a sudden you come flying down the lane on cue in a rickshaw to give me last rites. What's goin—"

I tried to divert him. "Speaking of which... You *could* show a little gratitude, Mooresby."

"A simple miscalculation." He looked embarrassed and rubbed his throat, then snapped, "What d'you want from me? I made a mistake."

"Are you hurt?"

"Nah. I'm okay."

"You don't look very okay."

"Hey, I'm... scared."

"Of the snake?"

"No... "

"Cat got your tongue?"

"Of you, I guess."

"C'mon. Big guy like you scared of a little green spot?"

"It's... There's something... about you... Something I don't quite get."

I snuggled next to him in the dappled sunshine. "Good. I like being a woman of mystery."

He drew back and tipped my chin, looking directly into my eyes. "Everywhere you go, seems like you stir up trouble."

"Mmmm... I like that even better. If a woman has magic powers, why not fly?"

But he wasn't listening. He was already worrying another bone. "Who'd want to kill him is what I keep asking myself."

"Rexworthy?"

"They're calling his death 'Accidental, pending further investigation.' "

"An accident? You mean I went through that whole Escape-from-Witch-Mountain routine for nothing?"

He cupped my chin in his hands, clamping my jaw shut, speaking harshly, "Eva, you were with him. He *must* have said something before he died."

"He was incoherent. Totally incoherent."

"He was *poisoned*. Hospital confirmed it this morning. *Tangena*. Slow death courtesy of a nasty little Malagasy seed pod."

I looked at him, wide-eyed. "Who'd want to poison a crazy *vazaha* biologist?"

Who, indeed? I could think of several. Michel Rakotomana, for starters. And there were plenty of disgruntled Malagasy who weren't keen on foreigners trespassing on their ancestral turf. Zoty certainly wasn't overjoyed that Rex had returned from Spirit Mountain alive.

"By the way," I probed, "Fred and Paul didn't happen to fly down with you this morning, did they?"

I felt Jack's arm stiffen around my shoulders. "Yeah, they did. What makes you ask?"

"Just curious. I thought they were going to stick around and survey the forest in Ranomafana, that's all."

"Something came up," Jack said, pushing back my headdress. "Artema, close your eyes. Lean back. Dammit, woman. You're so beautiful..." He pulled back my hair into a twist at the nape of my neck and held onto it like a rope while he nibbled my zircon studs. "Since the first night I saw you, I wanted to eat... you... up."

...like a little crab, before dawn... together with its shell.

My body quivered, every cell hollering tear off your clothes! Swim in the river! Jump! Drown! Breathe water. Become river head to foot. But I couldn't. This was Code Blue.

Something came up...

Jack swept his arm out over the beach that stretched away for empty miles to the north and south. "Look, it's a great day. Why don't we homestead a piece of sand and continue this conversation on the horizontal?"

"Thanks, but I have a date."

"A what?! You're kidding. Who with?"

"With... Salim."

"Where's this Salim taking you? To the movies?"

"No. To Ambohitsara."

"You're going to a circumcision in that rig?"

"Naturally" I said primly, "I plan to remove my costume first."

"Driver, stop here."

The rickshaw man pulled over in the shade. Jack stepped down and held out his hand.

"Come here. Right now."

I didn't budge.

His voice was husky. "First we're going for a little stroll on the sand, then we're going to have lunch, then we're going to find a hotel with a big bed and you're going to remove that rig and we're going to lie down on that big bed together, you and I, for the rest of the afternoon and maybe even the rest of the week. Salim is not happening."

"Yes. I mean, no. I have to leave by three."

"You're not going anywhere." His face was flushed, and the hand he held out was shaking.

"Come with me to the river," I said. "I'm sure we can find something to eat there."

"Artema, *where are your ears!?* I'm telling you something. I... want... you. Get down here, now."

I saw the rim of his penis rise and push against his faded Levis.

"Oh, Jack."

"I can't help it." His voice was barely audible over the surf. "I want you. Now."

"Damn you."

"Damn *me*?"

"I... I can't. No."

He made a strange sound and tipped his head back. "Christ almighty, Artema," he roared. "Don't you get it? I love you!"

"Mooresby, stop it."

"No!" He dropped to one knee, putting his hands around my ankles, holding them hostage.

"Don't..." I choked out the words, feeling faint. "Don't do this to me now." I touched the driver on his shoulder. "Please. Please continue to the river. I have a canoe to meet."

Jack groaned.

Maki whimpered.

Jack climbed back in and I put my arms around him.

Yes.

I held him like that all the way down to the river.

Yes.

It hurt so bad, the wanting.

On the other hand, it hurt so good...

...being a queen.

35

The entrance to the Mananjary River was a flat, tidal estuary bracketed by mangrove swamps and meandering watercourses that moved slowly out to sea carrying rafts of vegetation from a greener country upstream. Along the waterfront a ramshackle flotsam of shacks slumped on the mud at the high-water mark. A piebald dog teased the rind of a custard-apple and three gulls squabbled over a heap of broken shells near a collection of dark grey dugout canoes that lay strewn at odd angles in the muck, waiting for the tide to set them free. Farther out to sea, silhouetted under a cloudless sky, baskety fishing weirs leaned seawards, expecting the incoming tide to fill them. It was midday and very hot. Things dozed. Every now and then the breeze broke the torpor, stirring a glissando of coco fronds on the palms that fringed the lagoon.

I removed the nun's habit and placed it, together with the clodhoppers and a handful of francs, on the seat of the rickshaw. "Please." I shook the rickshaw driver's calloused hand. "If you would return these to the hospital..."

He took my hand in both of his, holding me thus for a long moment—long enough that I could see, hanging from a thong around his neck, a jagged crocodile tooth set in silver filagree. His chin was frizzed with white hairs but his handshake was strong.

"Whatever your wish." He bowed his head without taking his eyes off mine.

Jack tipped back his Stetson and surveyed the somnolent scene. "This guy Salim... he didn't exactly roll out the red carpet."

"Salim?" the driver overheard. "He is just there." He pointed along the row of wooden shacks to the farthermost end. A faded yellow *lamba* hung across the doorway, flopping lazily back and forth in the steamy air, bulging and shrinking like a fat man's stomach.

I tied Maki to the rickshaw and the driver led the way, stepping carefully on boards that had been scattered on the soft mud as walkways to keep from sinking into the ooze. He held the curtain aside while I stepped over a puddle blue with washing water and struggled up the slippery slope, grateful to tuck inside the shed out of the sun's glare.

"*Ça va, Salim?*" the rickshaw man called out.

Once my eyes had adjusted to the gloom I focused on a young, bare-chested Indian in army fatigues seated at a rickety table in a corner. At his feet were several makeshift crates surrounded by piles of shredded hemp and raffia. He was spreading rock salt crystals over something long, pinkish-white and bumpy that lay across the table, dangling down onto the floor behind him.

"Monsieur Salim?" I edged forward, not sure whether to extend my hand or not.

"*Si.*" He answered without looking up, digging into a jute sack for more salt.

"My name is Eva Artema. I'm interested in hiring a pirogue to take me to..." I was going to say the Blue Rainforest, but instead simply said, "I wish to go to Ambohitsara."

Salim raised his eyebrows and kept packing on the salt. The thatched roof rattled slightly. The wind curling through the loose slats was cool on my damp skin. From somewhere out back a propane generator spat and rumbled. Behind the counter next to a large cooler advertising Three Horse Beer sat a woman swaddled in a threadbare sari, the head of a nursing baby just visible in her fleshy armpit.

Jack pulled back the curtain and stepped inside, "C'mon Artema. Joke's over," he said curtly. "Let's get out of here."

"First, there is the question of petrol." Salim spoke to me while appraising Jack carefully. His French was clipped and heavily accented. "The Pangalanes Canal is wild country. There is no place to refuel, none at all."

"Refuel? I had expected... She... They mentioned a dugout canoe."

Salim leaned back and laughed soundlessly, revealing a mouthful of gold teeth. The butt of a pistol stuck out of the waistband of his fatigues. He slammed his chair back down on the packed earth. "Ambohitsara is 65 kilometers north. I presume you do not expect me to spend a week paddling, do you mademoiselle?"

"Just you lis—" Jack moved on him.

I quickly blocked his way. "No. Let me. If it's a question of money I'm quite prepared..."

I accidentally stumbled into a pile of raffia. It broke apart, scattering the contents across the dirt floor of the shack. They were birds—dead birds. All kinds of tropical specimens; red, white, black, yellow, blue, orange, in every conceivable colorful configuration. Their wings were trussed closely against their bodies, their wrinkled eyelids pinched shut, their clawed feet drawn up tightly underneath their feathered chests.

"I'm terribly sorry..." As I knelt down at the foot of the table and began picking them up, I happened to glance sideways into an open crate to my left. My heart stopped. For a minute I thought I was going to black out. Down at the very bottom was a wicker cage. Crouched listlessly inside was a pair of baby lemurs, rare white *sifakas* exactly like the ones Rasti had pointed out in Tzimbazaza Zoo. They looked dazed and uttered no sound when they saw me. Their eyes were dull, their pink tongues lolled out of their delicate black muzzles. A single, slender hand extended through the cage, palm up, unmoving.

I dropped the body of a white bird with a red beak onto a heap of raffia and tried to stand, reaching for one of the table legs to steady myself. In so doing I got a closer look at the other side of the long, bumpy object Salim was salting. It was an enormous, thick-scaled crocodile skin, at least eighteen feet long—the size of the Old Queen.

I lurched to my feet, my voice shaking as I pointed at it. "*Interdit!*"

Salim stood up and faced me. The handle of his gun shone bright black in the semi-darkness of the shack.

I stood my ground. "It is my understanding that the killing of crocodiles, like smuggling, is outlawed in Madagascar."

"Artema, what's got into you?" Jack barged in. "This is Malagasy business. Leave the guy alone."

Salim pulled out his pistol, slowly sighted down the barrel, then jammed it back into his trousers again. "In Tananarive, they make laws for Tananarive. On the Pangalanes, Salim makes the laws." He kicked the largest crate aside and strode past me outside into the sun.

I looked down. On the exposed underside of the box was stamped: Herr Jurgen Grindler, 151 Obergammen-strasse, Frankfurt 905BHP, Allemagne. That wasn't all. Stencilled in larger, bold letters were the words:

CANTEX INTL. MECH. DIV. 235B

NYSTAT HYDROSEALS. THIS SIDE UP.

Dead birds. Dead crocs. Dead Rex. Dead... James.

I grabbed the edge of the crocodile skin and jerked it off the table. How many bullets had Salim pumped into this queen before she finally died? I dragged it across the earthen floor, spraying a sparking white trail of salt crystals across the red dirt behind me.

Jack caught me at the doorway. "Eva! For chrissakes! Have you lost your mind?"

"I hope so."

I hauled the skin out into the sun where Salim stood and dumped it at his feet. A wind had come up, ruffling the brownish waters of the lagoon, carrying the faint sound of the white reefs offshore.

He turned around and looked down. Only a slight lifting of his chin betrayed any emotion. After a long silence, he said, "You will go alone, without your friend?"

"I will go alone."

"It will cost you 150,000 francs."

"I will pay."

"I cannot guarantee the petrol."

"Take paddles."

"Nor can I guaranteed your return."

"I'm hiring a boat, not a magician."

He tossed his head back and laughed soundlessly.

"Understand," I added, "if I had a choice, I would have nothing to do with you."

He put his hand on his gun and began to draw it out.

Beware the ferryman at the river's edge, he is not what he seems...

Jack came up behind me and grabbed my shoulders, turning me to face him.

"Eva, honey. Let's stop this kidding around." He opened his arms wide. The hot wind filled the air with his scent: toast, leather and hot cotton.

I shook my head. "No. Not honey. No time for honey."

"Please, baby," Jack pleaded. "Stay with me."

I swung my head from side to side, desperately fighting the desire to go to him, feeling that old kundalini energy surging up my spine, pressing on my forehead and behind my eyes, beating in my chest. I almost capitulated—I think I would have—had not my ears, my entire being, become filled with a soft, oceanic roaring, and from far away, like winds blowing from somewhere deep in my soul, I heard the thin, keening voices of the Vazimba, calling me home.

Jack took a step forward, lowering his voice to an urgent whisper. "You've done enough. Give up this bullshit quest. Nobody in their right mind would consider going into the Blue Rainforest alone, defenseless." He crept closer. "Hell, you've got no tent, food, clothes, *panga... nada.* Your brother's fine, I promise you. He's an experienced scientist. A pro. Wherever he is, I know he's doing okay. Guaranteed. C'mon now," he begged, reaching out for me.

I took a step backwards. "What are Paul and Fred doing here?"

"I told you, business." He extended his hand.

"What kind of business?" I stepped sideways, avoiding the salted skin.

"Upstream business." He closed in. "Artema, come off it. Come back to Mananjary with me."

I raised the flattened, eyeless croc snout from the mud with the toe of my tennis shoe and aimed it at him. "*Ciao*, Jack."

"Eva!"

"*Arrivederci.*"

"You can't leave like this!"

"Let's just say... something came up." I turned and bolted down the riverbank towards the line-up of waiting *pirogues*.

"Fuck!!" he yelled at the top of his lungs.

"I love you too," I yelled back. But I don't think he heard me, he was so pissed.

3b

Salim's *pirogue* turned out to be a blue fiberglass speedboat with a Johnson-25 outboard clamped to the stern. On a changing tide, a gang of children pushed us off into the flowing current and we were under way.

It was not a jolly farewell. Jack stood on the bank with Maki on his shoulder, one hand flung over his eyes against the sun in an awkward salute. Our final embrace was a full-court press that left us both shaking.

"You're sure I can't change your mind?" He'd grasped my hips with both hands and pulled my belly against him.

"No. Do you hate me?"

He buried his face in my hair. "For going, yes."

"I'll be okay. Promise."

"Hey, so... I guess... I'll be... seeing you around sometime."

I pulled back and took a deep breath, looking him straight in the eye. "Mooresby, you better not be lying to me."

"What're you talking?"

"You heard. Just what I said. Whatever's going on down here, you better not be mixed up in it."

He sniffed and twisted his mustache, straightened his hat, then pushed me away. "*Ciao*, kid."

It was a rotten goodbye, but I had an agenda.

Salim piloted the boat standing up with the tiller between his knees, like a bare-chested Rambo in a bad Indian film. We sputtered noisily north along the Pangalanes Canal. I opened my knapsack, peeled the last banana, rooting around for the packet of James' letters. At last I found the one I wanted, unfolded it, and began to read.

"The canal was built by French colonial engineers who linked together a placid series of freshwater lakes to create a commercially viable waterway. It's a man-made natural wonder, paralleling the entire eastern seacoast of Madagascar straight as an arrow for 650 miles, a fresh-water highway separated from the sea by nothing more than a narrow, sandy berm and mangrove swamps. Nobody ventures out into the Indian Ocean down there, not even fishermen, as the coast is infested with sharks, some so bold they even chase people all the way up onto the dry sand, snapping and biting."

There was a bruise-like smudge where he had broken off the sentence, leaving the aching trace of a fingerprint. I rubbed my own finger over it gently. One thing I've learned is that if you ever lose somebody, the most precious part of them that remains is their handwriting. Every ink blot and erasure draws them closer to you.

"In recent years the maintenance of the canal has been badly neglected and it has become choked with vegetation. In many places the sea has broken through the fragile dikes and the resulting contamination by salt water has devastated the freshwater game fish. The scuttlebutt here in Tana has it that a Dutch corporation that's been trying to restore the canal by

means of a massive dredging effort is having the devil's own time making headway. Like most high-tech projects undertaken here in Mad, it's probably doomed—difficulties in obtaining permits, costly bribes, local resistance, lack of amenities and replacement parts, malaria, cyclones—the usual hazo and tazo of trying to do business in the S.E. I don't give them long before they pack it in and return to Rotterdam with their slide-rules tucked between their legs. Myself, I much prefer to operate solo. It's easier to slip between the cracks and get lost in the field..."

My chest tightened. Slip between the cracks... lost in the field... Fateful irony!

"The failure of the Dutch may well be a blessing in disguise—certainly the wildlife will profit from an undisturbed habitat. Birds are particularly abundant in the sloughs, and it's said that Zaohitra Reserve (the locals call it the Blue Rainforest) is one of the few protected areas on the island where you can still find crocodilus niloticus. Thank God for the Reserves. If it weren't for them, half Mad's animals might already be extinct. Not so many years ago wild game was plentiful. I remember reading a report written in 1825 describing one of King Radama's successful hunting trips. It records that in 13 days of hunting they bagged 3063 wild cattle, 2235 wild fowl, 63 boars, 326 large amphibious turtles, 5 baskets of fish, 183 eels, 11 burrowing tenrecs, 7 tenrecs that do not burrow, 43 lemurs and 13 crocodiles!

"Island-wide, by now the crocs have been pretty well wiped out, slaughtered for meat or skins. Despite the embargo a good skin still fetches a depressingly high price on the black market. Legends about these big guys abound down in the Pangalanes, wild poetical fabrications about mythical twenty-foot monsters with eyes like torches. Seems like they're connected somehow to obscure circumcision rites and a sacred lake. The Malagasy are great spinners of yarns. They're nuts about folktales and old stories. 'Kabary mba?' they ask when they meet you. 'What news?' To which one ritually responds 'Tsy kabary', no new stories."

Kabary mba... I glowered at the well-oiled pistol Salim kept stashed in his waist, wondering what kind of grim stories it could tell.

He and I were the lone voyagers on the canal. The surface of the water was smooth and glassy, the color of a frog's back. The banks on either side were thick with bulrushes and an occasional stand of mangroves. Once or twice I saw a group of rectangular, palm-thatched huts on stilts huddled together in the hazy distance, but after that I saw no further signs of human habitation. The drone of the engine, the undisturbed sky, the beating sun all conspired to create a cocoon of melancholy languor within which I curled, clinging tightly to the sheet of lined, yellow paper, unwilling to let go of my brother... a brother whom I didn't really know.

Bibi, my darling...

Despite all the clues to his character, I had completely missed a vital, secret part of James' life. I studied the letter in my hand, his neat, scholarly cursive with its funny triangular loops going backwards underneath the g's and y's. It was so quintessentially James. The way the pen hit the paper, the controlled angle of the down-stroke, the precise peppering of dots over the i's, the even-handed crossings of the t's. Careful, shy James. All of him was there, present in his handwriting... all except passion.

I pressed the ruled paper over my knee, studying it the way an astronomer studies a satellite map of Mars, looking for signs of esoteric life. Where was Curtis Rexworthy hiding among the marching curlicues, in the forest of hoops and dashes? How had I missed the living clues, so central and so tender, to the geography of James' heart?

I trailed my hand over the side, letting the fluid contours of the murky riffles ease over my fingers, contemplating the murkiness of my own, unfulfilled love life. Take *famiglia* for instance... Oh, I talk great *famiglia*. But, I had to ask myself, how long had it been since I'd honestly participated in family love? A very long time—ever since Mama's death. After that it had just seemed easier to ignore Papa and the boys. Popi and Hermina had tried to get in touch with me, but I never returned their calls, except on Christmas. Grandfather Edwin kept sending me articles from scholarly journals filled with his cryptic marginalia, but I'd never bothered to answer him, either.

The green water slid over my skin, rippling around my fingers. I'd had a lifetime of opportunities to connect with my family, to respond and to share, and except for my intermittent correspondence with James, I'd retreated into a testy solitude. Small wonder I'd been a slam dunk for Rangita. From the very moment she breezed into my hotel room with that warm, knowing smile, accepting me, blessing me, putting my hand on her breast, calling me "sister", I was a goner. She was real. Open, unafraid, loving. I would have followed her anywhere.

Would have? I *had*.

I splashed my sunburned face with cool river. Hold everything. What about sex? Sex counted as love, didn't it? What about those cartwheels with Raul Pedregoza? Were they love? Whatever they'd been, the moment he left I'd folded, barricading myself behind piles of arty scrap and artful excuses. Then—surprise!—after a four-year estivation, out of the dry riverbed hops a frog prince named Mooresby. A little rough around the edges, but overall a righteous piece of work. A sincere possible, in spite of some overweening macho tendencies and some suspiciously shady CANTEX connections. Time to celebrate! And what had I done? I'd cut him off at the pass, dumping him on a muddy riverbank. What did that make me? A sexy, spiritual warrior, or a scared, stupid wimp?

I slapped the water angrily with the flat of my palm.

When it came to real, honest-to-God love, the frightening, whole-hog, mystery of love—I had to confess, it had completely escaped me. I'd been so busy trying to get love and keep love, that I'd never learned the most important thing: how to surrender to love. The only thing I knew for sure about love was how to push it away. Rangita had thrown down the glove in no uncertain terms: If I wanted to experience real love I had to persevere unswervingly and surrender. I had to bust loose and jump in the river.

Squinting back over our wake, I wondered: was I too late?

Had I missed the Love Boat forever? Maybe there was still time to go back to Mananjary, find Mooresby, and lie down on that big bed. On a reflex, I looked down at my wrist.

My Timex was gone. In its place, big, brilliant, golden as a new-laid goose egg, flashed a fat, fancy Rolex—Rangita's Rolex! The Big One. The prize of love. On *my* wrist.

I looked closer. There were no hands on the watch, or numerals. The face was as blank as the face of the moon. Of course! If time is a circle and we're always at its center, who needs hands? I let out a wild, wanton, war whoop, thrusting my fist into the warm wind. "Rangita, you mad-magician-mama! You time-blinded, crocodile-queen! I l-o-o-o-ve you..."

"Sala-a-m..aaa...." A faint cry echoed from the far bank. Across the canal, mired in a clump of mangrove roots, lay a beamy, wooden boat filled to the gunwales with Malagasy. "Sala-a-m..."

Salim stiffened and threw the throttle wide open. As we shot past I saw a white man on his hands and knees in the stern, tinkering with the engine. I couldn't make out his face, but his collar carved a snowy crescent against his red neck and a crucifix shone on his portly, black-robed chest. Motor parts were strewn on the deck around him like the innards of a sooth-sayer's chicken.

"Who's that?"

"Pere Soren, the Jesuit." He made it sound like a curse.

"Soren!? Turn back!"

"We cannot, if you wish to reach Ambohitsara before dark."

"Their engine's broken. They need help."

"Mademoiselle, I am the captain." Salim fixated on the canal.

"Monsieur, I am the client." I fixated on the overloaded ark, fast fading downstream.

Find Father Soren. He knows the way...

As far as I could see in every direction was nothing but sloughs, bulrushes, mangroves, and mud—a trackless, watery, tropical tundra. Reaching into the neck of my shirt, I pulled out the jagged croc tooth and bit its ivory tip in frustration. Instantly, a vision arose of the snapshot I'd found in the mission library. There was Curtis Rexworthy, his arm draped around James, Pere Soren's beefy, red face over his shoulder. Michel Rakotomana lurked in the background. I saw something else, something I'd missed the first time around. There was treachery afoot in that photo, and Father Soren was a part of it. I saw Rangita's words again, too, inked across a corner of the sky.

Courage. Andrebabe.

Blowing softly on the tooth, I let it drop back between my breasts. It was time to fish or cut bait. To walk the walk. I inched back slowly until I was crouched quite near Salim, who stood at the helm, scouring the canal ahead for snags and clots of vegetation. When I sprang up and snatched the pistol out of his waistband I caught him totally off-guard.

I cocked the hammer and levelled it directly at his naked stomach. "Captain, I order you. Turn this boat around. Now."

In a perfect world you could argue that fire power is a weak sister to spiritual power, but this was the Pangalanes, time was fleeting, and I lacked Rangita's bag of astral tricks to get my point across.

Salim got the message. He cut an angry arc and we flew back down the canal. I toyed momentarily with the idea of throwing the gun over the side, but it didn't seem queenly, deep-sixing a guy's *raison d'être* like that. It had served its purpose. And besides, real courage doesn't live in the barrel of a gun. As he cut the motor and we glided alongside the larger boat, I ceremoniously handed the pistol back to him.

"*Merci*, Salim" I told him.

He re-holstered the weapon, giving me a strange, stunned look.

Had I made a fatal miscalculation?

If so, it was too late to do anything about it now.

37

The afternoon faded as Salim and Father Soren did their best to revive the engine. The sun dropped lower and lower and finally got all tangled up in the mangrove roots on the western bank where we were moored. By the time the serpentine shadows had blended in a solid shawl of darkness, they gave up and chained the two boats together. It seemed like a hopelessly ambitious undertaking to try to tow this Kon-Tiki to Ambohitsara behind our lightweight, plastic bath toy. A 25-horsepower motor wasn't much of a match for a half-ton barge loaded with twenty-nine adults, eleven children, seven chickens, two goats and one overweight priest.

"*Moramora.*" Salim shrugged.

"*Oui, oui. Moramora, moramora, moramora,*" amended Father Soren, leaning over the side of the ark and passing his hand over Salim in a dishearteningly vague benediction.

Salim ripped the starter cord, the Johnson kicked over in a bilious display of stinking blue smoke, the chain slammed taut, and we were underway. The ark's passengers raised a few cheers while Josef, a young student who had been serenading us all afternoon with Malagasy love songs, frantically strummed his guitar.

Salim stood alone at the helm of the small speedboat, silhouetted in the dying light. If he harbored any resentment about being pushed around by a *vazaha*, he hadn't expressed it. Perhaps he simply accepted the enforced delay as his *vintana*. Kismet is a powerful force in Madagascar. Everybody knows Fate and the ancestors have stacked the deck. Einstein contended that God never loads the dice, but he'd never been to Madagascar. On this island it's just the opposite, I thought. Here, God's dice are always loaded. You can spend a lifetime trying to second-guess and appease the mysterious workings of a far-off deity, fruitlessly fending off the fateful   reverberations of your astrologically ordained destiny, but sooner or later, *vintana* will take you down.

Sunset segued into dusk. Venus appeared on the wrong edge of the sky and the rest of the stars started coming out, one by one, upside down and backwards, the way they do under the equator. Salim navigated carefully, guided only by the confetti flickerings of starshine on the dark water. After an afternoon of polite cross-examination, I was no longer a novelty. My fellow travellers had drifted away, content to chatter among themselves or to lean against sacks of rice and manioc as the night closed in, smoking and staring silently at the featureless banks of the ever-widening canal. At my elbow, a baby snored, hidden in the folds of a *lamba*. It was time to beard my *vintana*.

I moved across the deck and sat next to Father Soren. "I'm curious about Ambohitsara. I suppose you've been there many times?"

He made a place for me next to him. "No, I wouldn't say many. Perhaps three times in the last thirty years. It is a very small, very isolated village, not the sort of place one would expect a young and beautiful woman to choose for her vacation." He leered at me myopically. The thick, square lenses of his glasses reflected the deepening amethyst of dusk, reminding me of the clerestory windows in the domed library at his mission, and for a brief second I felt an urge to confess the stolen ambulance. His cassock rustled as he scooted closer. I smelled stale cigarettes, hair tonic and his sour breath as he whispered, "I don't suppose you'd have any whiskey on you, mademoiselle?"

"My name is Artema. Eva Artema." I took a long time fumbling in my pack in order for that to sink in. Then I added, "No. But I have some rum."

The priest's lower lip drooped on the right side as if he'd had a slight stroke, resulting in a peculiar, thrushy lisp. "Artema," he said, rapping his fingers nervously along the wooden gunwales. "Not a common name."

He seemed at a loss, and I felt a surge of power.

"My brother, James Artema, is not a common man." Why not cut to the chase? *Moramora* was for Malagasy, who had centuries to work out their destiny; I wanted to find James *now.*

I opened the bottle and handed it to him. He took a long swig, and then another, wiping his thick, unruly lip before speaking. "He always said you'd come." He said it so matter-of-factly I wasn't sure I heard him correctly. "He loves you, you know." Then he drank again and passed the bottle to me. It was firey, but it couldn't hold a candle to the blaze of joy he'd just lit in my heart with those five words.

I hunched closer. "Father, please, tell me about him. I want to understand."

Pere Soren fingered the crucifix suspended from his neck. "There is nothing to understand. He lost God."

It was my turn to drink.

"This isn't the first time it has happened to a *vazaha* on this island." He reached for the bottle again. "You see, when a man loses God, God turns away from him and his soul dries up, like a river-bed shrunken from drought. Cracks begin to appear, and before he notices, through one of them slips the devil." He paused and lit a cigarette. The match hissed as it struck the water below, momentarily extinguishing a star. "When a man loses God, he seems to have knowledge, but does not know. He seems to have memory, but does not remember. He bathes, but still he smells. He swims, and yet is never clean."

"Excuse me, Father, but I must ask, are you referring... I assume..." There was no way I could begin sensibly. Why try? "You knew about his friend... Curtis Rexworthy?"

"*Bien sur,*" he said, "I was his confessor." He brought his sweaty face next to mine, blowing hot rum across my cheek like an alcoholic blowtorch. "They were inseparable, *le deux, comme ci...*" He crossed his fingers and tapped the end of my nose with them. "*Lamban' akohs ka faty no isarahana...* Like the hen and its feathers, *that only death can separate.*"

Only death... I opened my mouth and closed it again. Oh, Father, if only you knew. How could I begin to describe those thin, white feet sticking out from under the sheet in that claustrophobic hotel room in Ranomafana?

"In the end, even Curtis could not dissuade him..." Pere Soren's lisp had become so pronounced I had to struggle to grab hold of each word. I knew I had to move quickly before I lost him to the rum.

"The devil... Father, you mentioned a devil."

"*Lemurs diaboliques.*" He spat the words. "Your brother became obsessed with finding these man-sized lemurs. When I last saw him, he was trying to convince Curtis to track them over Mt. Ambondrombe, into the Blue Rainforest." He paused, breathing heavily, and crossed himself vigorously several times. "I tried to warn him there would be trouble..." He stopped and took a deep drag on his cigarette.

"What sort of trouble?" I wasn't about to let him off the hook.

"*...kanefa tsy mihevitra ny fandrika, ary tsy matao-toraka...*"

"I'm sorry," I said irritably. "I'm not familiar with Malagasy proverbs."

"*He who is powerful gives no thought to the snare, and is not afraid of being stoned. He does not care, for he dies eating what he loves.*" He slurred the words, lurching towards me. "What's the most powerful and evil animal in Madagascar, that eats everything, that lives forever, growing larger and larger, feasting on weaker creatures, including men?"

Evil? A great heat rushed up and burned in my face. "I assume you are speaking of the crocodile."

"*Precisement.* Only something more powerful than that could cause a Christian to forget the Lord."

Every muscle in my body tensed as I waited for him to continue.

"That something is... the devil," he continued. "On this island the devil takes many forms; one of them is obsession, another is possession. It makes no difference; whatever guise he chooses, the prize is always the same... a human soul." He put his heavy, fat hand on my left arm, his fingers encircling my wrist, covering Rangita's faceless, timeless prize—her gift of love.

I felt sick and dizzy. I closed my eyes. Warm green water rushed past armored flanks, lightning flashed magenta and silver against banked clouds, and smoke... far off in the distance, I sniffed smoke... Possession... obsession... Lord God, James wasn't the only *vazaha* who'd lost it out here. Who owned *my* soul?

"The lemurs became James' *sampy.* That was his sin."

"*Sampy?*"

"Idols. Graven images. Until we brought Christ's Light to Madagascar, people worshiped the twelve *sampy.* They were kept in a box in the Queen's palace and brought out once a year to fill the heathens with enough terror to last another year. During Ranavalona's reign, thousands of newly baptized Christians were crucified in the name of these diabolical *sampy.* When the queen died, the terrible box was taken down and opened and do you know what was inside?" He loomed over me, blocking out the stars. "Nothing! Sticks. A bundle of plain, wooden sticks, wrapped in pieces of silk and smeared with castor oil." He flipped his cigarette into the canal. "As useless as an *ombiasa's ody.*"

Useless? My magic *ody*? I stretched my foot out, surreptitiously touching the edge of my knapsack with my toe, recalling the childish excitement I had felt when James' razor blade had sliced through the cecropia moth's cocoon, followed by my agonized tears when its brown, silken sides fell apart on his workbench in the closet, revealing the shocking, terrifying nothingness within. *Ody,* I thought, you wretched little bunch of heathen twigs, I won't abandon you now.

"Your brother idolized these mysterious lemurs," Pere Soren continued. "What did it matter if nobody else believed in their existence? He did. They were all that mattered to him. In the end, they meant more to him than God Himself."

I flared up. "Why is it that the Church has always found it necessary to turn pagan gods and ancient animals into devils and fiends?"

"*Les âmes,*" Father Soren's lisp turned nasty, making the sound of angry hornets as he wrapped his drooping lip around the words. "The Church exists for one reason—to win the battle for souls."

A heat flash raced up and down my entire body. That was it! That was exactly why *I* was here. To save souls. Mine, James', and the Vazimba's.

She who loses her life shall find it...

"Do you know where is he now?" I asked, wondering how the Church would cope with the news of James' recent astralization—organize an exorcism on Spirit Mountain?

"Gone," he said bitterly. "Gone to the Blue Rainforest, following the trail of his beloved *sampy.*"

"What if I told you I'm going there to find him."

"You..." The priest began to laugh—a raspy, nasal snort ending in a series of nicotine croakings. "Well, you will not be alone, my daughter."

"What do you mean?"

"There's one other man besides James who believes in *Hapelemur erectus.* He has tried, but he's never been able to capture a single specimen."

I waited, expecting him to say Curtis Rexworthy.

"His name is Michel Rakotomana." He pulled me across the seat next to him and whispered in a rummy voice. "*He* is a *voay.*

When God made this man, he bent down very, very low. But make no mistake: he gave him great power. Zaohitra Reserve is his private fiefdom, to do with as he wishes..."

"I fear no animal," I said fiercely. "Man or crocodile."

Father Soren cackled and lit another clove cigarette, striking the match on the rough metal edge of his crucifix. The orange flame lit up his doughy features like a Halloween mask. "Good," he said, exhaling a stream of smoke. "No doubt there will be many of them lying in wait for you between Ambohitsara and your destination."

It was my turn to laugh. "Well and good," I said. "They can have my body, but not one of them can touch my soul. Not even God."

He glared at me, shocked. "How can you be so sure of that?"

"Because..." I leaned over and confided directly into his ear, "Because I've already sold my soul... to the Vazimba."

Just then there was a shattering thump and a horrible scream. A splash, followed by dead silence. We ran forward, stumbling over chickens and sleeping children, and peered over the side into the black, marbled waters below. Impaled on the bow of our gigantic pirogue, was the blue fiberglass speedboat. It had been split completely in two. Apparently the greater weight of our towed craft had caused it to gain momentum, going unnoticed in the darkness when we suddenly overtook the little tugboat, ramming into it and destroying it instantly.

"Salim! Salim!! *Salaam*, Salim!" we shouted, listening for an answer. None came, only the sound of the water lapping against the hull of the torn plastic boat.

"Zsaleeeem..." Father Soren's lisp echoed into the dark night. "Zsalee..e..e..m..."

Platt... platt... platt...

We were adrift, lost on the Pangalanes Canal with nothing but some upside-down stars to show us the way to Ambohitsara.

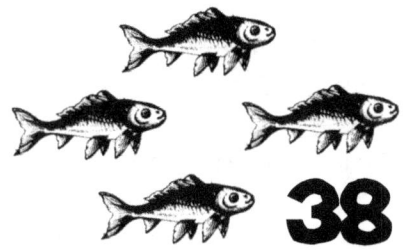

38

We floated for many hours, calling for Salim. No one had thought to bring a lantern so we had to make do with my flashlight. I swept it back and forth over the licorice waters, searching for signs of life, or a body. Our nautical disaster had thrown the passengers into a fearful, blue funk. It was obvious they were blaming Salim's grisly *vintana* upon the unwelcome presence of a *vazaha*. Pere Soren delivered a final, inebriated unction in mangled Malagasy and Latin while leaning over the gunwales. After that, we simply drifted. Back in the stern, the *sambatra* travelers huddled together, muttering darkly among themselves as the immense starry dome of heaven wheeled silently overhead. Hidden nightbirds trilled from the bulrushes, and every now and then a fish would jump, hitting the water with an unnerving, unexpected splash.

Josef, the musician, sidled along the rail next to me.

"We can't stay here all nigh—" I began.

"Shhhhh..." he put a finger to his lips. "I've come to warn you. We are passing the Place-Where-The-Fish-Jump. You must stay very still and say nothing. It is taboo to speak. If a fish should jump into the boat, do not move or call out. But most of all, whatever happens, *do not look into its eyes.*"

"Its eyes...?"

He put his finger against my lips, pointing over at the priest who was intently mumbling his rosary. "*Kokolampo*," he murmured. "This is their place."

Here? In this flooded wilderness?

He fidgeted and looked around anxiously. "They live at the bottom of the river, with their wives and villages and water cattle. Sometimes their white shapes can be seen under the surface."

I stared out across the trackless slough. A night breeze arose and roughened the surface until it resembled a freshly plowed field studded with clods of mica starlight.

"The people are saying the *kokolampo* have taken Salim." He paused. "They say he's not the first one." Josef was trembling. His bare feet shuffled nervously against the wooden deck. "Please, say nothing to the priest. It will only make him angry."

There was a low grumbling far off in the northeast, followed by a flash of sheet lightning. "Tell them we must try and paddle to shore," I whispered urgently. "We could be swamped in a big storm."

"You cannot tell them anything. If you could only understand their fear..."

Fear? I know all *about* fear, I wanted to scream at him. This canal is a cake-walk compared to the underground caves.

Another flash of lightning illuminated my companions. They were packed together, wrapped in their toga-like *lambas* in a terrorized, Biblical frieze. The wind picked up, and a driving chill blew at us off the top of the canal. I hugged my jacket around me, buttoning it at the neck, and heard the metallic chink of the filagree crocodiles on my necklace. A strange warmth hovered under my shirt where the tooth lay, directly above my heart.

"I will speak to them," I announced boldly. "A *kabary*. Will you translate?"

He shook his head emphatically: No.

"We'll need rum, and silver." I pressed on. "And music."

I was looking forward to this *kabary*...

"You will play, I will sing. Then they will listen."

...in fact, I relished the idea of it.

"I do not believe it will work, mademoiselle. They say that it is their *vintana* to die here, like Salim. And they fear that the spirits of their uncircumcised boys will be forced to wander eternally, forbidden a proper burial in the family tomb."

Souls again. More lost, doomed souls!

"For that we need a great deal of rum," I ordered. I grabbed my half-empty flask and dug into my jeans for some Malagasy coins. "Go to them quickly, before it rains."

"What about... the priest?" He glanced over his shoulder in trepidation.

"He has ears. He can listen."

Josef scurried back to the stern and there was a lot of stirring and muffled whispering, then silence.

Undaunted, I clambered over bags and freight as another wave of lightning lit up the sky and took up a position on top of a rice sack. I flung the coins into the water and poured the remainder of the rum in after them.

"Peace and blessings, honored mothers and fathers of Madagascar, and your sons, strong as bulls, who are soon to be celebrated as men before God and the Ancestors..."

"...*Andriamanitra sy ny razana*..." Josef finished translating.

"Blasphemer!" Father Soren roared drunkenly, attacking me from behind, pushing me forcibly aside, knocking me off my feet, throwing me down onto my pack in the sloshing bilge.

"Do not listen to this woman! She is not fit to say the holy name Andriamanitra." He straddled me, roaring incoherently as the rising wind ballooned the skirt of his black cassock. "*Mpamosavy*! Soulless witch!" He raised his crucifix against the night sky. "You and your brother... both of you, godless sinners!"

It was the third time I'd been cursed as a witch; first by a beggar, then by old One-Eye, and now by a rabid priest. *Basta!* A witch, was I? So be it. Time to call in the troops. I poked my hand into the top flap of my knapsack and felt around for the *ody*. The instant the tips of my fingers touched the bristles, I felt charged by a powerful vibration and I heard something pattering against the side of the wooden dugout.

Oh no, I thought, not rain. Not now.

The pattering continued and I raised myself up over the transom to see... hundreds of miniature silver fish flying through the windy darkness. Schools of them whirled through the night air like snowflakes in a child's globe. It was operatic, apocalyptic, angelically beautiful. The pint-sized *pescaditos* were everywhere, dive-bombing the priest, crash-landing on the cargo sacks, flopping around on the deck like thrown coins that had sprouted pairs of tiny silver wings.

"Frogs, pestilence, murrain..." Father Soren staggered across the deck, waving his arms, trying to defend himself from the piscene armada. Most bizarre, however, was the response of the Malagasy. Uniformly, they made no sound; not a peep. They crouched in a lump at the stern, with their *lambas* pulled over their faces, hiding their eyes.

That left Father Soren and me.

I stood up against him, facing into the wind. One side of the sky was filled with stars, the other with racing clouds—a shifting, celestial battleground with thunder drumming a wild tattoo between the two of us while the flying fish rained down like a plague of locusts.

"Your presence, O Lord, I seek. Hide not your face from me; do not repel thy servant!" Pere Soren stepped forward onto the slippery blanket of fish, skidded and crashed to his knees, arms whirling like egg-beaters. He fell forward prostrate on the deck, buried in smattering, pattering armies of silver.

I raised my arms on high, embracing the night, embracing the fish, embracing the coming rain. "The river is *mahery*, with a will of its own. You do not own it, you cannot tame it!" I declaimed over his body into the tempest. Spliced into the next flash of lightning and the wind, I thought I heard a mournful keening. My head throbbed with Rangita's litany: *Come home, my sister. It is time to come home...*

"Help!" a voice cried. "Help me! Someone help me, please!!"

I fumbled for my flashlight in the bilge and trained it over the side. Suspended in the obsidian water below was Salim. He was floating on a net of bright, silvery spheres—a fluorescent, underwater spider's web—that kept him from sinking.

Those balls of lights! Were they fish? Or...

I was hanging over the side, straining to see, when I felt something wet flap against my ankle. Down in the reeking gloom of the bilge was a flying fish, much larger than the others. It lay on its side, panting. Then it flipped sideways, using its finny wings for leverage, painfully attempting to turn its head in order to look up at me. Its round, glassine eyes strobed weakly on and off—yet still brighter by far than my halogen flashlight.

Beloved shape-shifter! Blessed little demon-fish! Even without her cloak, Noro couldn't fool me. Not with *those* eyes.

I leaned down and picked her up, cradling her ever so tenderly. One of her silver fins was broken and hung uselessly over her back. As I touched her she blinked, and then the light in her eyes flickered and dimmed. With a tired, gasping sigh, she made one mighty effort to squirm out of my hand, only to land with a pathetic *slappp* at my feet.

Scared and angry, I reached for her again. This time I put my hand firmly around her, but gently, so as not to bend her torn wing. What a different anger I felt now than when I'd tackled her on the sacrificial stone. This time I was scared and angry because I cared. This time I was the saviour, and she, the sacrificial lamb. It was then I noticed: she'd been lying on top of a carefully coiled, sisal rope.

What is a saviour, if not a fisher of souls?

I hoisted the heavy hawser and slung it overboard. It curled out, out over the water like a *do* uncoiling. Salim grabbed onto it and began to pull himself towards the boat.

"Awake!" I exhorted the huddled Malagasy. "Open your eyes, my friends! Salim lives. He is risen!"

I made sure they saw him before I opened my hand with the glowing fish in it.

I made sure they saw the fish before I dropped it over the side. Noro's eyes flickered feebly, all the way down until she struck the water.

We all watched the glowing net swim forward and surround her. Then, together, as one ball of light, the *kokolampos* sank from view.

After Salim's resurrection, we broke out more rum and people actually fought for a chance to paddle; everybody wanted to be part of the miracle.

"*Salaam vazaha, veloma* Salim..." Josef riffed happily, alternately pounding his guitar and my shoulders.

Feverish *kabary* and singing accompanied the paddling for most of the night. I slept in spurts, wedged between some bags of rice. Every time I awoke it seemed I was hearing the word *kokolampo, kokolampo*. A corner of the rain squall caught up with us and drenched us, but the havoc it created was a joyous one, providing an excuse for more rum, hugging and stories. I can vouch for it: people who survive miracles are as closely bonded as those who survive disasters—maybe more so. There's a sense of having been touched by the ineffable—I was going to say "the divine", but Father Soren would certainly not have agreed. He sat hunched in the bow reciting his beads while the party raged in the stern. When dawn came he was still there, twiddling away like a fat, black dung beetle. As soon as we scraped bottom, he tied his shoes together, hung them around his neck and leapt off the ark, hitching up his skirts, hobbling up the bank without a backward glance.

The relief and excitement was tremendous as the rest of the passengers prepared to debark. Not only was there the *sambatra* celebration to look forward to, but there was a miracle to celebrate and a fantastic *kabary* to report. They had been to the mountain, survived, and returned triumphantly home. Everyone, that is, except me. As I waited my turn to climb ashore in the midst of the homecoming frenzy, I burned with a longing for my brother and a village I had never seen, gripped by a Vazimba dream from which I could not seem to awaken.

The first rays of morning sun shot over the high sand dunes separating us from Ambohitsara. In the quickening dawn I noticed something bright pink hidden under a makeshift bower of dried palm fronds on the opposite side of the shallow bay where several primitive dugout canoes were beached. When you've been in the bush for a while and your eyes get used to seeing nothing but tan, green and brown, a color like pink—it jumps right out at you. I was curious. While the others were still unloading bales and livestock, I rolled up my jeans, waded across the still water and lifted up the thatch.

Some dugout. It was a brand new Kawasaki 650SS jet ski. On the side, hand-painted in flashy, ornate letters it said: RAKO II.

Rakotomana! It had to be his.

I dropped the branches and looked around to make sure nobody had noticed me, but they were still bustling around the ark. I trudged back across the lagoon feeling the warm mud squish between my toes.

Bastard. If Rakotomana controlled Ambohitsara and Zaohitra Reserve, who *else* was in his pocket? Paul Cummins? Fred Pearson? Jack Mooresby? Salim?

Salim? No way. Rakotomana might have owned him yesterday, but Eva Artema owned Salim today.

I caught up with my friends as they began their triumphal procession over the dunes to Ambohitsara, taking my place between Salim and Josef at the front of the line. That low-down *voay*, Rakotomana, might be powerful, but he had yet to tangle with a warrior Queen.

39

Botofino, the king of Ambohitsara, received us wrapped in a grey blanket while seated in the doorway of the *tranobe,* the Big House. Over the door hung a severed zebu tail and a frond of *ravenala*, the traveller's palm. On one side of the king were stacks of straw strips ready to be plaited into circumcision mats, and on the other, two giant conch shells. King Botofino picked one up and blew it three times. His cheeks distorted and his nose flattened with the effort. His scarlet cap fell off the back of his head onto the sand at his feet. Botofino was the first king I'd ever met and I was impressed, by his lung power as much as his dignity.

"There are hundreds, maybe thousands, of kings like him in Madagascar," Josef had informed me as our procession threaded its way through the village. "But in truth, today a king is just like a lemur—a symbol, soon to become extinct." In the wake of our miracle, Josef had taken it upon himself to become my unofficial guide.

"What about queens?" I inquired. "Are there hundreds of

those, too?"

His eyes narrowed and he shook his head, synchronizing his footsteps to match mine as we marched across the hot sand that separated the neat rows of identical thatched houses on stilts. I saw no power lines, no running water, no evidence whatsoever of the twentieth century, save an orange plastic bucket and some batteries that had been cast onto a heap of garbage.

"Queens? Oh, here and there in a small village I suppose you'll find one, but not like before. Female cabinet ministers, we have those. Councillors, professors, doctors, scientists, nuns... those too. But real queens? None since the French conquest."

Every now and then families would break off from the main troop of marchers, dashing from hut to hut to embrace friends and relatives they hadn't seen since the last *sambatra*, seven years ago. From one house came the lilting sound of women's voices singing. As we passed, I peeked inside and saw young girls, mothers and grandmothers, kneeling and plaiting mats of straw with flying fingers.

"But," I persisted, "the Vazimba were ruled by queens, weren't they? What about Queen Ranoro? Didn't she live just north of here on the shores of Lake Marovoay?"

Josef attempted a studied insouciance, but I could see the muscles in his jaw tense. "Extinct," he said flatly, slicing the air with his hands. "*Tout le monde*, extinct."

I turned and faced him. "And the invisible village? Is Andrebabe extinct, too?"

The discomfiture on Josef's face was acute. Why, I wondered? Was it because I'd broken Jack Mooresby's rule to never confront a Malagasy dead-on with a question? After last night, I couldn't believe that. Things had changed—or had they? Maybe it was still Code Blue, after all. From the look on Josef's face, I'd stepped over an invisible line, breaching an unassailable frontier of intimacy. Despite everything that had occurred, did he still perceive me as nothing more than a presumptuous, insensitive stranger? It was too late to back down now. I had to forge ahead.

"There's no reason to be frightened," I sought to allay his fears.

"The *kokolampo*s you saw in the water. They didn't kill Salim, they *saved* him." I paused and pulled the *ody* out of my pocket. "Josef, listen to me... The *kokolampos* came... *because I called them.*"

Josef stared at the amulet and then down at his feet, steadfastly refusing to meet my eyes. We had arrived at the *tranobe* and had to step aside as others streamed past us to greet King Botofino. "Mademoiselle Artema, it is time to meet the king." He bowed, speaking with the utmost formality as if he hadn't heard anything I'd said.

I'd gone too far, but I didn't give a fig. "Josef, you were raised in this village," I whispered as we moved closer to the *tranobe*. "You were circumcised here. You must know about Lake Marovoay and the sacred water. Perhaps, as a child, your father took you to explore the Blue Rainforest..."

"Come, mademoiselle," he said stiffly, "we must not delay. We will make the king angry."

"Talk to me," I entreated. "You can trust me."

"They say you can trust no one these days in Ambohitsara," he spoke quietly. "Not even the king. Ever since the arrival of the steel dragonflies..."

Mpakafo ride steel dragonflies... taboos are cracked and broken, useless... I had a sudden vision of Jack's helicopter and Rexworthy's empty stretcher hanging beneath it.

We'd reached the Big House. It was not impressive—nothing like a swooping Indonesian long-house. It might have been slightly larger, but other than that there was nothing at all to distinguish it from the other, identical thatched huts lined up facing northeast. King Botofino, however, was very distinguished. He was tall and reserved, with tufts of iron grey hair poking out from under that red skullcap, and when he extended his hand from the folds of the thick grey blanket for me to shake, he almost crushed my fingers as he welcomed me for the benefit of the crowd.

"I must translate," Josef said, bowing to the king, adding an aside to me, "Later, perhaps, we will talk."

Josef did his best to convey the gist of Botofino's flowery

phrases and my equally ornate responses. He was very nervous and I took it as a good sign; it meant that my questions had hit home and he had information that could help me.

"It would be appropriate for you to bow to him now," Josef told me after several minutes of *kabary* ping-pong.

I took a gulp of humid, Indian Ocean air and executed a deep, if somewhat ragged, curtsy in front of the barefoot king. It put me at eye level with his ankles, which were half-hidden under his robe. Both of them were wrapped in beaded thongs from which dangled a fringe of sharp, clacking, crocodile teeth. This was a promising development. I rose and met his gaze without blinking.

"We've heard rumors of your arrival," the king said.

No surprise, that.

"News travels fast on the Pangalanes," I replied.

"One does not need telephones if one has an *ombiasa* skilled in *sikidy.*"

...or an informer like Michel Rakotomana, with a high-powered jet ski, I thought silently, then added, "I've read that the most skillful sooth-sayers in Madagascar are from the Antemoro tribe."

Botofino nodded in agreement but said nothing.

"I've also read that the great *katibo* who advised Madagascar's kings and queens by means of astrology and divination were trained in these esoteric arts..." I waved my hand vaguely in a northerly direction, "...somewhere not far from here."

He drilled me with steady, unsmiling eyes. "You seem to be an ardent student of Malagasy history, mademoiselle. Have you come to Ambohitsara for the purpose of studying *mahay fomba*?"

Josef struggled to translate *mahay fomba*, finally deciding on "things Malagasy."

"I am..." I started to say "learning," but just then the king shifted his bare feet in the sand and the teeth around his ankles rattled softly.

I decided to chance it. Those teeth called for more than polite chit-chat. "Madagascar has given me no choice," I said slowly, emphasizing each word. "She is an uncompromising teacher. One must be prepared to give up one's life in order to share her dreams."

As I spoke, I saw something shift in him. His eyes, which had been opaque and glittering, now bored into me. He brushed away a fly that had settled on his knee with a zebu-tail whisk. "In the southeast we have many interpreters of dreams," he said, "as well as teachers, and priests."

I smiled. "Indeed. I met one of them yesterday. Father Jules Soren."

"Ah, yes..." he snorted softly. "Pere Soren. Our pastor is an infrequent visitor. The Jesuits used to maintain a small church here, but it has been closed for many years, however we still keep a house ready for their use."

"I presume then that Christianity is not a priority in Ambohitsara?" I spoke carefully and respectfully, hoping to draw him out, and at the same time not to insult him by the challenge hidden in my words.

"Ours is a very, very old village. No one knows how long it has stood here on this same, small spit of sand. It was established well before the Christians, certainly since the Arabs' arrival in the twelfth century, and very probably much earlier. Cyclones have destroyed it over and over, yet each time it has been rebuilt."

"There must be a great deal of power in this spot to make people want to rebuild year after year."

"We Malagasy are a ritualistic people. Ambohitsara is the gateway to..." he paused, his eyes locked on mine.

"...to the Blue Rainforest and Lake Marovoay." I finished his sentence for him. Then I went out on a limb. "Is it not also the gateway to... Andrebabe?" I held my breath, watching for the king's reaction, waiting for Josef to translate. But instead, he fell silent, staring over the king's shoulder, refusing to go on.

"Josef, please. This is important. Help me here."

I moved in closer and nudged him, but he studiedly ignored me, forcing me to follow his gaze down the sandy path between the row of palm-walled houses that extended east from the Big House. Approaching us, with the sun at their backs, were Michel Rakotomana and Father Soren. Rakotomana dwarfed the priest, towering over him and the black silk umbrella he was carrying to shade his bald head from the tropical sun.

"Andrebabe?" the king cut in.

"Josef!" I tugged on his shirt, anxiously watching the two men coming closer.

"Andrebabe?" Botofino repeated, not about to let it go.

"Your majesty," I bent forward, speaking quickly in a low voice, "Andrebabe is the reason I am here. My brother, James, is trapped there." I glowered at Josef, who had resumed translating in an unsteady voice.

Over Botofino's shoulder I could see beads of sweat dripping off Father Soren's rubbery red neck onto his black shoulders. Michel Rakotomana's khaki fatigues were stained with grime. The sleeves were short for his huge arms, revealing an intimidating amount of wrist and forearm. As they came towards us I could hear their shoes crunching in the soft sand. The king must have heard them too, for he turned his head slightly.

"King Botofino, sir," I dug into my blouse and pulled out my necklace, holding it up for him to see. Sunlight splashed on the silver filagree crocodiles. The bouncing rays created tiny spotlights that played back and forth at random across his dark, imposing face. "I need your help. Queen Rangita has sent me. The Vazimba are—"

I didn't have a chance to finish. The moment Rakotomana saw me with the king, he took charge. Stepping between us, he snarled an order to a group of men nearby who were leaning on long, pointed staves and *bingo!* without a word they snapped into action and surrounded me, trapping me inside a solid wall of spears. I was hustled away in lock-step over five long, empty sand dunes, through a couple of weedy patches of manioc and around a stagnant salt-rimmed pond. They marched me out, out beyond the pale, beyond the outermost edge of Ambohitsara to a palm grove near the sea, where they threw me into a bamboo cage. After twisting the lock. They turned and departed as wordlessly as they had come, jogging back over the dunes as one body, their sharpened staves *clickety-clacking* like mah-jong tiles.

I held onto the bars and looked out.

Mine wasn't the only cage in the grove. There were many; each contained a single lemur. It was a zoo—a smuggler's private zoo.

About twenty feet away stood another cage, similar to mine. In it was a black and white *indri-indri*. As soon as I made eye contact with those sparkling, yellow eyes it stuck its furry muzzle through the bars, opened its brilliant red mouth and let out the loudest, saddest, most bone-chilling howl I'd ever heard. Everything I was feeling, and more, was summed up in that *indri's* mournful wailing.

Artema, you were warned.

Unlike my fellow prisoners, I couldn't claim to be the hapless victim of a spear or a sling-shot, nor could I blame my fate on a cleverly set wire snare or even something so lowly as a well-aimed stone. No, I'd dug my own grave by stupidly spilling the beans to Father Soren.

The *indri* kept up its howling for a very long time, until—why not?—I stuck my freckled, sunburned snout out of my cage and joined in, adding some hominoid ululations of my own. I wasn't crazy up a banyan tree, but I was close. Very close.

40

The hours dragged by, clocked only by the crash of the ocean shredding itself on the shore, the dry palms fretting overhead and the melancholy cluckings from the trapped lemurs. Sometime around noon a trio of girls materialized bearing a long bamboo tube filled with water, bananas and some rice wrapped in a *ravenala* leaf. The youngest pushed the food through my cage on the point of a long stick. I felt like Gretel, inspecting the rice grain by grain before I ate.

At least I wasn't extinct... yet.

I'd tried everything to squelch that morbid fear, but it kept raising its head like a poisonous sea snake. I tried to sleep, but the cage was too short to stretch out in. I tried to meditate, but the bamboo slats made the lotus position impossible. I tried to pray, but my knees seized up. Worst of all: Botofino had my pack, and in it was my *ody*.

So kid, you wanna play hard ball.

Jack... *He* was the real torture. I kept hearing his voice, his cackling laugh, remembering how his gold-flecked eyes had slow-stripped me in the Chinese restaurant, how his mustache had tickled when he'd kissed me in the rickshaw, and—blissful agony!—his tongue in my ear.

The afternoon heat was unbearable so I took a clue from the lemurs draped slothfully in their cages, sleeping off lunch. I pulled off my shoes, shirt and jeans, rolled them into a pillow, and lay on my back in my underwear, putting my feet through the roof bars of the cage to catch the breeze, massaging my stomach a little, slipping my hand between my thighs every now and then, trying to imagine what kind of a lover Jack would have been, lying on top of me in a real bed, with real sheets. But try as I might, the fantasy bombed.

I rolled over into the fetal position and began to bawl. Way to go, Artema. Everybody's in town to celebrate a mass circumcision and you're so out of it you can't even imagine a guy in bed. Some warrior.

As I wept, I became aware of a dim, mechanical *whomp-whomping* coming up the canal from the south.

Helicopter!

I couldn't see through the plexiglass bubble, but the CANTEX logo was clearly visible on the tail. This time, instead of a stretcher strapped underneath, it carried a load of pre-fabricated steel struts—the kind used for oil drilling rigs. The engine made a tremendous racket, thrashing the tops of the trees and stirring up dust devils in the dunes as it circled once above Ambohitsara and then headed north. I clung to the bars of my cage, shouting, "Jack! Jack! Jack!" like a mad monkey. But of course he heard nothing, nothing at all.

"I see that you have made yourself comfortable, mademoiselle Eva," said a throaty voice behind me. "It is a warm day, is it not?"

Michel Rakotomana! How long had he been standing there?

I shrank into a half-naked ball in the corner of the cage, wrapping my arms around my thighs and belly, futilely trying to cover myself. He was leaning against the trunk of a palm tree, eating a papaya, spitting out the little black seeds like bullets onto the white sand.

I jammed my legs into my jeans, wriggling around absurdly in front of him, feeling like a hot, pink worm on display. "Is this what you call shooting birds on the Pangalanes Canal?" I hurled at him over my shoulder, struggling to button my fly.

"Some birds are too beautiful to be shot. They must be trapped, instead." He turned the papaya skin inside out, sucked off the last of the yellow meat, and tossed it into the bushes as he came towards me.

"And then, what? Sold to the highest bidder?"

I made a grab for my shirt, but he was there first. He snatched it through the bars of the cage and threw it across the clearing.

His laugh was slow and satanic, like dark thunder. "*Au contraire.* The best of the species one always reserves for oneself."

I crossed my arms over my nipples. "Did they teach you that at the University of Strasbourg? Or merely how to drink whiskey and steal from your country?"

He cracked his knuckles. "Science is a thirsty business."

"I gather it has become a dirty business, too."

He shrugged. "Where the demand is great, money follows."

"As I recall, in another lifetime, you once told me that in Madagascar science lay down before empty bellies. Apparently, that doesn't include Michel Rakotomana."

"The world thrives on new discoveries like *Hapelemur erectus.* It is in my best interest—and yours—to provide such *divertissements.*"

"And at what cost?"

He sighed. "A life here, a life there. A small pittance to pay for the glory of science..."

"...and the glorification of Michel Rakotomana."

"You are too harsh, mademoiselle. Believe me, many others prosper along the way."

"Tell me. Exactly how did Curtis Rexworthy 'prosper' along the way?"

"Ah, Curtis. An unfortunate sequence. He was so... defensive.

So protective. He refused to cooperate with my men, creating an unpleasant diversion, allowing your brother to escape to Mt. Ambondrombe. My superstitious trackers refused to follow. A ridiculous, unnecessary business..."

"Was that why you murdered him?"

"Murder is such an... *ugly* word. Let us just say he was overtaken by a jungle fever."

"A simple case of *hazo* and *tazo*, abetted by a few *tangena* pits, right?"

"Rexworthy knew too much. He was unwilling to share..."

"Share what? My brother James, or his lemurs?"

Rakotomana strode over, grabbed the cage and shook it, peering down through the bars at my naked breasts. "Mademoiselle, whatever else I am, it should be obvious that I am not a homosexual. It may interest you to know that Curtis Rexworthy's death has officially been recorded as a suicide."

"Suicide!?"

"It is not an unusual end for unusual lovers, even in your country. In Madagascar such suicides are quite a common solution..." He took out a rag and wiped his sweaty face. "You may even wish to consider the possibility that with this... academic competitor... out of the way, there will be fewer to share in James'––I should say— 'our'— discoveries."

"You're suggesting we make these giant lemurs a sort of... family affair."

"*Exactement.*"

"How very... charming." I indicated the caged lemurs scattered about in the shade. "In the meantime, I suppose it's business as usual."

"*Pourquoi pas?* Why disturb *l'arrangement?*"

"I see. The Blue Rainforest provides a steady stream of endangered animals for Rakotomana to smuggle abroad, CANTEX receives carte blanche from the World Wildlife Consortium to drill illegally in a protected Reserve, and...?"

"...and we both share in the proceeds from the sale of the

'equipment' they air freight to Europe and Asia."

"Ah... An international family affair."

Rakotomana shrugged. "One world. One tribe. One family. Very New Age, is it not?"

"Tell me, what does the Malagasy government think about this little family arrangement?"

More dark, thundering laughter. "You are a great deal like your brother, mademoiselle Eva. *Une idealiste.* Unfortunately, idealists are, like the aepyornis, a useless, flightless, rather clumsy and not very beautiful bird. One that has outlived its function and deserves..."

"...extinction?"

"Why jump to such a hasty and unnatural conclusion?" He circled the cage. Under the direct sun, the shadow of his overbite was horrible, like a gigantic, predatory gecko. I could smell the scent of over-ripe papaya on his hands, mingled with a rank, male sexual odor.

"Are you suggesting a more natural form of extinction? More... shall we say, Malagasy? Something like a spear? Or would you prefer poison?"

"Not at all. I would prefer something more leisurely. More... sybaritic."

"A sexual *quid pro quo*, is that what you had in mind? A woman in a cage? Some tricky *vazaha* S & M, in return for a few specimens of *Hapelemur erectus*?"

I threw open my arms, tipping my breasts up at him angrily. "Would you like me to lie down for you again, *sans* bikini? Or would you rather fuck me through the bars, standing up, like one of your lemurs?"

"Your *crudité* shocks me, mademoiselle."

"Coming from a *voyeur* and a murderer, I find that extremely amusing."

Rakotomana gripped the bamboo poles and pressed his thick bearded chin between them, purring dangerously, "Come, come. Let's cease this tiresome fencing. You are a courageous and determined woman to have journeyed so far for the love of a brother. And from what Jules Soren tells me, your brother reciprocates your affection. We Malagasy admire that kind of closeness in a family." He squatted down beside the cage and slid one enormous brown hand slowly up and down the bamboo without taking his eyes off my breasts. "Beside Curtis, you were James' sole confidante. He must have told you the location of his camp. I'm depending on you to lead me to him. He fears me, but he will not hide from you."

"Do you seriously expect me to become a decoy to trap my own brother?"

"Trap? I prefer to think that we have very sensibly joined forces to save him. A man cannot survive for long in a rain forest without... amenities. Not even a scientist."

"Maybe the Vazimba are taking care of him," I snapped.

He rocked backwards. "Your sense of humor is admirable. However, from someone in your position it would be reasonable to expect somewhat greater... cooperation." His voice dropped a notch and he rested his elbows intimately on top of the cage. "Eva, my little bird, I am not a savage. My hut is simple but well-appointed. I assure you, you will be most comfortable. You'll rest well tonight and we shall depart together for the Blue Rainforest in the morning."

"I'll... think about it."

He threw his head back and laughed.

"Ambivalence *is* a woman's prerogative, is it not?" I snapped.

"Ambivalence is a luxury reserved for *free* women. You are facing a long, uncomfortable night without the protection of a net. There are spiders, scorpions. Malaria is endemic along the canal. They say the *anopheles* mosquito delights in the sweet taste of a beautiful woman's blood."

"*Monsieur le Directeur,*" I pressed my face against my cage, "Believe me, I would rather die of fever or be eaten by a crocodile than sleep under the same roof, much less in the same bed, with a bastard like you."

"*Tres bién!*" he exploded. "I'll make sure that both your wishes come true—*after* we find your brother. I shall return for you when it is dark. Perhaps by then your ambivalence will have disappeared."

"It will not."

"Well then, I will take you anyway." He circled the cage slowly, casting a tremendous, black shadow, eclipsing me underneath him. "You are right, *ma chere*," he growled. "Caged animals do excite me. Why wait for nightfall, when I can have you now?"

He reached into his pocket, took out a key, unlocked the cage and lunged for me. Catching hold of my necklace, he dragged me across to him. I tried to wriggle free but I didn't have a chance; he had the croc tooth firmly in his grip. As he wrenched my face against his rough beard, I could feel the little silver crocs biting into the soft flesh of my neck.

Damned Vazimba jewelry!

He wrenched me closer until we were *dente al dente*, *voay* to *voay*.

"A fearless, blonde *vazaha*," he murmured, "is precisely the sort of challenge I enjo—"

Suddenly, I felt his cheek sag. His face twisted strangely and he crashed forward, his great khaki-clad bulk splayed out awkwardly half-in and half-out of the cage. He jerked spasmodically once or twice and then rolled slowly off me onto the sand. Jutting out of the back of his neck was a silver dart, no bigger than a bumble bee, fletched with fine, bamboo slivers.

41

A tiny, shriveled crone smothered in filthy rags came scuttling towards us. She moved very slowly sideways, creeping tentatively across the pale sand, feeling her way with claw-like hands and feet, like a hermit crab that has lost the sea. When she reached the cage, her hand shot out and she plucked the dart from Rakotomana's neck, fitting it into a small case fashioned from crocodile skin, taking care not to touch the needle-like point. Then she whirled around and made for the nearest thicket. I leapt out of the cage over the inert man and raced after her, grabbing my shirt as I ran.

The bushes were far too dense for a tall *vazaha* to penetrate and I lost her almost immediately. Realizing the canal was my only means of escape, I improvised from memory, taking a route around the edge of the village, zig-zagging across the dunes, circling around a clump of stubby doum palms, weaving in and out of thickets of seaside manzanita. I ran along the edge of a marsh, through a stand of reedy papyrus, stopping on a high dune to catch my breath.

It was crocodile country, all right.

I shivered, gazing down at the primeval beauty of the meandering, mirrored sloughs that fed into the canal. The slanting afternoon light burnished them copper as they snaked their way through rippling wastelands of bulrushes and wild grasses. Thrusting up from the northernmost edge of the swamps rose the somber, cloud-shrouded peaks of the Blue Rainforest.

"Andrebabe... James..." I murmured the words, as if speaking the names out loud would magically bring them closer, make them real.

A peculiar clicking arose behind me and I whirled about to find myself encircled by a band of the king's men—the same men who had earlier led me away to the cage. Now they were resplendent in ceremonial dress, wrapped in brilliant red robes with a long, finely woven white *lamba* thrown over the left shoulder. Each wore a small, square, raffia cap with pointed corners ornamented with tassels of red wool, and around each man's neck hung a crocodile tooth from a beaded thong. They stood rigidly at attention with their crossed wooden staves etched against the cobalt sky, forming a human crown through which King Botofino stepped, followed by Josef, Salim, and a fourth man who must have been the *ombiasa*, for he was laden with all kinds of beads, amulets and other magical paraphernalia. Shadowing them like a tattered roach was the crone.

The king spoke first. "Our people are deeply ashamed that your arrival in Ambohitsara has been marked by an act of violence. Hospitality is a sacred duty. Strangers visiting our village have always been treated as honored guests. Last year, when this man Rakotomana arrived from Tana with his guns and lies, everything began to change. Nobody knows what promises he made to the *vazahas*, or how much rum or money he gave, only that soon afterwards helicopters began flying north loaded with equipment, returning to Ambohitsara with animals."

Salim interrupted, "To have sold my skills to such a man! Of all the animals I captured, only a few left here alive, and none destined for Tzimbazaza. Stolen from the forest, they refused to eat, sickened and died. I am ashamed to tell you, mademoiselle. Out beyond those cages, on the beach, there's another ocean... of lemur bones. And still he drives on, determined to pursue this... this fantasy, the 'giant-with-the-hair-at-the-top.'"

Hapelemur erectus—the demonic man-lemur again! I couldn't seem to avoid them.

Josef leaned forward, "It's no fantasy what has happened to Lake Marovoay since the oil men began exploring..."

King Botofino reached into a covered basket and took out a large gourd strapped with silver chains and held it aloft.

"The Ancestors have decreed that every seven years we must send our strongest men north to gather water from the lake for our circumcision rites. Last week when they returned, this *arivolahy* was empty. The forest around the lake had been set on fire, the sacred water was black with cinders. Our men refused to dip the gourd." He paused, passing his hand over his grizzled face. "*Fady! Fady!* It is taboo to soil the lake!" His countenance was suffused with pain. "Without that water, there can be no *sambatra*. Our boys cannot become men or be buried in the family tomb." His eyes clouded. "Their souls will wander forever, crying like wild owls."

I had a vision of Rexworthy's white feet flying blindly through the night, hooting softly through eternity, desperately looking for a place to rest.

"A few have turned to Father Soren," Josef added bitterly. "But he has more respect for whiskey than *mahay fomba*. He merely scolds them and urges them to come to his mission and work in his hemp factories. The people whisper secretly among themselves, saying that because the lake is dying, the Ancestors have cursed them. They pray to the Vazimba to save them."

I gazed across the shimmering water, north to the deep green cliffs that plunged into the sea. "*The Blue Rainforest weeps bitter tears...*" I whispered softly. "*Bamboo breaks with the weight of a dying babokoto, mpakafo ride steel dragonflies, taboos are cracked, broken, useless...*"

Botofino leaned forward as Josef translated, hanging on to every word. "Where did you hear that?" he asked.

"They're lines from a poem given to me by a friend, a woman who calls herself Rangita, queen of the Vazimba."

"*Kai!*" He sighed and took both my hands in his. "The flying fish, the glowing net... I should have known. Only a Vazimba is powerful enough to command the *kokolampos.*" He bowed deferentially from the waist, then straightened. "I was right to defy Rakotomana's orders and send my men to free you. They were frightened to approach at first, then surprised and relieved to find the cage open and the big man lying on the sand, snoring."

Snoring!!? Bad news, indeed. For it meant Rakotomana was still alive and at large.

"Josef, please thank the king and ask him for his most powerful blessing. Tell him I must resume my journey immediately."

There was a hurried convo.

"He says he'll send some of his men with you. Mam'selle, can you paddle a dugout?"

I gulped, remembering the bare, arrow-thin skulls lying helter-skelter on the mud flats. "I haven't ever..." I began.

Just then a shot rang out. And another. King Botofino fell forward, blood staining his grey blanket.

Pandemonium ensued. The king's guards bolted back and forth, yelling orders and waving their sticks. The *ombiasa* clutched his amulets and moaned. I wished to hell I had my *ody*. On second thought, maybe it was asking too much of a bunch of beads and sticks to deliver me from a Luger.

Salim jerked my arm and I fell to the ground. We wriggled through the hot sand, dodging bullets. "I've taken your pack to the lagoon," he panted, "and a few things you'll need from the priest's house." We made it to a cane-break just in time to see Rakotomana staggering over the rise. Then we took off again and didn't look back until we reached the water's edge. Sure enough, nestled in the roots of a mangrove, was my old blue backpack. Strapped to it was a tent and some other stuff wrapped in raffia. In the chaos and shouting, it never occurred to me to ask Salim if he'd included a map.

"Hurry, Eva!" Salim waded out into the shallows, pushing a hollowed-out log no more than a foot wide.

I sized it up. With me and my pack, there'd be no more than an inch of freeboard. I could do better than that.

"*Sayonara*, Salim," I said, embracing him quickly. Then, shouldering the pack, I plunged into the waist-deep water, surging across the lagoon toward the pile of palm fronds that hid RAKO II, praying: *Be there. Be there. Be there.*

The mantra worked. The jet ski was still in place. I tore off the brushy covering, stowed my pack under the padded seat and climbed aboard, reached over and pressed the starter button on the right side.

Have gas, I prayed. You'd better have gas.

There was a nasty *whanggg* as a bullet tore into the thatch near my foot.

Now all I had to do was try to remember how to work the throttle. One summer weekend sporting with Raul on Lake Powell had taught me something about jet skis, if not love.

Another shot whistled through the trees above me.

"Surrender, Eva!" shouted Josef, running down towards the lagoon. "He means to kill you!"

"No way!" I yelled back over the roar of seven hundred and fifty Kawasaki cc's. "He wants me alive!"

I grabbed the hand grips and was just about to crank them when a foul-smelling tangle flung itself at me from the branches overhead. The crone! She landed in a heap directly behind me and immediately clamped her little hands around my waist. The sacred gourd hung from her neck.

"*Vite, ma soeur! Vite!*"

I cracked the throttle and punched it. The hull leapt full-bore out of the water, blasting the thatched hideaway to flinders. We shot up the canal like a hot pink bat, bullets plinking to the right and left like flying fish.

"Why didn't you kill him when you had the chance?" I shouted over my shoulder.

"We need him alive," she yelled back. "As bait for the trap."

"You could've made me disappear again. It would have been a hell of a lot simpler."

She laughed, "We need you, too."

"What for?"

"To spring the trap."

Our noisy, neon water-skater whizzed north on the broad canal. Its shiny pink plastic and flashy chrome seemed bizarre and exotic in this subdued, earth-toned landscape—an exotic, technological anachronism. Yet, in another sense it was hardly out of place; just another example of Mother Nature's grandstanding. Like the Comet moth—an excessive, Malagasy exuberance.

I looked back over my left shoulder. Rangita's tattered wrappings were flying off her one by one, floating away downstream like windborne ashes from a dead time, revealing her wrapped from head to toe in a spotless, white cotton cloak.

We were heading into a great green spot with no food, no medicines, no weapons. I began a mental check list of the hideous *hazo* and *tazo* that awaited me: poisonous frogs, slugs, spiders, centipedes, scorpions, stinging vines, fungi, bacteria, intestinal parasites, toe-rot, leeches, mosquitoes, polluted water, torrential rains... A twisted ankle could immobilize me. An infected bite could kill.

Directly ahead were the emerald mountains of the Blue Rainforest. Untold gallons of water vapor hung in the sky, leaking humidity into the air above an invisible village on an island in the middle of a lake called Marovoay. On the other side of the planet, a satellite's twirl away, tomorrow had already begun. The Bay Bridge was jammed with commuters fretting about dandruff and cellulite, deciding whether or not to apply for a platinum Visa card.

Rangita leaned out over the water, laughing merrily as our foaming wake dissolved from white to green. "*Coming, going, like water birds, we don't follow a path, we don't leave a trace,*" she sang out.

I suddenly felt sick. *No path... no trace...* Was I going to disappear again, this time forever? Be swallowed up, eaten alive by the jungle—just like James?

Rangita gave a deep, contented sigh, and leaned her warm, not-at-all-astral body against my back, tucking herself in, out of the wind. "Drive, sister," was what she said. "Take us home."

Lord, who is the savior, and who the saved?

I repeated those words again and again, until they lost all meaning and became the nonsensical sing-song of a madwoman banging her head against the asylum wall, chanting the phrase over and over as we skimmed across the water—*Lord, who is the savior, and who the saved?*—without the foggiest idea of where we were heading, lost in amazement that Rangita could trust in me as much as I trusted her, feeling her small body pressed against me, her arms wrapped around my waist, no division between us, closer to me than my neck vein, a unity of souls. Sisters, queens, going home.

How was I to know that Rakotomana was in the priest's hut on his radio, shouting orders at Jack Mooresby?

42

I'm no scientist. My journal from that time in the Blue Rainforest—was it hours, or days, I still can't be sure—is proof of that. It's an artist's jumble, rain-smeared ink jottings and pale, pencil sketches. Fragmentary attempts to wrap my brain around the ecstasy and the mystery of that green cathedral and its inhabitants. Feeble endeavors to decode events that now seem as distant and ephemeral as waking dreams.

Turning the pages, I come upon these quotes scrawled across a page: *The most beautiful thing we can experience is the mysterious. It is the source of all true art and science.* And again: *Every experience on the physical or astral plane is just a dream of the soul.* And yet... what happened was no dream! If you were here beside me now, I would show you the *ody* and Rangita's letters. I would place the crocodile necklace around your neck and you would hear it jingle and be amazed at the workmanship in those tiny silver beasts, clamped tail-to-tail. I would unscrew the silver lid on the hollow tooth, and overturn it into your hand. Then you would see the bullet they dug out of my thigh.

Thursday... Leave main canal. Enter northwest trib. Following, following, slower, narrow now, watch for hidden rocks, whirlpools. Around a bend, surprise! the river turns vertical, becomes a waterfall. No problem, no more gas. Abandon jet ski. Climbing up, skidding down. Fallen logs, mossy stones. Ford river once, twice, slip on tree-trunk bridge, hang over foaming torrent, squirming on belly to safety.

Rangita, like a bird, a moth, darts ahead beneath tree ferns twelve feet tall. Fleet of foot, a forest denizen, she hardly sweats, unaffected by the heat and humidity. Me, tall, clunky, too much skin. Heat-seeking leeches attack even through the eyelets of my shoes. Rangita, gentle, helps to pick them off, crushes leaves of a nearby plant, squeezes the juice to stop the bleeding.

Enough, magician! Give me ro and rice balls. Disappear me home! She answers, No. You must drown in forest in order to understand. But I don't want to understand, I whine. Leave your pack, she laughs. You don't need it. Leave it? It's my life! Your life? More laughter. You've already lost that, sister. But I refuse and soldier on. Trust in God, but tie your camel.

Friday morning... Light rain on Father Soren's plastic poncho. Bless Salim. Filmy mists drifting in and out the forest canopy high above. Down here sparkling dewdrops outline a glistening network of countless spider webs. Orb-weavers, tunnel-builders, trap-door crafters. Immense webs, diamond and silver trapezes, gauze the trail. Spiders like hairy golf balls, black and yellow, craggy six-inch legs, barrel out from underneath banana leaves. Passionate, quivering, defensive.

Rangita's delighted laughter. A chartreuse chameleon two feet long, horns on its snout, it creeps-creeps-stops, a dozen quick, nervous push-ups, it creeps-creeps-stops again, rotates its bulging, rusty eyeballs whoop-whoop, whoop-whoop, shoots its orange laser tongue and, wham! there's lunch.

Monotonous sitar drone of frogs and insects. Singing, sawing, sighing, rasping, drilling, chirping, clicking, wheedling, worming, buzzing, humming, shrilling, flapping, flitting, ticking, tapping, popping, boring, burrowing, biting, crunching. An undifferentiated, groaning OMMMM, arising from millions of unseen comings and goings, moltings and mountings, matings and dyings. A great mutual embrace, always happening, between the eternal and what dies. Life, in death, enduring.

Saturday or Sunday... We follow the river, pushing deeper up-country. A malachite kingfisher flashes brilliant wings, zealously guarding a tadpole pool. We dip and drink. The water's pure here. Will it lead us to Lake Marovoay?

Flurry of day-moths, black, blue, red, white and green—magnificent iridescence of oil slick rainbows. Ah... coming up river now, a bigger act. A swallowtail with neon wing-bars drifts, floats a moment in the sun. I put out my hand for it to land and it does, without a trace of shyness. The beauty! Oh James, you were so right. The beauty...

Fat, mottled zafu toad squats motionless, then burps, as ten inches of mahagony millipede roller-coasters over a log, Fuller-Brush legs whirling. A barrage of butterflies come down to watch, wings clapping like an audience. With every clap, orange eye-spots, dancing.

Beside a cork tree, Rangita points. I see nothing. She thumps the trunk as I prepare to move on, points again. Upside-down, pressed flat, immobile as a stone, a lizard eighteen inches long, bright reptile eyes overhung with tatters of skin, a nearly perfect camouflage. Rangita touches it lightly with a twig. Hisss! opens the bright red mouth! then whooshh it leaps! flies to the next tree, its barklike skin unfolding into leathery wings. "Tahafisaka," she calls it. I call it Lucifer.

On my sweating wrist the blank, gold Rolex, useless as a bank account or a blow-dryer. I laugh out loud, wind up and pitch it into the forest. Adios tiempo. Time already went out the window on the day Rangita said, "Why, we exist. As always."

A new morning... The Blue Rainforest. Not blue at all, but green. Intoxicating whorl of sun and shadow. Marching, stumbling, gulping humid air, sucking the sky down, drowning in the green seduction of a landscape undisturbed since the waters withdrew and fish began to haul themselves up out of the sea. Gondwanaland... I am feverish. Porous. Maddened by the excitement of this green life so driven by its own desire to exist. In the jungle of trees and creepers, clawing their way over each other, the slightest of sounds resonates in my cells. I am a wind chime, a water chime...

A cascade of sunlight illuminates a scarlet frog upon a blade—one blade—of grass. Aloha, little frog. Namaste. I see the god in you. In ancient cultures the word for hello and goodbye is the same. They understand something we are still learning—that arriving and leaving, living and dying, are two parts of the same thing... the One.

Today... Something has shifted, a change of lenses. My eyes tumble forward and adjust to subtleties. I begin to see past green, past the meaningless entanglements of vines and ferns, past the sameness of the vegetable confusion, past even the fear of death whose presence lurks in this fecund overkill of emerald, in the stinging nettles, lactic vines, poisonous berries. Details leap forth. So obvious. Why didn't I see them earlier? Today the path seems full of footprints. I notice a spray of white orchids, broken at a certain angle above a stone. A patch of lichen dangles unnaturally, torn from a log. A leaf from a travellers palm lies across a boulder, sliced by a blade, not teeth. It leaks fresh water from a hole drilled into the stalk. A basket, fashioned from twisted grasses, no bigger than a thimble. Signs. Portents.

Rangita, running ahead, then beside me, becomes more agitated. She seems to be growing smaller, darker, her flesh more dense. At times, she seems to glow, a bluish light around the edges of her body. Sometimes a mist plays about her, too. When I rub my eyes, it's gone.

The forest thins. Along the river, smooth black rocks, sand bars, sun. We drink and swim. Our naked feet leave black ovals on the hot, dry stones. Where are the crocodiles? I ask. Soon, she answers. Soon. Her elation is contagious. She begins to sing. It is the song of the morning of the world, before time began. I join in, feeling a river moving in me. A joy.

We're not alone. In the eucalyptus high above, a family of piebald Indris, glowing lemon eyes, doggy snouts, quit munching leaves and cut loose, too. Broken waterfalls of descending notes, the basso male picks up where his mate leaves off, eerie polyphonics echoing from hill to hill, a cacophony of thin, wild wails and mournful hootings. The music of Madagascar, the song of Eden.

Our trumpets arouse the kingdom. With eyes newborn, everywhere I look I see more lemurs. Grey, tufty ears, square-faced, one shreds bamboo so tough I saw it used for pipes in Ambohitsara. Another, higher up, round eyes in a soft grey face like a koala, nibbles contentedly on tender leaves. From a liana, hangs a family of fuzzy white-fronts, their eyebrows expressing perpetual surprise. They grunt-click their alarm while a band of gleaming red-ruffs, babies clinging to their mothers like moneybelts, pause and peer, curious and unafraid. In a hollow tree a mouse lemur, smaller than a chestnut, blinks and goes back to sleep.

Look! Rangita points upstream. Ahead, a strange miasma, a blueish fog... shimmering, palpating. It swirls, reveals a band of giant lemurs. Impossible to count... twenty, thirty... Dark, smooth skin, flat faces... something odd about their movements. And then they're gone, enveloped in that fog again. I run forward. They reappear, marching together through the mist, so... earthbound. Walking... upright. Yes! Could they... can they be? They are! What else? Hapelemur erectus! Run faster, panting: James, James, James... Promise, promise... won't lose them now... so close... Damn fog... or is it smoke? I smell smoke. What's that sound? They're singing! Running and singing... too much mist... can't see them, only hear. Follow music. Follow pipes of Pan...

I burst out of the deep woods onto the shore of a lake. In the middle, silhouetted against a patch of burning forest on the opposite shore, was an island hardly larger than a wooded rock. A hundred feet away, the giant lemurs faded in and out of a drifting blue fog, etched against the orange glow across the water.

I rushed forward.

The fog rolled in, they disappeared.

But wait... That singing! Yes. I knew that song. Massed wail of voices, it faded on a veer of mist, returned to fade again, a primal keening that combined time and distance into an aching present.

I was almost on top of them. The fog swirled. An opening... and I saw them clearly.

Heartrush of kundalini heat.

They were wrong! Wrong! All of them! James, Rex, Rakotomana. These were not lemurs. Not a new species, nor an extinct one. They were...

...*tiny humans.*

The Ones Who Came First.

The eternal, invisible...Vazimba.

I raised my arms and sang, walking into the fog toward the Little People gathered on the shore. Singing to them. Letting them sing to me.

Greeting, acclamation.

Antiphon, response.

Out of the blue mist, Rangita came forth.

She guides me in the right paths for her people's sake.

She took my hand and led me down to the edge of Lake Marovoay.

Beside the waters she leads me. She restoreth my soul.

The fog swirled around me. It felt cool and welcoming.

Yea, though I walk through the valley, I shall fear no evil.

It seemed only natural that when the crocodiles arose we should step out upon their backs, lightly, confidently, as if they were a dance floor, and let them ferry us across the water to Andrebabe.

When your head is submerged in the sea, how will your eye fall on the color of the water?

I didn't realize it then, but the moment I stepped onto those crocodiles' backs I had slipped through the veil of Time and entered another reality—a Vazimba reality.

I had entered the world of the ancestors.

43

"From here one can see everything."

I knelt down beside Rangita, resting my arms on the railing, following her gaze around the perimeter of the lake where plumes of black smoke arose. We were on the topmost gallery of the royal palace, sipping tiny cups of *tokagasy*, a potent brew made from fermented sugar cane.

Like every structure in Andrebabe, Rangita's palace was very small, built to fit the needs of little, forest people. It was a narrow, wood building consisting of a ground floor and two stories, surmounted by an extremely high, steeply pitched roof. The walls were framed with panels of diagonal wood and it was roofed with circular shingles, like a gingerbread Victorian playhouse built for a princess. The stories were surrounded by open galleries supported by columns of some kind of perfumed wood. Every joint was perfectly dovetailed, pegged with wooden plugs and wrapped with decorative rope. I didn't see a single nail. The ends of the rafters extended well beyond the roofline, dipping towards the ground with a graceful swoop, then banking up into the sky. Each was intricately carved in the shape of a swimming crocodile and marked with a single blue handprint—the mark of the artist. These rafters, as well as every window and door frame, had been hung with little silver bells that chimed with the passing breeze. It was a magical, harmonious, and deeply feminine building, more like a temple than a palace.

Below, the thatched houses of Andrebabe nestled like a clutch of contented chicks. The village was very small—I counted no more than twenty huts—and was well-concealed in a grove of ancient trees. Close by, tucked into the edges of the forest, were garden plots and rice paddies, irrigated by an intricate system of bamboo pipes and sluice gates that brought water up from the lake. The breeze carried the rhythmic sounds of splashing water, rice being pounded, and the faint, birdlike cries of Vazimba children. Farther off, down along the lakeshore, a brace of grey-green crocodiles lay sunning themselves, their snouts facing the water, tails toward the palace, guarding the island. I thought of the clanging cable cars, the freeways, the pell-mell rush and grab of San Francisco. The contrast could not have been more profound. Andrebabe simmered in a repose from which all fret of existence seemed to have ebbed away, an undisturbed umbilicus lost in the belly of Eden.

Rangita interrupted my reverie. "Sister, what you are seeing, across the lake, means the end of our world."

I stared across the water, trying to penetrate the rising plumes of smoke to a clearing where I knew the CANTEX camp, and Jack Mooresby, had to be, imagining heliports and pumping stations, dredged rivers and roads slashing through the forest. Who would stop them? And the fires they'd set to clear a spot for their camp? How long would they burn in a lonely green spot like this?

I knew the answer: until next January's cyclones extinguished them, or all the forest was gone. Whichever came first.

"I see a great deal," I said, "But I don't see everything. I don't see... James."

She frowned and pulled her cloak around her.

"*Does not the fish when it hears the sound of the waves, flip from the shore into the sea? Does not the hawk, on hearing the falconer whistle return, return, leave the hunt and return to the side of the king?*"

"Please," my voice trembled. "Stop this... this poetic doubletalk. Is it so hard to tell me straight out? He's dead, isn't he?"

She reached over and pulled a raffia strap that hung from a beam. I heard a bell ring somewhere downstairs and within seconds Noro appeared, gliding soundlessly across the polished gallery, igniting a burst of glowing sparkles from the hem of her cloak whenever it touched the floor. She was carrying a covered box made of finely plaited straw. When she approached me her eyes flashed on and off cautiously, with a measured *sobriedad* that I hadn't seen in her before. I could have sworn she was frightened.

"Open it," Rangita ordered.

I lifted the lid. Inside was something wrapped in a piece of blue silk.

I flushed. What was this? Idols? Some kind of Vazimba *sampy*? I unfolded the cloth and saw a notebook. On top of it lay a pair of bent, wire-rimmed glasses. *James'* glasses.

I burst into tears.

Rangita came and knelt beside me. Her oiled and braided hair gleamed like a crown. As she settled herself, I smelled her body heat, rich and sweet, like cocoa butter and tuberose. Suddenly I hated her, brushed her away and hid my face.

She spoke gently, "Eva, when your soul heard your brother's call, you didn't hesitate to release your life and fly to an unknown world. You spread your wings and escaped the cage of your reality, abandoning a stagnant pool to plunge into the running waters of life. Without understanding and filled with fear, you stubbornly persevered, determined to pursue your obsession, your dream of finding him.

"So what?" I whispered. cradling the glasses. "What does that have to do with him... now?"

"Everything." She stroked my arm softly. "Can't you see? James is no different than you, or the oil men. Or Michel Rakotomana. Dreamers, all of you. Each obsessed by your own private dream of the Blue Rainforest, believing you could find within it what you most desired—fame, wealth, animals, oil. And, in your case, a brother."

Some mixed-up fools even abandon love in pursuit of their dreams, I thought bitterly, remembering Jack. How he looked after the *famadihana*, on the top of that hill, waving his arms, with the bandanna on his head. A beautiful, Assyrian pirate. Or, kneeling with his hand outstretched beside the rickshaw, begging me, *Artema, I want you... I love you.*

Rangita reached up and took the *arivolahy* down from a peg where it hung from its silver chains.

"For King Botofino and the people of Ambohitsara, the forest and the sacred lake, the invisible village... these are more than a dream to be plundered for riches or ego. They are the dream at the center of the Malagasy world. Their continued existence maintains its timeless, unchanging stability. Educated people may dismiss Andrebabe and the Vazimba as primitive superstitions, but in the inmost heart of every Malagasy... it is a very different matter. They know. They believe. They need us, for we guard their past and protect their future. If the dream of the Vazimba should be destroyed, Madagascar itself will sicken and die."

...and become extinct, like a wild lemur. What was it Rasti had said? *The invisible village, I fear we shall lose it forever...* A scientist, far away in a cluttered laboratory on a hilltop in Tananarive—even *he* needed to believe.

"As you can see," Rangita indicated the rising plumes of smoke, "our forest has become a battleground. A place where dreams collide... and die." Her eyes began to glow with that peculiar blue light I recognized as Vazimba passion.

I clutched James' notebook, thumbing the worn edge of the cover. "And the dreamers?" I queried bitterly. "What happens to them when they collide with the Vazimba? Do they die, or simply disappear?"

"Sometimes..."

"Sometimes... what?"

She tugged her robes tightly around her until she resembled a small, white chrysalis. "Against a single intruder, here and there, we are powerful. But against so many... our magic is not sufficient. To battle the smugglers and these *vazaha* oilmen with their machines, their guns and their aircraft, we need more than *odys*. We need a warrior who can dream many dreams and bridge many worlds. A warrior who can fathom the mysteries of the *vazaha* mind and..." she flashed a smile, "the mysteries of *vazaha* men. For this we need a powerful *vazaha* woman."

It was the same, heady, seductive rap she'd laid on me before. But this time it seemed different. After everything I'd been through, I almost believed her.

"That's why, after Rexworthy's capture, we lured James away, tantalizing him with glimpses of 'giant lemurs.' We knew that inevitably you would follow."

"So, you used James as a lure to capture me."

"Yes," she said. "To save us."

Twisted Malagasy agendas! Rakotomana using me to find James in order to capture non-existent lemurs. Rangita using James to capture me, in order to destroy Rakotomana and CANTEX. It was Code Blue run amok, I buried my head in my arms.

"Don't think it was easy, Eva. It took all of our magic to bring you to Andrebabe. At every turn, with each test, we were in danger of losing you to fear and stubbornness." Her face broadened into a smile, "But now we can rest. We have our warrior."

I shook the spectacles at her. "Not so. I still don't have what I came for."

"Later, sister," she touched my shoulder, directing my gaze across the lake.. "First, the oilmen." The smoke was blowing to the west and for the first time I could see the CANTEX camp. The sunlight reflected off the yellow struts of the half-built drilling rig and the pre-fab, tin-roofed shack at its base.

Jack...

Rangita put a hand over my heart.

"Tonight is a full moon. There will be a *tsialinalina* celebration with much drumming and dancing. It is a time for love. Go to him," she whispered urgently. "Dance with him. Take him. Make him understand the folly of this project. He is the key."

"Jack Mooresby?"

"Without a helicopter and a pilot, the oilmen cannot proceed. They are doomed."

"But, Jack's not in charge. He doesn't act alone. He's just taking orders. There's Paul and Fred and God knows how many others involved."

"We have observed them from the forest. These other *vazaha* have no power. They are weak weeds blowing by the side of the road. Jack is a good man, Eva. A strong man. He loves you. Convince him to withdraw, and he will convince the rest."

"And you'll return my brother?"

She looked down. "I... can't promise you that."

"You can't... what?!" I twisted away. "Then forget Eva Artema! Without James, the Vazimba and Madagascar can burn in hell, for all I care!"

She sighed. "First, you must make me a promise."

"No!" I stood up, casting off her hand. "No more deals. No more agendas. No more promises! It's time for you to trust... *me*."

She said nothing, but her eyes were shooting electric blue sparks. I would have bet anything that mine were, too. The shoe was on the other foot. For once, I had *corazón*, and it felt good.

"Take me to James," I said. "*Now.*"

Noro led the way. She followed a well-worn path through frothy masses of magenta and pink periwinkles. We passed through a gateway formed by two upright plinths. The trail wound through a glade of tree ferns. Their curling tips brushed against my face, soft as sable watercolor brushes. Not far from the water's edge the path narrowed down and slithered into a dense stand of giant bamboo.

I squeezed between the stalks behind Rangita and the little *kokolampo*. Peering through the branches, I saw a thatched hut built on stilts, with a small verandah on three sides. On the porch, shaded by the overhanging palm fronds, was a stool and a rickety table. Seated at it, writing furiously, was James. Across from him, perched on the edge of the table about a foot away, sat a beautiful golden-brown lemur nibbling on a fresh, green stalk of bamboo. Its tail twitched every now and then, exactly like a cat about to pounce on a sparrow.

"Bibi!!" I shouted, rushing towards him. "Bibi, it's me! Evita!"

He was wearing his bright red Cornell T-shirt and had grown a full, blonde beard. His hair was long, too, tied back with a string. Straight-laced, nerdy James, in a pony-tail! He seemed fit, but thinner than I remembered him. With his pale myopic eyes no longer hidden behind those scholarly lenses, he looked angelic and transparently vulnerable. He kept on writing, absent-mindedly lifting his left hand to gently stroke the lemur's fur without interrupting his note-taking.

What the...? I knew he was near-sighted without his glasses, but was he deaf?

"*Mio fratello! Sono qui!*"

I sprang directly in front of the hut and threw open my arms in the wildest, warmest, most *famiglia* welcome you've ever seen.

But James didn't see. Any of it. He stopped writing, put down his pencil, stretched, looked right through me and walked slowly back into the hut. The brown lemur tagged along after him, like a tame puppy, dragging the stalk of bamboo behind it.

"James!! Wait! *Tua sorellina e arrivata!*"

I charged up the stairs, ready to follow him... And put my foot right through the step. I grabbed the table... It wasn't there. I reached for the lemur... My hand passed through its body as well.

"He's not... James... It's all a lie! He's not real!"

"*Tiens,* Eva," Rangita came up behind me quietly. "Of course everything is real. It is only that you and he do not share the same realities."

"No!" I kicked the wall of the hut as hard as I could.

Nothing! I was kicking thin air.

Rice balls and *ro*! "Either he doesn't exist, or I don't exist. It has to be one or the other."

"Does it?" Rangita smiled. "Why can't it be both?"

Both?

I hid my face, head pounding, trying to reshuffle the confused jigsaw pieces of reality so they made sense. Real people don't live in dreams, or on astral planes. In thin air. They live in real villages, towns, cities. Places made of wood and thatch, stone and steel. Places filled with huts, houses, offices, restaurants. Places like the Blue Rainforest. That was real, and the animals in it. I had the leech bites to prove it. But to "live" in an alternate reality? How do you do that? What happens to time? Do you get old? Do you eat? Do you see, do you hear? I had "heard" Rangita in the car on the way to Mananjary, even without "real" ears. Why couldn't James hear me? Or see me? Father Soren had it pegged: let a dream become your god, and you'll lose your soul, go mad, or die. James had been my obsession, my *sampy*. I'd staked my life on finding him, and now...

...where was he?

"Bibi!" I pushed against the thatched walls of the little hut. It was like trying to push a hologram, offering no resistance, no density, nothing but a quixotic shimmer of light and air, spinning out of reach on a different vibration.

"Come. The helicopter is landing. Soon I fear they will be lighting new fires across the lake. It is time to go down and meet our people."

I felt a fetid breath blow hot against my leg and whipped around.

Rangita had disappeared. Lying on the red earth at my feet was a great grey crocodile, older than God, bigger than Kon Tiki, with more rows of crooked teeth than you could count in a lifetime. If it wasn't the Old Queen, it was a more than reasonable facsimile. Noro sat crosslegged on her scaly back, wrapped in white *mufti*, like a little rajah without a *howdah*. She peeked out from under her hood, her dazzling, coin eyes going gang-busters. The Old Queen chuffed once loudly, thrashed her tail, spun around, and spraddled off through the forest, leaving a sinuous curve and a flotsam of croc-prints imprinted on the dirt behind her.

I looked back at James' hut. The outer edges of the roof glowed, the whiskery thatch radiated a blue light, as if backlit by a cobalt sunset. As I watched, my brother came out onto the porch. He was barefoot and smiling, holding the golden-brown lemur tenderly. There was another, woolly white *sifaka* with a long, black tail perched on his shoulder. A third, very small, dainty little lemur with suction-y prehensile toes and nut-sized, perfectly round, shining eyes, clung to the curls of his beard. Oh I loved James so terribly at that moment, so intensely. My whole being felt flooded with light, and love. He *isn't* dead, I kept telling myself. He still exists. It was unbearable not to be able to touch him, and talk to him. But what struck me the most—what I'll never forget—was how incredibly happy James looked. I'd never seen him that happy. Ever.

If only Papa and Rex were here to see him like this.

44

Rangita sat in the shade of a mighty banyan tree at the water's edge, surrounded by the Vazimba. It was easy to distinguish her in the deep, gloomish shadows because of her white *lamba*. The rest of the Little People, perched silently on the raised roots of the tree with their very dark skins and brown raffia garments, were almost invisible. Only their eyes gave them away, sparkling with the same iridescent blue as Rangita's. They could have been a tree full of owls, or night moths.

I sat down beside her. The Vazimba crowded in around us, jostling back and forth. I felt like a rough, rose quartz among polished, obsidian pebbles. My *vazaha* edges dissolved as the Little People pushed against me—my lurching pinkness, my long nose, my spinstery, angular, childless body and quick, brittle defensiveness; hard, First World edges, formed by another reality ten thousand miles away. Sharp edges, that had so plagued me here, that had kept me separate and uneasy, an outsider—began to disappear in the raffia rustle of the Vazimba body-pod.

"I believe you have met some of us already," Rangita indicated a grinning, gap-toothed man on her left.

I squinted to make him out in the shadows. It was Ratelifera, the herb-seller from the Zoma market. I hardly recognized him without his straw hat and red shirt.

He tipped his head. "How is your wound, mademoiselle? I trust it has healed."

Before I could answer, I felt a plucking at my sleeve, and a bony hand clasped my elbow. I turned and saw...

...the old hag from Lake Anosy!

"*Voici, la reine de Vazimba. Ici en Andrebabe.*" She creased up, her lined cheeks quivering with pleasure.

"Mademoiselle, you did not disappoint us," intoned a deep, male voice.

I had to stand up to see who had spoken.

The astrologer from the *famadihana* waved his stick in greeting. Seated next to him, dainty as a fallen thistle on the gnarled roots, was an extremely old man. He pressed his thin hands together and touched his forehead. "*Namaste,*" he wheezed.

Dr. Rabansoro... the old yogi.

Rangita waved at another, muscular man, who squatted in the shadows.

The rickshaw driver from Mananjary saluted me. "We are pleased you have reached your happy destination."

"We lack but one," Rangita said, surveying the group.

Not for long. From the forest there came a puffing, shuffling, hum-de-dumming. Out from under a giant fern trundled a portly little man wearing sprung rubber zoris. His raffia toga was rumpled and he had the distracted air of an absent-minded professor—which, of course, he was.

"Mademoiselle Eva!" Rasti's smile split his face wide open. He laughed and clapped his hands in childlike delight, hopping from one foot to another. "Welcome to our circle of magicians. Andrebabe is a pisser, is it not?"

Fortune goes up and down like a cartwheel revolving.

So, I hadn't been a solitary *vazaha*, after all. I'd had company all along on the path. On the up side, and the down side, my Vazimba *famiglia* had been with me every step of the way, weaving their invisible nets to catch me when I stumbled.

"*Namaste*," I said, bowing to one and all. "Andrebabe is a definite pisser." I was laughing and crying at the same time.

Noro, who had been taking in the proceedings hanging upside-down on a branch high above, let out a high shriek, turned one joyous cartwheel and plummeted to the ground in front of me in a shower of sparks.

That was a signal for the reunion to begin. Everyone started talking at once, and we didn't stop until the full moon had risen over the eastern mountains and I stood on the steps of the palace, perfumed and oiled, ready to lay siege to Jack Mooresby.

Rangita took my arm and led me down to a rock ledge overlooking the blue-black water. I reached up and touched my elaborately coiffed hair, braided and twisted and teased into a blonde cathedral. The ends of the braids, heavy with silver beads, jingled softly. Looking into Rangita's mirror, I had watched them line my eyes with charcoal and brighten my lips with henna. Even my bare toes and ankles had been blushed with rouge.

"If I fail?" I said. "What then?"

"Do not fail." The moonlight gilded Rangita's ebony cheekbones. "A warrior does not fail."

On the beach directly in front of us lay an ornate dugout canoe—Queen Rangita's pirogue. The uplifted Polynesian prow was carved in the shape of a leaping crocodile, like the rafters of the palace. Many blue handprints bordered the gunwales; every artist in Andrebabe had contributed to its creation. On either side of the boat the shoreline was ringed with crocodiles, pressed nose-to-tail in a thick, unbroken line, packed so close you could've walked all the way around the island and never stepped once onto dry land. From underneath them, every now and then, leaked a flickering tongue of incandescent blue mist.

"They are yours," Rangita said. "Command them."

She embraced me for a long time, holding me tight. I felt her strong heartbeat through the red silk of the *lambas* that two Vazimba girls had spent the afternoon creating, sewing four of hers together to make one large enough to wrap around me. "Don't worry, Eva," she whispered encouragingly. "When one is in love and jumps in the river, one achieves... miracles."

I tried to squelch a nagging fluttering of fear as the memory returned of the horrible cage and King Botofino, toppling sideways, blood pooling on his grey blanket.

"What if Michel Rakotomana is with them?"

Her eyes blazed and she struck a fist. "Bring him to me and I will eat him, before dawn, together with his shell."

Vazimba power!!

"Sister warrior," I slapped her five, "When this is over, you and I will dine on *that* Malagasy crab... together."

I turned out to be a master paddler once I got the hang of it. Josef and Salim would've been proud of me. Of course it helped to have an army of crocs swarming alongside, guiding the pirogue. In the time it took for the Vazimba to tune their *valihas* and get out their drums, the hull had bumped against the far shore and I was hiking up my skirts and wading towards the CANTEX camp in the warm lake.

It was eerie. Sooty black night, chiaroscuro light. Amber-orange flames in the burning forest. Silver splashes of celestial moon on the water. Yang and yin. Tugging. At war. I was barefoot, on my way to an assignation that was unexpected, uninvited, and quite likely unwelcome. I padded silently past the unfinished drilling rig, and the piles of struts awaiting installation, past the strange, hulking oddly shaped crates and equipment—the accumulated techno-rubble of a wildcat oil camp.

I heard them before I saw them. Loud male laughter and

shouts. Someone banged a bottle down on a table and let out a rebel yell. I sidled around and stood on tiptoe, peering in the lighted window of the shack.

They were playing cards—Paul, Jack, Fred and Rakotomana—seated on wooden crates around a table made from a cable spool. A gas pressure lantern hung from the roof, hissing steadily. Under its aluminum-bright light, they looked like four tin men. In the middle of the table lay a pile of Malagasy francs. There were Three Horse beer bottles everywhere and an empty bottle of Johnny Walker. Hammocks had been slung along the walls and in one corner, near a drying croc skin, a mosquito coil smoked sullenly, its red tip glowing like an evil eye.

"Eat *that*, flyboy," said Paul, slamming a fistful of cards on the table.

"I'm out." Jack tossed his hand onto the pile.

Fred Pearson smugly laid his cards down, face-up, took off his glasses, wiped them, blinked a few times into the too-bright light, and began to tidy up the pile of bills, stacking them so their edges matched evenly. He had a superior little smile on his thin grey lips.

"*Excusez-moi,*" said Rakotomana in a rumbling baritone, "This game belongs to me." He fanned a straight flush and laid it flat, covering Fred's cards.

"Motherfucker!" Fred let go of the money. It landed in a disorderly heap, a few, errant bills drifting to the floor.

Rakotomana waited.

Fred didn't move.

"Pick them up," said Rakotomana in a way that made me not want to know if that bulge under his left arm was muscle or gun.

"Mellow out, man. He didn't mean nothin' by that, did you, lil' buddy?" said Paul, and belched.

Fred looked anxiously to Jack for support. His nose twitched, a nervous, ratty tic.

Jack stood up and stretched. Very slowly.

Lord god...Yes. I pressed my nose to the glass. Sign me up. I'll take him. He was still wearing that black T-shirt and everything showed, tan and defined.

"Simmer down," Jack said. "No sense everybody getting riled up about a handful of francs worth less than five bucks."

"Yeah," said Paul. "Let's talk about the island."

I tingled all over.

"According to Pearson here," he continued, "it sits dead center on a monster field. Who knows? Maybe five, ten, twenty thousand barrels a day..." He walked over to a blow-up of a geologic topo that was pinned to the wall. "According to *this*, the island doesn't exist. Nobody knows the damn thing's here but us."

...and a handful of Little People.

I leaned closer, straining to hear.

"I say we do a reccie tomorrow. Think you can land the bird over there?" Fred asked.

Jack hesitated. "Like I told you before, I'm willing to give it a shot. It all depends if that ground fog lifts long enough for me to nail a flat spot—providing there is one. You saw it on the fly-overs. Looks like some pretty dense primary forest."

"What the hell then," Paul shrugged. "Why not drop some incendiaries and start a burn. A couple of days ought to be enough to clear a decent pad. We'll have to do that anyway if we're going to rig it and punch a core sample."

Incendiaries! Start a burn! In Andrebabe? I thought my heart was going to jump out of my chest.

"Hold on, Paul." Jack tried to rein him in. "Don't you think you're jumping the gun a little here?"

"Hell no, Mooresby. Take a look around you, man. Ain't nothing but empty jungle far as me and you can see."

"I don't like it..." Jack began.

"Shut up, Mooresby," said Fred Pearson. "CANTEX pays you good money to fly... where we tell you."

"Money!" Rakotomana slammed his fist drunkenly on the wooden spool. He wasn't finished with Fred. "Pick up the money." The gentleman's pose had disappeared. "Mother. Fucker." His eyes were narrow slits, but even so I could see that the whites were

Johnny Walker red. He stood up angrily, cracking his head on the lamp. It swung wildly back and forth. He grabbed for it and knocked it to the floor, plunging the shack into darkness. There was a lot of swearing and some heavy objects being thrown around. Then the door flew open and Jack staggered out into the moonlight. He unzipped his fly and began to relieve himself. It wasn't your classic invitation to romance, but hey.

"Mooresby!" I whispered, stepping out of the shadows.

The guy leapt about four feet into the air.

"Jesusfuckingchrist!"

It was him all right.

"Shhhhh... I need to talk to you. Quick. Before those bozos figure out you're missing."

"Artema? What the..."

Something smashed against the wall of the shack and broke. Probably a beer bottle. Maybe Johnny W. Possibly Fred.

I slipped past Jack, just close enough so that he could get a good whiff of *ylang-ylang* and jasmine but not so close he could grab me, and kept running down the slope towards the beach.

He charged after me.

I ran lightly, surprised at how agile and confident I was. Then again, don't forget that bivouac in the rainforest. Experience is knowledge.

When he finally caught up with me on the shore, he was panting hard. "Jeez, it's really you! In the moonlight back there, with that hairdo, buried in those *lambas*, I thought you were a goddamn Malagasy ghost."

I wanted to laugh hysterically, but instead I put my hand on the prow of the pirogue. "Would you care to join me for a paddle? The lake is very beautiful at night."

I'll admit it was awfully stiff and formal, but I was having trouble finding the language to match my royal attire. The same thing used to happen to me at high school dances. A schpritz of hair spray, perfume and some tulle. It never failed: high tea and a raised pinky. I lost a lot of cute guys going uptown like that.

Jack shook himself like a cocker spaniel after a bath, rubbed his face all over, pulled both ears, punched himself in the chest a bunch of times, and groaned, "Am I fuckin' dreaming or what?"

"Good. Get in. I'll paddle. And please, stop swearing."

"There's no way... where'd you get... how in the..."

I moved in real close. "Does that mean you'd rather stay here and duke it out with the boys?"

"I never said."

"So, c'mon. Hop in." I made sure he felt my nipples brush against his bare arm through the thin silk.

He did. His voice dropped a notch and he put one leg over the side. "Not before you explain..."

"Right," I said, picking up the paddle and shoving off. "Chinese it is."

As I dug into the dark water, I saw hundreds of half-sunken crocodile eyes glowing red in the reflected light from the burning forest behind the CANTEX camp. What I didn't see was Rakotomana, crouching at the edge of the shore. I probably thought he was a boulder or a bush. Even if I had seen him, the way I was feeling, it wouldn't have mattered. I had my prey.

45

Coming, going, the water birds leave no trace...

I paddled strongly, smoothly. The water rushed past, breaking into plumes of dark crystal against the prow. The rainforested mountains towered above us, immense and black, nudging the stars. Jack leaned back in the bow against a straw bolster and faced me with his arms folded over his chest. He had blitzed me with dozens of questions, only one of which I had answered.

"Where are you taking me?"

"*Tsialinalina*," I said, following the highway of moonlight across the water. I could hear the sound of drumming and singing floating across from the island.

He tugged his mustache and cleared his throat. "Artema, are you for real? Or is this some kind of alcoholic wish-fulfillment?"

"Both."

"Tell me I'm going to wake up passed out in a hammock tomorrow stinking of stale beer and pyrethrum."

"Probably."

"There's no way you could have made it through the rainforest alone."

"Of course."

"Which means you found your brother."

"Yes and no."

"Care to share?"

"Let's just say I've seen him, but he hasn't seen me. Don't ask me to explain."

He sighed. "You know Rakotomana's dangerous."

"I know."

"Dangerous. Armed. And angry. You shouldn't have come to camp. You could've been killed."

"*You* could be killed."

"Nah, he needs me."

"And you don't need him?"

He segued uncomfortably. "He's certain that you know where James is."

"I do. Sort of."

"Circles again... I don't get it. Every time I'm with you, something goes haywire, like... I've slipped on a banana peel and all of a sudden, I'm upside-down. Artema, you're a hell of a crazy-making broad."

I backpaddled, turning the canoe so he had a full view of the flames slowly licking the edges of the forest behind the CANTEX camp. "Jack, you want to know crazy. *That's* crazy."

"Is that why you brought me out here? To lecture me on the environment?"

"No." Soft, Eva. Walk softly. "I brought you here to dance."

"The hell... On water? Sorry. Best I can do is walk on that."

"They say cowboys are the next best thing to Jesus."

He laughed.

"...and pilots are... God."

He laughed harder, crinkling his mustache. "Yeah. So they say."

I stopped paddling. We could hear the insistent beating of the drums from across the water, punctuated by wild, warlike cries.

"Seems like the party's started without us," he said.

I smiled. "Maybe not."

I slid down into the center of the pirogue, knelt beside him and put my arms around him. My tongue searched the hollow of his neck where the blood beat, pressing him against me. I felt his penis stiffen.

"I don't want to move," he said.

"So, don't."

Wavelets collapsed against the bottom of the boat.

"Remind me to breathe," he whispered.

"Why?"

"I keep forgetting."

He held me at arm's length and ran his hands across my moonlit face. My beaded braids jingled. He played with the silver crocodiles on my necklace, moving his thumbs across my hardening nipples. "You beautiful, silver bitch," he murmured. "I'll bet you're silver all the way through, right down to your beautiful, silver cunt."

"They say." I sank down on top of him and put my hands behind his head. When I put my mouth over his mouth, I felt him smile before his tongue began searching for mine.

"Let's dance," I said, and unzipped his jeans.

"I... I don't disco."

"So I hear."

His hardness filled my hand and now I was the one afraid to move, knowing how close he was to coming.

He unwrapped my *lambas*, one by one, until there was nothing left but skin and moonlight. Then he straddled me, kissing my breasts. His mustache was soft and wet. "What planet does a goddess like you come from, anyhow?"

I caught his hands in mine, then his eyes. The trance was like a river, holding us under its steady surface. "Same place as a god like you."

A fish jumped. Was it Noro?

He knelt in front of me and the tip of his penis moved

342

erratically across my naked breasts, like a hot, wild bird.

It was hard to say whose body was burning brighter when I cupped my hands over his tight, cowboy ass and took him in my mouth. His fingers fluttered between my legs, beating in time to the Vazimba drums. The canoe rocked and I felt my insides swelling, bursting with wanting him, wanting him to never stop, go in deep enough to fill the crater that four years of emptiness had left deep in my center, wanting him to wipe out all the anger and the loneliness and the dried-out solitary nights and days, the TV dinners and the Sunday paper and the early-bird matinees and the piles of scrap waiting to be turned into art. Wanting him to take me, make me die, and resurrect me—bring me back to life.

"Come inside me, Mooresby. Now... now." I arched my back, ready for him, but instead he bent over me and I felt his tongue snaking over my belly in and out and in and out, there and everywhere, between my legs.

"Don't laugh," he said.

"It tickles."

"Hold still, I'm writing my name." And he kept on, and on, with his hands never leaving my breasts.

"Oh God, stop it, stop it," I moaned, wanting more.

"Mmmmm... No way. I want everyone to know, Artema. You belong to me."

You belong to me...

Lord, what those words released! A kundalini flash of serpent red flames roared up out of my spine. I became all mouth, all *yoni*. Yawning, open, desiring. Biting. Eating. Oh yes, I wanted to eat that little crab. Suck every bit of flesh from his sweet, rude bones. And when I pulled him down onto me into the devouring darkness I couldn't tell where his black curls stopped and the sky started, his shoulders and arms and belly moving over me like moving mountains blocking the heavens, my legs spread out on either side of the pirogue in a deep silvery V, strong as eucalyptus branches thrown against the moon. "I can't help it..." he kept saying. "I can't help it..." And coming to a brightness, like an imploding star, neither could I.

We awoke near dawn into a chill, milky-blue darkness. A deep fog had descended while we slept. The *lambas* covering us were soaked with dew, but my body was still as hot as a cooking stone. Our *pirogue* had drifted into a stand of bulrushes close to shore. They rustled gently, leaning protectively, making me think of Pharaoh's daughter leaning over the baby Moses.

Jack stirred and made a place for me on the bolster, murmuring, "So, how'd you learn to be so loving...?"

"Celibacy U. I was a four-year student."

He traced a finger around the edge of my lips. "With a B.A. in Blonde Witchcraft..."

"Jack..." I raised myself on both elbows, letting the point of the croc tooth trail across his chest. "Zaohitra is a protected Reserve. This CANTEX exploratory, the indiscriminate burning, the smuggled animals..."

"Come here."

"No." I pulled back. "Listen to me. It's wrong. It stinks. You know it."

"Honey, the deal's between Rakotomana and CANTEX. What's it got to do with you and me?"

"It's not too late. They can pull out now and save face. Nobody has to know."

"Eva, you're not hearing. I fly birds. Period. I don't make policy."

I sat up. "Refuse to fly."

"Hello. Earth to Eva."

"Don't take them to the island." My voice was shaking.

"What's got into you? Relax."

"Tell them it's not safe. You can't land. You can do it." I was shivering.

"Since when did you start hugging trees?"

"Since... since..." It was madness. How could I explain an invisible village, the palace, the Vazimba gathered under the giant banyan tree? "James," I said suddenly. "My brother James. His camp is on the island."

It was Jack's turn to sit up straight. "Holy shit," he whistled in disbelief. "No lie."

It wasn't a lie. Not really. But it did the job. It got his attention.

"The island is inhabited by... it's full of... lemurs, just like the Blue Rainforest, only different ones, rare ones. It's... it's a magic place, Jack. It's no place for oil derricks and drilling rigs. Leave it alone."

The bottom of the canoe bumped against the shore.

"I understand your wanting to protect your brother and his research," Jack said, "but sooner or later..."

"No. Not sooner or later. Never." I stood up naked and tall, astride him, trying to keep my balance in the unstable *pirogue*. "Say you won't do it. Lie to them if you have to."

His face flushed and I saw him growing hard again.

"Sonofabitch woman, you're an awesome piece of work."

"Say it, Jack. Say you won't fly them there."

"Okay, okay. I won't. I said it. Come here, you amazon queen." He kicked his legs up, wrapping them around my thighs, pulling me down onto him. "Promise?"

"What do you want from me? An affidavit? A blood oath? Human sacrifice?"

"All of the above."

I guided him inside me. "Will this do, for starters." And I began to ride him, moving slowly, rhythmically, feeling the length of him in the depth of me. "How'm I doing, cowboy?"

"You ride very well, mademoiselle," Michel Rakotomana said, pushing aside the rushes with the snub nose of his Luger. "Now, let us see if your stallion can fly. Get dressed, pilot. The three of us are are going for a ride."

46

I think the Old Queen made the first move, but I can't be sure. All I know is that something huge and dark rose up underneath the *pirogue* and *blamm!* Mooresby and I were upside down in the drink and the dugout slid forward and slammed into Rakotomana, who started hollering, "*Mamba, mamba!*" Then Jack was all over Rakotomana, punching and kicking him and trying to wrestle the gun out of his hand, shouting at me to get the hell out of the water, there were crocodiles, as if I didn't know.

It was dark and misty down there in the reeds, but I could see something he couldn't, and that was Paul and Fred running down the bank towards the noise of the fighting. I wasn't taking any chances whose side they'd be on, not knowing if they were armed or unarmed or what kind of deals had been made or unmade after the fracas last night, so I did the only sensible thing—I dove down into the rushes and swam out of sight.

Good thing, too. Because once Paul and Fred started mixing it up, Jack was a goner. They didn't hurt him too badly, just enough. I saw his left eye swollen and he must have been cut on his head because there was a lot of blood streaking down his neck from somewhere up under his hair. He fought, though. I tell you, that guy fought like a Tasmanian devil, calling my name over and over. They kept trying to yank him up the bank, away from the water, and he kept trying to get back to where the pirogue lay tipped over on its side, until finally Rakotomana got off a couple of shots in the air to show he meant business, Jack caved in, and they led him off not exactly in handcuffs, but he might as well have been.

I lay half-submerged in the rushes, treading water furiously, watching them disappear over a rise.

They took my man.

They were burning the forest. Looting, killing animals.

They took my man.

They were going to destroy Andrebabe, my brother, my sister, and my Vazimba family.

They took my man!

I felt something nudge my right ankle. Something rough scraped along my left thigh. Something scaly passed back and forth under my stomach, bumped against my knees. I dog-paddled around in a circle in the murky water. King Botofino's men were right about the sacred lake. It was choked with soot and ashes and nasty, dead things that had washed down from the burnt forest. It was also filled with some nasty, living things. Everywhere I turned I saw monstrous snouts, blowing hot, riffling the surface of the lake—a vast, underwater army of reptiles.

I swam through the bulrushes, side-stroked along the lakeshore, pulling my way hand-over-hand through nets of waving eel-grass until I floated at last, like a dead log, directly in front of the CANTEX camp.

They had taken my man...

...and they were going to use him against... us!!

I floated in the shallows, hidden in the thick veil of fog. From behind the camp came the stutterings of Jack's helicopter.

Vazaha bastards!!

My eyes were even with the surface of the water, hob-nailed and planked with scales, teeth, tails and eyes. *Voay* eyes.

They are yours. Command them.

"*Ny tody tsy misy, fa ny atao no miverina!*" I shouted, not knowing where the words came from or what they meant, but they were in my mouth for me to shout and I did. The Old Queen rose up underneath me and I went for a ride for the second time that morning.

If thine eye be filled with darkness, thy whole body shall be filled with darkness also.

It was. Believe me, it *was*.

I threw my fist into the air. "Things eat things in Madagascar!" We charged.

Slithering, scrabbling, thrusting. Powerful, stubby legs, clawed toes scrambling swiftly over sand and mud and rocks. A moving sea of knobbed leather and yellow fangs, more determined than a column of army ants, more unstoppable than flowing lava, we swarmed out of the mist and into the CANTEX camp. Gnashing and biting, we tore through the standing crates, splintering the wooden sides. Dragging generators, pumps, pipes, valves and seals over bushes and stones, across the muddy shore, we sank them deep in the lake. We took the steel struts in our jaws, snapping them up like french fries, tossing them through the air. They flew everywhere, dashed against rocks and trees. Some caught in the branches. Some fell to the ground, useless and bent, like pieces from a ruined erector set. Our lashing tails made short work of cable spools and drums of fuel, sent them spinning, rolling, bouncing down the slope to oblivion in the murk. Then we turned, in one body, and bulldozed the shack. Thirty battering snouts running full tilt abreast, you can bet it collapsed *whoompff!* in a hot minute, and we were up and over the other side, claws screeching metallica as we lemminged across the corrugated tin roof and into the clearing where the helicopter was warming up.

The fog hugged the earth as we came on, blue and thick and

cold. We ran swiftly, low to the ground, hidden beneath it like a writhing of boa constrictors let loose in an unmade bed. The only sound you could hear was the clicking of hundreds of crocodile claws on the charred stubble of dead trees and scorched dirt.

And then, bursting out of the mist, we were on them.

I jumped down and ran towards the helicopter. Out in front, leading the charge, I couldn't see Jack, but Paul and Fred, framed in the back window, were the two scaredest, whitest, *vazahas* I'd ever laid eyes on. Their mouths were gaping black holes right out of Edvard Munch. No doubt there were screams coming out of them, but who could hear with the noise of the engine and the rotors slapping the air.

Something stung my thigh. I stumbled and fell, amazed to see red running out of a hole in my leg. Michel Rakotomana leaned out the open cargo door, popping off shots one after the other, trying to keep the seething, snapping mob at bay. He swung down and with one, mighty arm, swooped me up off the ground and dragged me in through the open hatch. Jack revved the motor, threw the throttle and the copter pitched forward. One of my warriors made a tremendous, kamikaze leap and bit into a landing skid. The croc hung on for the longest time after we were airborne, twisting in mid-air, gnawing and biting. Rakotomana pumped a hail of bullets into it before it gave up, loosened its grip, and plunged to its death in the middle of the sacred lake.

We circled over the mist-shrouded island for long minutes, searching for a place to land. Paul and Fred fumbled with some gauze and disinfectant from Jack's kit and finally tore up a T-shirt and began wrapping my leg. I must have passed out, or maybe it was just the adrenaline rush, but I felt nothing; I went completely numb.

Jack hovered over the small, rocky beach that lay directly below the hidden palace, trying to maneuver the aircraft onto a flat spot between the jutting stones. The noise inside the helicopter was deafening and I could imagine the effect of the rotor's vibrations on the jointed walls of the delicate, wooden building and upon the Little People themselves, who must be inside, clinging to each other and their queen, terrorized by this disastrous turn of events.

Jack zig-zagged lower and lower, finally jockeying the copter to a bumpy landing on the rock-strewn beach.

Do not fail… Rangita's words echoed in my brain as the blades fanned slowly to a halt and Rakotomana unlocked the chopper's door. The sun was just breaking through the fog that still lay heavily on the island.

Warriors do not fail.

He opened swung it open and pushed me forward.

"Walk," he ordered.

"Hey, wait a goddamned min—" Jack lunged

Rakotomana swung the Luger directly at him. "Sit down." He waved it at Paul and Fred. "That means all of you. Mademoiselle Artema and I have a piece of unfinished, family business to attend to."

"The hell… She doesn't have to…"

I turned to confront Jack. "No. I must go alone."

"Eva, you can't!" Jack jumped up and tried to grab Rakotomana, but Paul and Fred pulled him back into his seat and held him there.

"Shut up, Mooresby," Fred growled. "Let her go. D'you want to get us all killed?"

Rakotomana signalled at the rising mist. "We're wasting time." He pushed the nose of the gun into my back.

I climbed down and began to limp along the shore.

"Artema!" Jack was leaning out of the cockpit. I could see it was taking everything Paul and Fred had to hold him back. The dawn highlighted each, edible inch of him. An electrifying charge of passion, pride and power surged through me. Love—I'm here to tell you—love puts an *ody* to shame.

I tipped an imaginary Stetson at the helicopter and started

walking into the rising sun. After limping a short distance, I paused and turned. "Say, Mooresby," I called back, "You dance pretty good. For a cowboy."

Rakotomana was right behind me. I heard his booted footsteps clomping over the rocks.

That wasn't all I heard.

A sibilant swish of water streamed over scales and there was a faint clicking of claws on granite. And I knew without looking that my soldiers of the night were crawling up out of the shallows where they'd been hiding, closing ranks solidly behind us like a ring of armored tanks, surrounding the helicopter, stranding Jack and the boys on the beach, imprisoning them in the bird.

Sniffing the barn, Rakotomana never bothered to look back. And neither did I.

47

I led him directly into the forest, keeping the palace and the village well out of sight. He staggered and stumbled often, knocking his head on branches and overhanging creepers, following a trail that was narrow and low, having been carved out for Little People. I made no attempt to slow my pace for him. My sole concern was what would happen when we reached the clearing.

Would James be there? Would Rakotomana be able to see him? Or were the Vazimba and I the only ones who shared that hallucination? More ominous by far—what would he do when I couldn't produce a giant lemur? I was consumed by these and other grim thoughts as I approached the bamboo grove and peered through the slender trunks into the clearing.

Everything was just as I remembered—the palm-thatched hut, the porch, the rickety little table and chair with the opened notebook. James was kicked back, his bare feet atop the desk, playing with two baby *sifaka* with black tufts on their heads. He was teasing them with a pencil, tapping it lightly on their muzzles and then hiding it from view, the way you'd play with kittens. They jumped from the top of his head to the floor and back as if on hidden springs. A roly-poly golden lemur dashed out of the hut with a shredded bamboo stalk in its jaws and disappeared into the forest, chased by a brilliant, russet-red mongoose with bright beady eyes and translucent ears. Something the color of buckskin snoozed on the palm-fringed roof of the hut. It appeared to be a small panther with doggy legs and feet. When it stretched, it curled its long tail, showing rows of sharp teeth. From under the stilts of the verandah lumbered a black and yellow tortoise the size of a television. It halted, greeted the dawn with a *hisss*, and cruised back underneath the house.

Rakotomana caught up with me, perspiring and breathing heavily. He grasped my shoulder, digging the gun into my ribs.

I held my breath.

He parted the bamboo, following my gaze. "Where's the camp?"

I pointed silently towards James' hut.

"Show me," he said, pushing me ahead of him.

I stumbled; he pulled me upright.

I stopped for breath; he forced me forward.

I tried to twist aside; he hauled me across the clearing after him like a rag doll.

"Where? I don't see anything."

And then he proceeded to drag me right through the middle of James' hut, stepping through the dream as easily as you'd step through the dazzling end of a rainbow.

I slumped to the ground in despair.

The inning was over. The cupboard was bare.

Hapelemur erectus was a no-show, and everything else was invisible. A chimera is a chimera. Not a porch, a lemur or a man.

"*Michel...*"

He was startled. I'd never used his Christian name before.

"It's... it's just the two of us now. Why... rush things?" I shook my beaded braids, attempting a flirtatious smile. It was a lousy, humiliating vamp, but maybe I could stall him long enough to allow the Vazimba time to escape.

Rakotomana towered over me, unleashing that gecko overbite. "Mademoiselle Artema, you are an enchanting, but treacherous, specimen." He yanked me up off the ground, "But not nearly so enchanting as a giant lemur. *Where is your brother!?*"

I wrenched out of his grasp.

"You're standing on him, you blind bully!"

He aimed his gun at my chest, his face mottled with rage and confusion. "*Merde!* What kind of *vazaha* trick is this? I will kill you for it!"

Beyond terror, beyond *corazón*, I closed my eyes and waited for the blast, praying, *Come to my aid, O saints of God. Receive this soul. Take me home.*

The shot never came. Instead, the air was rent by a fierce, keening cry, erupting from a thicket of ferns.

My eyes flew open.

A little person stood in the dappled shadows.

It was Queen Rangita. Gone were the royal robes, the sparkling silver ornaments, the arrogant self-assurance of a warrior. She wore a ragged, brown toga and her hair was matted. Everything about her was wild, dark, and primitive.

"*Mon Dieu! Incroyable!* It is... *Hapelemur erectus!*" Rakotomana whispered hoarsely.

As I watched in horror, he holstered his gun and from his pocket took a length of thong with a stone tied to either end. He whirled it over his head several times and slung it across the clearing.

Rangita didn't stand a chance. She collapsed to the ground instantly with the thong wrapped tightly around her neck.

He raced over to her and began to unwind the bolo.

She lay upon a broken fern branch. The leaves curled up around her tiny body, forming a soft, green bier. She blinked once, and then said meekly, "Big man, please do not kill me. I am Vazimba."

He led her through the forest on a leash like a dog. I followed helplessly, my mind a tumult of heartbroken questions, none of which mattered now that she'd given herself up. Rakotomana was ebullient, triumphantly making plans to exhibit her in Tananarive, Paris and New York. Calling her a Malagasy Ishi. A human ceolocanth. A missing link. A living Ancestor. Running on about academic honorariums, television appearances, and the *Légion d'honneur*. Trumpeting about a ministerial appointment and his face engraved on franc notes. There was no end to his bloated inventions. Rangita stumbled along behind him, downcast and beaten, her shoulders sagging.

I stopped and knelt by the side of the path, burying my face in a spray of magenta orchids, letting the dewdrops hidden in the waxy petals run down my face. What was the point of going on? Rangita could have astralized herself, becoming invisible. But she had chosen a different fate, choosing to remain on this plane, sacrificing herself... to save *my* life. She uttered a small cry and I looked up just in time to see her slip and fall. Rakotomana jerked the thong. She staggered to her feet and began trudging forward again.

Oh, the shame of her sacrifice! A Vazimba queen—an ancestor!—marched off as a side-show attraction to amuse the First World. It was no good telling myself I'd done my best. She'd entrusted the salvation of her world to a *vazaha* who couldn't cut it. The CANTEX camp lay in ruins, but what difference did that make now? My best hadn't been good enough, not for the Vazimba, or for James. And now, with the capture of Rangita he, too, would disappear forever. Lost! All lost, fallen prey to the oil men and the scientists and the smugglers who would pour in and exploit the Little People and their glorious garden, the Blue Rainforest.

I tore at my head, grieving.

My journey was over. Why not end it now?

I ripped out the tight braids until my hair stood out in a mad, buzzing aureole. I stripped off the earrings, the bracelets, the beads, all the trappings that meant Malagasy, Vazimba, queen, sister. I lifted the crocodile necklace off my neck, and held it aloft for one, last look, preparing to place it on the ground along with the rest of my costume. It was so incredibly beautiful. Graced by the morning sun, the little silver crocs twinkled playfully, and the great ivory fang, once so ugly, now seemed refined, almost... elegant.

I shook the talisman.

It rattled.

I shook it again.

It made a scratchy noise.

I pried open the silver lid and looked inside.

Something wretched in there. A bundle of sticks, beans, mud, blood.

I overturned the tooth. Out fell the *ody*.

I picked it up and held it tightly, pressing it to my cheek. "Ro, sham, po..." I sobbed.

The journey was over...

I squeezed and squeezed. "Ro, sham... Noro! Noro, where are you? Can't you hear me? I'm calling you!"

But nothing happened. No flashing, no glow. No balls of light, spitting sparkles. No cloaked *kokolampo* materializing at my side, eyes strobing silver delight. The sticks bit into my palm, all the power gone out of them. Worthless *sampy*... I bowed my head and wept.

The magic journey was over.

Gradually I became aware of a delicate whirring in the air, soft as the purr of a sleeping cat. I looked up and saw a comet orchid, suspended from a tree branch. It was pale and yellow and fragile as the moth it was named for, with a tubular nectary so deep that I couldn't begin to imagine what kind of insect would be capable of fertilizing it.

The orchid quivered. Hovering above it was a grey sphinx moth the size of a sparrow. As I watched, it unfurled its hollow tongue from somewhere deep inside its thorax. Long, longer... until all fifteen, shiny, black inches of it was uncurled. Daintily, with unerring accuracy, the hawkmoth dipped it deep into the nectary and drank.

I knelt, in awe, watching it sip. O marvelous creature! Ancestral spirit! *Lolo!* The sage battles with his own ego; the ordinary man battles with other people's egos. But the creatures of paradise have no egos. At every moment, in their infinite variety, they simply express God—a reminder that the miraculous is forever beyond the hand of man. It is through them we glimpse the Divine. That's reason alone to love them, I thought. And to save them.

"Traitor!" I jumped up. "Murderer!" I screamed at the top of my lungs, and began hobbling wildly down the trail after Rakotomana, bandages flapping.

I arrived at the ledge just in time to see him picking his way down the slope to the water, boulder-hopping from rock to rock, with Rangita in tow. Below on the shore sat Jack's helicopter, to my surprise no longer guarded by crocodiles, but by Little People. Everyone was there: the old yogi, the crone, Rasti, the astrologer, Ratelifera, the *pousse-pousse* man, plus a handful of women with babies slung on their backs.

A handful... all that was left of the Vazimba.

They stood in a circle, holding hands, facing outward, and when they caught sight of Rakotomana dragging their captured queen over the stones on a leash, a great, anguished wail went up, a high-pitched, funereal dirge that just about ripped my heart out. They swayed to and fro, singing to their doomed queen the song of their doomed homeland—the song of Andrebabe. They never stopped singing, even as Rakotomana and Rangita forced their way between them.

"Wait!" I called out, limping down the slope. I cut through the circle, wheezing, gasping for breath. "This Vazimba belongs to me. My brother James discovered her, and as his sister, I claim her in the name of Artema. We deserve credit for her." I grabbed the leash. "It's a family affair. She goes with me."

Rangita turned and looked at me. Her eyes were sunken and

dispirited, but in their depths I saw flashing tongues of blue, like lightning over a river at midnight.

Listen to me, I beamed at her desperately, without a clue if my mind was capable of reaching her in her abject state. *Don't just... give up. Fight back. Don't let this happen!*

Her eyes were dull. She looked through me. I felt the cold wind of death blowing through my heart.

Go, I beamed. *Get out of here. Evaporate into a ball of fire. Whatever magic you have left, use it, for God's sake! Leave this plane now.*

She answered with infinite sadness, *You do not understand. I cannot abandon my people. I am their queen, they are my tribe. I am their mother, they are my children. Andrebabe is our home. We anchor each other. We sustain each other. We are fianakaviana be—a big family.*

"Get over here," Rakotomana pulled Rangita towards the helicopter.

I limped to her and pushed him aside. Taking both of her tiny hands in mine I squeezed, hard, the way I'd squeezed the *ody*. I felt something peculiar stirring at the back of my eyes and I didn't need a mirror to know that they were glowing—alive and crackling with a blue fire.

Rangita. I'm here to tell you, you are not alone. You called me. You created me. There are two warrior queens on this island now... a vazaha and a Vazimba. And when two or more are gathered together, there is great power, great magic.

Rangita's hands grew hot. She began trembling, and her eyes flared.

"Let's go." The big man yanked on the thong.

She reached up and embraced me tightly. *Goodbye Eva,* she beamed. *Namaste.*

Oh Rangita, sister, queen, I wrapped my arms around her, *I love you so much.* I pressed her against my breast, feeling a hot, kundalini energy streaming from her heart into mine, and back into her, a continuous, invisible ribbon of heat and light and power, holding her like that until her breathing became my breathing, and mine hers, until we were one, glowing being.

She shuddered and drew back slightly, and I saw that her face was wet with tears.

Do not blame me for James, she beamed. *When we took him across, we had no intention of keeping him. But, there are those who would rather escape this plane forever than live a life without love.*

Our eyes locked and this time it was my Vazimba eyes that saw through her, to a clearing in a forest where a thin, near-sighted scholar in a Cornell T-shirt crouched underneath a makeshift shelter in the driving rain, happily scribbling in a notebook as a troop of lemurs cavorted overhead, dropping half-eaten fruits on the plastic tarp. I saw, and I knew. The truth was right there in her blazing, blue-rimmed eyes: James had chosen. He wasn't coming back. Ever.

My knees buckled and I would have broken down utterly, had not Rangita intervened.

It is not a tragedy, she beamed. *It is a miracle. There is no reason to weep. He jumped in the river and swam across. When he pierced the veil, he left sorrow behind and discovered everything he had ever desired. There, he found... paradise.*

"Enough!" Rakotomana took hold of our shoulders and separated us roughly. "The Vazimba is mine."

Rangita and I wriggled like two wild beasts, trying to break free.

Sister voay, I zapped her furiously, *I have a hunger in my belly that only the meat of a traitorous Malagasy crab will satisfy.*

I twisted around, bent down, and bit Rakotomana on the wrist as hard as I could.

He let out a roar, dropped me and tried to scoop Rangita up in his huge arms, intending to carry her several feet across to the waiting helicopter, but she flung out her hand and grabbed the croc tooth hanging around my neck.

I placed my hand on top of hers and together we squeezed. Yes. Yes! YES!!

There was a blinding flash, as powerful as a bolt of summer lightning. When I opened my eyes, Rangita had disappeared and there, half-buried in the mud, lay the Old Queen. She heaved herself up and headed towards us, snorting steam from her raised nostrils.

Rakotomana shouted *"Mamba!"* dropped the leash and ran to the helicopter, pounding on the cockpit door, demanding, begging to be let in.

A violent fist-fight broke out inside the copter between Jack and Fred and Paul. I could hear Jack shouting my name and trying to get to the door, but there was no way the other two were going to unlock it with a monster like the Old Queen on the loose.

Rakotomana let go of the handle and tried to make a run for it back up the slope, but the Little People stood their ground. Locked together, arm in arm, they transformed themselves into a glowing human chain, welded together as surely as the crocs on my necklace.

The Vazimba had drawn the line. Michel Rakotomana was trapped, caught in a pincer-play between his ancestors, great and small. He could not escape his *vintana*.

The Old Queen didn't rush; she was in no hurry. But once she lowered her snout, there was no turning back.

Ny tody tsy misy...

She opened her jaws and took him with a single bite.

...fa ny atao no miverina.

She dragged the big man down to the lake with both khaki-clad legs firmly clamped in her fangs.

There is no such thing as divine retribution...

She swam slowly out into the lake and sank beneath the surface of the water...

...but what is done, returns.

...leaving nothing behind but a trail of pink bubbles and a smear of red across the rocks.

Fred threw open the door and Paul held out a hand to help me up. "Christ almighty," he yelled. "Let's get outta this hell-hole before we all get eaten alive."

Rasti came forward. "Mademoiselle Eva," he said very quietly,

"Are you not forgetting something?" He held out my knapsack.

I took it. It seemed heavy, much heavier than I remembered. I heard water sloshing inside, and something metallic, clinking.

I bowed to each and every one of the Little People encircling the plane.

They bowed to me.

Namaste. Namaste. Namaste.

Goodbye...

Then Jack started the engine and the Vazimba scattered, blown away like so many autumn leaves.

I waved and waved as we circled the island for the last time, but not a soul waved back. Nothing moved except the ancient trees that hid the invisible village. The leafy canopy rippled gently in the morning breeze, easily, billowing and green, moving like a river in the air, changeless and ever-changing, flowing, just as it always had, ever since the beginning of time.

"Say, Artema," said Jack, as we gained altitude. "That little guy back there. He was a dead-ringer for Jerome, wasn't he?"

We swooped over the island one last time. I looked down. Lake Marovoay shimmered in the morning sun, small and insignificant as a silver coin—something you'd pick up off a sidewalk, wondering how it got there, and if anybody was missing it, before you put it in your pocket and moved on.

48

No one will experience in life what is not meant for him.

I wrote that in my journal September 30th, the day Papa died. I'd flown to Cleveland direct from Paris after an overnight flight from Tananarive—from the Island of Ghosts to Our Lady of Mercy.

Papa slept fitfully. Through a crack in the curtains, I saw a sliver of grey, a blighted elm, a gutterful of pigeon droppings and factory smoke belching over a dirty river. Imbrications of urban life.

He woke with a jerk, clawing at his face, struggling for air, harsh cotton blanket twisted in rubber sheet. Burning chest and back, icy legs and white feet. I placed and replaced the washcloth of ice against his blotchy face, and trembling back.

"*Evita, carissima,*" he croaked, "Tell me again about Bibi..."

He watched my hands as I took out the raffia box once again, unwrapped the pieces of silk, opened the notebook, and began to read...

"I'm beginning to understand. We foreigners come to Madagascar in order to find our personal utopias. To see not what Madagascar is, but what we would like Madagascar to be, so that we may satisfy our visions. Nothing new here. History contains a long list of such adventurers. Columbus was one. He wanted to reach India, stumbled on Latin America and saw... India.

"When you press beyond expressions of polite hospitality, the chasm between strangers and natives here is profound. For, unlike the Malagasy, who have placed their gods and spirits all around them, we vazahas have imprisoned our gods in ourselves and taken their divine attributes as our own. We look upon life from the point of view of the hungry chameleon, seeing ourselves as proud, victorious, rapacious. The Malagasy look upon life from the viewpoint of the fly, subject to the whims of unknown powers, fate and the Ancestors. It is the difference between predator and prey. Until we give up insisting on playing the role of predator, on satisfying our pre-conceived dreams, and learn how to dream theirs, we will never begin to perceive Malagasy reality, or fathom the Malagasy soul. We scientists especially are victim to this kind of thinking, considering man to be rational, competitive and inventive. That is our reality, not theirs. For all of our measurements and calculated observations, we are often the most misguided and understand least about the nature of the reality we believe we are 'discovering.'"

"No," Papa tugged my sleeve, "not that stuff. Read the part about the animals."

I flipped the pages.

"I'm getting closer every day to taming a female fossa who has claimed my thatched roof—very territorial, haughty and fierce, this girl-panther. She has an ancient lineage, harking back to a time before the other predators existed. I believe she's raising her young in the forest nearby. Occasionally I see her carrying water to them in the cup of her curled tail. Tomorrow I'll track her to her den."

Papa's eyes closed. Saturation 85. Blood pressure 128. Computerized red digits monitored the cellular war. Lightheaded, I tried to open the window. But there were no windows, just panes of welded glass. Pigeons wheeled, scattering the sun. Ten stories below, an ambulance squealed. I reached down and touched the bandage on my thigh, remembering how Jack bent over me at the clinic in Mananjary, holding me down while the nurse dug out the bullet. "Hang on, kid. I've got you. Don't cry. You're almost home." I wouldn't let them throw it away. Made Jack open the filagree lid of the croc fang and drop it inside. My *Croix de Guerre*. Later, the three of them closed the door to my room. Long, serious faces, they stood at the end of the bed. "What say we just forget about what happened out there?" Paul thrust the typed report at me to sign:

CANTEX camp: Destroyed by hostiles. Michel Rakotomana: Accidental death by drowning. Body unrecoverable. Oil reserves: Projections revised downward. Negligible to nil. Zahoitra Project: Recommend immediate abandonment.

Papa's doctor handed me the surgery permissions and I helped him sign, my hand over his, steadying the pen. Joking aides pushed his gurney down the hall, the IV bottle swaying, oozing life-giving, silver bubbles. Papa squinted into the too-bright lights as they slid him into the elevator. "Bibi's not too thin? He's getting enough to eat?"

"He's... he looks okay."

Rasping, whistling. "What kind of food they got over there? Plenty fresh fruit, I'll bet. Vitamin C. He needs that. Such a skinny little kid..." Drifting now. "...Always hiding in the closet... busy with his bugs."

I tucked in the sheet under his chin. "There's lots of tropical fruit in Madagascar, Pop. Mangos, papayas, bananas... things like that."

"Bananas," he wheezed. "That's good. Potassium's important."

He pinched my arm. "How's about his eyes? He's still wearing those hippie glasses?"

I quickly looked away. "No. The last time I saw Bibi he... he wasn't... wearing his glasses..."

"You see." A triumphant smile. "A professor. And for once he listens to his father. I kept telling him... eye exercises work."

We line up with other patients in the prep room, with monitors, machines, nurses with clipboards.

"He's got a girl out there?"

"Oh, Papa..."

"C'mon. He's in love."

"He has a beard. And a ponytail."

"Bibi?" Mumbled, a thermometer in his mouth.

"Shhhh... You rest, I'll read."

"Zaohitra Reserve contains a small crater lake and cascades. The area is unmapped and virtually inaccessible—no scientific studies have ever been conducted here; the flora and fauna have been undisturbed for over 100 million years. It is a place of immense peace and beauty. The clearing close to my hut is framed in white orchids and red hibiscus. Across the lake are the ragged slopes of the Blue Rainforest and Mt. Ambondrombe. It's said these jungle-ridden mountains are populated—not by people, but by Malagasy ghosts and spirits. Map-makers, scientists, experts in Tana, believe the forest to be wild and untrodden. Nothing could be further from the truth. Wherever I go, I find a ghostly network of narrow tracks, going into the bush and out of the bush, each one a path, leading home."

A nurse arrived take Papa's blood. Thin, thin arm, violet veins. He shut his eyes as the needle went in. "Read the poem to me again. Slowly."

I opened to the last page of the book. In that achingly familiar, thoughtful cursive, my brother James had written:

Great white lemur, you have climbed the sky.
What need now for trunks and branches?

Why do I bother to thrash about with words
When grief has made the space inside me full of light?
Your memory is wrapped in this light,
Yet still I call out your name at dusk.
Surely you are not deaf,
You, who heard the midnight tappings of the aye-aye
    in the upturned root.
You, who heard the cocoon being woven, the egg-case
    breaking,
And the slender tongues of night moths as they supped
    beneath the moon.
    Malemy, malemy.
The grave is a veil before the gathering of paradise.
Why should I mourn the setting of a sun or moon?
What seed goes into the earth that does not grow?
What bucket goes down and does not come up full?
Why do I doubt your arising into eternity?
You who have closed your mouth on this side
    and opened it in the beyond.
In the nowhere air between, I hear this song:
    Ny tany vadiben'i Zanahary:
      mihary ny velone
      manotrona ny maty.
    The Earth is the first wife of God:
      it cares for the living
      and embraces the dead.

In very small letters at the bottom of the page, James had noted:

for C.R.II   Friend, scholar, boon companion   1960-1999

"Let's roll you over now," said a burly male nurse. "There's a good fella." He slid a plastic tube into Papa's wrist and started the anesthetic drip.

"*Evita*," my father crooked a single finger at me.

I bent over him. My hair caressed his cheek. He smoothed it with the back of his hand. "So soft..." he said drowsily. "Like a bird's wing. *Que bella*. I had forgotten how beautiful you are..."

The nurses unlocked the wheels on the gurney, turned it to face the double doors of the operating room.

His voice grew very faint. "Eva, I wanted... I should've... told you... to come home... a long time ago."

"It's going to be okay, Papa. Don't worry. I'm here now."

His eyes fluttered. "Lucky... for me... and Bibi. To have a daughter... a sister... so strong and loving, like you."

"Sorry, Miss, time's up. You can wait in the Patient's Lounge."

"*Ciao, bambina.*"

"*Ciao*, Papa. I'll see you after. We'll have some ice cream."

"Vanilla," he whispered. "With jimmies."

And I thought he winked, but maybe it was just the lights, playing tricks.

AFTERWORD

The wind has died down. The stars are tired. One by one they wink themselves out against the dawn.

There's one more piece of Malagasy scrap I haven't wanted to look at yet. It's a photo. A group shot. Josef took it. I'd insisted that Jack land in Ambohitsara so we could free the caged lemurs. It wasn't until we touched down that I opened my pack and found the *arivolahy*. I pulled the silver plug and peered inside. The sacred gourd was full of fresh, clear water.

"Aahh," sighed King Botofino, raising it aloft with his bandaged arm.

"*Si*," said Salim.

"*Salaam tompoko*," said the mothers of the about-to-be-circumcised boys.

And the sambatra rolled, as scheduled. Everybody got drunk, the boys were blessed, we danced and had a ripping good time.

"*Mahay fomba*," sang Josef as we circled the *tranobe*, stopping at each corner of the Big House for King Botofino to blow the conch shell and staunch the bleeding of the new men. We were all together, the entire village of Ambohitsara and four *vazahas*, shuffling along underneath the moon in the sand, barefooted. Dancing, singing, swaying together. Babies, mothers, grandmothers, girls, in front of the pack. Boys and men at the rear, waving their brave, pointed sticks. Defying death and celebrating eternity.

"*Mahay fomba.*" Josef repeated, laughing and clapping. "It is the Malagasy way."

There we are, from left to right: Fred Pearson, Paul Cummins, Josef, King Botofino and his councillors. Everyone's smiling and mucking it up. In front, a line of wives. Then me. And next to me, Jack. You can't see his face clearly because he's got his arm around me like a vise, and he's bending down to kiss me. Oh, he wasn't taking any chances of losing me again.

What you can't hear is the thunder rumbling and the clouds sweeping in over the Indian Ocean from Antarctica. Somewhere up north in the Blue Rainforest, it's raining. Do we care? Hell no. In Ambohitsara, we're celebrating life. The rain... it's far away, hitting the high green mountains dead-on and dumping eight million tons of water onto the beginning of the world. Here, the sand under our bare feet is still warm from the day and the fruit bats are flying. Who knows? Maybe tomorrow, or the next day, someone will see a clump of leaves and branches floating downstream bearing the body of a lemur that got separated from its family and was swept away in the storm. But tonight—tonight we're celebrating life.

I know. You're looking at that bright white splotch down in the right-hand corner next to Jack. You're thinking: sun spot on the lens, inexperienced cameraman.

That's what I thought, too. Until I looked closely and realized it was really *two* spots, not one.

And if you look very closely, you can make out the outline of a cloak.

You tell me... Those *are* fins, aren't they?

APPENDICES

MADAGASCAR

ANTSERANANA
Anivorano-Nord
Ambilobe
NOSY — BE
Vohémar
Ambanja
Bealanana
Andapa
Sambava
Analalava
Antsohihy
Antalaha
Maroantsetra
MAHAJANGA
Port-Bergé
Mandritsara
Mananara
Soalala
Anbato-Boéni
Sitampiky
Tsaratanàna
Besalampy
Maevatanàna
Andilamena
SAINTE — MARIE
Lac Alaotra
Fénérive
Morafenobe
Andriba
Kiangara
Ambatondrazaka
Maintirano
Ankazobe
Aniozorobe
TOAMASINA
Antsalova
Tsiroanomandidy
Manjakandriana
ANTANANARIVO
Moramanga
Miarinarivo
Lac Itasy
Beparasy
Vatomandry
Soavinandriana
Faratsiho
Ambatolampy
Miandrivazo
Betafo
Antsirabe
Mahanoro
Belo-sur-Tsiribihina
Mandiambo
Morondava
Malaimbandy
Nosy-Varika
Mahabo
Ampasinambo
Ambatofinandrahana
Ambositra
Ambohimahasoa
Mananjary
Beroroha
FIANARANTSOA
Ifanadiana
Morombe
Ambalavao
Sahasinaka
Ankazoabo
Manakara
Ihosy
Ivohibe
Vohipeno
Ranohira
Farafangana
Sakaraha
Iakora
TOLIARY
Betroka
Vangaindrano
Midongy-du-Sud
Betioky
Tsivory
Bekily
Esira
Manantenina
Ampanihy
Antanimory
Beloha
Amboasary
Tsihombe
Ambovombe
TAOLANARO

⊕ Localités
. Sites
Échelle

. KMS .
0   100   200

Dr. Rabansoro's astral chart

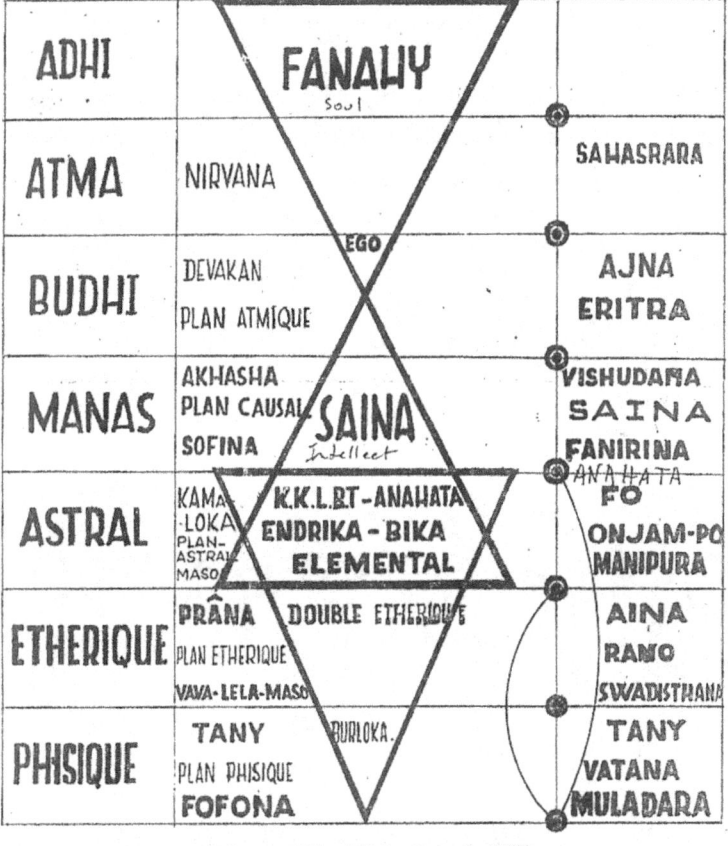

IZA MOA IANAO ?

ADHI	FANAHY Soul	
ATMA	NIRVANA	SAHASRARA
BUDHI	DEVAKAN PLAN ATMIQUE	AJNA ERITRA
MANAS	AKHASHA PLAN CAUSAL SOFINA	VISHUDARA SAINA FANIRINA
ASTRAL	KAMA -LOKA PLAN-ASTRAL MASO	FO ONJAM-PO MANIPURA
ETHERIQUE	PRÂNA PLAN ETHERIQUE VAVA-LELA-MASO	AINA RANO SWADISTHANA
PHISIQUE	TANY PLAN PHISIQUE FOFONA	TANY VATANA MULADARA

Inside the chart: EGO — SAINA Intellect — K.K.L.RT-ANAHATA ENDRIKA – BIKA ELEMENTAL — ANAHATA — DOUBLE ETHERIQUE — BURLOKA

TAT TVAM ASI

# DOCUMENTATION

0dfcMINISANSPORTS,
DU RAVITAILLEMENT
ET DU TOURISME

DIRECTION DU TOURISME

REPOBLIKA DEMOKRATIKA MALAGASY
Tanindrazana - Tolom-piavotana - Fahafahana

Antananarivo, le **18 SEP.**

A T T E S T A T I O N
-+++++++++++++++++++++++++++++++-

    i Je, soussigné, le Directeur du Tourisme, atteste
que Mademoiselle Artema est en mission à Madagascar pour
faire un reportage sur la civilisation malgache, plus parti-
culièrement sur le Tourisme et sur tous les aspects culturels

    Je serais reconnaissante à tous ceux qui peuvent lui
apporter leur appui dans la réalisation de son travail.

RAKOTOM-NANA RAZANAM-N
MAITRE ASSISTANT DE L'ENSEIG...
SUPERIEUR ET DE LA RECHERCHE